THE
ROAD
HOME

CHARLOTTE
BUELOW

PROLOGUE

"We must leave our beloved country." "We can no longer be persecuted for our religious beliefs." "Let us go to a new country where we can practice our religion as we see fit." "Let us go to the United States of America."

Mary and her friends were listening to a speech that was taking place in the village square of Killin, Scotland. It sat above the banks of Loch Tay in Perthshire and was nestled in the middle of Breadalbane. Things had been difficult in Scotland since the Highland Clearances which began around 1785 and reached a peak in the 1840's and early 1850's. Clan chiefs and other landowners created profitable sheep runs by clearing highlanders from their fertile land, they were forced to eke out a living in smaller plots of poor land; they were called crofters. Around 1834, the 2nd Marquis of Breadalbane burned out many of the land owners and the only reason a social uprising didn't happen was that many of the citizens decided to emigrate. Scots were leaving in droves sometimes even entire communities. They were lured by the promise of better opportunities abroad. Religion was another factor in the decision to leave their country. And so, in this historic parish village, many of the townspeople had gathered to listen, but for now the officials were busy trying to silence the leaders and break up the gathering crowd.

"Mary, Mary, come quickly, it is not safe to be out here." "Come with me, we will go home now," said her Father. Mary, always one to obey him, reluctantly said goodbye to her friends and followed her Father to the cart so they could go home. They had all congregated there after school to see what in the world was going on; she glanced over her shoulder and saw the crowd disbursing and heard the angry voices of the officials. This was the first of many gatherings, but it soon became apparent that those who were devoted Methodists, must hold their meetings in private to formulate plans of change and possible emigration for some of them. They were a peaceful people but stubborn and not willing to compromise their religion for anyone. However, it was not their intent to create public disturbances either, so they went their way peaceably. Many town hall meetings would be held in the future; the voice of the people would be heard.

As they walked in silence, Mary thought about William and if they might indeed have a future together. She wondered if he would approach her; after all she was seventeen now and it was common for most of the young women to marry at eighteen or nineteen; surely to have a beau. Mary had an eye for William since the sixth grade, he was very handsome, tall and lanky with blonde hair and blue eyes, a smile that was irresistible and he was good natured, usually teasing or joking with someone. She knew that a lot of other lasses had their eye on him too; there was lots of giggling and twittering when he was around; recently he had been paying her a lot of attention, pulling her hair, poking at her and looking at her when he didn't think she noticed. She noticed because she always had her eye on him too. Her best friend, Colleen, had been seeing, Harry Rutherford, for over a year now. Harry was of medium height with a shock of brown hair that always looked uncombed, he was a country lad, preferring to be fishing or working outside regardless of the weather; some might say he was handsome in a rugged sort of way. Harry and William were good friends so whenever Colleen and Harry were present William would be close behind.

Mary was a bonnie lass with long flowing reddish hair that fell in soft curls almost to her waist. She had green eyes and a wide smile that showed a straight line of white teeth. She was of average height and small in girth. All of the boys reaped attention on her but it was apparent that she wasn't interested in them; they heard she liked William and wondered what William was waiting for; apparently everyone could see it but him. Colleen was a redhead as well, she had freckles and she too was fun loving, good natured, and a little on the plump side. There were no secrets between the two lasses; they had been best friends for as long as they could remember.

Mary's Father was always hinting that Henry, a good friend of the family, would be an excellent catch for her but she wasn't interested in him; although he was good looking with intense dark eyes. He was older than her and had been away at school for a number of years now; coming home infrequently. She thought he might like her because she would catch him watching her with those unflinching dark eyes of his. "It's funny, she thought, I might be interested in him if it weren't for William." She saw him at the gathering today and supposed that he must be home on a break from school; he had caught her eye and gave a little smile and wave and she had waved back at him thinking that it was probably rude of her not to go over and welcome him home. There were such long periods of time between his visits that she never knew what to talk about, they had different lives now. Usually her Father gushed about his visits home, he hadn't mentioned anything to her this time; perhaps he didn't know. Henry and Mary's parents were longtime friends and there were many visits back and forth between the two families. Henry and Mary played together when they were young and were very good friends in those days. He was studying in Edinburgh now to be a schoolteacher; it was quite an honor to be able to receive higher education. Mary never gave much thought to Henry until she would see him again, he was always pleasant and courteous, but for Mary's taste, he seemed much too serious; nonetheless, she was proud of him and wondered if he had a beau.

Mary's Father was a crofter now because of the Clearances. There was still much talk about the unfairness felt towards those who took the family land away from the Highlanders and the bitterness had not worn off. Some Highlanders left for the coast where they became kelp farmers but now the kelp industry was suffering from new taxes being imposed upon them. Times were becoming hard and many of the younger generation thought about possible emigration to Canada and the United States where more opportunities and freedom awaited. It was said that there was land for the taking, more than you would even need, but there were also stories of the wilderness filled with hostile Native Americans who occupied the land and attacked the pioneers. The British government was offering incentives to go there, secretly wanting to get rid of the residents they thought of as lower working class. They also wanted to establish themselves and their government overseas and this would be a way to do so. As they drove north along Main Street and crossed the River Lochay on Pier Road toward home, Mary wondered how anyone could leave this beautiful village. To her, there was no place she would rather be. They passed the cemetery and made a left hand turn into the driveway to her home.

Mary found her mother baking bread in the kitchen so she tied up her flowing hair and hurried to assist her. She loved the warm homey kitchen and all of the smells, especially on bread baking day and she wanted to learn as much from her mother as she could so that when she had a family; hopefully with William someday, she would be the best wife and mother she could be. She also had a secret plan, one that she would keep to herself for the time being. "Mum," said Mary, "How did you and Da meet?" Her mother, who was kneading some bread answered, "Oh, I suppose we always knew each other, we went to the same school and our families were close." "It was a natural thing." Mary rolled a lump of dough in some flour and began the kneading process as well, "But did you feel anything different when you looked at him?" "Did you know that he was the one meant for you?" Mary's mother looked at her out of the corner of her eye. "It was meant to be, Mary," she replied. Mary nodded and went about her work. "Are you thinking, Mary, of anyone special yourself?" "Oh, not really," she said, thinking of nothing but William and wondering if and when he might ask her out. Colleen told her that Harry said William was going to ask her to the dance, she certainly hoped so.

CHAPTER ONE

William was driving the cart home slowly, thinking of Mary and how he was just ready to talk to her at the meeting until her Father came and summoned her home. Mr. Munro seemed to be a dour Scot, always serious as he went about his business. He knew that Mary liked him, he saw the looks she gave him and he just needed the courage to make his intentions known. Aye, he knew everyone looked at him as just a fun loving, outgoing person but when it came to affairs of the heart it was a different matter, he just couldn't find the way to make his feelings known. He would poke and tease Mary in his joking way but inside he wanted to let her know he was serious about her; he had never thought twice about any of the other lasses. He was aware that many of the other young lads would jump at a chance with Mary and it was just a matter of time before she lost interest in him and looked elsewhere. Likewise, many of the young lasses flirted with him and he knew it would be no challenge to court any of them; but he wasn't interested. The end of their school days was quickly approaching and it was time to think about a future and he hoped that Mary would be part of it. Oh aye, he had plans, and those plans did not include farming in any way. Many would not have guessed the depth of William, he might be fun loving on the outside, but inside, his head was always conjuring up ideas; he was not going to be a farmer, it wasn't in him.

William knew that his Father and Mary's were not on friendly terms. William's Father was able to retain his land. He had had maneuvered himself into becoming a tacksman, a position that was not popular with the crofters. The crofters were resentful, feeling that the tacksmen sold out just to obtain a higher standard of living. They struck a deal, so to speak with the sheep herders. It wasn't like William had anything to do with the bargain but feelings of resentment were strong. William had been able to avoid the distasteful task of rent collecting, which was part of the tacksman's duties. William's brothers accepted this task as part of their farming duties for their Father, and in some ways, William thought they enjoyed it. He was nothing like them, he wondered why. He knew his excuses would run out soon and he would be made to do the collecting just like everyone else but he just couldn't stand the thought of collecting rent from the good people who were struggling to make a living after they were burned out of their homes and had to start over. He didn't hate his Father; he understood that his Father had only taken advantage of an opportunity that was given to him in regard for his own family's welfare. His Father never spoke of it and William guessed that the burden lay heavy on his heart. He knew that his mother, his bonnie mother, felt ostracized from the women who used to be her peers and his heart broke for her; at least the children of the village didn't make judgments on each other.

William had a secret that he had not divulged to anyone but his mother. He was fascinated in the invention of the new power looms which were increasing productivity in the textile industry and he knew it wouldn't be long until the weavers in Scotland were using them. He wanted to be part of this exciting new development. He didn't understand where his fascination for textiles came from but it interested him nonetheless. He would soon need to have a talk with his Father to make his intentions known; he knew it would not be a hardship for the family; his three brothers could handle all the work easily. William wanted a different life, a life where he could learn new things and he was ready; it was a changing world. He had been spending many hours in the village talking with weaver George McGregor who was interested in sponsoring a young lad and sending him to Glasgow to tutor in the industry and bring back his knowledge to the shop. He too had plans of expansion and knew they could both prosper with the right training. Mr. McGregor knew William quite well; the boy had come into his shop for several years now asking endless questions about the fabrics, how they were made, and watching him work. He saw the need in him to learn the trade; unlike many other villagers, he saw a different side of the lad. They had many long conversations about where this new venture could take both of them.

As William neared home and the dreaded farm duties of the afternoon he made up his mind that he would take a trip over to Mary's and approach her Father for permission to take her to the Saturday dance that was being held in the town square in celebration of the end of the school year. If he didn't ask her soon, he knew that someone else would. He hoped that Mary's Father would approve but he wasn't sure, not sure at all.

CHAPTER
TWO

Two days later, William summoned up the courage to go over to Mary's. He was not a shy lad but he had to take a few deep breaths to accomplish this task. He drove into the yard and saw Mr. Munro by the shed. He jumped down and walked towards him, "Hello, Mr. Munro, how are you today?" he shouted. Mr. Munro looked up and saw who it was. He looked back down at his work as he replied, "William, what brings you over here?" William stopped a few feet from him, "Well, you see there's a dance on Saturday night in the town square and I would like your permission to escort Mary." With an audible breath, Mr. Munro looked up quickly, "Just exactly who will be going to this dance?" "Colleen and Harry for sure, hopefully other schoolmates and of course there will be adults there." Not looking at William, with his head down, Mr. Munro struggled for an answer. He wanted to say no but knew that Mary would be expecting to go with her friend and the last thing he wanted was to earn her disfavor right now. "Mary may go with you if you promise that you will stay at the town square throughout, in fact, I will request that Harry and Colleen travel with you to pick her up and I will expect you to have her home immediately after the dance." William closed his eyes in relief, "Of course, I would never disrespect your wishes, Mr. Munro." "Thank you, thank you so much, is there anything I can do to help you?" "No, I can handle it, thank you anyway," he replied gruffly. William took a few steps back and said, "All right, then, I guess I'll be going, is it ok if I stop at the house and tell Mary?" "As you wish, William, as you wish," he replied.

William turned toward the house, his heart pounding; he had all he could do to keep the grin off of his face. Now that the ice was broken, perhaps Mary's Father would see that he was polite and respectful. He knocked on the door and Mary's mother opened it. The shock of seeing him standing there showed clearly on her face. "William, what brings you here," she said as she dusted the flour off of her hands onto her apron. "My, I must look a sight, I've been baking." William smiled, "I can smell it, Mrs. Munro, and it smells good." "I've just had a chat with Mr. Munro and he gave me permission to escort Mary to the dance on Saturday night." "I was wondering if I might have a quick word with her to tell her the news; well, and of course to see if she will go." Catherine was a little surprised that John had agreed to this but she said, "A dance on Saturday, that sounds like a good time." "Of course, I think Mary's upstairs; I will call her down right away." "Come in now, come in and have a seat." She went to call for Mary thinking, "And John agreed, well, well." "I guess now I know who Mary has her eye on."

William stood in the entryway waiting. He thought how pleasant her mother was and imagined that Mary would be the same at her age. He knew Mary's mother was well known for her baked goods and by the smell wafting from the kitchen he could understand why, it was making his stomach growl. Mary's mother called up the stairs to let her know that William was there. She couldn't help but notice how swiftly the lass practically leaped down the steps; she could see from the look on her daughter's face that she was in love with William, there was no mistaking it.

It had been many years since she had felt that same way but she still remembered her first love, it was something that you never forget. For a moment her mind wandered back to those days when she was in love with David Clark. She had been quite the looker then with long red flowing locks just like Mary's. Over the years it had deepened in color and was now speckled with grey. David and she had made so many plans for their future. Then came the day that would stick in her gullet forever; the day she was told by her Father that she would wed John Munro. She knew John of course, he was a friend of the family, but never did she expect this. Of course, she refused, cried, pleaded all to no avail. She was to wed John and it did not matter how she felt. Shortly thereafter, her Father came to her and informed her that David had left the village. "Why?" she cried. "Why would he not tell me he was leaving?" Her Father just shook his head and answered, "One cannot know what is in the mind of another." She did not know that he had taken it upon himself to inform David that she would be getting married soon, it had all been arranged, and it was in his best interest to forget about her. Of course, when he found out, he left the village and she never heard from or saw him again. He didn't know why she had kept this from him, not knowing that she herself was never told. She had felt a coldness seep over her and the resentment grew in her not knowing why he would abandon her like that. In time, her heart softened and John courted her. He was kind and gentle and she grew to love him. No, it wasn't the same kind of love you feel when you are in love for the first time; it was a different, deeper kind of love. They married and her life with him had been good. Today she could honestly say that she loved him with all of her heart.

It was years later when her Father, on his deathbed, recounted to her what had happened. And yet, in those final hours, he still believed he had done the right thing. "So you see my daughter, what a blessed life you have had, and such a loving, caring husband." She leapt out of the chair by his bedside in shock and anger. She managed to control her outburst but quickly left his side and opened the door. She reached the stairs and slowly sank to the floor, holding onto the stair rail. "All these years, all these years I have wondered." "And this he has done to me." "My God, please forgive the thoughts I am thinking right now." She never held it against her husband, he had not been a part of it; she was sure of that.

Now, she was fearful for she knew that John had conjured up in his mind a relationship between Mary and Henry. He saw the potential Henry had to give his daughter a good life. She liked Henry too, she'd known him since he was a bairn but she believed that a lass should be able to choose for herself. Surely John would not be the man her Father was, he would never mislead Mary. She would see to it.

"Oh my," she said, turning from the window, when she realized she had been daydreaming. "How rude of me William, would you like to sit and have a piece of tayberry pie, fresh from the oven?" Mary smiled at her mother and William replied, "I can't say no, Mrs. Munro, me Mum likes to cook, just like you do." Catherine replied, "I'm fortunate to have an oven, William, many don't." "How is your mother, I haven't seen her for some time?" William looked down and then said, "She's good, you know, it's lonely up there." It went unspoken between them as to why, and she said, "You tell her to come down for a visit anytime, William, I'd welcome the company." He looked up, surprised, "I will, Mrs. Munro, I will." She continued, "Now, please, set yourself down, and we'll have a little chat." "Come on Mary, sit with us." "I can't refuse either," laughed Mary. They sat at the table eating pie, laughing, and having a good old time. Catherine could see why Mary had fallen for this happy go lucky lad. They heard the door open and John came into the house but instead of joining them, he headed to the sitting room without a word. The spell was broken and William graciously stood up and said, "Think I'd best be heading home now, me Da's expecting me to help with the chores, thanks for the pie, I truly enjoyed it." "You're welcome, William, you're welcome," smiled Catherine. "I'll walk you out," said Mary. William poked his head into the sitting room and said, "Goodbye Mr. Munro, thank you." "Goodbye," was all John replied, nothing more, as he sat looking straight ahead, neither turning his head left or right. When they had left the house he muttered to himself, "Of all the lads in this town, she had to pick Douglas Stevenson's son."

Mary walked with William in silence, holding hands, until they reached the cart. "I can't believe he said aye," he stated. "I was nervous about asking him, I'm so glad you agreed to go with me." She smiled shyly at him, "I was hoping you would ask me." "I wanted to ask you out before, but you know; I didn't know what you would say." "I would have said aye," she replied, smiling. He recounted to her all of the stipulations he had been given; that they were to remain in the presence of the other couples at all times and come home immediately after the dance. "He's just being protective, William, that's what Fathers do, it's not anything against you." "I know, Mary, I know," he replied but he had the feeling that Mary's Father didn't like him. He supposed it was because his Da was the tacksman. He could read people quite well and it was obvious that Mr. Munro couldn't even look him in the eye. No matter; he would change that in time. "I'll see you tomorrow at Colleens," he said and he gave a little squeeze to her hand. "Bye William," she said. "See you there." She turned and walked to the house but she felt like she could fly. William's touch had sent a flutter to her stomach, after waiting so long, he had finally asked her out. The worst was over, the ice was broken and her Da would see what a great person William was. Aye, it would take a little time, he was a stubborn man but he loved her and would see things her way eventually. She bounded into the kitchen where John was standing near the window and she ran and gave him a hug. "Thank you, thank you, so much Da." Unlike his usual response, either hugging her back or patting her shoulder, he stood woodenly and replied, "It's just a dance, Mary, just a dance, nothing more," and then he turned without another word and walked away. Mary was so elated that she barely noticed.

CHAPTER
THREE

The next morning Peter gave Mary a ride over to Colleen's where Colleen, Harry and William were waiting for her. The lasses buzzed about the dance, their last school dance, and how much fun they were going to have. They talked about marriage and babies as all lasses do, they would live near each other and their bairns would grow up together and be close friends just like them. Harry and William would keep busy outside while Mary and Colleen cooked dinner, then they would come in and all eat together. They went on, and on making plans. It was sad to see the end of their school days but they had much to look forward to. There was a small cottage in back of Colleen's parent's land where the couple would live and William was helping Harry with the renovation so both of the lads went over to the cottage to continue the work. The wedding was only two weeks away and they had a lot to accomplish before then. Mary and William would be in the wedding of course, and Mary's mother was asked to make the wedding cake and bannocks to which she readily agreed. It was common for Munro breads and sweets to be at every occasion in the area. Sugar was a scarce item so sweets were a treat; however, they had many inventive ways to replace sugar, using honey and sweet fruit when they could get it; even sweet potatoes. Mary had planned a bridal shower at her house for tomorrow night and William was in charge of 'stag night' which also would be taking place next week. They accomplished a lot today but there was still a list of unfinished projects.

The day for the wedding shower had arrived and everything was ready; they had all worked hard. Mary gave one last look around and was satisfied that there was nothing more to do. The men were all shooed out of the house for the afternoon; there was ale for them to drink outside or in the shed. Rebecca and Lillian were appointed servers to make sure the guests had tea and treats; they enjoyed helping Mary decorate and it was times like these that they bonded with each other; other times Mary considered them a nuisance because of their constant bickering with each other. As the guest of honor, Colleen arrived first with her mother and sisters. Mary took her by the hand and escorted her into the kitchen to show her what they would be serving. Catherine and Mrs. Hart chatted and Colleen's sisters went upstairs with Rebecca and Lillian. Soon the carts started parking in the yard and almost everyone who had been invited had now arrived. Everyone found a seat at which time refreshments were served and soon Colleen began opening her presents. Colleen's mother would hold an open house for the showing of presents after which time they would have 'hen night,' a long time tradition. Colleen would dress up and they would all go to the village where her friends would escort her through the town singing while banging pots and pans. Mary was happy for her friend and she wondered if or when her turn might come. The afternoon flew by and soon it was time to leave, the men were getting anxious to return home to their chores. "Thank you, Mary, Colleen said; giving her a hug, it was a lovely shower." "I'm happy to do it, she replied, giving her a kiss on the cheek, it won't be long and I will be calling you Mrs. Rutherford." They both laughed and walked arm in arm out to the cart.

On Saturday, Mary was up and down the stairs trying to decide what to wear to the dance and how to fix her hair. She appeared in the kitchen no less than half a dozen times asking advice from her mother. Mrs. Munro savored her time with Mary, it wouldn't be long and she would be off on her own, just like her oldest daughter Katie. Late afternoon the cart driven by Harry, accompanied by William and Colleen arrived to pick her up. Restraining herself, Mary watched from her bedroom window so as not to appear too anxious. William stepped out and came to the door to fetch her. John answered the door this time and opened it with a grim look on his face. "I've come for Mary, Mr. Munro," he said. "Colleen and Harry are in the cart as I promised you they would be." "I'm glad to see that, grumbled John, make sure you all stay together tonight." "I will call her, she's upstairs getting ready." He left William standing there with the door still open not asking him in. Calling up the stairs, he said, "Mary, William is here," then he turned around and headed for the sitting room; William remained standing in the doorway. When Mary headed down the stairs, this time entering like a young lady, he thought he had never seen such a bonnie sight in his life, she was decked out in her best dress and her hair was upswept with a couple of tendrils escaping on the sides. To him, she looked like an angel and his heart skipped several beats. He took Mary's hand and they walked to the door of the sitting room where he said, "I will have her home right after the dance then, Mr. Munro, Goodbye." This time, John rose and walked to the open door with them. "We'll be up waiting for her," he said and he gave a little wave to the waiting couple in the cart. Catherine's voice was heard in the kitchen, "Mary, Mary, wait. I've baked some scones for you to take." William took the plate from her, "Oh, thank you Mrs. Munro, I know everyone will enjoy them, I'm sure they won't last long." "I hope not, William, I hope not," she replied. "You're the best, Mum," said Mary and she kissed her on the cheek. They opened the door and Mary turned and said, "We're off then." Catherine gave a little chuckle, "Have fun," she said, and she closed the door then stood by the window watching them until they were out of sight. She thought what a nice, polite lad William was, this week she would make it a point to go up there and visit with his mother, Margaret Stevenson, after all they used to be friends; what a shame they had let the friendship drift away. She knew John would disapprove but in her Christian way she believed it was time and the right thing to do.

Off they were, not a care in the world. Mary relished sitting next to William in the cart and every once in a while he turned his head and smiled at her then he put his arm around her back and pulled her close. "Are you warm enough, Mary," he asked. "Aye," she said, and she looked at him and smiled. He wanted to bend down and give her a kiss but wasn't sure how she would react. They crossed the River Lochay and turned left on Main Street to arrive at the town square which was done up festively with decorations. There was a makeshift stage set up on which the musicians would perform. Lanterns were scattered around; there were tables and chairs set up for them to sit and watch the dancing. Couples were leisurely strolling around the grounds waiting for the dance music to begin and looking at the tables laden with food. William placed the plate of scones on the table along with some tea cakes that his mother had sent. Colleen and Harry followed with baked goods from their mothers. "Mary, let's not forget the plates when we leave." "We better not, she replied, they wouldn't be too pleased, would they?" "Oh me Mum would just about kill me, piped in Colleen, that's her best plate." They all laughed; Colleen was always so dramatic and funny. William and Harry went to get the drinks and the lasses found a table where they could all sit and enjoy the festivities.

A Piper was wandering around the square playing all the familiar Scottish tunes. William grabbed Mary's hand and they sat and watched more and more carts arrive; many of them their friends from school. Some couples stopped to visit, and then continued on their way. "You look so bonnie tonight, Mary, not to say that you're not bonnie all the time, well, you know what I mean," he said, a little embarrassed. "You don't look so bad yourself, William," she replied, reaching up and tenderly pushing a stray hair away from his eyes. He smiled at her, "I've wanted to let you know how I feel about you for a long time now." "And I you," she said shyly. Oh how she wished this night would last forever. Tom O'Donnell came by with Harriet and they stopped to talk. "Sit here by us, Harry said, there's plenty of room left at the table." Tom pulled out a chair for Harriet and they joined the couples. The music began with a reel and Harry and Colleen jumped up and pulled William and Mary, Tom and Harriet along with them; they all danced to the music, sometimes laughing so hard that they had to stop and catch their breath. Then a slow song began and William took Mary in his arms; they danced around the square, not wanting to let go of each other. Mary's dream had come true; it felt good in his arms. William thought that he had found the perfect lass for him. It was much too soon when the music ended. The couples gathered up their empty plates and leisurely strolled to the cart, holding hands and wishing the night would begin again. They talked and laughed on the way home about the evening and how some of the lads had taken a little too much ale; so much in fact that they were barely able to stand up. The lasses gushed about some of the dresses they had seen and planned to sew some like it if they ever got time. When they reached the house, William jumped out first and walked around the cart to help Mary down then he walked her to the door and gave her a sweet kiss on the lips. "Thank you for asking me William, she said, I had the best time." "Me too Mary, me too." he said, then reached around and gave her a hug before he walked back to the cart. She was just about to open the door when he yelled, "Wait a minute!" She turned and he held up the plate, they had left in the cart. "Wouldn't want to forget this," he said with a grin on his face. She smiled and took it from him, then stood and watched them drive away. She floated into the house wishing the night could have lasted forever. Unknown to her, Mr. Munro stood in the window of his room also watching them until they disappeared.

Harry pulled out of the driveway and turned left onto Pier Road for a short distance until he made another left at Finlarig Road where William lived. William sat in the back of the cart by himself thinking about the evening. Why did the time have to go so by quickly when you were having fun and so slowly when you weren't? Colleen was snuggled next to Harry chatting about the evening and the soon to come wedding. William was quiet, leaving them their time together, he was thinking about his future plans and he knew he would have to talk to Mary about them. He didn't want to tell her that it meant he would have to go away for a while and he certainly hadn't wanted to broach the subject until after the dance, not wanting

CHAPTER THREE

to put a damper on the evening. He wished he wouldn't have to leave and he hoped that Mary would understand and agree to wait for him, it was the only way he could think of to break away from his Father's business and stand up on his own as a person; there was nothing else here for him. What the future held, he could not know, but he hoped that Mary would be a part of it.

CHAPTER
FOUR

The next morning Mary flew down the stairs, still feeling elated from the night's events. She couldn't wait to share everything with her mother. As usual, Catherine was in the kitchen working. "Well there you are, young lass, how was the evening?" "The most dreamy evening ever, I can't tell you how much fun we had!" said Mary. "And you couldn't wait to tell me, could you, laughed Catherine, I'm glad you had a good time." Mary recounted the evening, even telling her mother that William had given her a light kiss at the door and how it was nothing like she had ever felt in her life. "Oh, we returned your plate, safe and sound, and of course empty; William was not going to let me forget it." "He's a sweet lad, Mary, a sweet lad." "Do you think so, really, I so want you and Da to like him?" "Aye, I think so; we'll have to work on your Da though because he's very protective of you." "By the way, I think I'll take a trip up to visit his mother Margaret soon, I miss our friendship and William was a good reminder of how long it's been." "Oh Mum, that would be wonderful, William would be so appreciative; he loves his Mum and worries about her." "You know Mary him being the tacksman and all has hardened people against them." "I know Mum, but still, it wasn't her doing." "So true, Mary, so true, it wasn't her doing." They both sat, lost in thought for a few minutes.

"Mary, most lasses go through a first love, sometimes they call it puppy love." said Catherine. "Oh, this isn't puppy love, mother, this is the real thing, laughed Mary, I just know it!" "I never told you this, said Catherine, but I felt the same way once too." Mary had never thought about her parents meeting or dating, it never entered her mind to think of them as an unmarried couple. "Did Da sweep you off your feet?" she asked. "Not exactly Mary, let me tell you my story." "You are a young woman now and I feel the need for you to hear this." This was so unlike her mother that Mary sat at attention, not knowing what to expect. She told Mary the story of her first love David Clark and what had happened. Mary felt a shock run through her, surely this couldn't be true, Mary's mother was devoted to her Father and him with her; she never heard a harsh word between them. "Why are you telling me this now," she asked. "So that you can always be strong, I want you to realize that there are many avenues open to you." "This is just a first love for you, there may be many more, you are still young." Mary's mother once again was lost in her daydreams so Mary slowly left the table, her mind reeling with the story she had just been told. She turned and looked at her mother, "I could never imagine a life with anyone but William." That night her dreams took her to a dark, swirling sea, and she kept trying to reach out and grab something over and over again, but it was always just outside her reach. In the morning she felt like she hadn't had any sleep at all. "Strange, she thought, you never really know anyone fully, not even your parents."

That Sunday, Mary's sister Katie and her husband, Ethan arrived for dinner, along with their three children. The lasses, Carolyn, Gretchen and a younger brother Donald were all hugs and kisses for their Grandmum and Grandda. Mary's older brother Richard couldn't come today because it was a busy time for him in his blacksmith shop but Sarah and baby Collin came along. Donald immediately latched onto Mary's brother Peter. Peter was a year older than Mary and Donald idolized him. He was good natured and let Donald follow him around wherever he went.

Ethan worked down at the mill which lay just south of the Falls of Dochart but lately Ethan hadn't been feeling well. It was damp at the mill and he had gotten a bad cold which hung on for some time until he developed a cough that just wouldn't go away. They had finally gone to see Dr. Traymoor who instructed him to rub menthol on his chest, drink a lot of fluids and try to get as much rest as possible. He had done as instructed and had seemed to recuperate for a time, but lately he had been short winded and started coughing again. Now Katie had insisted they go back to see him again next week.

"Ethan, Ethan, come and sit by the fire," said Catherine. "We have a seat ready for you; and mind you cover yourself with the quilt so you don't get chilled." "Thank you, Catherine, said Ethan, I'm sure this will go away but just in case we are going to the doctor again." Immediately he had a coughing spasm and Catherine could see that his condition was worsening. "Good, she replied, you must see that this doesn't get out of hand." She stood over him, patted his back and thought to herself, "He doesn't look good." She was fond of Ethan, he was a loving husband and a great Father; they had met when Katie accompanied John down to the mill to pick up some supplies. "Katie, she said, come with me in the kitchen and we'll fix Ethan up a nice hot cup of tea." "Ok, Mum," Katie replied, a worried look on her face. They both walked into the kitchen, and as they stood by the stove, Catherine said, "Katie, you make sure the doctor knows he has been coughing a lot, he can't go on like this." "I will, Mum, I want him to know that Ethan insists on going to work every day, he's not resting like he should be." "It'll be all right, Katie, it'll be all right, replied a concerned Catherine, but he must stay home from work." "I'll have John talk to him." "Come now, let's take him his tea, and then get on with the business of the kitchen." "I love you Mum," said Katie, "I love you too, Catherine replied, don't worry, we are here for you." "And I appreciate it, you know that," Katie said, a small tear in her eye.

Mary and her mother had been busy all week making bread, black pudding, powsoddie, oatcakes and shortbread along with stovies from yesterday's leftover meat, and haggis which they would serve with potato scones. Some of the food was left over from Friday night's bridal shower and the rest was made just for today's dinner. Once a year they had a big feast, their normal dinners were quite small. "Oh, I forgot to tell you, Mary, the MacAlduie's are coming today, even Henry is coming along, we haven't spent time together in such a long while." "It will be so nice to visit with them and catch up on all the news." "I'm sure that Henry enjoys his short time home from school, I understand he's almost finished and has been offered several positions but he's waiting to find one near here." "They say he is one of the most highly sought after new schoolmasters, Richard would have loved to visit with him, you know what close friends they were before he went off to school." "Are you excited to see him?" Mary shrugged her shoulders, "Actually, I did see him after school the other night when we were all watching the meeting in the square; he waved at me but it was much too crowded to go over and talk to him." "It will be nice to see everyone again; I miss Bethany and Marianne they always have a story or two to tell." "Aye they do, just like Lillian and Rebecca," laughed Catherine.

"Speaking of the lasses, I think we could use a little help, let me see what they are up to." said Catherine. She went to the foot of the stairs, looked up and called, "Rebecca and Lillian get down here and help us with the dinner please." She returned to the kitchen, wiping her hands on her apron, "They would stay up there all day if it would get them out of work." Rebecca came skipping down the stairs, her hair flying behind her; she was already looking a lot like Mary with long red hair, a tall and slender frame, and good looks. She danced into the kitchen holding a broom chanting, "Mary and William, Mary and William," then turned round and round with the broom until she lost her balance and fell on the floor, laughing. Mary piped in, "There you go; there you go, get up now and get on about helping us; stop worrying about what I have been doing." "You will have a beau yourself in a short time, so don't run your mouth." "Ugggg, no I won't," she shrieked "I don't like lads; they are mean." "Whose mean?" said Lillian, finally making her way to the kitchen. "Lads are, and I don't want anything to do with them," retorted Rebecca. Mary put her hand on her hips and said, "You'll be eating those words before you know it, I promise you." "Now let's stop all this tomfoolery and get on with the work, shall we?" "Oh Mary, she said you're just no fun anymore, no fun at all." Mrs. Munro turned from the stove, "Lasses, lasses, enough with you, come and get these dishes done we have much to do." Rebecca gave Mary a sly look as she got in one last quip, "Mary will have to work extra hard so she can keep house for William." Mary turned on her, "Enough, I said, now get yourselves to work."

It wasn't long before the MacAlduie family arrived, Mr. & Mrs. MacAlduie, Henry and the two younger sisters, Bethany and Marianne. Bethany was a year older than Mary and Marianne a year younger. They had their arms loaded with baskets of food and it was promising to be a very exciting day. Everybody was looking forward to the relaxation and companionship. Gretchen and Carolyn flew out of the sitting room at the sight of the lasses. "Well hello there, said Bethany, I haven't seen you for such a long time, my, my, you both have grown so, I must say you're becoming bonnie little lasses." The lasses looked at each other and smiled, the compliment was well received.

Mary was making her way over to where Bethany and Marianne were standing but Henry stepped in front of her and held out his hand. Mary reciprocated. "How are you Mary," he said placing her small hand in his. "I saw you in the town square and thought you're just as bonnie as ever." "I'm just fine Henry, and yourself," she replied removing her hand from his as quickly as was polite. She couldn't look at him, those eyes of his made her uneasy and his touch was electric. "I'm sorry I didn't come and speak to you in town, there was such a crowd." "Yes there was, he said, I understand." "I'm glad that school is almost finished, I'm looking forward to returning home, I've missed it around here." "You should be proud of yourself you've accomplished a lot, Henry." "Thank you Mary, what are you going to do now that school is over?" "I have some plans but nothing certain right now," she replied. "Oh, you do?" he said, somewhat surprised. "I hope you're not thinking of leaving the area, I'd love to hear about your plans sometime." "No, I don't think I could ever leave here, it's too beautiful, but then I've never been anywhere else have I?" she laughed. "Right now it's best I get back to the kitchen and help; Mum and I have been cooking all week; I hope you enjoy the things we have made." "I'm certain I will, Mary, I hear you are taking after her." "Thank you Henry, but I think it will take some time before I am up to me Mother's standards, I'll see you later." He touched her shoulder and she turned around again and looked at him. "I've been thinking a lot about you lately, Mary, I hope to secure a teaching post near Killin, and I'm just waiting to hear something from the board." Mary smiled at him and said, "Aye, Mum told me; how wonderful for you; it was good to see you again, we must catch up some time, but for now, please excuse me." "Later then?" questioned Henry. "Aye, later," she said and hurried on her way. Why was it, she thought, did he always make her nervous; after all they had known each other forever.

The men wandered outside with their tobacco and talked while the women were busy with the table and food. Ethan remained in the sitting room with the children, coughing periodically. There was certainly going to be enough food to go around with all that they had made combined with Mrs. MacAlduie, Katie, and Sarah's contributions. The lasses whispered, and laughed, talking about the lads they liked, clothes, and plans for the future; it was always fun to be around them. Mary looked out the window and daydreamed, imagining William standing there amongst the group of men and her in the kitchen with the women; maybe even a bairn.

Catherine opened the door and yelled, "Dinner is ready." Everyone ate until they could eat no more; the conversation at the table was light and merry; every so often another dish was passed around. Mary sat with the lasses at one end and Henry was at the other with the men; she would turn her head and find him looking at her; he certainly was attractive, it was unnerving. The men gathered in the sitting room with their ale and the women could hear them talking as they all pitched in together cleaning up the kitchen. They exchanged recipes and talked about bairns and their children growing up. "Henry often speaks of you Mary," said his mother Alicia. "Oh, in what respect?" asked Mary, curious as to why he would talk about her. "Oh, you know, just about the old days and how much fun it was when you were all younger." "Aye, Mary chuckled, we did have fun and Henry took the blame for all the trouble we got into because he was the oldest." Talk then turned to the weather and how it would soon be too cold to do much of anything except sit in the house and work on needlework; Mary drifted in and out of daydreaming wishing that William were here and wondering what he was doing. She caught Henry's glance every so often from the sitting room and wondered why he didn't he have a beau by now, lasses must be attracted to him for his looks and intelligence, maybe he had been too busy with school to care.

The kitchen work was finally done and the women took a well-deserved break, they made some tea and just sat around glad to be done with the chores for a while. Sarah was breastfeeding their infant, Collin, who was only three months old. Alicia, Henry's mother, asked about Richard. Sarah nodded her head, "I wish he could have been able to come along but, as he said, "I must work when work is available." "Lord knows it's hard to get by these days." "The farmers are getting all their horses ready for the next planting season now; Richard really could use another hand in the blacksmith shop."

"Mary, said Alicia, it's about time for you to find a beau, don't you think?" "Well, I do have my eye on someone," Mary said, looking sideways at her sister Katie. "Oh who, they all asked?" She laughed "I'll keep it to meself for now." The mothers exchanged a smile between them. Catherine added, "Mary went to the dance with a group of friends the other night; they had a good time." "Oh, aye, said Alicia, I heard the Piper was out that night, we should have gone too, I so love to hear him." "You can hear him soon, he'll be at Colleen's wedding," said Mary. "That's right, the wedding is coming up soon isn't it, Alicia said; Aaron so likes Harry, they often meet up at Lochay where they both fish; that Stevenson boy too."

The stories and laughter carried on into the early evening hours and soon the group was making plans to head back home. "What's this talk, and who is it that you have your eye on," said Katie, as the two of them stood side by side finishing up the dishes from the meal. Mary missed her big sister Katie. They had always been close but since Katie had married and now had children, they didn't get to spend much time together. Sometimes she went over to Katie's after school and Peter, her brother, always ready to visit with Richard in his shop, would bring the cart to town and pick her up. Mary could tell Katie anything. Mary smiled and said, "I think I'm in love, Katie; of course I've liked William for quite some time, and he me, but now we've made our intentions known." "Da doesn't like him, solely because he's Mr. Stevenson's son." "Oh dear, oh dear, said Katie, only you would pick someone to get Da's goat." "Well you can't help who you fall in love with, can you," laughed Mary. "No, I guess you're right, Mary, you can't." "Good luck with that, you will have to keep me updated, she said, and she yelled into the sitting room, Gretchen, mind that you keep an eye on your sister and brother now, you hear?" "Aye Mum, shouted Gretchen, Grandda is entertaining them right now." "Gather your things together, we will be leaving soon." At that, Catherine came into the kitchen. "Katie, take some of the leftover food home, especially the broth, it will do Ethan good."

"Sarah, you come and get some food for Richard too, I so wish he didn't have to work so hard, I know he would have liked to visit with everyone" "Aye, he would, she replied, maybe next time." "Oh, we understand completely dear, said Catherine, you tell him that he was missed by all and that I will send Peter in with something special for him next week." "I was going to mention to you that Peter has taken an interest in Richard's blacksmithing work." "Aye, Richard and I were talking about that just the other day," Sarah replied. "Every time he comes over he bolts out back to the shop and doesn't come in until Richard does." "Richard said he was going to talk to John and see what he would think of Peter coming in a couple days a week and he would start training him. Lord knows, Richard has enough work for two people after the smithy in Kinnell passed away." "He's been working his fingers off trying to keep up." Catherine smiled at her, "My children are all growing up Sarah, it seems like yesterday they were just wee tots." "My mother says the same thing Catherine, there's only Donny left at home, and the rest all have homes of their own now." "How are your parents Sarah?" "I don't think I've seen them since they visited you on St. Fillian"s Day." "They're well; they would love to see you again." "If you and John happen to go to Stirling, you should stop and see them, they would be thrilled." "As I would, should they come here," said Catherine. "Well, we'd better go see to our other guests they are all getting ready to leave."

MacAlduie's were saying their goodbyes and Henry once again approached Mary. "I haven't been able to spend any time with you Mary and I have to leave for school again next week, would you accompany me on a cart ride tomorrow evening so we can catch up?" "I would love to Henry, but my week is looking pretty busy, we have a lot of bannocks and the wedding cake to make." "There will be plenty of time to do something together when you are back home again." "Oh, Mary, if I didn't know better, I'd think you are trying to avoid me," he laughed. "Surely you can allow me one little cart ride; its ok, Mary, I've already spoken to your Father about it, and he agrees as long as I don't keep you out too late." "Well then, I guess it's all arranged, she said dourly, I will see you then, perhaps your sisters could accompany us, we really didn't get as much time to talk as I wanted." "Perhaps, replied Henry, I'll be looking forward to seeing you again, Mary my dear, and by the way, I'll be interested to hear about your plans." Mary nodded, then turned and walked away. "Mary my dear, Mary my dear," she thought as she stomped into the house. "It's all been arranged has it?" "Me Da left me with nothing but to be rude or comply but this will stop, it has to, William will not approve." "It's a good thing he is going back to school, by the time he returns perhaps William will have asked me to be his beau." Mary was miffed at herself that evening because she just couldn't get

Henry off of her mind, she'd have to tell him about William, but then what could she say, William hadn't asked her to be his beau, not yet anyway.

Katie and Ethan, with their children, were also getting ready to leave. Mary thought that Ethan looked pale and tired; she was concerned. Catherine swept Katie aside and said, "Katie, get news to us as soon as you can about Ethan, after you see the doctor, in fact, I'll have your Da drive over to your house when you return." "He will bring some more broth and other food for you and the bairns, and we'll pack up some salted meat and vegetables for you." "I know Ethan has missed work and its best he doesn't return until he is completely well this time." "If you need anything before that, get word to me, you hear." "Thank you Mum, I know I keep saying it but we really appreciate all you do, I love you." "Listen, Katie, why don't you have the bairns ready when your Da comes and they can stay with us for a while until Ethan feels better, maybe it will be quieter at home and he can rest more, you will be able to get more rest too." "Oh, Mum, they would love that, but are you sure it's not too much for you." "Nonsense, Katie, we would love it, and we have Rebecca and Lillian to tend to them, they need something to do." "Ok, then, I won't say no, you know Donald, he would live here permanently if he thought Peter would give him some attention." "He so looks up to his uncle and Peter is so patient with him and all his questions." "Your Da will be glad to spend some time with his grandchildren; he misses them, as do I." They waked together outside and Catherine gave her a hug, "Off you go then, Ethan, you stay covered up in the cart now, you hear?" "I promise," he said, then immediately had a coughing spasm again. "Bye everyone," waved Katie. "Bye" was heard around. Rebecca and Lillian ran behind the cart trying to keep up until it disappeared out of sight. They fell to the ground laughing and out of breath. "Would you look at the two of them," Catherine said to John. "Now they are still children, it won't be long until they are young women." "Aye, he said, just like our Mary." They stood together for a while watching the lasses frolic and play. "It was nice to have everyone here," he said. "Aye it was, but I'm so concerned for Ethan, I told Katie that you would take some food in for them and the children can come back with you, they can stay out here so Ethan can rest." "Good idea, he said, and the children will enjoy it." "Pray for him John, if you still pray," she said, then turned and walked to the house. He snapped his head around and watched her, "Of course I still pray, why would I not," he shouted across the yard. Without turning and looking at him she lifted her hand up indicating she heard him; then opened the door and went inside. He stood there for a moment, then muttered, "That woman is getting stranger every day." "Come lasses, let's go to the shed and see what Peter is up to." Off they went, running as usual, John following behind.

Mary was sitting at the kitchen table when Catherine entered the house. "He doesn't look good, Mum," she said. "No he doesn't, I agree with you," she replied. "I'm sure he just needs some rest and stronger medicine." "I do so love that little one of Richard and Sarah's. I could hold him all day, it won't be long and he'll be running around, it seems they grow so quickly." "I told Sarah to have Richard keep checking on Katie when he can, until Ethan is better." "She said he goes over there quite often anyway and he would be happy to do it, they've become pretty good friends." "Next week I'm going to have Peter take me over to Richard's so I can spend time with the baby, with all the cooking going on today, I hardly had time to look at him." "It was a great day, don't you think Mary." "It was, wasn't it, she replied, it's always so good to have the family together." "I just wish Richard didn't work so hard." "Aye, what a shame, replied Catherine, I told Sarah that Peter was interested in blacksmithing and she said he's always out in the shop when Richard is there." "I can see that, said Mary, aye I can see he would like that kind of work." "He's always looked up to his big brother, something like Donald looking up to him." "By the way, Henry is coming by tomorrow; he wants me to go on a cart ride with him before he goes back to school." "I tried to refuse but he said Da had already agreed to it, so what could I do?" "It would have been nice if Da had asked my opinion first." "What can it hurt, Mary, one little cart ride, you wouldn't want to hurt Henry's feelings would you?" "No, I guess not, Mum, but he likes me, I mean more than just friends, I can tell." "You're a bonnie lass, Mary, lots of lads will be waiting to court you; it's not unusual, not unusual at all."

That evening Catherine and John were in the sitting room talking about the day. "As usual, dear, you outdid yourself with the meal," he said, taking his wife's hand in his. "Now, now, John; Alicia, Katie and Sarah brought some mighty good food too and our Mary was so much help, it wasn't all my doing, oh no." "You're right, dear, but I am prejudiced," he said as he kissed her hand. "Oh John, you flatter me too much," she laughed. "It's well deserved, my dear, and I must say my daughter is a miniature of you." "Aye, she loves to cook as much as I do." "She'll make a fine wife," he said. "That she will; that she will." "Speaking of Mary, Catherine said, she wasn't happy that you made arrangements for her to go on a cart ride with Henry." "What could a little nudge hurt dear, he said, maybe she will see a different side of him now that they are all grown up, you never can tell." "True, she replied, you never can tell." "By the way, you know, Ethan is still trying to work and he was told he shouldn't, if he wants to get well he's going to have to stop, Katie says he's stubborn and insists on going." "Well, John said, he's a man and feels he must support his family." Catherine retorted, "If he gets any sicker, he won't be supporting anyone." "I'm sure it's nothing more than a bad cold, he'll snap out of it, now stop worrying until the worrying is necessary." "We'll see to it that they have what they need, and so will Richard." "You're a good man, John Munro, a good man," said Catherine. "Think I'll tidy up the kitchen and head for bed soon, I must say I'm a little tired." "Me too, he said, but I think I'll go outside and make sure everything is in order, I'll be in soon." He walked out of the room and he thought, "She's a wonderful woman, my wife, I'm lucky to have her."

CHAPTER
FIVE

In the morning, Catherine packed up a basket with bread and headed out to the field where John was working. "Where might you be off to, this early in the morning," he said when he saw her. "Just going to have a long past due visit with Margaret, she replied, I've readied everything for dinner and will be home to serve it." "Margaret, Margaret who," he asked. "Margaret Stevenson," she said, nothing more. "Oh, no, oh no, I'll not have it," he shouted. "You don't have a say in the matter, John, she replied sternly, her up there lonely, since practically all the crofters have ostracized her." "As well it should be, as well it should be," he said dryly. "John, she said softly, if you are a Christian, as you say you are, then have a heart and see that this woman was not a part of what has happened." "This is all because of that boy, William, you have taken to him, just like Mary," he replied. "John, John, enough of that now, she chided, listen to you blaming everyone." "What's done is done and you had better reconcile yourself to it, it's eating you up John," and with that she turned and walked away. He watched her drive off in the cart, thinking, "Bye, she's a stubborn woman." She had never defied him in any way before, what in the world had gotten into her? He couldn't stand the thought of her going up there.

Margaret, as usual, was sitting on the bench by the cottage, when she saw someone coming up the hill. Her eyes remained fixed on the figure until she could see that it was a woman. "I wonder who that would be?" she thought to herself. "When the figure reached the top, she saw that it was Catherine Munro." "Well, I never, she thought, why is she coming here?" and the first thing in her mind was that something had happened to William. She stood up and yelled, "Catherine is everything ok?" Catherine looked up and gave a little wave, "Hello there, I've come for a short visit if that's ok, and everything is fine." She parked the cart in front of the cottage. Margaret, relieved, smiled, "Welcome, it's so good to see you." "It's good to see you too, replied Catherine, it's been too long." "I must tell you that William is such a nice young lad." "Thank you, she replied, of course, I must agree with you." "He's my joy, I love my other sons too, but William is the most like me; he reminds me of my Father, a gentle man." "My Mary is quite smitten with him," replied Catherine, smiling; here, I've brought you some bread." "Thank you, Catherine you didn't have to do that, you could have come empty handed and I would have been just as glad to see you." "Enjoy," she said, handing her the basket. "Come in, said Margaret, I hope you can stay for a while, and have some tea." "I would be most happy too, laughed Catherine, we have a lot of catching up to do; I've missed you." "And I, you," said Margaret sadly. They made small talk while Margaret readied the tea. "You have a nice kitchen, said Catherine, isn't it wonderful to have an oven?" "Oh aye, said Margaret, I love it." They sipped their tea and talked about the old times, both avoiding any mention of the Clearances and what had transpired. They talked of their children, cooking and getting older. "My, my, I must be going, the time has just flown, hasn't it?" "I have to be home to ready dinner, said Catherine, and I'm sure I'm keeping you from seeing to yours." "Not at all, Catherine, not at all," said Margaret. Catherine stood up, "I must say that I have enjoyed my visit, now you must come and see me." "I will, I will," she replied. "Well don't let too much time pass before you do, laughed Catherine, I go to town some days to visit Katie and my daughter in law, Sarah, other than that, I'm home most of the time." "You could always send word with William." "I'll do that, it will be nice to get out, replied Margaret, I'll walk with you; these old bones need some exercise." "As do mine, as do mine," Catherine replied. "Goodbye, old friend, I'll see you soon." "Goodbye Catherine, and thank you, it meant a lot to me." She stood and watched Catherine drive down the hill until she was just a small dot, then turned and walked in the house her heart lighter than it had been for many months. She made no mention of it to Douglas or her sons that evening, some things were better left unsaid.

As promised, shortly after the supper hour, Henry drove into the yard in the cart. He strode across the grass and came to the door. Catherine answered and invited him in. "Henry, it's good to see you again, so soon." "I'll call Mary down, John's in the sitting room, why don't you go and have a chat?" "Thank you, I will," he replied. She went to the stairs and called, "Mary, Henry is here to see you." Mary was sitting on the bed in her room not wanting to go downstairs at all and definitely not wanting to go on that cart ride. "I'll be there in a minute, Mum," she replied.

Mary's sister Rebecca peeked into the room. "Mary has another beau, Mary has another beau, I'm going to tell William," she chanted. "Wheesht. Rebecca, Mary retorted, Henry is not my beau, and never will be." "Aye he is, aye he is," continued Rebecca in her usual annoying way. "You have two beaus, William and Henry, William and Henry." "You don't know anything; you can't have two beaus," said Mary and she slowly rose from the bed and made her way down the steps to find that Henry was in the sitting room with her Da. How she hated it that they seemed to be so close and full of secrets. Instead of continuing to the sitting room she went to the kitchen where she found her Mum at the sink.

"There you are, said Catherine; Henry is waiting for you in the sitting room." "Aye, I know Mum, I don't want to go; I don't feel good." "Nonsense, the fresh air will do you good, you must go, Henry has come all this way." "It's only one cart ride, Henry will be going back to school, and we are friends with the family." "I know, I know, Mum." With that, she made her way into the sitting room. Catherine observed her demeanor and felt for her daughter, she knew that Mary had no interest in spending time with Henry; she had been fine all day until now. She couldn't help but compare Mary's leaping entrance down the steps when William came over, to the slow, almost dragging entrance she made upon Henry's arrival. She debated whether she should have a talk with John about it or let it lie. She decided to leave it alone because John wouldn't understand anyway, his mind was set.

Mary stood in the doorway without saying a word. "Mary, said John, there you are, Henry's here." "I see that Da, she replied, how are you Henry?" She held out her hand in greeting. "Fine, Mary, just fine," said Henry and he took her hand gently, not letting go. "Your Da and I were just having a little talk." "Did your sisters not come then," she said, disappointment clearly showing in her voice as she removed her hand from his. "Truthfully, Mary, I didn't ask them, I thought we could spend some time alone." "I'm sorry to hear that, Henry, she said aloofly, we might as well go then, it's getting late." "Mary; cautioned her Da, watch your manners!" "I'm sorry, Da, she replied, I just meant that it will be quite dark soon." "I'll have her home safe and sound in a couple of hours then," said Henry. "I know you will, have a good time, replied John, if I don't see you before you go back to school, have a safe trip and we'll see you when you come home again." He was obviously quite pleased with the evening there was a lilt in his voice. Mary was upset that her Da didn't put the restrictions on their outing that he had done with William and she was annoyed that he seemed to be so pleased about it.

They reached the cart and Henry grabbed Mary's hand and elbow and gently steered her into the cart seat. "For heaven's sake, Henry, she said, you don't have to be such a gentleman around me after all we grew up together." "We did, didn't we Mary?" "I guess that's why I still feel such a bond with you." "Things change; we are not the same now as we were back then." "No, I suppose you're right, said Henry, now we are all grown up looking ahead to new lives." "I must say, you have grown up bonnie." "Thank you Henry, let's be on our way, shall we." "At your service, my dear," he laughed, picking up the reins. It was obvious that he was in quite a joyful mood. "Oh boy," she thought to herself.

They rode in silence for quite some time. Mary couldn't help but compare the difference in being with Henry from being with William. With William there was no uneasy silence, no need to conjure up something to say for the sake of talking although it seemed Henry had a lot to say. He talked about his life in the city where he was studying and how different it was to the quite life of Killin. Mary listened politely, drifting in and out of daydreams and glad that she was not required to comment. They rode through the town, past Lochay Road where Colleen lived, all the way down Main Street to Manse Road where they took a right and then another right on Stewart Road only going a short distance further when Henry stopped and parked the cart by a grassy field. "Shall we, Mary," said Henry, reaching for her hand to escort her from the cart. "Thank you, Henry, she said, so here we are at Fingal's Stone." "Aye, replied Henry, I brought you here because it reminded me of how many times we came out here when we were children, and all the stories we made up about Fingal and his stone." "Aye we did do that," laughed Mary, starting to relax a little. "I will have to tell the story of Fingal to my students when I start teaching, he said, I want them to remember the stories of Scotland, I think it's important for them to know all about our heritage." "Oh, I do agree, there is so much history here, she said, and what will you tell them, Henry?" "I will tell them that outside the lovely village of Killin, Scotland, lies a field wherein lies a stone by the name of Fingal's Stone." "The stone marks the burial ground of a mythical Celtic Warrior known to be a giant; this giant, named Fingal, died on an island in Lake Dochart after a courageous battle with an arch enemy over the hand of a woman." "His body was found downstream and he was carried to Killin where he is remembered by the stone forever named Fingal's Stone." "Ah, said Mary, that's a very good story indeed; your students will like it." "I think you will be an exceptional teacher, Henry." "I also brought you here, Mary, because, just like Fingal, I am hoping for the hand of a woman." "You are an educated man, Henry, you must have your pick of women," said Mary. "Yes, I could have had my pick in Glasgow, Mary, but I was not looking for anyone there, I've always only loved one woman." "And whom would that be?" she asked, and immediately thought, "Oh no, why did I say that?" She had been trying to keep the conversation lighthearted but he was so charming that the words just slipped out. "I think you know," Henry said quietly. "I don't know, she replied, sometimes what we want is not attainable and we have to look in other directions." "Thank you for bringing me here, Henry, it was good to remember the fun we used to have; I'll always remember those days." "I think we had best be on our way home now, before it gets too late." "I suppose you're right, Henry said, but it seems the evening has flown by and we had such little time together." "I had hoped to talk more with you." "There will be lots of time for more talk, she said, after all, my schooldays are over and yours are nearing an end." "We are both ready to start our new lives soon." He said, "I am looking forward to teaching but it's nothing unless I can share it with someone." Quickly she spoke, "And I have plans to start a bakery with Mum in Mr. McPhee's old store, I haven't asked them yet so please keep it to yourself for now, I haven't told anyone else except Colleen." "Of course Mary, whatever you wish," he replied. "If they agree and we do it, you will have to stop in and see us from time to time." "Well, well, I must say, you are quite ambitious, Mary, most women would be ready to settle down and have bairns." "I know, she replied, times are changing." Henry decided not to push the conversation as he was detecting a dismissal tone in her voice. He hoped that she was just anxious to get home; hopefully there would be another time. He felt at a loss for words and simply said, "Come, Mary, I'll take you home now." The bakery had thrown a wrench in his plans, would she be willing to leave and move to another town? He wasn't sure where he would get a position but it most likely wouldn't be in Killin as they already had a schoolmaster. Mary chattered on the ride home, telling Henry about Mr. McPhee and how they had formulated a deal with each other. She said she was excited be doing something that could help the family with their financial situation. She well knew what had been on Henry's mind and didn't want to let the conversation flow in that direction again. On the ride there, she had barely said a word but now she was talking nonstop hoping he wouldn't start talking again. He listened patiently, his mind reeling at how differently things had turned out than what he had expected. Mary was the only lass he had ever considered when he thought about taking a wife and he dreamed about her on those lonely nights so far away. There were many eligible lasses in Glasgow and he'd been invited to quite a few dinners where the host hoped that he would court their daughter but he was never attracted to any of them, his mind was always on Mary. When they arrived back at the farm he escorted her to the door and asked if he could call on her when he came home again. "Hopefully things will work out and I'll be at the bakery she said, I have a feeling I'll be spending most of my time there." That wasn't what he hand in mind, but he dropped the subject. Before he could give her a hug or a kiss on the check she said, "Thank you Henry, for the evening, it was good to see Fingal's Stone again, I haven't been out there in years." "Have a good trip back, I'll see you soon." She opened the door and went in never turning to look behind her. Clearly Henry was disappointed, he was aware that Mary had deftly changed the conversation. Had he waited all this time just to be turned away now? He hoped not.

Mary didn't sleep well that night, she felt badly that she had been so rude to Henry, he was obviously in love with her and it scared her. The last thing she wanted to do was hurt him.

School was over and the wedding was fast approaching, Mary and Colleen spent their days together getting everything ready. William and Harry were still furiously working on the cottage but the work was nearly done. Sometimes they would all meet at Mary's house and sit out front chatting and talking; other times Catherine would hail them into the kitchen for a snack or they would all go for a walk. John tolerated this but kept an ever watchful eye on them. One evening they went up to William's house and surprised Margaret. Mary liked her instantly and Margaret felt the same about her. Colleen and Harry invited her to the wedding and she promised to go.

Mary headed off to Colleen's with Peter. She wanted to get there early and help; besides they were going to the cottage and see what remained to be done. Colleen was waiting outside for her and they laughed about the upcoming stag party for Harry. They knew William would go all out with it because of the fun loving person he was.

CHAPTER
SIX

Mary decided it was time to make her plans for the future known and she wanted to tell her mother what she had been planning with Mr. McPhee. "Hey Mum, the shower went well, don't you think?" "Oh aye, she replied, very well, what nice gifts Colleen received." "Listen, Mum, now that school is over I want to talk to you about something." "I have an idea but I need your opinion, and of course, your approval." "Oh, and what's that Mary?" "You know the fish market went out of business when Mr. McPhee's health declined." "Aye, I know Mary; the market will be missed by the villagers, it's too bad they never had any children to take over for them." "They lost two bairns you know, when they were very young." "I didn't know that, Mary replied, what a shame, he is such a kind man; his wife is quite frail now too." "Mary clasped her hands together and said, "The shop is waiting for a new owner and I would like us to start a bakery." "Everyone says we have the best baked goods in the area, we already send them to weddings and special occasions; I just know we could make a go of it." "Oh, and Mr. McPhee said the one in Aberfeldy burned down just last year." "That's right, Catherine said, I forgot all about that." "Oh Mary, I had no idea you were thinking along those lines, aren't you the secret one." "Has your Da heard of this?" "No, not yet, I wanted to talk to you about it first." "Where would we get the money for this venture, we haven't been able to accumulate any savings and now with Ethan sick we're going to have to pitch in and help." "Not to worry, said Mary, I've already had several discussions with Mr. McPhee and he has a plan that I think will work for all of us; seeing the shop sitting there idle was hard for him and no one else has approached him to rent it out."

"I told him my idea and he made a proposal to me." "He says he's well aware of our reputation for baked goods in the area and he has no reservations whatsoever." "He told me he had savings just collecting dust and he would fix it up with the ovens and shelves that we need and also pay for the supplies until we are able to do it; in return, we would pay him a 30% commission on what we make until his expenses were covered; after that time, he will charge us rent and perhaps someday would sell it to us." "He made it clear, in his teasing way, that he would expect us to make him some highland scones once in a while and maybe a spot of tea each day." "He says it would be good to have some activity around, he's going crazy in the silence; after all, his life has been spent waiting on customers day after day." "He said, (and at this comment Mary hunched her shoulders and squinted her eyes in an imitation of him), Mr. and Mrs. Munro are good people." Catherine chuckled. "I told him that we would be there to look in on Mrs. McPhee once in a while, she must get lonely." "Oh, and I told him that he shouldn't have to worry about fixing breakfast and dinner, we would see to it." "He says he is an amateur carpenter and he would be able to do a lot of the remodeling himself." "He suggested that we might want to also serve breakfast and dinner but, of course, that would be up to us; he pointed out that there is room for at least six or seven tables and chairs." "You know, Mum, even in Killin, a lot of people still don't have ovens, they have been taking their dough to bakeries out of town to get it baked; even as far as Kinnell and Comrie." Catherine replied, "Aye, many of them do that when they go for other supplies, I was just telling Margaret how lucky we both were to have ovens." "Margaret?" questioned Mary. "Aye, William's mother, she replied, oh my goodness, with all the fuss going on lately, I forgot to tell you that I had made a trip to see her." "Remember, I told you I would, we had such a nice little visit." Mary grabbed her mother's hands, "Oh Mum, you don't know how that pleases me." "It was good for me too, Mary, she replied, of course your Da didn't take it too well, but I went anyway." "Now, I must say, you have been very busy and I am a little taken aback by this idea of yours; but it is exciting and I'm willing to do it; however, we must speak to your Da and get his opinion, so don't get your hopes up just yet."

That evening Catherine approached John. He too, was shocked but the wheels began to spin in his head. It seemed as if Catherine's baked goods were already in demand for the weddings and festivities in the area; every week she was baking for one event or the other. He had no doubt that they would succeed but he hoped it wouldn't be too much for her. After giving it much thought, he agreed to the venture and they would tell Mary in the morning. Since the Clearances, it had been difficult to eke out a living on what they were able to make on the little croft farm they were allotted. And to think that Douglas Stevenson, William's Father, sat up there on his perch as a tacksman making money was more than he could bear. He would have to do something soon about this fascination Mary had with William, before it got out of hand. He had other ideas for his beloved daughter and William had nothing to do with it. He wasn't a man to judge someone because of who his Father was but William did not come across as having any goals for his future. Mary needed someone who could take care of her properly and he was going to make sure that his daughter had a responsible husband. Now it was obvious that Mary had a head on her shoulders; many women would never think of starting a business, much less, someone as young as his daughter. "Aye, he thought, times were changing, maybe for the better." Catherine was unaware how he feared for the future. They were just getting by and now that they needed to help Ethan and Katie it would become harder and harder to make ends meet. He drifted off to sleep in the sitting room chair thinking that they finally had a chance to make something of themselves and all because of his Mary.

Next morning Mary was up early hoping that she would have her answer. She hurried down the stairs and found her mother as usual in the kitchen. "And why would you be up so early this morning," said her mother laughingly. "Well, you know, I'm an early riser, Mum." "That's good to know, said her mother, because bakers have to be up early every day." "Are you saying we can do it?" smiled Mary. She grabbed her mother and turned her around and around several times. "Aye, we can do it, Mary, your Father thinks it's a good idea if we are sure it's not going to be too much for us." "He wants to talk to Mr. McPhee and thank him for the opportunity and your Da says that you have a good napper on yer shoulders." Mum, if you agree, I have been thinking about a name and sign for the business, 'Munro's Bakery, Confections and Eatery', and then below that, 'Come in and have a seat'. "Aye, aye, I like it Mary, there is no stopping you, you are always thinking." "I've had some time to think about it; now we have to make it happen." "No doubt, no doubt, said her mother, and so we shall."

Mary was elated and couldn't wait to see William and tell him the news. She wasn't sure what he would think about the bakery but she assumed he would be happy for her. When it was time for bairns, the bakery would already be established and they could hire someone to replace her. Rebecca and Lillian were getting older and they could pitch in as well. 'Goodness, she thought, I'm already planning bairns and he hasn't even asked me to wed him yet." Peter dropped her off at Colleen's house early so they could get a few pending things finished. He would meet her later at Katie's as he wanted to see Richard that afternoon. Mary found Colleen and told her that everyone had agreed to her idea. Colleen was not surprised; they had talked about it many times. She knew that Mary had been to see Mr. McPhee and a few times she had accompanied her there. She wondered at Mary's need to do this. Most lasses their age were only worried about getting married including her. Lost in thought, they both walked to her soon to be new cottage not talking but lost in thought. Colleen was thinking about the discussion between herself and Harry the other evening. She had asked him if William was going to approach Mary and make known that he wanted to wed her. Harry said he didn't know but he was pretty sure that William had a few things he wanted to do before he was wed. William had talked to him about his plans but he didn't feel he should repeat them; not even to Colleen; that was for William to do. Colleen wondered what plans he would have. She liked William a lot but like most people, she didn't see the depth of him and the last thing she wanted was to see Mary hurt. She turned and looked at her friend and said, "Mary, if you ever need help in the bakery and I still am without bairns, would you consider me?" "Of course we will dunderhead, she replied, I hope that it will be a success and we will need lots of help; and of course, as my best friend in the whole world, you are my first choice." "Will Harry allow his wife to work?" "We both want bairns but we've talked about trying to wait until we can get a little ahead financially, we have to try and save up a little money and that will take time." "If we're going to have bairns, I want them to be well provided for." "Harry and I want you to know how much we appreciate all the work that you and William have done to get the cottage ready, the bridal shower, and everything else you've done" "William says he is all thumbs when it comes to carpentry but Harry said, no matter, he did all the lifting and hauling that Harry asked him to do." "I am so glad that they are good friends, just like us." "What if William asks you to wed him and he wants to start a family right away and not have his wife working in a bakery?" asked Colleen. "I don't know, Colleen, but he hasn't asked me yet and I feel like I have to make plans for my future now." "If the bakery is a success and William asks me to wed him, then I'm sure someone else can step into my place." Colleen threw her head back and laughed, "Oh, Mary, you said if it's a success, of course it will be." Changing the subject, Mary said, "Here we are, let's get the measuring stick for the curtains, your wedding will be here before you know it." "Aren't you excited?" I'm very excited and I'm going to wear me Mum's wedding dress, we had to do some alterations but we've finished it, I'll show it to you when we go back to the house." "I can't wait to see it, I'm getting a dress from Katie to wear, and I hope you like it." "I will, Mary, you would look bonnie in anything." "Did I tell you that Harry is going full out and wearing the Highland Dress; kilt, jacket, dirk and sporran?" "Oh my, laughed Mary, won't he be the elegant Scotsman?" They finished measuring for the curtains, then hurried back to the house to see that guests had started arriving for the open house. Mary saw her mother with Rebecca and Lillian just getting out of the cart. "Come with me upstairs quick, said Colleen, I want you to see the dress." "Oh, Harry will just die when he sees you, you are going to be the most bonnie bride," said Mary. "I don't know about that, Mary, but I do know Harry loves me just the way I am." "And that's just perfect," replied Mary. They hugged each other and then went back downstairs. They had a fun afternoon and everyone admired the presents, then the food was served. It wasn't long before the carts were heading back home again. Mary rode back to the village with a friend from school and they dropped her off at Katie's house.

CHAPTER

SEVEN

William drove into Munroe's yard. Mary saw him coming from out her bedroom window and ran to meet him. "Let's take a little walk, if you can," he said. He grabbed her hand. "First of all Mary, I think you know that my affections for you are more than friendship, I want to make you my wife someday and spend the rest of me life with you." "And I feel the same," replied Mary. "I don't want to be a farmer or tacksman like me Da, I can't stomach the rent collecting." " I want to apprentice in the textile industry and learn about the power looms; in order to do so, I must go to Glasgow for a couple of years and study; I hope you will understand." "I know it's not right for me to ask you to wait that long but I don't know of any other way to make a better life for us and I believe this is what I need to do." "I will be able to come home now and again during that time but if you don't want to wait that long, I understand, I really do."

Mary felt she would faint for a moment, but then caught her breath." "Oh William, two years is such a long time, of course I will wait for you but I had no idea, I mean, that you were planning this." She thought that it had been silly of her to assume he would be a tacksman like his Father. Her mind was racing and she stood there thinking, not saying a word. The thought of her being a tacksman's wife had never even entered her mind before. Her Da would never have stood for it. She knew that the bakery would take a lot of her time and she hoped that the two years would fly by quickly. "Was she doing the right thing?" Her mind started spinning, but of course she was; her family needed this as much as she did. William touched her arm, "Mary, are you ok?" She looked up at him, tears in her eyes. "Aye, I'm fine, just shocked, that's all." "I thought about asking you to marry me and come to the city but it wouldn't be practical." "I have nothing to my name and I wouldn't be able to take care of you." "I understand William, I really do, you must go and do as you have planned we have our whole lives ahead to be together." "We are young now; it's the right time to do it, you may never have that chance again." "Thank you, Mary, I just knew you would understand," he said, relief in his voice. She wondered what he would have done if she had told him that she wouldn't be willing to wait, but of course, she never would have. He hadn't told her about his plans and she hadn't said anything to him about the bakery. Perhaps he thought she wouldn't understand, and maybe she felt the same about him. They really did know so little about each other.

As they walked back home she told him her plans. "So you see, William, the two years will fly by quickly, I will be busy at the bakery and you will be busy learning a trade." Then they were silent, it was the first time they were without much to say to each other, both lost in thought. "Come in," she said when they reached the cottage. They entered the kitchen. "Sit, and I will get you a cup of tea," said Mary. Rebecca came into the kitchen and stopped short when she saw them sitting there. "Oh, hello, she said, I didn't know you were home." Mary smiled at her, "Aye, here we are, where's Mum?" Rebecca sat down beside them, "She went to Sarah's today, to see the bairn and visit with her." "Peter went to pick her up and he should be back any minute now, in fact, here they come in the cart." "I'm in charge of supper tonight." "You are now, laughed Mary, good for you, good for you." "And will you be staying for supper, William?" Rebecca asked. "No, but thank you for asking, I have to be on my way soon, chores you know." "Aye, I know a little bit about chores, Mum is good at thinking them up for me," Rebecca said, and they all laughed.

They heard the door and Mrs. Munro came into the house, went to her bedroom to drop her packages and then came into the kitchen putting her apron on as she did so. "Well, well, what a surprise," she said, as she saw William and Mary sitting there. "What are you two doing today?" "Well, Mum, it seems William has been making some plans too," said Mary. Mrs. Munro thought to herself, "Oh no, oh no, he's gone and asked her to wed him, and John will never stand for it." Out loud she said, "Plans, and what might they be?" "Shall I tell, William, or shall you?" said Mary. "I'll tell, Mary," he said, and squeezed her hand. "I haven't said anything until now, but Mr. McGregor and I have been having talks for quite some time, you see, I have no interest in farming or collecting rents, it's not something I'm interested in." He laughed, "Me Da is always after me about it." "Linen has been the primary industry but recently the cotton industry has been on the rise and there are going to be massive changes in the textile industry." There are new power looms that will increase productivity and a new technique called sprigging that I am interested in." "Glasgow is renowned for its plaids, and many of the weaver's cottages in Stirling and Aberdeen are using looms to weave tartans." "It's my desire to apprentice in Glasgow and Mr. McGregor wants to sponsor me, it will be to his advantage as well." "He intends to build onto his shop and hire some workers." "Of course, they will have to be trained in the new machinery, and that's where I come in." "I'm sorry, he ended, I'm probably boring you to death." "No, not at all," said Mrs. Munro, she was relieved and surprised all at the same time. "I can see that your generation is ambitious, Mary has plans, you have plans, oh my!" "I must say I admire your goals, how long will this apprenticeship be?" William sighed and said, "Mr. McGregor says around two years but Mary said she will be busy with the bakery and she doesn't mind waiting for me." "You see, Mrs. Munro, we want to be wed someday." "Well, well, you don't say, Catherine replied, two years is a long time." He smiled and looked at Mary, "I think I'll be able to come home once in a while but I'm not sure." "Of course, I'll send a post every week." Mrs. Munro looked down and softly said, "I wish the best for you, William, we were just getting to know each other, I will miss you." William stood up and took her hand in his. "Thank you, Mrs. Munro, for understanding, I must be off for home, I still haven't told me Da, it's something I'm not looking forward to doing." "Of course me Mum is happy for me; and sad at the same time." "My Father is another story." They all walked to the door. Catherine patted William on the shoulder. "It will all work out, things usually do." "Good luck, William, and tell your mother hello, we had a nice little visit the other day." "I'm expecting to see her come here soon." "You don't say, said William, she never mentioned it to me." "Then again, we've all be running henny penny with the wedding and all." "I'm glad you are friends, it will be hard for her when I leave, me brothers are closer to me Da but I must confess I'm a mama's boy." "There's nothing wrong with that, William, nothing at all."

Mary walked William down the drive to the cart, holding hands as they went. John was coming out of the shed and they gave him a wave. He waved back, but said nothing. He thought to himself. "What is he doing here again, and look at them holding hands." "I suppose Catherine is catering to him as usual."

Rebecca was busy as a bee in the kitchen, she was proud to show everyone what she had made and she thought she had done a pretty fine job. She called up the stairs, "Lillian, get down here and set the table for supper, everyone will be in soon, so hurry up about it." Lillian flounced into the kitchen, "Just because you are cooking, doesn't mean you are me boss." "No, I'm not your boss, Rebecca replied, but mother is, right Mum?" Catherine was just turning the corner into the kitchen,

"What's that?" she asked. Rebecca looked at Lillian and said, "As I am doing the cooking tonight, it is only right that Lillian set the table." "Sounds fair to me," said Catherine. Rebecca gave Lillian a look that said, "Told you so." The family sat down for supper and Peter had to get in his say, "Rebecca, are you sure the food it fit to eat." "Now, now, said John, enough of that teasing, I'm sure Rebecca has done just fine, it smells pretty good to me." "Thank you, Da," said Rebecca. They finished eating, everyone congratulated Rebecca on her first meal, then Peter and John went out to finish their chores and the women cleaned up. "Mighty fine job, Rebecca, you can cook any time you want to." "You see, said Rebecca, I have been watching you; Mary is not the only one who can cook." "That's good because we will be depending on you to cook much more when the bakery opens, I hope we can count on you," said Catherine. "Of course, I will do whatever you need, Mum," she said proudly. "Furthermore, said Catherine, Lillian, you will be expected to help too." Once more Rebecca gave that look to Lillian who ignored her. They all wiped their hands on their aprons and sat down for a final cup of tea for the evening. "I think the lasses are growing up, Mum, said Mary, they really did work hard." "Did I hear you right Mary, said Rebecca, I never thought I'd hear those words coming out of your mouth." "Love must change people." "Oh, for heaven's sake, said Mary, you always have to have the last word." "I'm going up to bed, goodnight everyone." "Goodnight," they all said in unison.

That evening John and Catherine were in the sitting room and he asked, "What was that Stevenson boy doing here again?" She replied, "He wanted to tell us about his plans for the future." "Plans, what plans," he asked. "Mr. McGregor is sending him to Glasgow to learn how to run new machinery looms, then he plans on expanding his shop and William will train everyone." "You see, John, William isn't interested in the farm or in collecting rent." "You don't say, you don't say," replied John, trying to hide his surprise and mirth. "And how long will he be gone then?" "He says about two years," she replied. "Hmmm," he said, two years is a long time, a long time indeed, when you are young." He stood up and looked out of the window thinking that you never know what lies around the corner in life. There was a bounce in his step that evening and a glint in his eye which didn't go unnoticed by his wife.

CHAPTER
EIGHT

John Munro was finished with his work for the day, he stood by the outside pump washing his hands and he ran his fingers through his thinning brown hair. He walked to the house and called, "Catherine, Catherine, where are you?" There was no answer, so once again he stepped outside and walked around to the back where Catherine often spent time in the garden. "Oh, there you are," he said. Catherine smiled and stood up, removing her gloves. "Were you looking for me John?" "Aye, aye, he replied, I thought we could take a ride into town to talk to Mr. McPhee about the bakery." "As you wish, John, but shouldn't Mary come as well, after all it was her idea?" "Of course, of course, replied John, where is she now?" "Tending to the wash, let's see if she has finished." They both walked to the back where Mary had just emptied the dolly tub in the washhouse and was placing the possing stick inside. "There you are, Mary me lass," he said, an uncharacteristic smile on his face. "Here I am, Da, just me and my wash, smiled Mary. "What are you two up to, looking like the foxes who ate the chickens?" "I see you have just finished up the last of the wash, said Catherine, your Da thought we should make a trip to town and talk to Mr. McPhee." "Oh, aye, that would be alright, but I've some stew on the fire that needs tending to." "No matter, Mary, said Catherine, we'll fetch Lillian and Rebecca down to watch the kettle, it will be a good experience for them." "That's if we don't come home to scorched stew, laughed John, them with their heads in the clouds." "I'll just run in and change my frock then, said Mary, I'll meet you by the shed." "Ok, said John, Come along then Catherine," and he, grabbed his wife's hand. Catherine was so surprised by his action that she had to hide a grin. She thought to herself, "My, he's like a changed man, so lighthearted." She hadn't seen him this way since before the clearances; it was turning out to be a good day, a good day indeed!

Mary hurried out to the shed quickly. She was excited that her plan was starting to become a reality. John and Catherine were waiting in the cart and he reached down to take his daughter's hand and help her. "Thanks, Da," said Mary. "You're welcome, he replied, and off we go." They traveled a short distance through the beautiful countryside, down Pier Road, across Lochay Bridge then left onto Main Street, entering the Village of Killin "Won't be long until the cold sets in," John said. "Can't stop the seasons," replied Catherine. "Too bad you can't stop the old bones from aching either," he laughed. "My, my, thought Mary, what in the world has gotten into him, he's never this jolly." Truth was that John was relieved since the idea of the bakery had been agreed upon, and who would have thought that his bonnie daughter would have dreamed up this plan." "Bye, she would be a welcome wife, she had a head on her shoulders it was too bad she didn't have the same knack for picking out suitors. He turned his head and asked, "How did your ride with Henry go?" "Fine, we drove out to Fingal's Stone, I forgot how beautiful it is out there, remember you used to take us there." "I remember those days when you were all wee tots; we all went, the MacAlduie's too."

They turned left on Lyon Road and then stopped in front of McPhee's. John jumped down and went to the door and knocked. He stood waiting for a few minutes and then turned to the cart and said, "I hope we haven't come at a bad time, perhaps he's not feeling well today." "No Da, Mary said, pointing to the door, here he comes now." Mr. McPhee opened the door smiling and said, "Well, well, if it isn't the Munro's, come in, come in." They shook hands, "Are you sure you have time for us right now?" asked John. "Aye, aye, I was just finishing up some dishes, these old ears aren't what they used to be, I thought I heard someone but wasn't sure." "We'll have to get that bell hooked up again; I took it down when the shop closed." He waved to the women in the cart, "Come, come, ladies." Mary jumped down and then assisted Catherine and they all went into the shop. Mr. McPhee pointed to a long table in the room and asked them to have a seat. Once they were seated, he said, "I've been eager to hear if you have agreed to the plans that Mary and I hatched up." He laughed, "You didn't know we were having secret meetings did you?" "No, replied John, I must say I was shocked, but also pleasantly surprised and we have thought about it and the answer is aye, it was very kind and generous of you to make such an offer." Mr. McPhee snorted, "Nonsense, he said, it's all of you I should thank, it was breaking me heart that this poor old shop would be left all alone with no one to attend to her." "Now, enough of the thanks and howdy doos, let's get down to business, shall we?" He threw back his head and laughed again, "It's obvious that a bakery has to have ovens and I can have someone here next week to put them in, you see, I was pretty sure you would say aye so I went about the business of finding someone to do it." He chuckled, "This old dunderhead of mine is still pretty quick." "My suggestion is that you need two ovens but if you want more, we can arrange it." "I can pretty much assure you that one of them will be filled most of the time with village folk wanting their bread baked." He rubbed his stomach, "We all love our bread don't you know." He looked at the women and they looked at each other. "Mum," asked Mary? Catherine said, "Two ovens will be quite enough, we can work our schedule around the busy time." "I see you are a practical woman, he said, what else will you be needing?" Of course, as I've discussed with Mary, I will see to the supplies until you are able to do so." John said, "This won't be all on your shoulders, Mr. McPhee, I will help, and my sons Peter and Richard are pretty good with a hammer." "Good, good, Mr. McPhee said, let's stop with the formalities, shall we, you can call me Charles." This time John let out a long chuckle and reached over and patted him on the shoulder, "Charles it is then, when would you like to begin the work?" Charles gave another laugh and said, "No sense putting off til' the morrow what you can do today, why don't you stop in early next week and we will see how the ovens are coming along, once they are in we can begin our work." "We wouldn't want to get in the way and impede their progress, huh?" "Once everything is done, the women can come in and pretty things up," he said, laughing merrily again. "Nothing like a woman's touch I always say." This time they all laughed. Mr. McPhee was such a funny, jolly, little man that it was impossible not to like him, his laugh was infectious. Catherine stood up, "Charles is your wife Nancy up and about?" "I wonder if it would be ok for me to stop in quickly and say hello to her, I thought we should get reacquainted as we will be here every day." "Aye, aye, go ahead in, she's probably reading the good book, she has to make up for my sins," he said, which brought yet again another round of laughter from him. "Seriously, she would be thrilled to see you, she doesn't get much company these days." "We'll have to change that," Catherine said and headed to the back of the house calling out, "Mrs. McPhee, it's Catherine Munro, would it be ok if I come in and visit with you just a short time?" She heard a feeble voice call from one of the rooms and found Nancy sitting in a chair with The Bible lying in front of her. "Catherine what a nice surprise!" "Charles told me that I might be seeing a lot of you in the future." "I don't get around much anymore, but it will be lovely to have some activity in the shop again, please, forgive my appearance." Catherine reached over and patted her hand, "You look just fine to me, rest assured, Mrs. McPhee, Mary and I will stop in and see you every day, we're so appreciative that you and Charles would take a chance on us like this." "You're a blessing in disguise, Catherine I'll look forward to seeing more of you and having some activity in the shop again." "Charles is so good to me but I do yearn for some female companionship and frankly, he doesn't know what to do with himself all day, he loves people so." They caught up on the past, mostly talking about the villagers who were still with them and some who had passed on to the better life. Finally Catherine stood, "I'll let you get back to your reading, is there anything I can do for you right now?" "No, thank you for asking, I have everything I need right now." "Alright then, I think we'll be leaving soon so I'd better get back out there, it was so nice to see you again." She turned and walked back to the shop thinking that their lives had all taken a new path; hopefully a better one.

She found everyone looking around the shop discussing where and what they should do to change it when John grabbed her arm and steered her to the back of the room. "Charles says, if you want, we can widen this doorway and put up tables for your work and shelves for your supplies, the doorway will be wide enough to see when someone comes into the shop but it will hide all of the work in progress." "It's only a suggestion, Charles piped in, and whatever will work best for you ladies is fine with me." She smiled at him, "And a great suggestion, don't you agree, Mary?" Wholeheartedly," she replied. "We can put the counter out here in front of the ovens, from the door almost to the work room." "The tables can all go over here by the windows for customers to sit; we can put pretty tablecloths on them; I'm getting so excited!" She grabbed Charles and gave him a big hug, "It's all because of you," and she kissed him on the cheek. For the first time in his life he didn't know what to say. His face turned a bright red but he had a smile from ear to ear. "Oh Mary, he said when he recovered, you have brought a light back into me life." On that note they all said their goodbyes and headed home. "What a lovely little man," said Catherine. "I agree," said John. "I agree too," said Mary and they laughed most of the way home. Charles' bubbly personality had infected all of them. They arrived home and were getting ready for bed when an idea popped into Mary's head. "Mum, Da," she said, "Mr. McPhee has been so generous to us." "Aye, aye he has," they agreed. "Why don't we change our sign and call it McPhee's Bakery, and then under that we can put *serving Munro breads, sweets and eats.*" "What a lovely idea, Mary, said John, Richard can make the sign, he's good at it." Mary smiled at him, "Let's keep it a secret from him until we put up the sign." "Aye, Catherine laughed, can't you just see his face when we tell him?" "He will be all puffed up about it." All of them chuckled on their way to bed.

CHAPTER NINE

William's mother, Margaret, was sitting outside the cottage on her favorite bench thinking about her four sons. What a shame she hadn't had a daughter. She wouldn't trade any of her sons, she loved them all, they were part of her, but a daughter would have been lovely. Her eldest three were hard hearted and ambitious like their Father. Douglas was always strong willed but since he saw his chance at tacksman he had taken on a rougher persona. She supposed he would have to, collecting rent from those he had lived side by side with all those years. She would never know and could never have imagined he would have done it. He had butted a few heads in the past with his personality, but nothing serious. On the rare occasions that there had been meetings in the village, he had practically appointed himself head of the project; he certainly didn't have any problem giving orders. William was her salvation, he was like her, in fact he was a lot like her Da; softer, more sensitive, and they had a special bond. Her life could be divided between two things; before the clearances and after. Before, there were fun times when all the women would get together, especially when they went to the shielings in summer. They planned festivities and food they would prepare for events like St. Fillian's Day and talked and gossiped about their menfolk. "Bye, how she missed those times." After, things had changed dramatically there were no more trips to the shielings and no more invitations. It was an unspoken thing but she could feel the avoidance from the villagers. She lived in a different world than they did now, but was it a better one? She didn't think so. She didn't hold it against anyone she wasn't that kind of a person but it still hurt. "Oh well, she thought, life is as life does."

Of her three elder sons, only Michael had a beau, Nellie. She had only met her once in the village and she seemed a nice lass. Margaret lived for the days when the cottage would be filled with the sound of little bairns. She would welcome having a daughter in law and she wished that Michael would bring Nellie for a visit but he didn't seem to spend much time with her. In his usual brusque way, everything else came first. The other two sons apparently had several lasses or so it sounded from the conversations she had overhead. Her mind wandered to Catherine's visit. Catherine would never know how much that had meant to her, she would reciprocate soon, and gladly.

Looking up, she heard her son coming up the hill home. He jumped out of the cart and made his way to the cottage with his long, strident steps. Late as usual, he'd have to answer to Douglas for it, but in his good natured way, he would brush the rebuke off lightly as usual. She watched him, "Oh, how she loved this tall good looking boy." The minute he spied her, a huge grin spread across his face. "Hi, Mum, are you waiting for me?" "Just out catching some sun," she said, smiling too. "Where have you been so late this time, at Mr. McGregor's again?" "No, not this time, he said, I've been with Harry making last minute wedding plans and then over to Tom O'Donnells, to plan the stag night." "Stag night, she laughed, I'm sure Harry will be feeling poorly the next day, now don't you go and make it too hard on him, you hear." "Would I do that, Mum," he replied, a twinkle in his eye. "Aye, son, I think you would." "Bye the way, he said, I told Mary about my plans." "And what did she think?" "She was sad but she understood, at least I think she did; she said I have to do what is best, oh and you'll never guess she has plans too." "You don't say what kind of plans?" "Mr. McPhee is letting his shop out and Mary and her mother are starting a bakery." She clapped her hands together, "What a nice addition to the village, I'm sure it will be a big success, you say that this was Mary's idea?" "Yup, all hers," he replied proudly. Margaret closed her eyes in a thoughtful way, "That Mr. McPhee is a lovely man, and his wife too, it's such a shame they never had any children to pass the business on to." He looked at her and said, "You should go down and visit with Mrs. Munro sometime she's really a nice lady." "Oh William, she laughed, I forgot to tell you that she came here for a visit." "Aye mum she told me, I'm so glad." We had such a nice time; she invited me down to her house." "I hope you become good friends; you know Mary is just like her."

They sat there for a few more moments enjoying each other's company in the way good friends can without saying a word. "William, you had better go have a talk with your Da soon about your plans with Mr. McGregor, there will be repercussions if he finds out from someone else." "I suppose you're right, Mum, I'll go and talk to him now, where is he?" "Out in the field behind the shed, I assume, and he's probably already miffed at you for being late again." "My, the time has flown by today, guess I'd better get up and see to supper." William reached down for Margaret's arm and helped her up. "See you later, Mum," he said, and gave her a little kiss on the cheek. "The light of my life, she thought, how will I stand it when he leaves?" She rose and walked slowly into the cottage.

William wandered out to the field where he found his Father. "Da," he said. William's Father looked surprised to see him. It wasn't like William to seek him out, especially in the field. Unlike his brothers, William didn't seem to have much interest at all in the farm. His brothers were always ribbing him, saying he was a dunderhead and lazy, keeping it up until William got angry and stomped off elsewhere. "Where have you been again, William," he said, you know that I count on you to be here on time for chores." William hung his head, "I know, time just always seems to get away from me, and I had some business to attend to." His Father gave a loud laugh, "Business, what business would you have to take care of?" "Plans, I have plans, Da," he said, looking up. His Father stood and looked at him for a moment and then turned and said, "You'd best be getting over to the shed now and see to your chores, your so-called plans can wait a while longer." "Aye sir," William said and he slumped off to the shed. Mr. Stevenson watched him go and chuckled to himself, "Now what plans would a lad like him have with his head in the clouds most of the time." He resumed his work in the field, shaking his head.

Supper ready, Margaret rang the bell outside the door. Her strapping lads would be in shortly and everything was ready. First in was Michael, "Hands, Michael, hands," she said. He gave a nod of his head and went to the sink to wash up. He looked up and said, "Mum, do you think it would be all right if I brought Nellie by for supper on Saturday?" Margaret smiled, "I think that would be just fine, Michael, just fine, is there anything special you would like me to make?" "Could you make Cullen Skink, I've had a taste for it and you haven't made it for a long time." "Cullen Skink it is then, I'll make some biscuits to go with it." "We'll have to take a trip over to Aberfeldy for haddock now that Mr. McPhee's fish shop is closed, but that's ok, an outing will do us good." "Thanks Mum, you're the best," he replied. She wiped her hands on her apron and said, "You'll never guess what William just told me, Munro's are starting a bakery in the old fish shop." "You don't say, he replied thinking to himself, "Bye, that William sure did know what was going on in the village, no wonder he was never at the farm helping." Why he got away with it, he couldn't say but he'd just about had enough of it.

They all sat down for supper and talk centered around the farm as usual; William and Margaret not contributing much to the conversation. There was a lull and Margaret said, "Michael tells me that Nellie will be joining us for supper on Saturday, isn't that nice." "Very nice, very nice indeed," said Douglas. "We'll tell her all about Michael's bad habits," laughed Patrick, always the jokester. "Right, and how he fell in the mud plowing and when he walked up to the house we didn't know who it was," chirped in Joseph. Michael stood up abruptly, "Haud yer wheesht, you'll do no such thing, Mum tell them they must behave." "That's right, lads, we don't want to scare the poor lass on her first supper here," she scolded. Douglas just laughed; his lads could do no wrong.

"By the way, William, what plans were you going to tell me about earlier?" William looked up at him, but said nothing. "Well?" William put his head down and said, "I don't know, nothing." Everyone sat there looking at him when Margaret suddenly stood up. "Oh, for heaven's sake, Douglas, some things are private." "Can the boy please talk to you alone?" Douglas smiled and looked around the table. "Now we have secrets?" "Good Lord, he's probably gone and asked that Munro lass to marry him, how is he going to support her, he has no interest in the farm?" This produced guffaws from the other boys. William suddenly pushed back his chair. He looked at Margaret and said, "I'm scunnered, now you know why I can't talk to him," and out the door he went. For the first time in her life, Margaret raised her voice. "I could give you boys a thrashing, you're all a bunch of uncouth, selfish men but none of you would recognize it because you're too busy looking at yourselves." "I'll tell you something you can't seem to see; William has a head on his shoulders." "He has a vision outside of this farm, and I for one, support him." "Oh, and by the way, he's not getting married, not at this time." "Douglas, you owe the boy an apology." She too pushed back her chair and exited the kitchen leaving them all to sit with their mouths open, for once not knowing what to say.

CHAPTER
TEN

Middle of next week, mid-morning, John came into the house and yelled, "Hey, you women, I thought we could take a trip down to the bakery and see what the progress is, who wants to come?" "We do, we do," said Rebecca and Lillian, racing down the stairs. "I'll be right down, yelled Mary, give me a few minutes." "John and I will be outside waiting, called Catherine, I just have to take this pot off of the fire so it cools." "Ok, he replied, I will get the cart ready and be waiting outside." Catherine turned and said, "Lasses, if you're going, no dillydallying." "Not to worry, Mum, Rebecca said, I'm ready now." She turned to Lillian, "Lillian, stop fussing with your hair, we're only going to the bakery." Lillian turned and looked hard at her, "You stop worrying about me you did your hair while I finished all the dishes." Rebecca, exasperated, went into the kitchen. "Mum, does she have to go?" "Aye, Catherine replied, if one goes, you both go, don't be a wee clipe now." Rebecca flounced her hair, "She picks on me, so I pick on her." "Oh dear," Catherine thought.

William was making his way down the hill to see Mr. McGregor in the village. He still had not talked to his Da and his Da had not asked him anything further, nor had his brothers. It wasn't in William to dislike anyone, but at this moment he wondered if he liked any of the lot except his mother. He wondered why he was so different from them, his Mum said he was like her Da, gentle and sensitive; he supposed she were right, he couldn't remember them. Maybe he should just leave for Glasgow and not say anything to his Da at all. No, he couldn't do that it wouldn't be fair to his Mum; she would reap the repercussions for it.

He passed Mary's house and thought about stopping and asking her to go with him but decided to wait, she might be bored at McGregor's, maybe he would see her later at Colleen's. Two more weeks and the wedding would be here. Two more weeks for them, two more years for him and Mary; he hoped the time would pass quickly. He saw someone along the road near the village and looked up to see his friend Tom O'Donnell coming towards him so he pulled the cart over to the side. "Hey, William, where are you going?" "Down to Mr. McGregor's for a while." "Oh, he replied, I haven't seen you around since the dance, what have you been doing with yourself?" "I've been up at Colleen's with Harry, we've been fixing up the little cottage in back for them to live in, and you know the wedding is only two weeks away." "I know, he said, the first of our classmates to be wed." "You should have asked, I would have come and helped too." "I'm coming to the wedding, hope to see you there." "You will; Mary and I are in the wedding." "Oh, so you are still seeing each other?" he replied. "Aye, of course, said William, in fact I'm going to meet her as soon as I'm done at McGregor's." "That's strange," Tom said, "Strange, what's strange?" William asked. "Well, I guess you're not betrothed to each other are you?" "No, not formally, he said, I'll be going to Glasgow to learn how to run the power looms soon, that's why I'm heading to McGregor's now, he's sponsoring me." "I'll be gone two years." "Two years, that's a long time," Tom replied. "It is, Mary is willing to wait for me, they're opening a bakery in town, you know." "No, I hadn't heard about it." "When?" "Not sure, as soon as the renovations are done I guess." "They're going to serve food in the morning and for dinner." "You don't say, that will be a welcome addition to the village; for sure I'll be stopping in there." "So long then, I'll see you at the wedding," Tom said. "Wait Tom, where are you going?" "I can give you a lift." "Thanks, I'd appreciate it," Tom replied, jumping into the cart. William picked up the reins and then turned and said, "Say, by the way, what were you talking about that was strange?" "Maybe I shouldn't say anything, but I saw Mary and that older guy, I think he's a MacAlduie, out in the field by Fingal's Stone last week." "It was just before dusk and they must have come in a cart because there was one sitting by the road." "No, it must have been someone else," said William. "No, it was her, come on, William there aren't many lasses in this village who look like her." "Gotta go or me Da will kill me, you can drop me off right here; thanks for the ride." "Are you sure you want to get off here? William asked, I can drive you all the way home." "That's ok, he replied, I want to stop at Harriet's, she might be outside." "I see, laughed William, I'm never one to come in between a romance; so long, Tom, I'll see you at the wedding," he clicked his reins and went on his way.

Tom watched William drive away and thought, "Two years is a long, long time, anything could happen." "You never know, maybe I'll have a chance with Mary yet." William was a good friend of his so he had always stayed in the back ground out of respect, just like most of the other village lads. Of course, he would never make his intentions known if William were still courting her, but if it became known that they were no longer involved, he would be the first one stepping up, he was sure of that. He wondered about MacAlduie, he heard that he was close to becoming a teacher now and he certainly was good looking; could Mary be seeing him on the side and William just didn't know about it? He thought, "Maybe I shouldn't have let the cat out of the bag."

"What in the world, thought William as he drove along, Mary never said anything to me about going on a cart ride with anyone." "It could have been Henry he saw, I know he was home from school last week, I saw him in the village when we were there, and then he remembered, "That's right, I saw Mary wave at him and I noticed him looking at her all the time." "Could it have been her?" "No, Tom must be mistaken." William reached McGregor's and entered the shop. "There you are me laddie, smiled Mr. McGregor, you aren't here to say you've changed your mind are you?" "No, no, of course not sir, I just wanted to make sure the date I'm leaving is still the same; I'll be leaving the week following the wedding?" "Same date, same time, laughed Mr. McGregor, get your thinking cap on, William, you'll be in for a lot of study." "Don't just stand there, come in; I'm not busy right now we can have a little chat." "Wish I could, Mr. McGregor, but I have to go over to the Hart's, we are finalizing the wedding plans." "Ok lad, stop in sometime next week and I'll have the travel schedule ready for you." "I'll be looking forward to it, see you next week."

That done William was once again on the road thinking about Mary, surely Tom had made a mistake, and it couldn't have been her. He took special notice of everything around him; the trees, the flowers; the buildings. He wanted to remember how everything looked so that when he was gone he would have a picture in his mind. He knew it would be hard, he had never been anywhere outside of the area before but he could do it. No he would do it. William drove into the yard just as Mary and Colleen came out of the house on their way to the cottage. "Where's Harry," he asked. "He's already over at the cottage working, Colleen said, we were just going over there to take some more measurements." "I see he answered, I'll just drive the cart over there." Mary thought something was off, William didn't seem his usual self and he looked upset about something. "I wonder what's wrong with him, he seems distracted," Mary said to Colleen. "Aye, Colleen said, he's probably got a lot on his mind before leaving." "I suppose you're right," Mary replied. Colleen went in the cottage and Mary stayed outside to wait for William, "I'll be there in just a minute she said." "Are you feeling ok?" she asked him. "Aye, why?" he replied. "I don't know, just asking, you seem mad or something," she said. He shrugged his shoulders and walked past her and entered the cottage. She stood there perplexed, then said to herself, "Colleen must be right, he has a lot on his mind right now, that's all it is."

Mary remembered that she had to talk to Mrs. Hart so she slowly walked back to the house and found her in the kitchen. "Me Mum says to tell you Peter will deliver the bannocks and wedding cake whenever you want him to." "Your brother is such a nice young lad she replied, we could have sent someone over for them; did she mention how much we owed her?" "Me mum says you don't owe her a thing because Colleen and I have been best friends forever, this is their wedding present to her." "Oh, how generous of her, all of you, please, tell her thank you for us, she said, she didn't have to do that." "Of course, I'll mention it to her when I see her." Mary smiled, "They wouldn't have it any other way, she says that's what friends are for." "They want you to drive out some evening and visit." "Tell them we will, after this wedding is over." "Thanks, Mrs. Hart, she replied, I'm going back over to the cottage now, William just arrived." "Have fun dear, I'm sure the lads will be glad when the renovating is finished." "Aye, said Mary, Colleen is anxious to decorate it."

William found Harry nailing some boards on the outside of the cottage. He told him he had seen Tom O'Donnell and Tom said he would be going to the wedding. "Oh good replied Harry, he'll have a good time, he always does." "He said he was stopping by Harriet's if she's home, maybe he'll bring her." "I wonder if he's serious about her, said Harry, he's the type who likes all the lasses." "I don't know, William replied, he never said anything to me." William never mentioned what Tom had said about seeing Mary with Henry. They finished up the work and Harry opened the door to the cottage and told the lasses they were going back to the main house. "Wait a minute, Colleen yelled, we'll come with you." As they waited for the lasses, Harry grabbed William's shoulder and gave him a big hug, "I couldn't have done it without all your help." "Ah, sure you could, smiled William, but thank you for saying so." Harry grabbed Colleen's hand and they all walked back to the house, William walked next to Mary but didn't look at her or attempt to take her hand. They entered the house and Mrs. Hart told the lads to go into the kitchen for some milk and tea cakes. Mr. Hart came and joined them, he thanked William for all the work he had done on the cottage. "I was glad to do it, Mr. Hart." "I hear you're going off to Glasgow to study," Mr. Hart said. "Aye, William replied, I'm excited to go but apprehensive about leaving." "I'm going to miss you, friend," said Harry. "Not as much as I will you, William replied, when I come home you'll probably have a bairn or two." "Maybe one," replied Harry. "I guess everything is set for the big day, said William, everything except the stag party, can you come, Mr. Hart." "Wouldn't miss it," he replied, a twinkle in his eye. "Darn, said Harry, I was hoping you'd forgotten about it." "Don't let him be too hard on me, Mr. Hart." "Don't look at me, he laughed, the party is in William and Tom's hands, I had no part in the planning." "Oh Lord, said Harry, I'm in for it, I just know it." He sat there with his head in his hands and they all laughed at him. "We should be on our way," said William standing up. "Thanks for the snack, I enjoyed it," he said, extending his hand to Mrs. Hart. "Til the wedding then," she said, holding his hand for a moment. "Til the wedding," he replied. The lasses came downstairs and Harry patted William on the back. "We'll walk to the cart with you." He grabbed Colleen's hand and they all went out. William walked in front of Mary and she trailed behind not knowing what to think. She got into the cart, as did William. Harry and Colleen stood, hand in hand, watching them drive away. "I wonder what Mary really thinks of William leaving, she hasn't said a word about it," said Colleen. "I don't know, replied Harry, William said she was ok with it but two years is a long time." "Did you think they were a little off with each other today?" Colleen asked. "I didn't notice, he said, come on love, let's go inside, I have to say my goodbyes and get home meself."

William and Mary drove in silence for a time. She couldn't figure out what was wrong with him, he had been so sullen tonight, not usual for him. "Did you talk to your Da?" "Tried to," was all he said. She looked at him, then put her head down and thought, "That's all it is, his Da again." After a time, he said, "He didn't want to hear about my plans." "What plans could you have?" he said. She grabbed his hand and he pulled her to him then she reached up and touched his hair. "I'm sorry William, he should have listened." He squeezed her hand and said, "No matter, Mary, he only sees the other three, that's all he ever has." He pulled the cart to the side of the road and stopped. "Mary, I must ask you something." "What is it William?" "Today when I was going to town, I ran into Tom O'Donnell; we talked and he mentioned that he had seen you with someone at Fingal's Stone the other night." "He thought it was Henry MacAlduie but I told him it couldn't have been he must be mistaken." "He was, wasn't he, Mary, mistaken that is?" She dropped her hands and said, "Oh dear, William, I am so sorry." He interrupted her, "So it's true then, it was you he saw?" "Why wouldn't you tell me Mary?" "My God, for me to find out from someone else, I never would have imagined you were seeing him too." "Were you just waiting for him to get out of school or me to leave?" "No, William, you have it all wrong," she cried "How could it be anything but," he snapped. He sat straight up nearly pushing her away and clicked the reins. "Let's go, I need to get home." "No, William, you haven't let me explain, I deserve that much." He stopped the cart again and sat there looking straight ahead, "Explain then," he said. She turned in the seat, looking at him. "It was me Da, I didn't want to go; he all but arranged it." He turned his head and looked at her. "Let me get this straight so I understand correctly." "We couldn't go to the town dance without being supervised by another couple, yet he let you go on a ride, in the evening, all alone with an older man." "No, she cried, I mean aye but you don't understand, I didn't want to go; I asked Henry to bring his sisters along and he didn't." "But you went, you could have refused." "No, William, I couldn't; it's complicated, they've been friends of the family for years." "My Father likes Henry, he always has, I don't know why; well, I mean, he's a great lad but I'm not interested in him." "Look, William, it was nothing, there was nothing romantic about it, we are just friends, we grew up together." "I love you, do you understand me; I love you, only you." His heart softened and he took her hand in his once more, there were tears in his eyes. "I believe you, Mary; oh, how I love you too, I was jealous, he has so much more to offer you than I do." "That's not true William; all we need is each other." They held hands the rest of the way home and he walked her to the door where he held her tight, then kissed her." She threw her arms around him not wanting to let him go. "I'll come tomorrow if I can," he said softly. "Try, William, I'll be waiting for you."

CHAPTER
ELEVEN

John and Catherine approached the store and saw some men carrying materials out with Charles close behind looking pleased as punch. "Hello there, I was hoping you'd come by, come see, come see." He walked up to the cart and offered Catherine his hand. "Thank you, Sir," she said. They locked arms together and walked into the store leaving John to follow behind." "Here we are then," smiled Charles. "Oh my goodness, I can't believe it," she cried. "The ovens are finished and what a fine job." "Aye, repeated John, a fine job indeed." "If I may be so bold, I'm quite pleased meself," laughed Charles. John admired the ovens and then walked outside, looked at the front of the building and then walked back in the door. "Charles, do you happen to have a ladder and a measuring stick?" "Of course, of course," he said, we've been using them, they're right over here." He pointed to the ladder and carried the measuring stick with him. "Let's go back out, Charles." "I want to measure for the sign, then I'll stop at Richard's with the dimensions." "Did you know my son was a good artist?" "No, I didn't, Charles replied, but I heard he's a good blacksmith." "Is it ok to start work tomorrow then, John asked?" "Of course, of course, Charles replied, the sooner the better." "What time would be good for you then, we wouldn't want to disturb Mrs. McPhee too early in the morning." "Not to worry, Nancy is always up early, besides, she's a little hard of hearing, like me," he laughed.

Catherine admired the work that had been done already. This was beginning to look like a bakery and she couldn't wait for Mary to see. All the shelves and counters were finished in the work room. "Bye, they wouldn't run out of space, that's was for sure." She walked to the door and called outside, "I'll be back I'm popping in to say hi to Nancy." "Aye, aye, she's in the sitting room, go right in," Charles yelled back. Catherine walked into the back and when she called out Nancy's name the old lady looked up and smiled. "Catherine, how nice to see you so soon again, I'm going to like these daily visits." "John and I stopped by to see the ovens, they are wonderful." "Aren't they now, replied Nancy, I saw them too." "I can't wait to smell the baking, there's nothing like the smell of bread baking, I used to make a good loaf meself and that was in the days when you didn't have an oven." "You'll be the first one to have a slice then but you'll have to come out and have tea with us and keep us company." "I will, you can be sure of that, I will." "Well, I just wanted to peek in for a second and see how you were doing, I'll be off now." "See you later Catherine," she replied.

John was waiting for her, he was anxious to stop at Richard's to deliver the board and paint for the sign. He stuck out his hand and said, "See you tomorrow then, Charles." "Tomorrow, Charles replied, I'll be looking forward to it." "Goodbye Catherine." "Goodbye, she said and she reached over and gave him a hug. "Now where have the lasses disappeared to?" They all walked over to Richards," John replied.

They headed for Richard's and saw the lasses walking and stopped to see if they wanted a ride. "No, we're enjoying the walk," they said. "It's starting to look like a bakery, John." "It is, wait until we get the finishing touches done." "I can't wait," she said. They pulled the cart in front of Richard's house and Sarah came out to greet them, a solemn look on her face. "Sarah, whatever is the matter?" Catherine said. "Come in, come in, we'll talk," she replied. Richard came from around the house and helped Catherine down from the cart. "You ladies go into the house, Da and I will get this wood and paint unloaded and then come in." The women walked into the house and Catherine stopped to look at the sleeping bairn "Such an angel, she said, I miss him so." "What's wrong, Sarah, I can tell it's something from the look on your face." "Come into the kitchen, I'll fix some tea, have a seat." They were quiet while Sarah fixed tea and then sat down beside her. "Catherine, Richard just came from Katie's and Ethan is getting worse." "Richard went to get Doctor Traymoor but he's out on a call right now, his wife said she'd send him over there right away when he gets back." "It's bad Catherine." Catherine looked down and said, "John and I will pick up the children now, John was going to get them earlier, but they weren't ready." "Katie will have all she can handle taking care of him." "Good idea," said Sarah. John and Richard came in from the back. Richard had already told John the news, it was a sober visit. The wheels were turning in Catherine's head thinking of what they could do to help. "Let's go to Katie's and pick up the children now John." John grabbed Richard in a bear hug. "Listen, Peter and I will get started on the bakery early in the morning, when you find out what the doctor says, come over and let us know." "I will Da, I will." Richard said. "We'll all get through this, he will beat it; all he needs is more time."

The ride to Katie's was a quiet one; even the lasses had nothing to say; they were all worried and lost in their own thoughts. Katie came to the door and they could tell she had been crying. She grabbed her mother and held onto her. "Have faith, Katie," "He's coughing so much, Mum, it's wearing him out." John said, "Get the children's things, Katie, we're going to take them home with us until Ethan is stronger." "Rebecca can stay here with you and I'll have Peter bring her things in later." "She can relieve you so you can rest, Catherine said, we can't leave them both at the same time, they quibble so." "When Rebecca comes back, we'll send Lillian and then Mary." "Don't feel alone, we are all here to help you." Rebecca hugged her big sister, "Aye, Katie, we're all here for you." Katie had tears in her eyes but looked a little more relieved, 'You don't know how much we appreciate what you all do." "That's what family is for, Katie; someday we may have to count on you." "Ethan's Father is bringing his mother over soon; she'll stay with us until he is better." "That's wonderful, Katie, she's a good woman and will be a comfort to you and Ethan."

They went into the bedroom where Ethan was propped up in bed. "Don't say a word, Ethan," said Catherine. She walked over to him and patted his shoulder. "You'll beat this Ethan, we are all praying for you." John walked over and grabbed his forearm, "You have us, son, be strong!" Ethan nodded.

The children were all packed and ready. "Go say goodbye to your Da, Catherine said, but mind, you don't make him talk, it will just get him coughing." The children, one by one, gave their Da a kiss on the cheek. Ethan gave them a weak smile and a small tear ran down his face. They all left the room turning one more time to wave goodbye to him. John grabbed Katie in his arms and held her tight; he couldn't say a word because he had a huge lump in his throat. He turned away from her, blinked his eyes and said, "We're off then, we'll see you tomorrow, watch for Peter, he should be along with Rebecca's things soon." "Bye, I love you." "Bye children." "Bye mum," they all yelled, one by one. Katie watched them out the window then turned and hurried back to Ethan.

The children chatted all the way home. In their blessed way, they were somewhat unaware of how serious their Father's condition was. Catherine and John did their best to keep the conversation light and happy. Catherine thought the day had been both high and low. It was hard to be excited for the shop when her heart was so heavy for her daughter and Ethan. John pulled up in front of the house and Catherine went in to find Peter. "Children, set your belongings by the stairs, we will take them up later, Lillian, go upstairs and gather the things that Rebecca will need." John came in the door and Catherine said, "Peter's not in here, he must be out in the shed." "I'll go fetch him," said John. John found Peter in the shed and told him what had happened. "Oh no, said Peter, I was afraid something like this would happen, I knew he didn't look good." "I'll go right away." "Thanks son, John said; you're a good lad I can always count on you." Catherine asked Mary, "Can you stay here tomorrow and help with the children, Lillian will be here to help too?" "Of course, I will Mum, we all have to pitch in together now." "Come, let's get these children situated for bed, and then retire ourselves, we're going to need our rest." "You go up, Mum, I'll see to the children, I'll give them a scone and some milk, that will help them sleep good." "Ok, thank you dear." Catherine had to admit that she was tired; bone tired from the day's activities, and stress tired from worry. She went to make her way to the bedroom, then suddenly turned and said, "Mary, I forgot to tell you, the ovens are done and they look marvelous, they are planning on starting the other work tomorrow." "Oh good, everything's coming along well then," said Mary, and she went to gather up the children. "Come in the kitchen, we'll have a snack before bed." "Yeah, yeah," they cried. She smiled, she loved these dear little bairns, and they were always so good. They all raced into the kitchen, "Grandda, Grandda, we're having a scone and milk, you want some too?" "I'd love to, but I've already had mine, you enjoy, I see Peter is home, I'm going out to help him." "Can I go, can I go," said Donald. "You stay here, you can see Peter tomorrow, ok?" "Ok, Grandda, he said with a sad face, but I'd really like to go."

Mary got them all settled in bed then came down to tidy up the kitchen. Peter and her Father entered the house. "Peter," she called, would you like a snack?" "I would, Mary, thanks." Mary fixed a scone and milk for Peter and then sat down beside him. "I see you and William are becoming friends." "Aye, I like him Mary, he's easy to talk to and fun to be around." "That he is," she said. "He's coming over early tomorrow, he wants to help us," he said. "What will Da say," she asked. "With Richard tied up in the morning, he should welcome the extra hand." "For what it's worth, Mary, I can see why you chose him?" "Thank you, Peter, that means a lot to me," she said. "Don't get mad at me Mary, but I really like Henry too and he's always been fond of you." "I know, Mary replied, but sometimes your heart leads you elsewhere." "I guess," Peter said, smiling at her. "Maybe you could go up and tell the bairns goodnight, Donald has been waiting for you." He laughed, "My shadow, I will right now; goodnight, I'll see you tomorrow." "Good night Peter." Mary sat at the table a while longer thinking about how angry William was over her little ride with Henry. She supposed she would feel the same way if he had been seen with another lass and hadn't told her about it. She wondered if Henry would find someone, it would be a shame if he didn't, any lass would be lucky to have him.

CHAPTER
TWELVE

They all woke early with much on their minds, and lots to do. John and Peter were already outside finishing up some chores so they could be on their way. Mary was bustling in the kitchen. She had fed the men and was now getting things ready for the bairns. Lillian was still sleeping, she would let her stay in bed, no need for her to be up this early today; it would be a long one.

"Peter said to his Father." "I'm just going to fetch William, he wants to help today." John said nothing, just nodded his head. He thought, "First Mary, then Catherine and now Peter; the lad must have put a spell on them all." He went to the shed and scrounged for what he thought they could use; boards, tools, and a saw. He placed them into the cart and then had a seat on the bench to wait for everyone. He was thinking that the bakery couldn't have come at a better time and they would have to try and ready it as soon as possible. Although he wouldn't let on to anyone, even his wife, the burden of extra mouths to feed with the children, Ethan and Katie would have a huge impact on their already straining budget. He didn't begrudge them, oh no, he would have it no other way; his children were the world to him. Everyone came outside just as Peter was returning with the cart, William sitting by his side. William jumped out and went over by Mary. "I'm here to help, it's the least I can do." "Peter told me about your sister's husband when I saw him yesterday." Mary took his hand, "We're very appreciative, William." Peter jumped down to help his mother into the cart and Donald ran to him. "Peter, I've been waiting for you," he said. Peter smiled, picked him up and set him in the cart. "I can't take you today, big boy, but I promise you we will do something fun soon, ok." "I guess," said Donald, clearly disappointed. "Look, you are the man of the house today, so help Mary take care of things, won't you." "I am," he said, a smile crossing his face. "Aye you are, isn't that right, Granda?" Peter said, looking at his Father. "That's right, Donald, we're counting on you." Peter picked him up and set him down on the ground. "I'll see you later." Everyone was in the cart and John picked up the reins. William walked to the side of the cart, near him. "Mr. Munro, if it's ok with you, I'd like to come along and help." John turned his head and looked at him, then extended his hand. "We could use another person today, hop in." William's face lit up so bright that he could have illuminated an entire room which caused John to suppress a smile himself. He turned around to the back and said, "Thank you William for taking time out of your day to help us." William replied, "I can't lie and tell you that I'm a good carpenter but I'm a mighty good fetcher and hauler, so you just tell me what to do and I'll do it." John winked at Catherine and replied, "That's ok, any help at all will be welcome, shall we be on our way," and with that he clucked his tongue and they were off. Catherine gave William's hand a little squeeze. She raised her eyes and said a silent prayer. "Thank you, Lord, the ice is finally broken." Mary, standing there watching, saw what had transpired and silently said, "Finally, he sees him for what he is." William turned to Catherine and said, "I told me Mum about your son-in-law, she said to let you know she was available if you need help of any kind; just call her if you need someone to watch the bairns or laundry; anything." "You have a considerate mother, William, I think we're covered but I sure might need some friendship and a visit when things settle down." "She'll do that, I'll tell her," he said. Not much more conversation was had on the way to town; everyone was lost in thoughts of what needed to be done and unconsciously of Ethan and Katie too. John thought, "I have a good woman, she was right, I've harbored ill will against William and the boy hasn't done anything wrong." "He seems good tempered, has not taken any liberties with Mary and still offers to help me when I haven't exactly been civil to him." "I think I've misjudged him."

They arrived at the shop and the men jumped down and unloaded the cart. "Peter, take your mother over to Katie's and tell Richard not to hurry, we have an extra hand helping today." With that he looked at William and smiled. Mr. McPhee saw them and propped open the door so they could bring in their things. John shook Charles hand and introduced William, "This is Mary's beau William, he said, he's helping us out today." Charles held out his hand, "Nice to meet you William, I hope you know that you have a fine lass in Mary; if I was forty years younger you would have some competition on your hands, she's one in a million, that lass." "William replied, "Don't I know it, Sir, I surely do." Charles looked at him and said,

"I know what a tall good looking lad like you are thinking, what would Mary see in a funny little man like that but I have me powers of persuasion, I do; my Nancy was a mighty fine looker in her day too." William chuckled, "Now, now, Mr. McPhee, I was thinking no such thing." "Call me Charles, call me Charles," he replied. William patted Charles on the back, "I think we're going to get along just fine," he laughed.

They got right to work, and as promised, William was worth his weight in gold. Charles said, "I've been to the ice house and when you get thirsty, we have cold ale, just help yourselves." "You're the best, Charles, you really are," said John. "Naw, laughed Charles, it's only because I have a taste for the brew meself." "Now just because I'm old doesn't mean I'm useless, I'm a pretty good carpenter, I'll get started on the storage room." On the sly he said to William, "You didn't know that's why I kept the ale in there did you?" William looked at the funny little man and doubled over with laughter, it wasn't just what he said but the way he said it that made everything he did so funny.

It was much more restrained at Katie's. Rebecca opened the door for Catherine, and gave her mother a hug. "Did Katie get any sleep," asked Catherine. "I think so, Mum, the doctor brought some cough medicine for Ethan." "He said it won't cure him but it will lessen the cough and help him sleep, he can have it every two hours if he needs it." Katie wouldn't go to bed but she kept falling asleep in a chair near him." "Richard is bringing over a small bed to put in the room, he says that's the only way we will get her to lie down, if she's near him; I've been trying to help as best I can." "I know dear, I know, said Catherine, I want you to go in the other room and rest now too, later today, we will have Peter take you home and Mary or Lillian can stay here." "You'll need your rest to help with the children at home." "Ok, Mum, I'll try to rest, I love you." "And I love you my dear."

Catherine walked into the room where she found Ethan sleeping and Katie propped up on a chair next to him. She quietly exited the room. If they were both asleep, she would see what else could be done in the house. She went into the kitchen and found things to make a dinner and when she was finished she made a cup of tea and sat down. Her mind wandered to the bakery and she wondered what progress was being made. She thought of John, he must feel liberated now that some of the anger was gone, why he was downright friendly to the lad. She loved her husband, he could appear to be gruff on the outside but inside he still had a heart of gold.

She heard coughing so she rushed into the bedroom to find Ethan in a coughing spasm and Katie holding a rag to his face. "That's good, Ethan, get it out, get it out." It seemed forever before the coughing stopped and he lay back spent. Katie looked up, "It's good you're here, the doctor. says he needs to get up several times a day, even walk if he's able, just to keep his legs strong and his blood flowing." Catherine put a hand on his forehead, "We'll let him rest for a few minutes and then we will get him up." "Come in the kitchen with me, he'll be ok." They went into the kitchen and Catherine fixed a bite to eat and some tea for Katie. "I'm not hungry Mum," she said. "Nonsense, you must try to eat, you won't be any good to him at all if you both get sick." They talked while Katie tried to eat what she could. "Give me the full report from the doctor," Catherine said. "He gave him cough medicine; it's very strong and makes him sleep." "He said he doesn't want to stop the cough completely, he needs to get the fluid out of his system." "Other than that, he said to keep doing what we are doing; there is nothing more he can do for him." "He said that it will be up to the body, Ethan, and God." "He said if he beats this, we shouldn't even think about him working for at least six months after, it's taken a toll on him." "I'm going to have to find work, Mum, we can't go on like this." Catherine held her daughter in her arms for quite some time and then gently pulled her up and they went back into the room. Ethan had his eyes closed but opened them when he sensed someone was there. "Ethan, said Catherine, do you think you're strong enough to sit up in a chair?" "Don't talk dear, just nod your head." "Katie, you get on the other side, we will sit him up in bed first." They sat him up and propped his back with pillows. "Now, just let him sit there for a bit, until he catches his breath, we don't want him to strain and start coughing again, at least until he's in the chair." They waited for at least five minutes and Ethan pointed his finger towards the chair indicating he was ready to move." "He was pretty unsteady on his feet but with a woman on both sides of him he was able to sit in the chair without too much effort." "Katie, Catherine said, I'll strip the bed, I think the cool sheets will feel good to him." "Once that is done, we'll see if he can walk around a little." They finished the bed then Catherine hunkered down in front of Ethan and took both of his hands in hers. "I've made some of my famous broth Ethan; I want you to do your best to eat as much as you can, it will do you a world of good." "We all love you, be patient, this will take some time but if you do as the doctor says, you will get better." He looked at her and his lip moved in an attempt at a smile. She wasn't sure that her words were entirely true but they must remain positive. There was a ruckus in the sitting room and Catherine rushed out to see what was going on, it was Richard bringing in the small bed. "Richard, she said, why don't you leave that for now and come in the bedroom, we are going to try and get Ethan to walk a little." They managed to get him standing. "I won't let you fall, Ethan, said Richard, can you take just a few steps?" Ethan felt dizzy but he was able to slowly walk around the room several times until a coughing fit took over. "Get him in the chair now, Catherine said, he's had enough." He coughed and it seemed like he would never stop. Katie looked at her mother with a scared expression on her face. "It's all right, Katie, the coughing is good for him." "If he can walk a few times a day and stand the coughing after, then I think he'll get it all out." "He's stopped coughing for now, Katie, let him sit quietly and I'll go and fetch some broth." Katie knelt on the floor by Ethan, her head in his lap. He took his hand and laid it on the top of her head. They stayed that way until Catherine scurried back into the room with the broth. "I know you're not hungry, Ethan, but please, do your best to get as much down as you can." He managed to sip about one-half of a cup until he gave a sigh and his head dropped to his chest. "That's it for now," Katie, let's get him back into bed, go and fetch Richard." Richard and Katie came back into the room and all three of them managed to get him comfortably in bed. "Leave his head propped up on the pillows, Catherine said; it will be better if he doesn't lay flat." Ethan had yet another coughing spasm and they held him until he stopped, then gave him the medicine. "He will sleep now, Catherine said, Richard, let's get that bed in here and made up so Katie can lie near him." Everything was done for now, Ethan and Katie seemed to be resting comfortably and Catherine and Richard collapsed in the kitchen. "We've got a long way to go, son," she said. "We'll do it, Mum, we all have to pitch in. I have to leave now, but I'll stop back later." Richard left but not before he found Rebecca and made it clear that she was to help so that their mother didn't get too worn out." "I will, I promise Richard," she said. He patted her head and then left. He was anxious to get home as he knew Sarah would be waiting for news. Catherine kept an eye on the couple but they both remained sleeping or appeared to be. She sent Rebecca in the other room to rest as well. They must all take advantage of the quiet times. Catherine nodded off to sleep herself; she awoke when she heard a noise. She went to the bedroom and saw that Ethan was awake. She sat beside him and touched his hand, he curled his finger around hers and drifted back to sleep again.

Richard drove up to the shop and saw quite a bit of activity. It appeared as if there were several men coming in and out carrying various boards and tools. He walked to the door and saw his Father near the back of the room so he made his way through the mess on the floor until he was beside him. "Hey Da, doesn't look like you're lacking for help." He smiled, "It's amazing, people would stop by to see what was going on and then stay and help." "It appears that Charles has a lot of friends in this village." "We'll probably be able to finish by the end of the day tomorrow." "Let me get Peter and William over here before you update me, no sense having to repeat it to everyone." "Peter, William, come here a moment would you?" The lads had been so busy working they never noticed Richard come in. They looked up, then looked at each other and headed to the back." Peter was the first to speak, "How is he?" "Stable for now, but it's not good, there was nothing more that the doctor could do, it will just take time." "Either he will beat it or he won't." Peter hung his head, he was hoping for better news. William patted him on the back, not knowing what to say. Peter looked up and put his hand on William's shoulder, pushing him forward. "Richard, I don't think you've met William, he's Mary's beau." Richard put out his hand, "So nice to finally meet you, you'll have to come by for supper some night when things settle down." "Nice to meet you too and we'll definitely take you up on that invitation if we can make it before I leave." "Leave?" "After Colleen's wedding I will be going to Glasgow for a couple of years, Mr. McGregor is expanding and he's sending me for apprenticeship." Richard shook his head, "I'm sorry to hear that but I'm happy for you," he said. "Thank you," William replied. "Let's take a tour, shall we," said John. "You've made a lot of progress," said Richard, looking around. "This is the prep and supply room, said John, they have two long tables to work on and more shelf space then they will ever need." "It was Charles suggestion to widen the doorway so they could see customers coming into the store." Charles came out from behind the shelves with his hand extended. "Good to see you again, Richard, can you believe all these good people came out to help us." "It was unexpected, but I'm not surprised, said Richard, there's no better folks than in Killin." "Aye, aye, to that," replied Charles and he disappeared behind the shelves again. "Come," said John. Richard followed behind. "These are the ovens, obviously." Richard nodded his head, "I can't believe they got them done so quickly." "Aye, said John, the hearth was already here and it's a nice, big one." "This has to be finished yet, but it will be a long counter and we'll have shelves on the inside." "And here, he swept his arm the length of the store in front of him, will be the tables." "Most of them are done, they are finishing them outside." "So you see; we have made unexpected progress today, except for the finishing touches." "I can't wait for Catherine and Mary to see." "I'll keep it a secret so as not to ruin the surprise, Richard said, it looks good, it looks really good."

Just then a voice was heard from the back. "Stop your work, gentlemen it's ale time." Everyone stopped and looked up to see Charles standing in the back, his arm raised with a bottle of ale in his hand. "Come and help me, William, let's pass them out." It seemed that Charles had taken a shine to William; he was constantly over by him telling a joke. The ale was passed and another voice was heard. "Let's have a toast to a successful bakery." The clinking of bottles and the sound of aye, aye,

aye, could be heard throughout the store. "Thank you, Charles," they all cheered. John climbed onto the first rungs of the ladder and raised his ale. "Thanks to each and every one of you for helping, you'll never know how much we appreciate it!" "Listen Da, said Richard, I feel I need to get back and help Mum." "Of course, we're doing fine here, you go and I'll send Peter out to get Lillian in about an hour."

"Peter, said John, you'll have to stop for now and pick up Catherine and Rebecca, you can bring Lillian back she'll stay at Katie's tonight." "I just need another hour and I'll have this done, Da." "I'll go, said William, I mean, if you want me to." "Well, sure, if you don't mind, then Peter can finish." "Thanks William, said Peter, I really hated to stop right now." "No problem, said William, I'll be back as soon as I can," and he went out the door. He came back in the door and stood there. John looked up from his work, "William?" "Silly of me, he replied, where does Katie live?" There was a roar of laughter from everyone. John gave him the directions; just go out on Lyon Road until it takes a fork to the right, they will be the first cottage on the right hand side." "By the way, William, keep this a secret, will you, we want to see their faces when they find out how much we have done." He nodded his head and once more went out, this time his face a bright red.

William knocked on the door and Rebecca answered. "I've come to take you and your mother home," he said. "Come in, we'll just be a minute." Catherine came from the bedroom with a bowl of broth in her hand and said, "Hello there, I just have to help Katie get Ethan back in bed and then we can go." "Can I lend a hand," he asked. She stopped, "Do you mind?" "Of course not, I don't mind at all, in fact I'm glad to help." Catherine touched his arm, "We have a lot to thank you for today, come with me." "No need for thanks, no need at all." Once Ethan was settled, Catherine said; "Katie, give me the sheets, we'll get them laundered and back tomorrow." Katie handed Catherine the sheets, then threw her arms around her mother and held her. Catherine gave her a kiss and they left the room. William held the door, then turned and said, "I'll be back with Lillian soon." "Goodbye, see you later," she said, then hurried back to the bedroom.

William took the sheets from Catherine and put them in the back of the cart, then helped her in. Rebecca was already in the back and they headed for home. "I bet you're tired," he said. She leaned back in the seat, "I really am, it's exhausting, but don't get me wrong, I'm glad to do it." "Of course, you are," he said softly. "So what's been done at the shop today?" she asked. "It's coming along well; some of the townsfolk came to help." "Really, how nice of them." He smiled at her, "Charles is a pretty popular man in town." "He's one of a kind," she replied. They pulled into the yard and entered the house. Mary came to the door and immediately went to

William. He put his arm around her and they all went to the kitchen and sat down. "I'll make some tea, we'll catch you up with the news, Mary, and then William will take Lillian to Katie's, I don't think we should leave Katie alone too long." "Lillian, have you got your things together?" "Aye Mum," she called from the sitting room. At that, the children ran into the kitchen, "Grandmum, you're home." "That I am," she said, and threw her arms around them. They had their tea, caught up on the news and then the lasses and William brought their things and they were off again. They didn't talk much on the way, their minds were full of the last couple of day's events and William didn't want to let any secrets out about the progress of the shop. They entered the house and immediately heard Ethan coughing again. "I'll help, William said, see to your things." When all was settled, William said, "I should be getting back to the store, they will wonder where I am." Mary grabbed his hand and walked to the door with him; Katie called from the bedroom, "Thanks for your help William, you're a Godsend," William grabbed Mary and held her, gave her a kiss, and then left.

He entered the store to find that most of the men had left and Charles, Peter and John were seated at the tables they had brought in having some ale. "William, come and have a seat," Peter beckoned. John rose to get him ale. "Here you go William, have a drink with us, I can't tell you how much we appreciate all you've done to help us today, I mean that." William sat down with his ale and looked around. The floor had been cleared and there was nothing more to do than a few finishing touches. "Looks good," he said. "It does," they all replied. "Tomorrow we should be able to hang the sign." "I never would have thought we'd get this far in one day, not with everything else that's going on," said John. "I was told the village is eager for a bakery," replied Peter. "Well I for one am," laughed Charles. "Hear, hear," they all said and clicked their ale together in a toast. "Charles, said John, extending his hand, it's been a pleasure, you're a good man." "We'll see you tomorrow midday, don't make yourself a dinner, we'll bring something in and have a little celebration, that's if you agree." "I hope that Mrs. McPhee can join us." "I won't refuse, oh no, I won't refuse, and I'm sure Nancy will be glad to come if she's up to it," he replied. "Tomorrow it is then." "Goodnight Gentlemen." "Goodnight," they all replied in unison. Each one of them turned at the door to look at the finished work and then exited. They hopped into the cart, all of them weary but satisfied. "A good day's work, lads." said John. They made small talk on the way home and laughed about the surprise they had for Charles; by putting his name on the sign. John pulled up by the house and the boys jumped out. "Goodnight lads, and thanks again," John said. "William, "I hope you can join us tomorrow for dinner." William was shocked, "I, um, well, I'd love to, Mr. Munro, I'll have me Mum cook up a dish to pass." "Tell you what, William, if she wants, why don't you have her come along, she might like to see the shop and I understand she owes us a visit anyway, Catherine will love the company." "I'll send Peter up with the cart around ten to get you." "Are you sure?" "I mean, aye, aye, we'll be ready, and thank you." William got his horse, hopped in the cart and headed for home. "Bye," he thought, it was a day of highs and lows. They made him feel like family and oh, he was scared for Ethan.

He was afraid to go in the house as once again he had missed his chores; it really was irresponsible of him. He sat on the bench outside the cottage summoning up the courage. What a turn his life had taken today. His mother always told him, "Be kind and kindness will come back to you in full." Well, kindness surely had come back to him today, and to think they had invited his mother, he couldn't wait to tell her. He stood up and stretched, it was a good day's work and his body felt it.

CHAPTER
THIRTEEN

Margaret was in the sitting room, Douglas and his brothers were nowhere to be seen. "You're sitting her all alone, then?" he said. "Aye, I just finished up everything and was thinking about going to bed." "They're not back from rent collecting yet?" You know how they like to stop for ale." "How did it go today?" she asked. William grinned, "Good, really good." "Remember I told you that Mary's Da was a little cold to me?" "Aye I remember." "Well, it's just like you said, Mum, today he was like a different person, and he was pleasant to me." "I'm not surprised, she said, anyone can see what a fine lad you are." "Thanks Mum, everyone except me Da." "Listen, we almost finished everything today so they're having a dinner there tomorrow, Mr. Munro invited me, and you too." Her head snapped up, "Me?" "Aye he said he understood you were past due for a visit anyway." "Oh, my, do you think I should go?" "Aye, aye, he replied, I think you should go, and I told him you would bring a dish to pass, Peter will pick us up in the cart mid-morning." "And how is the brother in law doing," she asked. "Not good, mum, not good." "We'll have to pray extra hard then tonight, she replied, I'll see you in the morning." "Ok, he said, "I love you."

He sat down in the sitting room, the day running through his mind. He may as well wait for his Da, maybe he would tell him his plans tonight. If he didn't approve, no matter, his mind was set. He drifted off to sleep in the chair when he heard them come into the house. They were noisy and loud as usual not minding that they may be disturbing anyone. Douglas walked in the room and in a sneering voice he said, "There you sit, again." "Where have you been all day, avoiding work as usual?" In an uncharacteristic manner William jumped out of the chair and in a loud voice he replied, "Aye, aye I have." "I'll not be part of collecting rent from the poor people below." "For your information, I have been busy working all day for people who actually appreciate it." "You won't have to worry about what I'm doing or not doing because as soon as Harry's wedding is over I'll be going to Glasgow and you'll be rid of me." "I would have talked to you about it before now but you didn't want to listen." With that he went out the front door and slammed it. Margaret heard the conversation and part of her was glad, the other part sad. She was glad that William finally stood up to him; he had been bullied long enough. She was sad because she knew he was hurting inside by his Father's rejection of him. Douglas remained standing there with his mouth gaping open as did the three brothers. He scratched his head and went into the bedroom where he found Margaret sitting on the edge of the bed. "Well, I suppose you heard, your addle-brained son says he's going to Glasgow, have you ever heard such a story," at which he laughed. "Laugh all you want, Douglas, but it's not a story, some people see the potential in him." "Mr. McGregor is sponsoring him, he is going to Glasgow, to learn a trade, he's been trying to tell you for a month now but your mouth was running so much you didn't listen." "I've had to keep me mouth shut many times at your antics but this time I'll have me say." "And by the way, you can all find your own dinner tomorrow, I'll be out." She lay down in the bed, her heart pounding and closed her eyes to the sight of him standing over her. "Woman, he said, I'll not have you talk to me that way in me own house." He turned and walked out of the room. She closed her eyes but had a hard time falling asleep; sometime later that night she heard him come into the room and crawl into bed beside her.

William went to the shed and lay down in the straw where he fell asleep. He slept fitfully all night and he dreamed that Mary was walking in front of him down the road and he was running after her but he could never catch up. In the morning he woke and was surprised that he had slept there all night. "I'd better get cleaned up and ready," he thought, and hurried to the house. "Where have you been this early?" she called from the kitchen. William poked his head in. "I fell asleep in the shed and didn't wake up until now, I suppose you heard the ruckus, I'm sorry." "Don't be sorry, she replied, it was long overdue." "I've had me say too, I think we're cut from the same cloth." "There's no finer cloth I'd rather be cut from then," he replied, smiling at her. "Sit down; I'll get your porridge." "What are you cooking?" he asked. "Fisherman's Pie and jam roly polys, will that be all right?" "It's better than all right," he said. He ate his porridge quickly then said, "I'd best be getting out there and doing the chores, I've twice as many since missing last night." "See you later," she said. "I'll be in to clean up when I'm done," he replied, and out the door he went.

He was busy raking in the shed when his brother Patrick came in and stood there watching him. He put his head down and kept raking. "Look who decided to come and help today, are you sure you don't have better things to do?" asked Patrick, trying to evoke an argument. "Were you with the Munro lass yesterday?" Again, William made no response. "How'd you ever get a lass like that anyway, a good looker like her?" "I wouldn't mind having her for my beau maybe I'll take a drive down there and ask her." "Let her know what a real man is like." With that statement, in one fell swoop, William dropped his rake and pushed Patrick up against the stanchion and held him pinned there. "You can say what you like about me, but you keep Mary out of it." "If I ever hear you talk about her again, you'll rue the day you did, I promise you that." "Besides, she's a smart lass, she'd never have a loudmouthed lout like you." Patrick pushed William off of him and exited the shed shouting behind him, "You're crazy, William." Just like any bully who had been confronted, he didn't agitate the argument further. William finished his chores and with a heavy heart, he headed to the house to clean up. In some ways he could understand the animosity felt against him. He didn't do his part, he knew that, but it wasn't because he was lazy, it was because he detested it.

He entered the house to the smell of food cooking. "I've some hot water on the hearth ready for you," called Margaret. "Thanks Mum, I've finished me chores, I'll clean up now." "I don't want Peter to wait when he gets here; by the way, food smells good." He took the kettle of hot water to the wash room and filled the tub, then came back, pumped some cold water and poured that into the tub too. He locked the door, removed his clothes and sat there soaking and relaxing for some time; then took a vase and poured water on his head and scrubbed it. He lay there savoring the warm water and almost fell asleep; he was tired after his fitful sleep in the shed last night. When the water cooled, he rose and got dressed, then emptied the tub. "I'm going outside to wait for Peter, he called; I'll let you know when he's here." "Ok," she replied, I want to leave the food on the hearth as long as possible so it stays warm."

She made everything as ready as she could for now then opened the door and came outside. She looked at William and said, "I'm going down to find your Da and let him know the foods on the hearth." "Last night I told him he'd have to find his own dinner but on second thought I don't need to listen to the nippin for the next six months." She found Douglas behind the shed and simply said, "William and I will be leaving soon, dinners on the hearth." "Just leave the dishes and I'll clean up when I get home." He nodded his head without looking at her and she left without saying more. He wondered where they were going but out of stubbornness would not ask. William watched her come up to the house and it seemed to him that there was a new lightness in her step. She looked at him and said, "Well, that's done," and then went back into the house. She set the table with dishes and then sat there to wait. Soon, William stuck his head in and yelled, "I hear Peter coming with the cart." She took a large towel and wrapped her food, then came outside. "Here, let me take that for you Mum," he said. The cart stopped in front of the house and William helped her up. "Mum, this is Mary's brother, Peter." She put out her hand, "I'm so happy to meet you, thank you for coming to get us." "We're happy to have you join us today," he said; William did us a big favor yesterday and I must say he's a hard worker." Douglas had heard the cart too and he stepped around the shed to see who it was but he didn't recognize the lad driving, which perplexed him even more. "Must be one of William's friends," he thought, then dismissed it from his mind and went back to work.

They rode along in silence until Peter said, "I don't know what you have back there Mrs. Stevenson, but it smells mighty good." "I hope you like it, she said, its Fisherman's Pie and jam roly polys." "I'll have to slip one on the side, he said, I love roly polys but me Mum doesn't make them." "Well here's the driveway, we have to stop and get the women, Da left some time ago with the other cart to get Richard, and they want to bring the sign." William turned to Margaret and explained. "Mary suggested that they name the bakery 'McPhee's Bakery' to honor Charles for all he's done." "He doesn't know about it, it's a surprise." "Have you ever met him?" "Oh aye, everyone in the village knows Mr. McPhee." "As the saying goes; you can always get a fair deal from Mr. McPhee." "I like Nancy, his wife, she's polite and very quiet, maybe because he talks so much," she laughed and they all joined in. "Shame on me for not going to visit her, I hear she's not feeling well." They pulled into the yard and Peter said, "There she is, already waiting along with my sidekick, Donald, I'm sure she's excited to see the shop." "Don't let on that the work is done." "Hello, hello, she cried out, Margaret, I'm so glad you have come." "Let me go get the other children and the food, I will be quick about it." "We'll help, Mum," said Peter and they both jumped down from the cart. "I'm going with Peter, said Donald, right Peter?" "Aye, Peter laughed, but if you come with me you have to help." "I will, I will, he cried, me Da says I'm a big boy." "Well your Da's right, you are." They went into the house and they marched out one by one, each with something in his hands. Margaret laughed and yelled out, "It looks like we're having a parade." With that she got down and took the items from each one as they came, then packed them in the back of the cart. "Oh my, she said we'll have to squeeze the children in; there's so much food." Catherine was the last to reach the cart. "Thank you, Margaret, I see what you mean, good thing it's not far." "Rebecca and Gretchen can sit in the back and steady the food, Carolyn can squeeze in between the two of us and Donald can sit up front between Peter and William, that's where he wants to be anyway, he's Peter's shadow." Margaret laughed, "Oh how I wish I had little ones around, it's so quiet at my house you can hear a pin drop." "That is when the lads are out." They had a jolly ride to town, the children chattering the whole way and the adults either commenting or laughing. "Bye, Margaret thought, it's so good to be around happy people again."

John's cart was already at the shop when they pulled in front. They could see that the sign was in the back. William and Peter helped the women and children down and they started handing out items to each one. "Let the parade begin again," laughed Peter. "Is me Da here," said Donald. "No, I'm sorry, he had to stay home, but we are going to get Mary, you can come with us and see him if you want." "Ok Peter," he said. Charles came and held open the door and they all made their way in. There were squeals of delight when they saw that the tables had all been set up and the work had been finished. "I can't believe it," said Catherine, running from corner to corner. "How in the world did you manage it?" "Because we're good," said Charles which got everyone laughing. "I'm glad that you have all these beautiful counters, said Margaret, there is so much food here." "Oh, Catherine, it is lovely." "You know this was all Mary's idea." "Aye, William told me, he's so proud of her." John stood in the middle of the room and called out, "Everyone please have a seat, let's have dinner before the food cools down." "What matter, Charles shouted out, we have a hearth and two ovens." Once again he had them all laughing. Catherine took Charles aside. "Have you talked to Nancy, will she come and join us?" "She wants to, but may not stand it for long." "Why don't we give it a try, hum; I'll go with you." "Children, find a seat please, everyone, help yourselves to the food, we'll be right back." "John and Richard, come with me, we may need a little help, let me go in first." They walked to the back and Catherine cried out, "Mrs. McPhee, it's Catherine, may I come in?" Her weak voice responded, "Aye, please, come." She looked so small and frail sitting in that big chair. Catherine put a hand on her shoulder and said, "We would like you to join us for dinner, do you feel up to it?" "Oh, she replied, I don't know if I'm strong enough to make it all the way out there." "No matter, said Richard, I will carry you." Nancy looked startled as Richard reached down and picked her up in his arms. Charles said, "You always wanted a handsome prince to carry you away, now you have one." They placed her in a chair at a table and Margaret went over to talk to her. "Do you remember me, I came to the fish shop every time we were in town." "I do remember your face, but I apologize that I can't remember your name." "It's Margaret Stevenson, and I'm so happy to see you again, Mary is seeing my son William." "May I visit you some time?" "I would love to have you visit, anytime." "Good, then I will, I have a feeling I'll be getting out more in the future." "I'll leave you to your dinner now."

Everyone filled their plates and the ale was once again brought out. When they were finished eating John stood up, "Let's all say a prayer for Ethan." They bowed their heads and John continued. *"We thank you Lord for blessing us today with this new shop, plentiful food and loving friends." "Please send your healing hand to Ethan; a good man and faithful servant." "Give us strength and courage to make it through the hard times and the humility we need in good times. Amen."* "Amen, Amen, was said by all." Then Charles stood up, with his hand on his wife's shoulder. "Nancy and I want to thank everyone for making our lives full again." All stood up and clapped their hands. "And now," John shouted above the noise, "Mary has a surprise for Charles and Nancy." Charles looked at Nancy and said, "Did you hear that, Mary has a surprise for us?" He grabbed her hand and there were tears in his eyes. "Everyone sit, John said, we will be right back." Peter held open the door and Richard and John came in carrying a huge piece of wood. They walked to the center of the room and then John said, "Are you ready Mary?" "Ready," she replied. She also walked to the center of the room and said, "Charles and Nancy, out of the goodness of your hearts you trusted in me and my idea and now it's become a reality." "There are few people in this world who would take such a chance on a young lass like me." "The name McPhee means something in this village; that's why everyone came out and helped put this together so quickly." "The only way we know to show our appreciation is to name the bakery after you, I promise we will not let you down." With that they raised the sign. "And so, we've named the bakery, McPhee's Bakery." Charles stood up, he was clapping and his eyes were full of tears. In his usual way, he said, "It's a good thing you put, "Munro baked goods, sweets and eats, on the second line, I ran a good fish shop but I can't bake." Laughter ensued. Nancy obviously had enjoyed herself but she was beginning to tire; "I think I need to go back now," she said to Charles. Charles motioned to Richard, "Would you mind?" he asked. "Certainly not, I must get Cinderella home before midnight." He grabbed Nancy's hand and kissed it." "Oh you," she said. "Lead the way, Charles." Richard picked her up and carried her into the bedroom and sat her down on the edge of the bed." "Thank you, she said, I've had a grand time." More ale was passed out and the men sat around talking while the women cleaned and packed up the dishes and food. Catherine fixed

76

some food for Charles and Nancy then went back and asked if there were anything more she could do for them. "No thank you, said Charles, she's all settled and will probably nap soon; I'll come out and visit with the men." Catherine went back and sat down with Margaret and Mary. "I guess all of our lives will be changing soon," she said. "Mum, said Mary, I feel bad that Katie, Lillian, and Sarah are missing out on everything." "What if I go and sit with Ethan so they can come, even if it's just for a little while, I feel guilty celebrating when he's over there so sick." Catherine replied, "Don't, they would be happy for you, listen, let me go, I want to see how he's doing anyway, I'll see if Richard will drive me." "William and I will take you," Mary said. "Why don't I go and keep you company, Catherine, said Margaret, that's if you don't mind." "Are you sure, Catherine replied, I don't want to take you away from William, you have such little time left with him before he leaves." "It's ok, I don't mind," she said, as long as I know he is happy and healthy, that's all I need." Catherine squeezed her hand "You're a good friend, why have we let our friendship go all these years?"

They all got in the cart, and were off to Katie's. Sarah came to the door, and was delighted when she saw them. "We've come to relieve you for a while; this is my friend Margaret, William's mother." "Sarah took Margaret's arm, "It's nice to meet you, come in." Just then the baby, Collin, started to fuss. "Can I?" Margaret asked. "Of course," Sarah said. Margaret picked up Collin and gently rocked him in her arms, he immediately closed his eyes and went back to sleep. "What a darling bairn," she said. Margaret gingerly sat down in the rocking chair with the bairn and Catherine went into the bedroom to see how Ethan was doing. He was resting comfortably. "We'll stay here and you can go over and see the shop, it will do you good to get out of the house for a while." "How is he doing?" "Better Mum, not good, but better." "He's eaten a little more today and has been able to sit up longer." "They walked into the sitting room and Catherine introduced Margaret who was still rocking the baby. "This is William's mother, Margaret." "Nice to meet you, Katie said, we really like William, he's such a nice lad." "It's nice to meet you as well, I'd extend my hand but it's a little tied up right now," she said nodding at the bairn. "How is your husband?" "Some better," replied Katie. "That's good to hear," she replied.

William was relaxing in the cart, waiting for the women to come out. He thought the evening had been grand, he now felt more a part of this family than he did his own. It was a bonus that his mother was present and he knew she was enjoying herself too. She was much too gentle of a person to be stuck up there with those unfeeling, selfish men. He wondered if his Da had always been that way, he couldn't imagine what attracted her to him. The door opened and Sarah and Lillian came out with Katie behind. William jumped out of the cart and helped them in. He asked how Ethan was doing and she told him a little better. "Good, he said, "I'm so glad to hear that."

They entered the shop and everyone came over with hugs. The lasses ran to see their mother. "Mum, mum, we've missed you but we're having fun at Grandmum and Grandda's." She knelt down on her knees and embraced them all. They admired the shop and were surprised that it had been completed so quickly; they didn't stay long but it was good to get out and see everyone. The shop was cleaned, everyone said their goodbyes and they were off for home. Charles waved goodbye, locked up and then sat down and enjoyed another bottle of ale by himself. He finished, rose, unlocked the door and stood outside admiring the sign. He muttered to himself, "These are good people I've struck a bargain with." "Good people indeed." He entered the back and found Nancy still reading. "Did you have a good time," he said. "Very," she smiled. "I'm glad dear, it's good to see you enjoy yourself; they've left some food, so when you get hungry, just call me." "I will dear, thank you," she said and then went back to reading.

The children were excited to see their Da; even Donald forgot about his uncle Peter momentarily. They rushed into the house where Catherine met them, "Ssshh, children, your Father is sleeping right now you'll have time to see him when he wakes." She went to Katie and took her hands, "I think he's some better, he was able to get down almost a cup of broth and he had a spasm which brought up a lot of fluid." "We'll keep doing as we're doing and rotate so no one gets too tired out." "Mary and I talked and we'd like you to join us in the bakery, we're quite sure we'll need an extra hand." "There's no need, at this time, to find work elsewhere, we'll all manage." "It's quite possible that Ethan's lungs have been so damaged that he won't be able to work again." "Katie sat down next to Margaret with a sigh, "I couldn't get through this without each and every one of you." She turned to Margaret, "and how was Collin?" "He's the best little angel, barely fussed at all." Katie took her hands, "We're happy to have you as our friend; I see why William is such a nice young man." John came in the door, "Here are Rebecca's things, she will stay the night again, it's best the rest of us head for home, chores are waiting." "The children, Katie cried; have they time to peek in on their Da?" "Of course, of course," said John. Like good little children, one by one they stood by the bed and touched their Father's hand. Ethan patted each one on the head and smiled. "Come now, Katie said gently, let him rest." Goodbyes were said and they were once again on their way. They talked about the day, the bakery, Ethan and the children on the way home. Catherine turned to Margaret, "I'll probably be at the bakery most days; there or Ethan's; you are welcome to come visit anytime." "She replied, "I've truly enjoyed me day, you have a remarkable family." They pulled into the yard and everyone helped unload all of the food and dishes. "Thanks for bringing dishes to pass, Margaret, Catherine said, your food was truly enjoyed, I'll have to get that roly poly recipe from you if you don't mind sharing it." "Not at all," Margaret replied, I'll come in some morning and we can make them."

Peter dropped William and Margaret off at their cottage. Once again Douglas was scratching his head wondering where they had been off to. William changed his clothes and headed out to do chores. Margaret went into the bedroom to change then got her apron so she could clean up the dinner dishes and start supper. That night at supper Michael asked where they had been. "With Mary and her family," Margaret said, nothing more. William sat mute and didn't comment.

CHAPTER
FOURTEEN

Catherine, Mary and Peter, along with Lillian and the other children headed to the store with John early in the morning. They had all their linens; tablecloths, curtains, etc. with them, it was an exciting day. Charles as usual was up early and let them in then gave them a key, "You're on your own now," he said. "Listen, Charles, Catherine said, would you have time to help us with the supply order, we could use your expertise." "Of course, laughed Charles, I thought you'd never ask." John was busy with finishing touches then stated he would run over to Katie's to drop off Lillian and pick up Rebecca. The rotation of extra hands to help Katie would continue over the next several months, this time the children got to spend more time with Ethan. John was satisfied that things were progressing; he found Ethan sitting up and eating broth. They left with the children and headed over to Richards to drop off Peter who was excited as this was the first day of his training as smithy. Donald, of course, showed his indignation at the fact that he wasn't allowed to stay with his idol, Peter.

The ordering had all been done. Everyone was stunned at the transformation of the shop, it looked bright and cheery. They had recruited Charles to put up the poles for the curtains and he was beaming from ear to ear because he had been of service. It was agreed that they would open on Monday and each day would close after the dinner hour once things had been cleaned up. Charles was told to no longer concern himself with dinner or supper; they would see to it that Nancy and he had food to eat. "Oh, I couldn't be such an imposition on you," he cried. Mary touched him fondly on the shoulder, "You have no choice we've already arranged it."

Margaret had been thinking all evening into the next morning about William. The wedding was next week and he had grown so that he didn't have a decent suit to wear. She had packed away her egg money and decided that they would go to the village and she would insist he get a new suit. She knew, in his unselfish way, he would refuse, but she would get her way this time. He came in from chores and she asked if he had plans for the day. "Not really, I thought I might drive down to Mary's." She said, "I'll go with you, I want to go to town and we can pick Mary up on the way." "I'm telling your Da we want the cart today." "Ok, he said, I'll change my clothes." She walked down to the field and approached Douglas. "William and I are taking the cart today, I need to go to the village and get some things." He turned around and looked at her. "Now you and William are running off again?" "What are the two of you up to, anyway?" "It's of no concern to you, she said, don't bother with your lectures, I've had me fill of them." "I'll leave your dinner on the hearth as before." She turned and walked away. "You just wait a minute," he called after her, "You've had your fill of me, you say?" "Well, let me tell you that I've had me fill of your attitude and that son of yours too." "Long overdue, long overdue," she replied, and off she went leaving him standing there wordless again.

They pulled into Munro's and William went to the door; Catherine answered. "Is Mary home, me Mum and I are heading to the village and wanted to know if she'd like to go along." Catherine looked out the door and waved at Margaret sitting there. "Listen, William, we have to make a switch of help at Katie's, would you mind taking us over there? "Of course not," he replied. "Tell your mother to come in, we'll have some tea while the others get ready, that is if you're not in a hurry, I don't want to disrupt your plans for the day." "Not at all, William said, Mum just wanted to do a little shopping." "I appreciate this, John was going to take us but he's had a little trouble with one of the animals so we've been waiting on him." "I'll run out and tell him you're going with us," said William. "Thank you dear, your milk and scone will be waiting for you when you come back in." He turned and smiled at her and she thought he had the most irresistible smile. Catherine and Margaret were enjoying their tea; Margaret told her why they were going to the village, but that she hadn't told William because he would say no. She said she wanted him to look nice at the wedding and he couldn't go to Glasgow looking like a country boy. "It must be hard for you, knowing that he will be leaving soon, I know that it's hard for us, we've grown so fond of him." "It is hard, Margaret said, what keeps me going is that he won't end up like the rest of them up there." "I'm sorry, I love all me lads, but the rest are not like William, they're a rough lot." Catherine put her hands on top of Margaret's. "I understand."

CHAPTER FOURTEEN

She thought to herself that it was a shame Margaret hadn't had a daughter; she would never say it, but she knew Douglas and his sons, and Margaret was right, they were ruthless. William came in and wolfed his scone and milk down. They heard squealing and the children came racing down the steps. "Careful children, Catherine said, someone will fall and get hurt." They all left the house for the village and William dropped them off at Katie's. Mary stayed behind, wishing to spend more time with William and his mother.

"Where do you want to go first, Mum," he said. "To the clothiers, please." "The clothiers it is, then," he said. They stopped in front of the shop and after William helped them down he turned to walk back to the cart. "Wait a minute, Margaret said, you're going in too." "Aw, Mum, you know how I hate that." "This time you must, I'm ordering you," Margaret laughed. Mary joined in, "You can't disobey your mother now can you?" William unwillingly walked to the shop and held the door open for them. The clothier asked if he could help them. "Aye, said Margaret, my son is in a wedding and he needs a proper suit." With his mouth wide open, William cried, "Mum, you've played a trick on me." Mary laughed. "Have a seat ladies, smiled the clothier, I will see to the lad." Good natured as he was, William followed the man to the back of the shop. Margaret and Mary made small talk while he was gone. "I'm so glad William found you," she said to Mary. "Thank you, Mrs. Stevenson. I'm glad too." William came out with a suit on that obviously would need a little tailoring. "What do you think of this one?" asked the clothier. "It's very stylish, replied Margaret, would it be fashionable in Glasgow?" "Glasgow?" the man asked. "Aye, she replied, my son is going there to become a textile apprentice." "I see, he replied, I have another one that is the newest style right now but it also is much more costly." "No matter, said Margaret, I want him to have the best." "Mum, said William, this one is just fine." "No, she replied, try the other one on." He came out and the women looked at each other and shook their heads. "That's the one, Margaret said, fit him to it." "That's definitely the one," repeated Mary. William looked transformed from a village lad to the pictures they had seen of the city businessmen. Margaret paid the bill and the clothier told them that the suit would be ready early next week. They left the shop, William still shaking his head. "Thank you, Mum," he said. Margaret winked at Mary and stated, "Only the best for my son." William parked the cart and the rest of the morning they ran in and out of various shops, even peeking in to wave at Charles. He came to the door and said, "Aye, may I help you?" They laughed and Mary said, "I'd like two loaves of bread please." Margaret piped in, "And I would like a tayberry pie." "Sorry, he said, me bakers are out of town." They talked a moment and then continued on

83

their way. People were walking by the bakery looking in the windows. They had posted a sign on the door stating that they would be open on Monday at 7:00 AM.

"It's been fun, said William, best we be getting back to Katie's now." Katie lived just past the bakery on Lyon Road so it only took a minute or two to arrive there. Mary jumped off to let them know they were there but came back out immediately. "Mum said to come in, she has dinner ready and wants us to eat." They had a nice meal during which the atmosphere was much lighter for all now that Ethan seemed to be rallying some. They made plans for the coming week; Richard would take Katie to the bakery in the morning and one of the lasses, either Rebecca or Lillian would be there to help Ethan's mother who was expected to arrive soon. Peter would drive Catherine and Mary to the shop and then head to Richard's to work. John would pick up the slack on the farm. This was the plan they would repeat, the next coming months.

William and Margaret sat on the bench after supper. "I'm going to miss you lad," she said. "And I'll miss you too, but what choice do I have other than to stay here doing work I hate?" "Thank you for the suit, it sure is grand but I wish you would have spent the money on yourself." "You look all grown up in it," she replied. William stood up, "I think I'll take a little walk, I want to remember how everything looks here, my time to leave is getting closer; do you want to come?" "No, I think I'll sit here bit longer" she replied. William walked along, much on his mind. He saw Ben Lawers towering above him, he thought about the magic of Dochart Falls where Harry and he liked to fish during the salmon run, and the mill where Ethan had worked. He stood on the hill overlooking Lake Tay and wondered if Glasgow or anywhere else on earth could compare to this beautiful place. It was funny, he thought, how he loved the land but he didn't like working it. He had been sure that he wanted a taste of the city life, but now he wasn't so sure. This had been a week of change, he felt he had found a family who accepted him, he further alienated his Father and brothers and he had mixed feelings about leaving his mother behind. Could he change his mind? No, what was there for him here but the farm. Mr. McGregor had taken a chance on him, he couldn't let him down; he wasn't that kind of person. Would Mary wait for him? His brother had brought it to light that she was a bonnie lass; he knew there must be many other lads just waiting to take his place. What about Henry? He was educated and handsome with a good reputation and a promising future. He believed Mary had no feelings for him, but two years was a long, long time.

CHAPTER

FIFTEEN

Monday morning was here and the house was alive early in the morning. Mary and Catherine had gone to the bakery on the weekend to ready things and start batches of dough to rise. They felt they would be able to fill the shelves, not as they hoped to in the future but at least a taste of what they would be offering. It was hard to judge how much to make until they had acquired more experience.

Peter dropped them off and they started working immediately. "I'll start the bread, Mary if you can get the mutton stew on the fire." They would serve only one choice each day and had decided on mutton stew with vegetables and a pudding today. They had ample supply of ale, tea and milk for drink. The ice house delivered ice as promised, shortly after their arrival. Katie came in and was directed to start some tea cakes. "I think I'm going to like this," thought Mary. "What could be better than to spend me days with me Mum and favorite sister?" Katie reported that Ethan was still progressing, slowly, but progressing nonetheless and that Richard and Peter would periodically check on things during the day. Charles wandered out to the store. "My, my, he said, I must have died and gone to heaven, what with the smell wafting to the back." "Is Nancy up yet?" Catherine asked. "Aye, she's been up for a while." "I'll send some porridge and tea back, why don't you go and ready the table?" "And mind, leave the dishes after, we will take care of it." "As you wish Madam," he said, and disappeared again. By six-thirty they had the shelves filled with bread and other sweets, the stew was simmering on the hearth and so they decided to take a little break. They made tea and sat at the table drinking it, admiring their work. Just before seven Mary said, "Oh my, Mum, look," and she pointed to the window. They stood up and saw at least four women lining up outside the door with baskets in their arms. "Let's open the doors, business has begun."

Mary went to the door and opened it, "Good morning, come in ladies, please." They came into the store and one by one, were waited on. As predicted, during the day, women brought their dough to be baked. "Mind you don't mix them up," said Catherine. "No, Mum, I'm being careful," said Mary. All the dough was placed in the oven and the women were told to return for the baked product or just have a seat and wait if they preferred. Most had other errands to do and returned later. "Thank you for the business," they were told as they left the store. There was a steady stream of customers throughout the morning it was proving to be very promising. They scurried to mix up more products to bake and put on the shelves. The mutton stew and pudding were ready; it was nearing the dinner hour and soon men and women alike came and sat down to be served. Catherine took a plate in the back for Charles and Nancy fearing they would run out. Tables were filled and they were getting compliments on the food. There was literally only one serving of stew left when lunch was done. They would have to do some early morning baking to replenish the shelves again, but they were not complaining. "You know, lasses, said Catherine, I've asked Margaret for her jam roly poly recipe, Mary says they were a big hit at the dance and they disappeared quickly the other day." "Aye, everyone in my family loves them," said Katie.

This was their daily routine. On occasion, when she felt up to it, Nancy made her way out to the bakery and found she truly enjoyed the company of the ladies, often visiting with her prior customers from the fish shop; many of them would sit and chat with her over a cup of tea. It truly did her a world of good. Of course, Charles was always there with a joke or comment to make everyone laugh. It would have been hard to find a more joyful shop in Killin.

CHAPTER
SIXTEEN

Mary was getting ready for hen night. Tomorrow night the men would celebrate stag night. Peter came into the house and called up the stairs, "Lasses, are you ready to go." Lillian called down, "Just a minute, we're still cutting streamers." Mary had been to a hen night before but the lasses hadn't so they were excited. Catherine had given them some old rags and they were busy cutting them into thin streamers. The streamers would be placed all over Colleen; they had decided to forgo the traditional custom of dusting the soon to be bride with flour and soot. Rebecca flew down the stairs to scrounge the kitchen for any available pots and pans. When all was ready, they merrily said their goodbyes and were off, laughing and singing on the way. John looked at Catherine and said, "Oh my, I hope Peter has a lot of patience." Catherine laughed.

They turned the cart down Main Street at which time the lasses took pots and started banging them together, letting the village folk know what was soon to take place. Peter uncharacteristically yelled, "Stop, lasses, you'll frighten the horses and we'll end upside down in Lochay." They immediately stopped the banging, but not the laughing, they turned right onto Lochay Road and pulled up in Colleen's yard where they all momentarily jumped out. Peter waited because he would drop them off in the village and then meet William and Harry at the pub where they were waiting with Tom. It was their intention to secretly peek out and see the lasses. The yard was filled with lasses already waiting and other carts on standby to take them to town. Some of the lasses who lived in the village would meet them in the Town Square; others would come by cart. Amid chattering, laughing and squealing, they all managed to get into the carts and they were off. Once in town, the drivers happily dropped them off in the square. Peter parked the cart and went to meet William and Harry. Mary and her sisters gave everyone a bag of streamers; they immediately starting pinning them all over Colleen. They took some dye and painted her face and arms with it and then with ribbons, they grabbed pieces of her hair and tied it; when they were finished her hair was sticking up in every direction which brought another fit of laugher. With Colleen reluctantly at the head, they took their pots and pans, bells, whistles and cans, banging them together for noise as they paraded around the Town Square. Then the procession marched down Main Street and when they got to the end, turned around and marched back. The street was lined with people all laughing at them and egging them on. The lasses saw William and Harry peeking out of the pub and this caused embarrassment and more laughing. When they were spent from parading around, they all collapsed on the grass and Mary, with her sisters helping, passed out treats and drink. They spent another hour or so just talking and then disbursed for home. Colleen was congratulated and all were on their way calling and shouting to each other until no one was in sight. Colleen and Mary sat on the bench in the square watching until everyone had left. Rebecca and Lillian had run off somewhere unknown. Mary turned to her. "Now you've had a proper hen night, we had a good turnout." "That we did, that we did," said Colleen. "As embarrassing as it was, I'm glad you didn't soot and flour me." "We wanted to, laughed Mary, but I just couldn't do it, mind you remember that, in case I ever have a hen night." "I'll remember, Colleen replied, I won't make any promises though." "Oh you, Mary laughed, did you see William and Harry spying?" "Fair is fair, Colleen chuckled, we'll do the same on stag night." Mary patted her on the shoulder, "That's a plan, we will; now where did those lasses run off to?" "Peter will be miffed if he comes to fetch us and they're gone off somewhere." "I don't know, replied Colleen, but we might be the ones to fetch Peter at the pub." "Maybe, said Mary, but it's good to see him enjoy himself, he's always the responsible one." They sat, perhaps another hour, just enjoying each other's company when the lasses finally returned; they heard them coming; skipping and laughing on their way. "There you are, said Mary, I was wondering where you had run off to." "We had such a good time, Colleen," Rebecca said. "Yes, Lillian piped in, I've never laughed so hard." "Good, good, said Colleen, I'm glad." They waited a little longer and then saw the lads all coming from the pub. "Here they come, said Colleen, do you think they're tipsy?" "Maybe a little, said Mary, laughing, I hope they've saved some room for more ale until tomorrow night." Peter went to get the cart and William, Tom and Harry came over by the lasses." "See you tomorrow," said Tom. "Wait,

Harry called, we'll give you a ride." "Goodbye Mary, and thank you," said Colleen. "Bye, I'll see you tomorrow," she replied, and gave a little wave. William asked if she wanted to ride home with him, "Of course, I do, silly," she said. Peter came with the cart and the lasses jumped in. "See you in a bit," said Mary. "They drove off to the sound of the lasses singing, Mary and William, Mary and William." "I swear, said Mary, those lasses are always trying to get a rise out of me." "Their time will come, laughed William, you should have seen Harry laugh when he saw Colleen all painted up." "She was lucky we didn't soot and flour her." "That she was, that she was," said William. "Tomorrow's stag night you know." "Yes," she said, I know, then the wedding, my how time flies." They drove in silence for a while, both thinking, how time truly does seem to fly and both dreading when William would be leaving. He grabbed her by the waist and pulled her to him and she laid her head against him, savoring the feel of him next to her. They passed the cemetery and turned left into the driveway when he stopped the cart. "I'm not going to be able to stand it away from you, he said, am I doing the right thing?" "I wish it were us getting wed." At that, he pulled her to him and they kissed, then held and fondled each other until he suddenly put his hands on her shoulders and looked at her. "What?" she asked. "I'm drinking you in," he said." She laughed, "Drinking me in?" "Yes, he replied, so that when I am thirsty for you, I will remember what you looked like tonight." "Don't, she said, you will make me cry." She touched his face and let her fingers lie there for a moment, then said, "We'll be ok, our love will keep us going." "See that star up there, the bright one?" "When I look up there and see it, I will think of you." He replied, "See the star below it, when I look up and see it I will be reminded that we are meant to be together forever, just like those two stars." This time he smiled at her, then clicked the reins and drove to the house. "Do you want to come in?" she asked when they stopped. "Yes, I want to, he said, but I'd better get home, tomorrow's another long night." She gave him a kiss, then jumped down and went to the door but turned before she went in and blew him a kiss goodbye. Peter was already home with the lasses when she went into the house, they were telling John and Catherine all about the night.

It was a busy day again at the bakery and they planned on going to Katie's afterwards to visit with Ethan and have supper there. One of the lasses was already there, helping Ethan's mother get everything ready; Peter would bring everyone else later. Ethan was making slow progress, but he was still very weak; they ate supper and talked with Ethan's mother; they hadn't seen her for some time so it was good to catch up. Ethan was still not able to sit for long but he could now have a short conversation without having a coughing spasm, they were giving him steam treatments every day which helped keep the cough loose. They heard a knock on the door; it was Colleen coming to get Mary because they were going to town to see if they could catch any of the stag night carrying on. This they would do on the sly, and they were already laughing about it. The lasses both begged to go along which Catherine allowed, but for a short time only. "Oh Mum really, cried Mary, I'm not putting up with their bickering tonight." "Lasses, said Catherine, mind that you behave and don't bother Mary and Colleen tonight." "We won't Mum," they said, ready to make any promise in order to go along. Peter dropped them off (always the coachman). John and Catherine would return in about two hours to pick them up as Peter was going to stag night and would spend the night at Richard and Sarah's. Mary was spending the night at Colleen's and William at Tom's. William had informed everyone to meet at the pub and Margaret had cooked up a variety of food including breads and sweets for him to serve and of course there would be plenty of ale to drink. William did not invite his brothers, fearful that they would try to pick a fight with someone. They were secretly jealous that William was so popular; they themselves had few friends because of their rough nature. William picked up Tom and then turned around and went back up Manse Road and took Stewart Road on the left all the way past Fingal's Stone to Harry's house. Harry came dragging out, certain that every prank they could think of would be forced upon him tonight. They arrived to find that many lads were already there, joking it up and having a good time. When they saw Harry, a shout went up and the bottles of ale clicked together. Some of their friends had a band and they were setting up, getting ready to play. The bar maidens were going to have a lot of work to do tonight, they put the food that William and Tom brought in on a table and it wasn't long before the lads attacked it. A shout went up and Harry was brought to the middle of the floor while all the lads stood in a circle around him. He was given a big draught of ale and expected to drink it all at once. This continued throughout the night. The musicians commenced to play and they danced around the pub, sometimes the lads would grab the bar maidens for a reel around the floor. Some of the maidens grabbed William and he obliged with a dance and although it was clear they were interested in more, he didn't encourage them. When the night was half over and Harry was becoming tipsy, they dragged him out to the street and paraded him around the Town Square, then tied him to a lamp post and let him sit there by himself. Scottish tradition in the past sometimes stripped the groom of his clothes before he was tied to the lamp post and sometimes tarred and feathered or left tied up all night long. William wouldn't have it, so after a couple of hours they went and got him and partied a few more hours before they called it a night. They never saw the lasses spying on them from down the street. The musicians stopped playing and one by one the lads staggered out of the pub for home. William and Tom helped Harry into the cart and he half laid and half sat up in the seat. William went back in and got Margaret's dishes, thanked the owners and musicians and they were on their way to take Harry home. "Well Tom, I guess this is the last big party we'll have together for a long time," said William. "I guess so, he replied, I'm glad school is over and sad for the friends I won't see as much." "Thanks for letting me stay over, William said, it's a long drive home out to Finlarig Road." "Glad to do it, Tom replied, I think we'll all sleep well tonight, especially him." He nodded his head towards Harry, already asleep in the back. They arrived at Harry's and jumped out, one on each side of him to get him into the house. Once more, back in the cart, Tom said, "He won't be risin until midmorning tomorrow." William just laughed. "It was a good party, William." "That it was, I can see the bar maidens were interested in you," he replied. "Aye, William chuckled, I saw you spin around with a few yourself."

Next morning William headed for home, there was much to do for the wedding tomorrow. He hoped Harry was feeling ok this morning. Mary was also busy, she was putting together wedding bouquets; Lillian and Rebecca had collected heather for them, a sign of luck. They would make a ribbon from tartan cloth. She was excused from the bakery today to get everything ready; her days were so busy at the bakery and with the wedding that she hardly had time to worry about William's soon to be departure. Rebecca and Lillian were excited; this would be the first wedding they had attended since they were wee bairns. William would pick up Mary tomorrow and drop her off at Colleen's and then head to Harry's house himself. Harry wouldn't see the bride until he arrived at the church.

CHAPTER
SEVENTEEN

The bakery would remain open for wedding day with only Katie to tend to customers. Ethan was able to get around in the house now and his mother was there to attend to his immediate needs. Donald was proudly appointed helper to Peter and he wasted no time letting every member of the family know. Gretchen and Carolyn had new dresses to wear and they were upstairs where Rebecca and Lillian were helping them get dressed and fix their hair. Mary had made little pins of heather for them all to wear. It was a festive day. "Donald, me man, are you ready to go?" called Peter as he entered the house. They were going to the bakery to get the cake and sweets for delivery to Colleen's house. Donald came running, a huge grin on his face. "Here I am." "We'll be back for everyone in a little while," said Peter, and they were on their way. "My Da is getting better now," said Donald, looking at Peter. "I know, that's wonderful," Peter replied. "Would you like to stop over there and tell him you are working today?" "Oh, aye, I would," smiled Donald. "Well, I think we have time to do that, so we shall," replied Peter. "I like to sit up front in the cart by you," Donald said. "Mind you hang on tight and stay away from the side," said Peter. "I will, I'll be careful, Peter," he replied. Donald kept up a steady stream of chatter all the way to town. They turned left on Lyons road and drove past the bakery. "Peter, the bakery," said Donald. "I thought we'd stop at your house first, he replied, that way we don't have to leave all the baked goods in the cart." Donald nodded and smiled.

They stopped at the house and Donald jumped out and ran to the door before Peter could even step down. They knocked and Ethan's mother answered but before she could say anything, Donald interrupted, "Grandmum, I'm working today with Peter and I'm all dressed up for the wedding and Peter said I could stop and show me Da." "Donald, I didn't even recognize you, she laughed, aren't you looking like a little man today." She smiled at Peter and waved her hand toward the living room. "Sit down, Peter, can you stay for a while. "Just a short time, he replied, we are headed to the bakery, we have to deliver items to Colleen's for the wedding today." "I'll get Ethan," she said. "Don't disturb him if he's resting," Peter replied. Soon Donald came; racing out of the bedroom with his Da following slowly behind. Ethan extended his hand to Peter. "Peter, how nice to see you, thanks for bringing my little man to see me, I hear he's working for you today." "He is, and the best little worker I've ever had," Peter replied. "You look much better, are you starting to get your strength back?" "Some, but I'm still weak," he said, sitting on the couch beside them." They made small talk for a short time and then Peter rose and said, "Come on Donald, we have to go get the cakes now." Donald threw his arms around his Da and they hugged for a moment. "I miss you Da," he said and then once more they were on their way.

Peter stopped at the bakery, only a short way back on Lyon Road toward town. Donald ran in the door, heedless of customers in line, yelling, "Mum, mum, I'm helping Peter today and we've come for the wedding stuff and I saw Da and he said I was a little man." Everyone in the store smiled and laughed. Charles came from the back, "What in the world is the racket about?" "My son, Donald has made an entry into the store," said Katie. "Your son, Charles said, I thought it was another businessman come to see us." At that, everyone in the store started laughing again. Donald, never one to mince words said, "No, I'm not, I've come for the wedding items." "Oh, well then, we'd best get them loaded," Charles replied. "Have a seat at the table Peter, Katie said, I'll be with you in a minute." Once Katie had everyone waited on in the ever increasingly busy bakery, she came over and sat down by Peter. Donald was busy munching on a snack and glass of milk that Charles gave him. "Ethan looks much better," said Peter. "Aye, he has a little more color back, she replied, he's still quite weak but any progress is encouraging." "Just hang on Katie, he said, he's come a long way already, we have to take it day by day." "Thanks, Peter, she said, and thanks for letting Donald come along." "It's not a problem, he replied, he's a good lad, I enjoy him." "Well, we had better be on our way then before they think we got lost." "Are you ready, young man?" Donald ran to give Katie a kiss and then he was running after Peter, helping him to carry the small items. Everything was loaded and Peter said, "I couldn't have done it all without your help Donald, hop in now, let's go." Off they went, Donald waving at his mother standing in the doorway.

They pulled into Colleen's yard just as Mary and William were getting out of the cart. William came over to help unload the cake and bakery items and Mary took the bouquets and went to find Colleen. The house was a flurry of activity. Mr. Hart and Harry had gone to get the carriage. Mrs. Hart and the rest of the family were busy getting ready and putting the final touches to their hair. Mrs. Hart came running up to Mary, a bundle of nerves, "There you are, she said to Mary, how lovely you look." "And the same to the mother of the bride," said Mary. "These bouquets are wonderful," Mrs. Hart smiled, taking them from Mary's arms. "Thank you, I was hoping you would like them," Mary replied. "Mary, Mary, called Colleen from the top of the stairs, come up here." "Well, I must go see the bride, said Mary, I'll be back later." She hurried up the steps to find Colleen in a state of undress, she didn't have her gown on yet and she was still fixing her hair. "Oh Mary, she cried, jumping up and down, I love your dress and your hair." "Thanks, Colleen, but now let's get you into yours." They got her into her dress and Mrs. Hart was called up to give the final approval. "You are bonnie, dear," she said with tears in her eyes. "I second that, said Mary, you look gorgeous." Although Colleen didn't have the stunning beauty that Mary did, she was a pretty lass with creamy skin and bright eyes; she had a great personality and was always cheerful. "Now we just wait for the carriage," said Mary. "Oh Mary, in a few more hours I will be Mrs. Harry Rutherford, I can't believe it." "You have a good man, Colleen, said Mary, you are a lucky lass." "Aye, I feel lucky, she replied, I want you to be just as happy, Mary." "I am happy, Colleen," she replied, but Colleen could see the sadness in her eyes. The lasses were waiting for the carriage to come so they sat in Colleen's room talking about the past and future until Mr. Hart yelled up the stairs. "Lasses, the carriage is here to take you to the kirk" Colleen called down the stairs. "Is Harry there, I don't want him to see me." "No, her Father called, he went to the cottage with William to wait." "Ok then, coast is clear, she said, we'll be right there." They went down the stairs, Mary and Mrs. Hart helping to hold the gown so it wouldn't get caught and rip on something. "Maybe you should have gotten dressed at the kirk," Mary suggested. "Too late now, Colleen laughed, I want to peek at the cake." "It's here in the kitchen," said her mother. The downstairs had been decorated with white tablecloths and flowers and there were chairs and tables for people to sit at inside as well as outside. All neighbors pitched together on occasions like these and the men would be in charge of picking up and delivering all available chairs and tables. Weddings were always a community affair. "The cake is beautiful, Mary," said Colleen. "I'm glad you like it," she replied.

They left the house and carefully got into the carriage. Peter was the driver with Donald sitting proudly at his side. Mr. Hart had gone on ahead to see to the Piper. The wedding was to be held at St. Fillian's Episcopal Kirk on Main Street not far from Breadalbane Park. When they neared the kirk they could hear the Piper playing as guests arrived; he was in full Highland dress. Peter pulled up in front of the kirk and jumped down to assist the women from the carriage. Mary and Mrs. Hart once again held the gown so it would stay off of the ground. They went into a small room in the church to wait for the ceremony to begin.

William and Harry headed to the kirk and made their way to the front where they stood to wait for the bride. The parents of the couples were escorted to the front pews and everyone anxiously awaited the beginning of the ceremony. Harry looked resplendent in his Highland kilt and sporran. He had a piece of tartan fashioned into a bow on his lapel. Both of the men had a piece of heather attached to their jackets as a sign of good luck. William smiled as he spotted his mother seated in a pew; Richard had graciously offered to pick her up and bring her to the kirk; he then headed to the bakery to get Katie who had brought along a change of clothes and was waiting for him at the door. They had invited Charles and Nancy who declined because they thought it would be too much for them. Richard and Katie were seated just moments before the ceremony began.

Guests heard the Highland Wedding tune begin and all stood and turned to watch the wedding procession. Mary was first down the aisle. She looked bonnie in her dress which was plain but elegant. She carried a wreath of heather wrapped with a tartan bow. William felt a great burst of love when he saw her and a deep sadness in his heart that he would be leaving so soon, he didn't know how he would be able to do it; nonetheless, he kept a smile pasted on his face. He looked handsome and stylish in his new suit; it was a perfect fit. Colleen entered, her arm entwined in her Father's; she looked gorgeous as she came down the aisle, her veil trailing behind, she held a bouquet of heather tied with a tartan bow. Harry smiled from ear to ear, he loved this lass with all of his heart and he would do anything he could to be the best husband. Mr. Hart gave his daughter a kiss on the cheek and then turned to sit by his wife in the pew. The Piper, now silent, stood like a soldier at the back of the kirk.

The wedding vows were given and Harry placed the ring on Colleen's third finger. This was a Roman tradition, it was believed that the third finger ran directly to the heart and so it was bound to love and life. The Quaich was presented and the couple both took a drink. The couple was pronounced husband and wife at which time a cheer went up from the guests and a long kiss took place between the couple. William and Mary smiled at each other both wondering when it would be their turn. They assisted Colleen and Harry as each ripped a piece of tartan; Harry's from his lapel and Colleen's from the bow around her bouquet. They held the two pieces up for all to see and then Harry tied them together, each one taking an end and raising their arms up; another symbol of the two families joining together. The Piper began his music again and came down the aisle, then turned toward the guests and the processional march began. First down the aisle was the newly married couple, greeting guests as they went, and then William and Mary, arm in arm, trailing behind. The couples followed the Piper out of the kirk followed by the guests; they formed a line outside with the Piper who was once again silent, standing sentinel beside them where they accepted good wishes from the guests. Once all of the guests had given their greeting, the Piper led the couple to their waiting carriage. Mary and William found Margaret and took her with them. Peter and Donald were the first to leave with the Piper so that he could greet everyone with music as they arrived at Colleen's house. A beaming Donald said, "It was a nice wedding, wasn't it Peter?" "Aye, Donald, a fine wedding indeed!" Donald turned to look at the Piper somewhat apprehensively, "That's a funny music bag." "It's called a bagpipe," the Piper replied. "I would like to try it," Donald said. "Well then you shall, after we alight," smiled the Piper. Donald looked at Peter and grinned.

Margaret grabbed Mary's hands, "You look bonnie today, dear; and your friend was a gorgeous bride." "Thank you, Margaret, I am so happy for her and I'm happy you came too." They rode virtually in silence to Colleen's house. It was a festive day to be sure but also the beginning of a new life for all of them. They heard the Piper playing when they arrived. Guests were already seated at the tables and most of the men were drinking ale; some were standing around smoking and talking. The wedding party was seated and the ladies began to pass around the wedding feast. Catherine brought Margaret over to sit with the family and Margaret said, "It was a lovely wedding." "We're so glad that you came," Catherine replied. They made small talk, even John joining in at times. Mr. Hart stood up and said, "Let us have a prayer." Then the Minister began as he said, *"May the Lord keep you in his hand and never close his fist too tight upon you." "Today you will share your first meal together as a married couple, let us bless the food."* Everyone bowed their head in prayer. *"Dear Lord, thank you for bringing all of these friends together today in celebration of Harry and Colleen's wedding." "Please bless this couple as they begin their life, may they live together in peace and harmony with each other, Amen."* Everyone began to eat and the Piper went from table to table playing tunes. Soon they heard a clinking of bottles and Mr. Hart stood up again. "I'd like to make a toast to the bride and groom." "Although we are losing our beloved daughter, we are gaining a wonderful son in law; Harry, we welcome you into our family." "I know that you will cherish and care for our daughter as we would." With that, that there was more clinking of bottles and hear, hear was said all around. Next Harry stood up. "I want to thank my new family for welcoming me, I will not disappoint you." "To my bonnie new wife, I will cherish and love you to me dying day." More cheers and claps were heard from the guests. Finally William stood up. "Harry, you have been my best friend for as long as I can remember, I can assure your lovely new bride that you have been anxiously awaiting this reunion and will cherish Colleen to the end of your days." "She is lucky to have you and likewise you are lucky to have her." "Colleen, I have never heard a discouraging word out of your mouth and I know that you will make Harry happy, I have no doubt at all that you will be a caring and devout wife." "I can't wait until you have wee little bairns running around." He reached down and grabbed Harry by the shoulders and gave him a hug. Harry stood up and they embraced. "Hear, hear," everyone shouted again. Finally the Minister stood up once again, *"May the road rise up to meet you. May the wind be always at your back and may the sun shine warm upon your face; the rains fall soft upon your fields and until we meet again, may God hold you in the palm of his hand." (Traditional Gaelic blessing)*

Guests mingled throughout the afternoon. The ale and food kept coming, and it wasn't long before the musicians arrived. Mary and William had little to say, they sat together holding hands and watching the crowd; enjoying each other's company. Tom and Harriet came by and visited for a while; it seemed they were becoming a couple although he was known to tally with other lasses. A cry was heard in the crowd, "Gather round everyone, time to cut the cake." Harry and Colleen stood over the cake and Harry guided Colleen's hand as she cut the first slice. They both were giddy and had a hard time trying not to laugh. They fed a piece to each other and then plates of cake were passed around to all of the guests. Harry said, "Colleen and I want to thank everyone for celebrating our wedding today, it meant the world to us." "We want to thank William and Mary for consenting to be in the bridal party." "William, thank you for all the help you did on the cottage and for being the best friend any lad could want. Tom and William for the stag party, and thanks for not making it too hard on me." At that, everyone laughed. Colleen said,, "Mary, I couldn't have gotten everything ready for today without your help, the bridal shower, all of the bouquets, and just being there when I needed you." Then Harry and Colleen grabbed hands and Harry said, "And last, but not least, thanks to our

98

parents for all of the support, to Reverend Grady for officiating with his beautiful words, to the Munro Family for the wedding cake and baked goods, to Rebecca and Lillian for finding all the heather, and to the Piper who made the ceremony special." "Thanks to God for blessing each and every one of us who are present here today." "Now, everyone, please stay and celebrate with us this evening, the musicians will be ready in just a short time, but before that Colleen will throw the bouquet so all of the young lasses, please gather around her in a circle." The Piper led the way and all the lasses gathered in a circle around her. Mary tied a towel around Colleen's eyes and turned her around a couple of times. She threw the bouquet as hard as she could and it was caught by Harriet. Tom made no comment, he was thinking about William leaving Mary for so long, "My, two years is a long time."

For the final time, the Piper led the musicians. Harry and Colleen started the first dance of the night and soon all couples joined in; even John and Catherine. Margaret watched the festivities with William and Mary by her side. She couldn't help but wish that her family was as fun loving as this one, and oh, how they had welcomed her. All of the children, young and old were on the dance floor having the time of their lives. William walked over to Margaret and held out his hand, "Come, Mum, dance with me." "Oh no, William, I couldn't." "Yes you can, come on now." He led her to the floor and they danced while Mary looked on smiling. "I love you Mum, he said, you look bonnie tonight." "I love you son," she replied. It truly was a memorable wedding. For the last slow dance, William held Mary tight, and she him, neither knowing what the future held for them and their life together.

As the evening drew to a close the guests started leaving, one by one. William and Mary said their goodbyes to the bride and groom and with Margaret by their side they headed for home. It was a lengthy trip for William all the way out to Finlarig Road and they were tired from the past week's events. When everyone had left but the immediate family, Colleen and Harry headed on foot to their cottage, holding hands as they walked. The men would worry about the tables and chairs tomorrow; the leftover food was packed up and put in the icehouse. When they reached the door to the cottage Harry picked up Colleen and carried her over the threshold.

Mary sat close to William on the way home, savoring the feel and smell of him. Margaret sat in the back thinking how much fun she had; more than she could remember in a long, long time. She liked Mary and her family and was glad her son had chosen her but she hoped that they would be able to sustain their relationship with such a long absence. Two years was a long time. They pulled into the yard and William jumped out and walked Mary to the door giving her a kiss before he turned and walked away. John and Peter were still outside putting things away and he gave a wave to them and they in turn waved back. William would return tomorrow to spend one final day with Mary before he left for Glasgow. Neither of them, bone tired as they were, would sleep well that night.

Arriving at home, Margaret entered the house and William went to put the cart away. The house was quiet; all had gone to bed already. When Margaret entered the bedroom, Douglas awoke and asked, "Did you have a good time, then?" "Aye, aye, I did," she replied. "With the lad leaving soon, maybe you'll stop all of this gallivanting around and stay home once in a while, like a good wife should." She turned to him, "I am a good wife, I would have to be to put up with the likes of you." With that, she slipped into her night clothes and crawled into bed beside him. Douglas merely gave a grunt and turned his back to her. It was not lost on him or the other lads that William had left in a stylish new suit. Where or how he had acquired this was curious to them but he would not ask; he was sure Margaret must have had something to do with it.

CHAPTER
EIGHTEEN

William headed for town the next morning to see Mr. McGregor and find out what his itinerary would be. Mr. McGregor; a plump, balding man, was working on a new pattern and he looked up as William entered the shop. "There's me lad, have you recovered from all the wedding activity?" William smiled, "Aye, but I must admit I've barely slept all night." Mr. McGregor looked up thoughtfully, and then spoke, "Was it loss of sleep over the lass or the festivities?" William looked down and then ran his fingers through his hair. "The lass, but don't worry, Mr. McGregor, I won't let you down." Mr. McGregor rubbed his chin in his hand, "Will she wait for you then?" "Aye, she will wait, of course I've told her I'd understand if she couldn't." Mr. McGregor knew Mary and her family and he was aware that she was an exceptionally bonnie lass. He wondered how many other lads would be waiting to court her once William was out of the picture and he couldn't say that he blamed them. "Sounds like you have a good woman there, laddie." "Now, let's get to the itinerary, shall we?" "You need to be here tomorrow at six in the morning, you will take the coach to Perth." "The trip will be long with a lot of stops so you should have your mother pack you a lunch." "I've made arrangements for you to spend the night at The George Inn in Perth and the next morning, make sure that you are at the railroad by nine in the morning; it's within walking distance from the Inn." "The Inn will give you breakfast and a lunch to take with you." "Make sure that you get up early enough, ask at the desk for a wakeup call." "The train will take you to Glasgow and you'll arrive at Enoch Station." "There may be some transfers along the way so make sure you ask someone if you are getting on the correct train for Enoch Station." "Glasgow is a very large city, as is the station, so it may be easy to lose your direction." "There will be lots of people there you can ask for directions if you get confused." "Mind you hang tight onto your belongings, a large city like that has a lot of pickpockets just waiting to find an unsuspecting victim." "Keep aware of your surroundings." "You will spend the night at the Enoch Hotel, it's all been arranged." "Your supper and breakfast will be provided; you will not need any money for them." "Next morning, take a carriage from the hotel to the Templeton Carpet Factory at 52 Templeton Street." "Here is the address, I've written it down for you in case you forget." "Don't lose it." "This is where you will receive your training."

"When you get to the factory, ask for Isaac Campbell, he will tell you what to do." "You will stay in a flat with some of the other lads who are training at the factory. It's possible that some of them may be a rough lot, don't let them take advantage of you, and keep your valuables on you at all times." He gave William a little slap on the back, "I will meet you here in the morning, I have some money for you to live on until you receive your monthly allotment, you may need it for food and carriage service." "I wish you luck, I can't believe our dream is finally coming to fruition." He laughed, "If I wasn't such an old sod I'd be goin' meself." "I know you will do me proud; the want to learn is half the battle."

William reached out his hand. "Thank you for everything, Mr. McGregor." "As I've said, I promise to work hard." Mr. McGregor smiled. "William, you are a man now, I think it's time you call me George, I have no doubt you will do well, and I have faith in you." They shook hands and William left to pick up Mary at the bakery. George stood by his window watching him leave. "What a nice lad he is; too bad that Father of his is such a know-it-all." "I hope his lass waits for him, two years is a long time when you're young."

Catherine, Mary and Katie were finishing up the baking for the morning and as usual, there were a number of customers in the store. Mary had been quiet all morning, even peaked looking. Catherine observed her daughter, "Mary, why don't you go and sit down for a while, you look ill." "Oh, no Mum, I'm ok, I just didn't sleep well last night."

Katie was at the hearth working on the soup they were going to serve for dinner and she was thinking about Ethan. He was much better but it was clear that he was still very weak and it would be some time before he would be able to work, if ever, and probably not back at the mill where it was damp. She wished there was something he could do at home that wouldn't expend too much energy but she was at a loss as to what that might be. He was getting restless for something to do; she'd have to talk to her Da and see if he had any ideas. "Katie, Katie," she looked up startled. "Yes Mum?" "Katie, I've been talking to you and you haven't heard a word I've said." She laughed, "I guess I was daydreaming, sorry." Catherine had a worried look on her face. "What's wrong Mum?" "I took lunch back for Charles and Nancy and he said she wasn't feeling well." "She hasn't been out here to sit for a few days and I know how she enjoys it." "Has Charles called Dr. Traymoor?" "No, not yet, but if she's still poorly tomorrow, he said he would." "I felt her forehead and she doesn't seem to have a fever; she doesn't have a cold, she's not coughing and she says she doesn't hurt anywhere but that she gets dizzy when she's up." "Did you ask Charles if he wanted someone to stay here with them tonight?" "Aye, but he said no, they would be fine." "She hardly touched her food." "Well, hopefully the doctor will get to the bottom of it if she's not better tomorrow."

Just then, William entered the store but his usual smile was missing. Catherine looked at him. "Well hello there, Mary is just finishing up in the back room." "I must say, the wedding has done you both in, you look just as peaked as she does." "No, I'm fine, he replied, just a lot on my mind right now, I've been to McGregor's to get my itinerary." "You leave tomorrow then, as planned?" she asked. "Aye, I'll be leaving at six in the morning." "Oh William, we will all miss you so." "Between you and me, Mrs. Munro, I was so sure this is what I wanted to do but now that it's here, I'm not so sure." She smiled sadly at him, "You know, you can always change your mind, there's still time, no one would think less of you." "That's the thing, I can't, and it wouldn't be right to let Mr. McGregor down, he's so excited about this and has so many plans now." She patted his hand. "I respect that William, I really do, don't think about it so much then, things usually work themselves out." "Now, give me a hug, will you, and make sure you send a post every week so we know how you're doing." He gave her a long hug, seemingly not wanting to let go. She left him sitting at the table looking about as lost as a lamb. He felt like a little lad again with a big lump in his throat. Mary came out of the back room, dusting off her hands on her apron. "Give me just a minute more William and I'll be ready to go." He looked up and smiled at her. "William, called Katie, would you be wanting a cup of soup before you leave, it's ready now?" "Thanks, Katie, but no, I'm not too hungry right now; ate too much at the wedding yesterday." Katie walked over and stood beside him. "I'm truly glad we got to know you, Ethan says Mary picked a fine lad; we'll miss you." "Thank you," he said, and patted her arm. "Oh come on now, William, give me a hug too." William stood up and gave her a hug. There were tears in his eyes but he brushed them away without anyone seeing.

Mary came to the table and sat down. "What did you have planned for today?" she asked. "I'm not sure maybe for starters we could go down to the Falls of Lake Dochart." "What would you like to do?" "Just be with you," she replied. They left the bakery and Catherine couldn't get them off of her mind. "Katie," she said, "It just doesn't seem right that William is leaving." "Like he says, Mum, what else is there for him here to do, he detests farming." "What a shame, Catherine replied, I understand why he is doing it but I feel for Mary." "Mary will be fine, Mum, she's a determined lass, besides, the bakery will keep her busy and there's nothing more healing than that."

They traveled down Main Street all the way down to Dochart Road. The roar of the water could be heard as they approached, even before they saw it. The falls weren't high, by waterfall standards, but they were spectacular as they created a roar when the water crashed over the smooth black rocks. It was a soothing sound and that's just what the couple needed right now. The horses were tied in a field where they would stay cool and could nibble on lush grass. Mary and William held hands and walked to the old narrow bridge. There they stood for a long time, not speaking, both just watching the water. They were subdued, neither knowing what to say, both afraid to let their emotions out. Mary was not the clingy, crying type of lass but she was close to tears now. "Come, Mary, let's sit in the grass over here." There was a deep pool beneath the falls and there were several men fishing there. "You know," he said, in season, Harry and I spent a lot of hours down here fishing for salmon, it's a resting spot for salmon when they are spawning, before they swim up the rushing river." "Aye, Peter and Richard come down here then too." They sat close together, he had his arm around her and she rested against him. William took her face in his hands and stared into her eyes; then he kissed her. Their kiss lasted for a long time it was all he could do to break apart from her. The last thing he wanted was to lose control and take advantage of her; it would be so easy to do right now; they were both full of passion and longing. "I love you so much, he said, I can't believe I'm doing this." "And I love you, she patted her chest, this heart belongs to you forever." "It will be alright, I will write to you and you will write to me." "When I read your letters I will try to pretend it's you beside me talking, you will get to see and learn so many new things." "Take advantage of your opportunity and try to enjoy yourself; don't waste your time worrying about me, I will be here waiting for you and will be just fine." William thought she was the most remarkable lass, always thinking of everyone but herself. "You're right, I made the decision and now I need to abide by it, but that doesn't mean I won't miss you" "Let's go down to Inchbuie Island, shall we?" Mary stood up and put her hands out to pull William up. "I'll race you," she laughed. She had a head start on him and was through the gate before he caught up with her. Laughing, he grabbed her hand and they went down the steps. "Careful," he said, they're slippery, I don't want you to fall." "Oh, I forgot how beautiful it is down here," she said. The island was shaded by groves of various trees and the way the light played on the ground, it looked golden. They took the path to the MacNab burial ground and came to a stone enclosure where the remains of the Chiefs of the MacNab Clan lay. The stone of Frances McNab was carved with a mediaeval knight. One of the oldest stones was dated 1574. They walked outside the enclosure where the common members of the clan were buried. The feeling was almost surreal as they stood there, making one feel as if they had entered another magical world. Mary laughed, "Colleen and I used to come down here and then she would always say she saw a ghost and we would scream and run back out like we were being chased." William smiled, "I can see the two of you doing that, remember when she told us that she put milk out so the Urvisk (*Brownie*) wouldn't bring bad luck to the family." Mary smiled and shook her head, "That's our Colleen." William grabbed her around the shoulders and kissed her, Mary put her arms around his neck and they leaned into each other until William broke apart. "Mary its best we're not alone now, I'm afraid what might happen," he said, his voice husky with emotion. Shaken, Mary nodded. "Let's have lunch at the bakery and then go up to the foothills of Ben Lawers so we can look down on Loch Tay, said William, I so love it up there." "Good idea, we're having leek soup today with tattie scones and you're in for a treat because Katie made some Dundee cake." "How is your Mum doing," Mary asked. "She's putting on a brave face, me mind will rest easier when I'm gone knowing that she is getting out more." Their mood had somewhat brightened, they were both determined to enjoy the day.

"We're back," Mary said as they entered the bakery. The tables were almost full with customers and they went in back and filled bowls with soup; took their tattie scones and sat in back at a table. "I hope they have good food in Glasgow or I'll come home skinny and you might not know me." Mary laughed, "You're already skinny." Catherine came by and Mary asked, "How is Nancy today?" "Worse, she replied, Charles brought the doctor and he said he thought it was her heart, just to let her rest and try to get her to eat something." "He said there was nothing more he could do, she might have to go to Edinburgh for better treatment." "Nancy said she would do no such thing, she wasn't going to have those high faulting doctors poke and prod her." "On the side, Dr. Traymoore said the trip might be too much for her anyway and Charles is quite distraught." "I'm sorry to hear that, said William, they're both such nice people." When they were finished eating, Mary said, "I'm full now, should we take our Dundee cake and milk with us and have a picnic in the hills." "Aye, let's," he said. They had a long walk up the foothills to view Loch Tay but the walk was worth it. Ben Lawers loomed in front of them; it was Perthshire's highest mountain, just under 4,000'. They stood looking down on the Loch and William said, "I think this must be the most beautiful place in the world." She took his hand. "We are blessed to have been born here; some people will never get to see it, what a shame." "This is where I always want to live and where I want to raise my children; she looked at him and smiled, our children." "I'm not even gone and this is where I want to return," he agreed. He turned and put his hands on her shoulders and stood looking at her once more. "I know it's customary to ask your Da for your hand first, but as soon as I return, will you marry me?" "I'll be waiting with my wedding dress on," she smiled. They grabbed each other and stood together kissing; she pressed her body against him until William found it necessary to break apart once again before things got out of hand. They ran around the hills, chasing each other and picking herbs and wildflowers until they tired. "Let's have our Dundee cake and milk now, shall we?" "This will be our last meal together for a while," she said. "It's so good, if it's my last meal ever, I would be satisfied." "Aye, she replied, it's not something we make often." "You have milk on your face," she said, and took her hand and wiped it away, letting her fingers linger on him. "We could go and see Harry and Colleen but they probably want their privacy today." "They wouldn't mind, they'd welcome us; but I agree they need to be alone today." "Has your Da said anything?" "Not a word." "What about your brothers?" "Nothing." Mary couldn't understand a family like that, how did William and Margaret stand it? When they married, would any of them come, she wondered, well of course Margaret would. "Peter could take you tomorrow morning, he would be glad to, he goes to Richard's anyway." "Thanks, but me Mum wants to, you know, spend the last few minutes with me." "I understand, she said, can you pick me up at the bakery or shall I meet you at McGregors?" "Of course we will stop and pick you up; we'll be there shortly after five in the morning." "That's ok we're always there that early baking." "Guess we'd better head home, it's getting late." "I guess," she said and they walked slowly back down the hill holding hands.

They arrived at Mary's and William came into the house with her. They all gathered around the kitchen table and visited, even John. Eventually William stood up, "Guess I'd best be heading home, I've some packing to do and me Mum's probably waiting up for me." Rebecca and Lillian jumped up and gave him a hug, telling him how much they would miss him. Catherine held his hand and said, "We've had our goodbyes earlier, good luck son." Peter shook his hand, "I'm so glad we're friends now, don't get too used to big city life, you hear?" "Never," William replied. John followed him to the door and to everyone's surprise he grabbed William around the shoulders and hugged him. "I know I gave you a rough time of it at first lad, you're an outstanding man and I truly respect you." "I hope you don't harbor any hard feelings against me?" "None, sir, it means a lot to me that your family has welcomed me and me Mum, I'll never forget that, never in a million years." "Good, good, replied John; take care William."

Mary took his hand and they went out the door. Rebecca and Lillian were just ready to run out after them when John stepped in front of it, blocking them. "Hold on there lasses, give them some time alone." "Oh Da," they said and both ran upstairs to look out the window. William and Mary stood by the side of the cart in a tight embrace, an embrace that would have to last for two years in their memory. "Don't be sad, he said, remember we're always connected by those stars up there." "I'm not sad, I'm happy for you." They kissed and hugged then William hopped in the cart and left the yard. Mary stood there without emotion until he was out of sight then, all the emotion she had held back the last few weeks came flooding out and she fell to her knees in the grass. There was no sound coming out of her but she was doubled over as if in physical pain. "Mum, what's wrong with Mary," called Rebecca from upstairs. Catherine went to the window and saw her daughter out there and it broke her heart. "She's ok, she called, let her get it out, it's been brewing for too long." Unknown to anyone, William had stopped the cart down the road and he too was bent over in agony. When he had gotten under control again, he picked up the reins and headed home. Margaret was in the kitchen waiting for him. "Well son, I guess the time has come, huh?" "Did you enjoy your day?" "Aye, we went to Dochart Falls and then up to the foothills below Ben Lawers to look down at Loch Tay, bye, it's beautiful up there." "It was nice, but sad too." "You'll have to get packed and then to bed early, I'll wake you about four in the morning." "Come, I've got something for you." Margaret went into her bedroom and came out with a satchel. "Look, I thought you could use this, it was one of your Grandda's prize possessions, see, it has his name engraved on it, Sean Ferguson." "It was given to him by a good friend." "Oh, I couldn't, he said, it was your Da's." "You can and you will, she laughed, besides what would I do with it, it's been sitting around collecting dust for years, I'm glad it has a use now, he would be happy to see you use it." "Thanks Mum, you're the best." "Well, get packed and then off to bed you go, or do you want a snack first?" "No thanks, I had one at Mary's." "Is she doing ok with this?" "Aye, she's a strong lass, she'll be ok, and she has her family and the bakery to keep her busy while I'm gone." He turned and gave her a kiss on the cheek, then went to his room, packed what few things he needed then went back to the kitchen where Margaret was cleaning. She looked up when he entered. "I forgot to ask you, Mr. McGregor said I should bring a lunch with me tomorrow; he said it's a long, tiring trip to Perth." "Of course, I'll fix it up now so it's ready in the morning." William went up to bed; sleep would come easy for him tonight he was so exhausted.

Douglas came into the kitchen and sat at the table. "Would you be wanting a snack?" "Aye, I would," he replied. "Is the lad really leaving tomorrow?" "Yes, I'm waking him at four in the morning, he has to catch the coach to Perth by six in the morning; it would be nice if you would accompany us." "Of course, I'll go; the whole village would talk if I didn't; I might not have such a fancy suit to wear as my son though." Margaret slammed the milk down on the table. "You never stop thinking about yourself." "What's happened to you?" "What's happened to us?" She left him sitting there by himself and went to bed. The other boys weren't home yet they were always carousing around at night, either at someone's house or the inn.

Douglas sat there sipping his milk and thinking. "She's right, what has happened to me?" He had a conscience, oh aye he did. When he took on the job as tacksman he thought it was a good opportunity for the family, he didn't think about having to collect rent from those he had worked with and was friends with all those years. Oh, he knew how they despised him; especially John Munro, the Father of William's lass, Mary. He had hardened himself to the task and it changed him. He loved all his sons but William was not like the others, he knew the other boys actually didn't mind the rent collecting and William had always looked down on him for doing it. In time, they had grown apart; they were too different to understand each other. He finished his snack, then went to the bedroom, undressed, and crawled into bed. He turned to her, "I'm sorry for what I said, wake me up in the morning, I'll go with you, the lads can see to the chores." She turned towards him, "Thank you, I really mean it."

CHAPTER
NINETEEN

The morning came way too early for all of them. "How does Mary do it," William thought; getting up so early every day." He wondered what she was doing at this very moment, a habit that would continue for many months to come. He dressed and then headed to the kitchen with his satchel, not realizing that he looked quite professional. Everyone was already seated at the table and the lads had been admonished not to start the picking and nagging today. "Come, sit down and have a bite, said Douglas, otherwise you'll be hungry in a few hours." "You're going then?" "To town I mean," William asked. Douglas patted him on the back, "Of course, I'm going." William sat down next to him, a little stunned. The boys, for the first time, questioned William about his training and it was the first amicable meal they had together for a long time. Margaret thought how sad it was that it had come to a parting for them all to get along together. She rose from the table and went to the icehouse to get the lunch she had prepared for William. "I suppose we should leave soon, better to be early than late, the coach won't wait for you." Douglas rose, "Lads, you know what to do this morning, don't be lollygagging around, get to the chores right away, and don't be nippin at each other." "Aye, Da, we won't," they replied. They came to William, one by one hugging him and wishing him good luck. Then Douglas and William went to get the cart. "Look, son, he said, I haven't understood you, I guess I still don't, but I love you and I'm proud of you just the same." "I'm sorry for the things I've said." "It's ok, William replied, I haven't exactly done me share around here either, I guess I deserved it." In his wildest dreams, William never thought he would hear those words coming out of his Da's mouth. He stopped and put out his hand. "Thank you, I hope I make you proud someday." "You already do, son, you already do." William turned from him so he couldn't see the tears running down his face. Margaret said a silent prayer that William didn't have to leave on bad terms with his family.

They brought the cart up to the house and to everyone's amazement Douglas actually jumped off and assisted Margaret into the cart. William felt relieved, maybe his Mum would be treated with respect now; he always felt he had to show her respect because she didn't get it from any of them. It was a beautiful day and they had a nice ride into town. The turn to Mary's house didn't go unnoticed by him; it would be a long time before he saw it again. "Da, would you mind stopping at the bakery to pick up Mary?" "No, of course not," he replied. When they arrived, William jumped down and went in to let Mary know he was there and say a final farewell to Catherine and Katie. When they came out, Douglas thought to himself, "My God, she's a bonnie lass." He smiled and nodded his head and they were off to McGregor's. William immediately grabbed Mary's hand and held it tight. He would never let on to anyone, but he was becoming a little frightened, he had never been out of Killin before except to Aberfeldy and Comrie.

They pulled up in front of the shop and Mr. McGregor waddled to the door and unlocked it. "I see you've brought the family with you, come in, come in, I'm so glad to meet you all." "Let me get the pot going and we'll have some tea, we'll be able to see the coach when it arrives." He pumped the water into the pot, put it on the hearth, and motioned for everyone to sit at the table. He then went to Douglas and extended his hand in welcome and the same to Margaret and Mary. Then he sat down by William. "Do any of you have questions about what William will be doing?" Douglas asked, "I know that Glasgow is a large city, William won't get lost will he." "No, said Mr. McGregor, not as long as he asks for directions if he's not sure where he's going." "There won't be a lack of people for that," at which he laughed. "And living conditions?" asked Douglas. "He will be staying with several other lads who are also training at the factory." "I am told they are not fancy, but clean and adequate." He rose to get the tea and cups and Margaret and Mary went to help him. "I even have some shortbread from McPhee's Bakery," he said, and then winked at Mary. "You know, the food is good there, but it's not helping my girth." Mary smiled at him, "I see you've become one of our regulars at lunch, it's good to see you there." "It's getting to be a club every day, I like the companionship, Charles and I have been good friends for a long time, you know." "I can see why," she replied, he's quite a remarkable man; you both are."

CHAPTER NINETEEN

Soon the coach rolled into town. Mary suddenly felt sick to her stomach and she had a lump in her throat. William turned white and squeezed Mary's hand. They left the shop and walked outside. William and Mary were the last out the door as he grabbed her for one last moment alone. Two passengers were seated in the coach and they stepped out to get some exercise. Mr. McGregor shook the driver's hand when he alighted; they exchanged words and Mr. McGregor gave him an envelope. "William, give the driver your satchel," he instructed. William handed it over and the driver secured it on the coach. The passengers asked where they could get some ale and were told that it was too early, no one was open yet. Mr. McGregor went inside and got a bottle for each of the passengers, William and the driver. "Thank you, that wasn't necessary, they said. "It's nothing," he replied. "We'll be leaving in five minutes," the driver called; then turned to William, best say your goodbyes now." William bent down and hugged Mr. McGregor, thanking him for everything, then turned toward his parents. Margaret was determined not to cry; she threw her arms around him, then kissed him on the cheek and tousled his hair. "God Speed, Son." Douglas also hugged him, "Good luck Son, if you need anything, anything at all you send a post or telegram right away." William nodded his head then turned to Mary. They held each other and he kissed her. "I love you, remember that." "I will," she said, with a feeble attempt at a smile. The passengers climbed into the coach first and William stepped in after, sitting across from them. He held the lunch Margaret had made on his lap like a little lad. The driver clicked his reins and they were off. They all stood in silence watching the coach until it disappeared into the trail of dust that lingered behind. Mary turned her back to the others, not wanting them to see the tears in her eyes. Margaret stood with tears running down her face and Douglas pulled out his handkerchief and wiped them away, then wrapped his arm around her. Mr. McGregor invited them in again; they thanked him but declined, stating they had to be on their way home. None of them knew the agony that was yet to come.

They stopped at the bakery to let Mary off and she asked them to come in for a moment, wanting to hang onto anything of William's as long as possible. "Come in and have some tea or milk before you leave." Margaret looked at Douglas expecting him to refuse but instead he jumped down, went around to her side and helped her down. "That's kind of you, Mary," he said, still awed by her beauty. Mary held the door for them and they entered. She pointed to the tables, "Have a seat anywhere you like." They picked a table and sat down. Mary went back to the workroom where Catherine and Katie were kneading bread. "I've invited William's parents in for tea before they head home." Catherine nodded and came out to greet them, wiping her hands on her apron. "Margaret, how good to see you again, I wish it could be under better circumstances, how are you holding up?" "We're ok, you remember my husband, Douglas?" Catherine offered her hand, "How are you Douglas, we think the world of your son." He smiled at her, "Thank you that means a lot to me coming from you." Mary came with a tray of tea and fruitcake. They visited for a short time, keeping the conversation light with talk of the bakery and weather, avoiding any conversation that would remind them of the recent parting. Douglas was the first to stand up, "I think we'd best be on our way, I'm sure you ladies have work to do." "Aye, the customers will be lining up soon, I'm not complaining, mind you," Catherine said, smiling. Mary gave them each a hug and they left the store. Without another word, she cleaned up the table, walked to the workroom and put on an apron. Work would be her salvation, keeping busy and not having time to think would get her through, day after long lonely day. She would spend her nights outside the house looking up at the two stars. The light had gone out of her she was only a shell of her former self, and a slow anger was building up in her at William for leaving her behind.

CHAPTER
TWENTY

The coach rolled along mile after bumpy, dusty mile. The man across from William extended his hand. "I'm Albert and this is my wife Susan." William shook his hand, "Nice to meet you, I'm William, where are you headed?" "We're going to Perth, to meet our new grandson, our daughter lives there and she just gave birth." "Congratulations, where do you live?" "We live in Achmore." "I've never been there but I've heard the name." "We like it but of course we've lived there our entire lives." "Killin is a lovely village, what I've seen of it." "I think so but I'm prejudiced, I hate to leave but I'm going to Glasgow to learn a trade." "Good for you, what trade?" "Power looms, the gentleman outside the store is sponsoring me he wants to expand his shop." "It is a changing world, something new every day, I wish you luck." "Thank you, I'll need it." Conversation stopped for the time, the boring trip had lulled them all into near sleep; they would periodically doze off and then be awakened by a bump in the road. Now and again they would pass another carriage or cart on the road and they would lean forward to look out the window. "Have you been to Perth before," William asked. "No, first time for us, they were married in Achmore but he got a job with the railroad, I wish they lived closer, it's such a long trip."

The coach made several stops along the way; the driver would dismount, check the horse's hoofs and inspect the wheels to make sure that everything was as it should be. During these times the passengers would get out and stretch their legs. They had come to the outskirts of Crieff and the driver announced that they would be stopping for about 30 minutes to make a change in horses. There was an inn next to the stables so William walked over and bought ale to drink with lunch and one to take with him. He walked back to the stables and found a grassy spot to sit and eat lunch. The ale tasted cool and refreshing after the hot dusty ride. He opened his lunch and ate it. He felt tired and lazy from sitting in the coach all morning. He smiled as two young boys ran through the grass, sticks in their hands; it reminded him of Harry and himself years ago. He thought about the stories he had been told of Crieff. He could see where the name came from because there were groves of trees everywhere. (*Crieff means among trees in Gaelic*). His Da had told him about Sir John Drummond of Drummond Castle and how his family and the Campbells were feuding with the Murray family and had set fire to the old church at Innerpeffray, just west of Crieff. The entire Murray family was burnt to death. He was told that Crieff was considered the Gateway to the Highlands because it was a main cattle trading town and the town had a history of violence, mostly due to cattle raids and payments for cattle. There were many hangings in the town and the timber used in the gallows was preserved in the Town Hall. Still, William thought it seemed to be a nice town now, at least what he had seen of it. William's head jerked up, he had almost fallen asleep in the grass, daydreaming about the old stories. He decided he'd better get up and walk around a bit before he fell asleep and missed the coach but he supposed the driver would have awoken him. Still, he needed the exercise so he walked to the stable door and looked in just as the driver was coming out. "That's a huge stable they have here," he said. "They house the horses for all the coaches on this line." "How many coaches do they have?" "I'm not sure, but at least six of them, there are more between Perth and Edinburgh." "I'm taking the railway from Perth to Glasgow." "Glasgow you say? Have you been there before?" "Oh, no, never, William replied, I've never been this far before." The driver smiled, "Better hop in, we will be leaving soon." William opened the door and to his surprise there was another passenger sitting there, a young lady who must have boarded when he had dozed off in the grass. "Hello," he said. She extended her hand, "Hello, I'm Kristine." "I'm William, nice to meet you." He smiled at the couple. "Did you have lunch?" asked Albert. "Yes I did, me Mum sent one along with me, I sat on the grass and ate it, it was good to stretch and I got some ale at the inn, my mouth was dry from the ride and the cool drink helped." "The man smiled, "We had some ale too, I agree with you, we ate at the inn and the food was tasty." Susan smiled at the lass, "Where are you headed to?" Kristine looked up, "To Perth where I live, I've been helping my sister who just had a baby." "As have we," Susan replied, well sort of, our first grandson was just born and we haven't seen him yet, so we are going to Perth too." "Congratulations, where do they live in

Perth?" asked the lass. William had closed his eyes and fallen asleep listening to the drone of voices and the clip clop of the horses as they plodded along. He dreamt of Mary, they were in the field, chasing each other and her long hair was flowing behind her. He must have slept for quite some time because when he woke, with a start, he could see there were more and more cottages around, they must be getting close to the city. He could see that the lass was awake and staring out her window so he gently touched her arm. "I'm sorry to disturb you but I wonder if you could tell me how to get to The George Inn when we stop." "Oh, you are in for a treat, it's very elegant but far from where we will be stopping." "My Father is picking me up so we'll give you a ride there" "Thank you, but that's not necessary, I'm sure I will find it, I don't want to trouble you." She smiled at him, "Nonsense, we have to go right past it anyway, we live on Glenearn Road." "It would be silly of you to have to make other arrangements we would be pleased to do it." "Now, if you're catching the railway to Glasgow tomorrow it will be only a 10-15 minute walk; that is if you want to walk." "Oh aye, he replied, I do." "Then from the right side of the hotel just follow St. Leonard Street, you will cross a bridge and the railroad station will be on your left, you really can't miss it." "Thank you," he said, I appreciate your help, and it's kind of you." Susan was observing them talking and thought to herself, "They would make a lovely couple, she is so bonny and he is quite handsome, that smile of his is a heartbreaker."

The coach came to a stop and they all exited and waited for the driver to give them their belongings. The couple was the first to leave as they spotted their daughter's husband waiting. "Goodbye everyone, they said, it was nice to meet you." William said, "Goodbye, enjoy that baby." "We will," they replied, excited smiles on their faces. William looked at the lass; she was bonnie and had dark black hair and eyes, a slim build and a full mouth. "I guess you're glad to be home again," he said. "I am, but I'll miss the wee bairn, my sister and I are close and I miss her now that she's married and gone from home." "They live a much simpler life than we do here in Perth, it's nice, and I like it." William nodded his head, "I have three brothers, but we're not close at all, we're too different." "Different in what way," she asked. "They love farming and I don't, I'm going to Glasgow to learn a trade, I'll be gone for two years." "That's a long time, won't you get homesick." "Aye, I will, I hope I can stick it out, I have a lass waiting for me; her name is Mary." "Will you marry, when you return that is?" "Aye, I've already asked her, she says she will be waiting with her wedding dress on," and he laughed. She laughed too but was thinking, "I hope she waits for him, he seems a nice lad but two years is a long time." She had been in a similar situation not long ago. Her fiancée' had gone to Edinburgh to study for a year. After six months had gone by, the posts were coming less and less frequently until one day she received the last one. She could almost recite it by heart; she had read and re-read it so many times that the paper was frayed. *My Dearest Kristine. I find it hard to write this to you today, I know that it will come as a shock. I have met someone else here and we plan to be married next month. I never thought it would turn out this way, it just happened. Please know that I will always hold you in the deepest respect. Yours Truly, Gavin.* Of course she was devastated at first and then she told herself that it was a good thing it happened before they were wed; maybe he hadn't loved her after all. She wasn't one to wallow in self-pity and she recovered quickly assuring herself that it just was not meant to be.

She looked up with a start from her daydream, realizing that her Father had arrived with the carriage. "Come, William, she said, my Father is right over there." He followed behind her and assisted her up into the carriage. She leaned forward and gave her Father a kiss on the cheek, then said, "This is William, we traveled in the coach together, he is going to The George Inn and I told him we'd give him a ride." "Of course, hop in lad." William stepped into the carriage and they drove off. "Where are you from lad," he called from the front. William leaned forward, "Killin, but I'm going to Glasgow to learn the power looms." "A good trade, a good trade, up and coming now." he said. "Glasgow will be very different from Killin and it will take you some time to get used to the city." "That's what I hear," he replied smiling at Kristine. Kristine was taken aback; she felt something flutter in her stomach at that smile of his. Kristine's Father continued, "If you like, we would be happy to have you for the evening, we can take you to the station in the morning, I assume you're traveling by train?" "Aye, I am, but my room has been arranged as have my meals." "Thank you for the invitation anyway, I appreciate it." "Very well then," he said. William sat back in the seat and looked at Kristine. "I hope everything works out for you," she said. "If I meet as many nice people there as I have today, I'm sure it will," he replied. The coach stopped in front of the hotel and William grabbed his satchel then turned to the lass, "You were very kind to of-fer me a ride, I've enjoyed getting to meet you." "Goodbye, maybe we'll meet again someday." She almost wished he had come to their house for the evening, it was the first time she had felt an attraction since her rejection. "Goodbye, it was nice meet-ing you too," she replied. He opened the door and stepped out, then looked up at the Father and reached out his hand. "Thank you for the ride, sir." "You're very wel-come, I'm glad we were able to do it; good luck to you." William stepped back and the carriage drove away. He watched them until they turned the corner of the street and he noticed the lass looking out the window behind her. She was a lovely lass, a lovely lass indeed. He spotted the front door of the Inn and headed towards it.

He stood in the lobby, amazed by the grandeur of the place. "May I help you?" a bellboy asked. "No, aye please, I'm checking in." "You have a reservation?" "I do." "Follow me; may I take your bag?" "Thank you, but no, I can manage," said William. He followed the bellboy who took him to a lady behind a counter. "What is your name sir? "William, William Stevenson." "Yes, Mr. Stevenson, we have your reservation right here, this is your key, you will be in room 16B the bellboy will show you the way." "I was told to ask for a wakeup call at seven in the morning, I'm catching the train at nine in the morning, the one to Glasgow." "Of course, we will ring you in the morning the train station is within walking distance from here, if you don't mind the walk, otherwise we can arrange a carriage for you." "I will walk, said William, but thank you." She grabbed a piece of paper, "I will write the directions for you." She wrote them down and then handed him the paper, "Would you like supper in your room or shall we set you up in the dining room?" "My room, if it's not too much trouble, I've been traveling all day." "No trouble at all, we will send something up, is thirty minutes ok with you?" "That will be just fine, he said, thank you for everything."

He followed the bellboy to his room and was pleasantly surprised by how lovely it was. "It's very nice here," he said. The bellboy nodded, "Did you know Queen Victoria stayed here just two years ago in 1848?" "I didn't, said William that must have been quite an honor for the Inn." "Aye, he replied, it was, quite an honor for the Inn indeed." "I'll leave you, if you need anything else, please ring for me." "I hope you enjoy your stay, you have a view out your window of the Blackfriars, a Dominican friary, prior to that there was a castle but it was destroyed in the flood of 1209." "Did you know that James I was murdered over there." "No, I didn't know that, William replied. "Would you be interested in the story?" "Aye, very much," replied William. The bellboy recounted the story, *"In 1463, The Monarch and his party were celebrating Christmas at Blackfriars." "On February 21 he was playing chess and had supper around 9:00 after which he enjoyed some entertainment." "He changed into his nightgown and had joined the Queen and her ladies in conversation before the fire when they heard the noise of armed men in the passage outside." "An attempt to bar the door failed as Robert Stewart, the King's nephew had removed it." "One of the Queen's ladies put her arm through the brackets while the King, using a poker, raised some floorboards so they could slip below into the cellar." "They were unable to escape because the passage was blocked and subsequently, the Queen's lady, Catherine, received a broken arm when the door was pushed open." "The King tried to hide but they found him and stabbed him 16 times." "My* goodness, said William, and all of this happened just across the street?" "Yes, said the bellboy, it's hard to imagine now." The bellboy left and William found himself alone for the first time that day. He smiled to himself, the Inn was nice and he had a history lesson to boot.

William didn't think he'd have time to bathe before his food arrived so he sat at the little table and watched the goings on out the window. It was quite a busy street with people and carriages. He wondered what Mary was doing and stood up to see if the stars were out but he couldn't see any. He sat there almost transfixed until he heard a knock on the door. When he opened it there was a waiter in a white jacket with a cart which he wheeled into the room next to the table. "Can I get you anything else, sir?" "No, thank you, I think I have all I need." "Very well then, when you are finished you can just wheel the cart out into the hallway and we will get it," he turned and left the room. William couldn't believe he was so hungry; after all he had virtually done nothing all day long. He sat at the table and lifted the cover off of the first dish. It was haddock in cream sauce with little round tatties. There was a basket filled with biscuits. The food was delicious and he ate everything then finished his milk with a small piece of cake. He wheeled the cart into the hallway, undressed and ran water for a bath. He thought how nice it was to be able to just turn a handle for water. This is something he had never experienced before and he wondered if it would be the same in Glasgow. He supposed so. He thought about the black haired lass who had been so kind to him. She was certainly a beauty; he imagined she must have a beau. The soothing warm water relaxed him and he nearly fell asleep sitting there. He immediately poured water on his head and shampooed it, then rinsed off and climbed out of the tub. He donned a nightshirt, brushed his teeth and climbed into bed. In only minutes he was fast asleep and never woke until he heard the bell in the morning. He felt refreshed; he dressed, gave the room one more look to make sure he hadn't forgotten something and left. He went down to the front desk and asked where breakfast was served. It was a large dining room and he picked a table by the window. He ordered milk, porridge and a scone. While he waited he watched traffic and pedestrians outside. It was so different from Killin, there were people everywhere. Had anyone slept the night? When he was finished eating, the waiter asked if he needed anything else and he asked if they could pack him a lunch as he would be catching the train to Glasgow today. "Yes, the waiter replied, is there anything special you would like?" "Anything will be fine," he replied. He found his map to the railroad station while he waited. The waiter brought his lunch and he asked where he could settle his bill. "The front desk, sir," he was told. He went to the front desk and was told that everything was settled, there was nothing due. "I've enjoyed my stay here," he said. "Thank you, sir, have a good trip." He left through the same doors he had entered and stood in the street to get his bearings. It was still early so he had some time to find his way. He walked along sure he was going the right direction. He enjoyed looking in the store windows; it was amazing how many different stores there were. He saw a shoe shiner setting up on the street and looked down at his own shoes thinking they could use a shine, but he didn't stop. He must be getting citified already because he never gave a thought about the shine of his shoes before. It took him about twenty minutes to get there but it was easy to find, he saw the clock tower from quite a distance away. He wandered around until he found what appeared to be the main counter. There was a gentleman behind it. "Excuse me, he said, I'm to catch the train to Enoch Station in Glasgow at nine o'clock can you direct me to where I need to wait?" "Do you have your ticket?" the man asked. "No, he said; it was all pre-arranged by my mentor." "What is your name, sir?" "William Stevenson," he replied. "Very well, I'll go and check, please wait here." He saw the man talking to someone and hoped that there wouldn't be a problem, he had some money but wasn't sure if it would be enough for a ticket. The man disappeared and then came back and handed him a ticket. "Here you go, he said, we don't usually have prearranged tickets, I'm sorry for the wait." "No problem, William replied, I'm just glad you were able to find it; this is all new to me." The man smiled, "I understand, don't lose the ticket, the conductor will take it after you are seated on the train." "See the sign way over there that says Platform Two?" "Yes, I see it," said William. "That is where the passengers to Enoch Station will load, there are benches there where you can sit and wait." "You will know it's the correct train because they all have signs on the front of them to show the destination, furthermore, if you would happen to board the wrong one, the conductor would know by the ticket." "Just a word of warning, Glasgow is a big city and pickpockets hang around the station watching for unsuspecting victims so watch your belongings very carefully." "Thank you for the ticket and the advice," said William and he went to find the benches; he was nervous that he would miss the train even though he knew it would be at least another forty-five minutes.

CHAPTER
TWENTY-ONE

Abonnie young lass with black hair and black eyes scurried into the station. She wasn't sure why but she felt compelled to see the man she had met on the coach again. She went to her Father and asked him to take her to the station and he reluctantly agreed. He knew his daughter, and when her mind was set to something there was no changing it. "I suppose, he said, if I don't take you there, you will find another way on your own." He dropped her at the station and told her he'd return in an hour, he had some shopping to do down the street. She stopped at the front desk and talked to the clerk then turned and looked around. She let out a sign of relief when she saw him sitting on the bench by himself so she hurried over to him. She came up behind him and said, "Hello William." Startled, he quickly turned around and was pleasantly surprised to see her standing there. "Kristine, what are you doing here?" "I don't know, she said, I couldn't get you out of my mind, you looked so alone when we dropped you off at the inn." He smiled at her. "Sit down, I'm glad to see you." "You are, really?" she asked. "Aye, really," he replied, amused. "However did you get here?" "I talked my Father into bringing me, he had some shopping to do anyway, he's returning in an hour." William confessed to her, "To tell you the truth, I was a little scared when you dropped me at the Inn, I wasn't sure what to do, never having been in a city before, you know." "Yes, I suppose it could be frightening, I've grown up here so I'm used to it." "The Inn was amazing, everyone was very helpful." She shook her head, "I've been in there before; after Queen Victoria's visit they had tours there." "I'm glad you found your way around then; did you find the station easily?" "Oh aye, I enjoyed the walk."

"You can't miss the clock tower; that is if you're going the right way in the first place." He laughed and she joined in. "I know it's very forward of me to have come but I felt almost like we were becoming friends and I know so little about you." He patted her hand, "I'm glad you came and I don't think you're forward at all, I was a little lonely here all by meself." "Why don't you tell me about yourself," she said. "There's not much to tell, I'm from a small village called Killin, I think you know that already," he laughed. "Me Da's the tacksman but I'm not interested in that kind of work, there's a textile merchant in the village, Mr. McGregor, a round jolly little man, you'd like him; I went into the shop a lot after school and talked with him, he took an interest in me and is sending me to learn how to run power looms." "When I come back, he wants to expand his shop and hire workers, I will train them." "What a great opportunity for you, I just know you'll be good at it." "I hope so, he replied, Mr. McGregor is spending a lot of money on me." "I've been to Killin before," she said. He smiled, "No, really?" "Yes, about two years ago, my Father had a great aunt who passed away and they had business to take care of, it's a nice little village, everyone was very friendly." "We went to The Falls of Dochart, it's very enchanting there and we also went out to Fingal's Stone." "My fiancée, Mary, owns the bakery in town but it wouldn't have been there then, it's new, it used to be McPhee's Fish Market." She looked down and smiled, "Where will you stay in Glasgow?" "I don't know yet, but I'm told it will be in a flat with other lads who are also training there." "Then you won't be alone, that's good." "What about you, tell me about yourself," he said. "Well, let's see, I'm a spoiled rich lass." "My Father is a tobacco merchant and he says I'm too forward and not prim and proper like a young lady should be." William doubled over with laugher at that statement. She sat up straight in the seat and pursed her lips. "My Mother is always dragging me to socials, hoping to find a young man for me, but this time I will find one for myself." "I was engaged but he went to Edinburgh for a year to study and one day I received a post from him telling me that he was getting married, he had found someone else." "I'm sorry, he said, that must have been hard on you." "Yes, it was at the time but it doesn't matter to me now, I'm glad I found out before we were married." "Oh, I almost forgot," she pulled a package out of her bag and handed it to him. "I brought you some tea cakes; I made them myself because I like to cook." "My Father said to put in a bottle of ale you would get thirsty on the train." "Thank you, and thank him for me as well, it was very kind of you." "It seems I'm always thanking you for something, I wish I could return the favor." "You already have, she said, you've brought a little light back into my life." "I'm glad, he replied, you've brightened me day too, I needed someone to talk to, it's very lonely in a big city where you don't know anyone. "You know me now," she said. "I do," he smiled. She caught her breath again at that smile. She looked up and then with a pout said, "Oh dear, I think this is your train, you said Enoch Station didn't you?" "Aye, that's it, the time has flown by." He reached down and gave her a hug. "Take care, William," she said, here, I've written down my address, if you need anything, send me a post, and please, let me know how you're doing from time to time." "I will, I promise," he said. He put the paper in the pocket of his suit. She watched him step into the train then the conductor motioned with his hand toward the seats and William picked one by the window. He looked out and saw her still standing there. "What a nice, strange lass, he thought, if it wasn't for Mary, I would be tempted." Yesterday he was the one who felt lonely, today she looked the same. He hoped she would find happiness some day because she seemed to deserve it. The conductor came by and asked for his ticket, he looked at it, then pulled out a punch and punched it, moved on to the next passenger and did the same until all tickets had been retrieved.

Kristine left the station to find her Father. She couldn't understand the sense of loss she felt over this lad she barely knew. Maybe he would write to her, one never knew what turn life would take next.

William was excited about getting to ride on a train; he liked the sound it made. "Sure beats a coach ride," he thought. He had the seat to himself so he stretched out and relaxed, it had been a long two days. He wondered what Mary would think of this adventure; she, like him, had never really been anywhere else but Killin. He wished they had married so she could have come along but he knew she wouldn't have, not with the bakery, she wouldn't have left her mother with all the work to do; after all, it was her idea to open it in the first place and he respected her for that. What a surprise it was that his Da had taken him to meet the coach and his brothers seemed genuinely sorry to see him go, maybe because there would be no one to pick on. He shouldn't think like that, it wasn't nice. He thought back to when he was young and he and his Da had gotten along just fine; he would try harder when he came back home. He moved his hand and felt the package she had left him so he opened it and took the bottle of ale; it was still cool so he drank it. It seemed that traveling made you thirsty for he could have downed another. What a nice gesture it was of her to come by the station and see him off, he hoped she didn't have the wrong idea about him but he had told her all about Mary. It was a shame her fiancée' left her and hard to believe he wouldn't hold on to someone as nice and bonnie as her. He closed his eyes but couldn't sleep; he'd gotten a good rest last night. What a grand inn that was, Mr. McGregor had spent a fortune on him; he hoped he would make him proud. He sat there, his mind thinking about his future and his past. He was becoming bored, it was too bad the lass wasn't along to keep him company; she didn't seem to lack for conversation. In fact, she was very entertaining. He smiled just thinking about her and supposed she was quite a handful for her parents. Funny but he couldn't get her off his mind. Once again he picked up the package and opened it. He took one of the tea cakes, wishing he had some milk to go with it. If he didn't stop all this eating he would come back as roly poly as Mr. McGregor and Mary wouldn't recognize him. The tea cake was good, he was impressed. He leaned back in the seat and the steady drone of the engine and the sound it made caused him to fall asleep. He woke to the sound of the conductor calling, "Enoch Station, five minutes." He sat up and gathered his things together, then waited for the train to stop. Once stopped at the platform the passengers were instructed to leave and William rose and stood in line behind the others. He thought he would sit in the station and eat his lunch it would be one less package to carry with him although he wondered how he could possibly be hungry again. He saw an attendant and asked if there was a place he could get some milk or perhaps ale. The attendant pointed off in the distance so he walked that way, hoping he would find it. He didn't see anything, so once again he asked someone who was passing by. "You've missed it, they said, you need to go back and then take the hallway to the left; there's a little stand there where you can buy refreshments." He did as instructed and found the little stand. He asked if they had milk and ale. "Aye we have both, which would you like sir?" "I'll have both of them please, he said; how much do I owe you?" He gave them the money and then left to find a bench to sit on. First he drank the ale; he seemed so thirsty he just couldn't seem to get enough to drink. He remembered the warnings so he took the handles of his satchel and slipped them over his ankle while he was sitting there. If anyone tried to grab it they would have to take him along with it. He opened the lunch and was pleasantly surprised. He saved his milk for the scones. When he was finished he looked around realizing that he had made so many turns trying to find the stand that he wasn't sure which direction he should go. "Oh well, he thought, at least I don't have to worry about missing a coach or train this time." "I can find me way in me own time." He thought about home and how he could walk for miles and never see a person and yet not be lonely; here, surrounded by people he felt as alone as he ever had. He opened the satchel and put the rest of the tea cakes in, then took the directions to the hotel and factory out and put them in his pocket. He closed the satchel and made his way out of the station. If he thought Perth was a busy city, it was nothing compared to Glasgow. He walked for some time in what he believed was the right direction but the street seemed endless and he hadn't spotted the hotel. He was wondering if he was going the right way so he stopped a pedestrian and asked what street they were on. "Argyle Street," the man replied and he rushed off before he could ask where the St. Enoch Hotel was. "This isn't right, he thought, I don't think the paper said Argyle Street." He was starting to panic thinking he was lost so he reached into his pocket to get the note with directions but the wind caught it and blew it out of his hand. "Oh no," he cried and ran after it. He was just about to reach for it when he heard the carriage and he tried to move aside but it was too late. He never heard the whine of the horses, the shriek of the wheels or the screams of pedestrians. He didn't see the driver fly out of the carriage onto the street or the look of horror on the faces of the passengers. He was unaware of the lost directions on the little piece of paper, happily skipping down the street in the wind. He laid there a broken, twisted, bloody mess beneath the carriage. Shouts of, "Get the medic, get the medic," were heard. A nurse on the street came running over to help. She crawled under the carriage and felt for a pulse then yelled out, "He has a faint pulse but he's badly broken, he'll have to have a board." "Get someone here from The Royal Infirmary now, and hurry!" A group of men gathered around; they unhooked the horses, assisted the passengers out, then took a stance around the carriage and lifted it away from his twisted body. Another group of men were trying to get the horses back up onto their feet. they were alright but frightened and uncooperative. The driver was sitting up, he was bruised and battered with an apparent broken arm but conscious and alert. A crowd was gathered around the scene. It was fortunate that The Royal Infirmary was only a short distance away and they soon arrived with a cart and a board. William, still unconscious but holding on to life, was gently moved. His leg lay at an odd angle and there was a visual broken bone sticking out. His arm appeared to be broken and his hand hung loosely suggesting his wrist may be broken as well. His face was bleeding badly, it appeared he had a gash but it was hard to tell where. They quickly got him into the cart and raced down High Street to The Royal Infirmary which stood near the Glasgow Cathedral. He was taken directly into surgery. There would be no one in the waiting room praying that he would survive, no mother crying at night hoping that his bones would mend and no one holding his hand when he woke except a little nurse who sat vigilantly by his side night after night. When they had cleaned his face it was badly gashed all the way from the ear to the corner of his mouth and would have to be stitched back together. They set his arm; it was broken at the elbow and wrist. Three of his fingers were badly crushed, it was doubtful that he would be able to use them again, if they healed. His leg was so badly broken and twisted that they discussed whether to set it or amputate. They fixed it but if it hadn't been for the recent work and research of Lord

Joseph Lister they would never have tried to save it. They wondered if they had made the right decision and hoped because of his youth he would heal; for him to walk again normally would be a miracle, the most he could hope for was to use a cane to get around. He would never be the tall, lanky boy with the long strident steps again. When they were done they wheeled him back into his room, his fate now lie in prayers, strong will, antiseptics and a lot of luck.

Abigale worked at The Royal Infirmary; she was also the nurse on Argyle Street where William had his accident. She was a small lass with light brown hair and an unremarkable face but she was the sweetest, most caring person one would ever meet. She had been passed over by lads and had never had a date in her life. Her mother died in childbirth bearing another sibling when she was five years old, the sibling hadn't survived either and she had no other siblings. She lived with her Father on High Street above a cigar and men's accessories shop owned by her Father. It was called McCleary's Cigars, Tobacco, and General Men's Emporium. They sold cigars, tobacco, cigar boxes, spittoons, neckties, cravats, hats, caps, eyeglasses, socks, underwear, razors, watches and shaving brushes among other items; all for men. It was quite successful and busy. Her Father had a knack for supplying items men wanted. She took care of the house and did all the cooking but she was lonely, her Father worked a lot of hours and he didn't like her in the shop with men hanging around. She always came straight home from school to prepare supper and never had a best friend. Her Father was good to her but had failed to see that she hadn't developed the social grace and femininity of other lasses her age. He loved her and was proud of her, never considering that she needed more social experiences in her life. Lately he hadn't been feeling well and she felt he would have to slow down his pace. More than once she had asked him to train her in the shop but he had refused, "It's not the place for a young lady." Finally she had resigned herself from trying and instead had gone to school to be a nurse. She loved her job and her days had been much more fulfilled since working. She asked the head nurse if she could be assigned to Shawn's room and was granted the request. Someone had brought William's satchel to the hospital after the accident; since it had the name Shawn Ferguson engraved on it, he was registered under that name and everyone assumed that's who he was. It was little matter at this time because he still had not gained consciousness.

CHAPTER
TWENTY-TWO

Back in Killin not much had changed. Mary was counting the days to when she thought William might send a post. They were all sitting at the tables in the bakery after they closed and the subject of Ethan came up. Charles, always the thinker, with his chin in his hands looking up at the ceiling, said, "What about the spare room at the back, he could have a little store of some sort, everyone has to wait for the traveling salesman to come with his kitchen wares, he could sell a variety of teas and then expand to tea cups, teapots, saucers and the like." "There's no end to what he could have in there and we've already got the customers coming here." "My supplier can get him anything he needs." "Hmmm, John said; let's take a peek, shall we." He walked to the room with Charles. "Aye, Richard and I could put a counter and shelves in here in no time at all." "I'm sure Catherine and Katie could pretty it up a bit." "Alrighty then, said Charles, let's ask Ethan and see what he thinks, if he goes for it, I'll send a telegram to my supplier and place the order." "We could draw up an agreement similar to the one Mary has for the bakery and I'll fund the initial investment," he continued.

Ethan was all for it, excited actually, he needed to do something to help support the family. They had the room finished in one day, Katie and Catherine put up cute little curtains and Richard made another sign for the front of the building, 'Ethan's Tea & Kitchen Mercantile.' Rebecca and Lillian made little cards to put around the bakery so word would get around. Next week the supplier showed up with a variety of teas, some sets of saucers and cups, teapots, and a combination of other kitchen items. When he left, Ethan sat at his little table and marked everything then handed the items to Charles and he placed them on the shelves. When they were finished, they sat at the little table admiring their work; the shop was open for business. Ethan grabbed Charles hand, "Our family has a lot to thank you for, we couldn't have done any of this without your help, and you are such a remarkable and generous man." Charles laughed, "I'm a shrewd businessman, that's what I am, don't worry, I'll get me money back and more." Ethan shook his head and laughed at him. It took a few days, but once the word got out, customers were flocking in and buying the tea and kitchen items. The items were flying off the shelf and Ethan couldn't believe he had to place another order already.

One day Margaret came to the bakery in the early morning. "Hello stranger," Catherine said. "Douglas dropped me off; he has to go to the mill and has other errands, then he's coming back here for dinner, is it a good time to show you how to make the jam roly polys?" "Yes," they all said, excited to learn a new recipe. Mary came out of the workroom with an apron, "Better put this on." "Thank you dear, how are you doing?" "I'm trying to keep busy and I'm always wondering what he's doing, if he likes it, if he misses me." Margaret touched her shoulder, "Of course he misses you." Mary smiled at her, "And you?" "How are you doing?" "I miss him too, but it's a funny thing, Douglas is like a different man, we sit at the table talking late into the night, he sits outside with me or we go for a walk." "I can hardly believe it meself." Mary touched her arm, "I'm glad for you, Margaret, I really am."

They got busy working on the roly polys in between waiting on customers and getting things ready for dinner. Margaret checked out the tea shop and purchased some to take home with her. "I like it, she said, we needed a shop like this in town." "Whose idea was it?" "Mine of course," piped up Charles, and they all laughed. "He's right though, said Catherine, it really was his idea." "You're a smart man, Charles," said Margaret. He sat at the table with his hands folded on his chest smiling, you wouldn't find a more pleasant man, he didn't show what was troubling him but he was worried about Nancy, she wasn't getting any better and she refused to go to a city doctor.

"Margaret, we'll pack up some of these roly polys and you can take them home for your family." She waved her hand, "No, that's not necessary we have them all the time, maybe you could pack just a few of them and I'll take them over to George McGregor, I'm pretty sure he would like them and I want to see if he's heard anything from or about William." "Good idea, said Mary, if you don't mind, I'll go with you." "Do you have any more secret recipes, Katie asked, that was fun." Katie was much more lighthearted now that Ethan was feeling and looking better and now had something to occupy his time as well as bring some income into the household. Charles would never know what a relief it was that he wouldn't be tempted to go back to work at the mill, the dampness down there would have killed him in time; he didn't have the lungs for it.

Mary and Catherine took off for McGregors. He opened the door, glad to see them, and invited them in. "Would you like some tea?" "No, don't bother, we've had our tea, said Margaret, we've just made a batch of jam roly polys and thought you might like some." "You bet I would, I haven't had them for a long, long, time no one makes them anymore." Mary looked at Margaret with a little grin and said, "No one used to make them but Margaret was kind enough to share her recipe so we will have them in the bakery now." "Yippee," shouted George, roly polys for a roly poly man." They laughed, no wonder he was such good friends with Charles, they both had a keen sense of humor. "I was wondering if you've heard anything from or about our William." "No, I can't say that I have, Mrs. Stevenson, but I didn't expect to yet." "I wouldn't worry if I were you, there will be a lot of getting used to a schedule and finding his way around, he's probably bone tired by the time the day is over and hasn't had a chance to even find a piece of paper, much less a post office." "I'm sure you're right, she replied, we'll have to give it a little more time; I so want to hear from him though." "Well anyway it was nice to see you again, we have to get back to the bakery, are you coming in for dinner today?" "Yes, yes, I think I will, I wanted to talk to Charles, I understand he's pretty worried about Nancy." "You know it's been ten years since me dear wife passed away." "Let's hope she pulls out of it, Margaret said, she's a lovely lady." "That she is, that she is, I'll see you ladies later."

Back at the shop they were busy and the tables starting filling up for dinner. Margaret had visited Nancy and came back worried, "She's not looking any better Catherine." "I know, Catherine replied, every day she seems weaker." "I've offered to stay here at night but Charles won't have it, he wants to tend her himself but I think it's wearing him down too." "It's his way of coping with it," Margaret replied. Just then the door opened and Douglas came in. Margaret took her apron off and they found a table and sat down. Catherine was happy for Margaret, it would be easier on her now that William was gone to have a closer relationship with her husband; she was a nice woman, she deserved to be treated well.

Mary had finished up and was sitting at the table with a glass of milk and a jam roly poly; she was daydreaming again and hadn't paid attention to who was coming and going. "Hello Mary, it's been a while since I've seen you." She looked up and saw Henry standing there. "Henry, you're home now?" "Yes, I've secured a position in Comrie; it's the closest one they had to offer that is near Killin." "May

I sit with you?" "Of course," she said, and waved her hand toward the other chair. "It must be nice to have finished school?" "Yes, I've always liked learning but I'm ready to do other things now, I hope I make a good teacher." "William has left for Glasgow, he's going to learn how to run power looms for Mr. McGregor, he was quite excited to get the opportunity but he also hated to leave." "I see, and he'll be gone two years?" "Yes, we haven't heard from him yet but he's only been gone little over a week." "Say, have you seen Ethan's new shop?" "No but I saw the sign when I came in; I'll have to get something for Mother, she'd like that." "How are your Mum and sisters, I haven't really had a chance to talk to them for a while." "They're good you should come over with me sometime they'd love to see you." "They were in here last week but you know how it is when you're busy, you don't get time to stop and talk." "Where are you staying in Comrie?" "I have a little cottage, actually not so little, there are three bedrooms, and I like it." "How many students do you have?" "Only twenty, when they come; they don't come every day?" "The little ones do but the older boys sometimes have to help on the farm." "I see," she said. "Are you hungry, I could get you something?" "Yes, actually I came here for lunch I hear it's quite popular." She laughed, "We have regulars they come every day, I'm not sure if it's because they like the food or the company." "It's a cheery little place I can see why they enjoy it here." "Stay put, I will get something for you," she said. She went to the back and dished up some food for Henry. Catherine said, "That's Henry sitting over there, I must go over and say hello." "Yes, I know Mum, Mary said, this plate of food is for him." They both walked over to the table together. "Henry, nice to see you again," said Catherine, extending her hand. He stood up and gave her a hug. "It's good to be back, well in Comrie that is." "You are teaching in Comrie?" "Yes," he replied. She smiled at him, "We'll have to have a family get together again, the last one was fun; John would like it." "My Father too," he said. She continued, "We'll invite the newly married couple, Harry and Colleen." "The Hart's too," said Mary. "Aye, the Hart's too." "Let me know, Henry said, I'd love to come, it gets a little lonely over in Comrie." "Better eat your food, Henry, before it gets cold, said Mary, I'll be back with dessert; we have a special treat for the first time today." "Oh, what's that," he asked. She laughed, "You'll have to wait and find out." He smiled and then began to eat. He thought to himself, "My she's in a pleasant mood today; much better than when we went on the carriage ride." Soon Mary was back with another plate, this time she was all smiles. "Here you go Henry." Henry looked at the plate, "And what might this be?" "Jam roly polys." "I don't think I've ever had them." "It's a new item we made for the first time today, William's Mum showed us how." "You don't say, let me try them." Wait, wait," she said, and she ran back to the kitchen. He watched her with a puzzled look on his face. She came back with another glass of milk "You have to have milk with them, they taste better that way." She sat there with her head in her hands watching him. "Ok, here goes," he said, and took a bite. "Ummm, those are good," he looked at her and smiled. Mary smiled and then felt a blush cross her face. He took another bite and then some milk. "I could get used to these, may I purchase some to take home, I'd like my Mother to try them?" "No, you can't purchase them, not today anyway, I'll fix you a plate to take." "Really, that's not necessary," he said. "Just take them Henry, I want you to." He looked at her and shook his head, his heart doing a couple of flips; "Thanks Mary, I will then." Once again Mary blushed and thought, "What is the matter with me, I wish he wouldn't look at me with those eyes of his." When he was finished she took him back to show him Ethan's tea shop. Henry was quite impressed with the selection and purchased some tea for himself and his Mother and then a tea set for his new home. "Now if I get visitors, I'll have a nice set to serve them with, I think his shop will be a success." "I'll tell them in Comrie about the shop, I understand they used to have a bakery there but it's closed now." "I'm not a very good cook but the ladies in town are always sending the schoolteacher food, so I have plenty to eat." "She replied, "Lillian and Rebecca made some cards; let me see if I can find more, you could take them, that is if you don't mind." "No of course I don't mind, I'd be glad to." Mary thought, "He must be quite popular over there already if they are cooking for him." Henry touched her arm, "I'd best be getting over to see the family, they'll be expecting me." She almost jumped at his touch but smiled at him, "I'll get the plate of treats; you can return the plate next time you come in." She disappeared again and then came out with the plate and handed it to him. He tried to gather everything in his arms but nearly dropped the tea set. "Here, let me help you, she said, give me the tea set before you drop and break it, I'll go out with you." She carried the tea set to the cart and carefully set it where it wouldn't get jostled too much. "Thanks Mary, maybe I'll stop in again next week." "Ok, see you then, she said, don't forget the plate." She turned to go back into the store but once more turned around and looked at him. He was standing there watching her too; she smiled, gave a little wave, and went back in the store. Catherine was observing the two of them and couldn't help but think what a nice couple they would make. She hoped a post would come from William soon; a young lass can get mighty restless.

CHAPTER
TWENTY-THREE

Abigale had a mission. She was determined to help Shawn recover. She came in to work early and sat with him and she stayed after her shift and sat with him again. She talked to him, read to him and sometimes quietly sang to him. The doctors would come in and check him, shake their heads and leave. When she asked if he was improving they would say, "Give it some time, only time will tell." It had been about a week and a half and although he had emitted some groans and his hands twitched periodically, he still wasn't conscious. His face was swollen, it was hard to tell what he might look like, but to her he was handsome. In the short time she had been caring for him, she had fallen in love. She knew nothing about him, but it didn't matter to her, she didn't think about the possibility of him being married or having a family; right now, she had him to herself and she didn't look beyond that.

The head nurse came in and checked him, then asked her why she was still there. "Hasn't your shift ended hours ago?" "Yes," she said, but I thought I'd sit here a while in case he wakes, it would be sad if no one was there." "Don't get too attached now, the nurse warned, remember what you've learned in nursing school." "I won't," she replied. "Listen, the nurse asked, has anyone gone through his bag and pockets, maybe there is some identification in there." "It's strange no one has called about him, although he did have the satchel with him, he may have been traveling." "I could go through his things if you want," she offered. "All right, the nurse replied, if you find something helpful, let me know."

Abigale opened the satchel first. There was a package at the top and she unwrapped it, there were tea cakes in it. She set them aside to throw away. She pulled out the clothes and checked the pockets but there was nothing in them. She found the toiletry items but they held no clue either. She didn't find anything of interest so she closed the satchel and put it away. She glanced up and saw the suit hanging there. Maybe she would take it to the cleaners and see if they could clean it up and fix some of the tears that had occurred in the accident. It appeared to be of the latest style, it was a shame it had been damaged. She checked the pockets; inside one of the pockets she found a paper with a name and address on it so she set it aside to give the nurse. She checked Shawn one more time and then went to the desk. "I've found an address," she said, and she handed her the note. "Thank you Abigale, best you be heading home now, it's getting late." "Yes, madam," she said and left the hospital. She caught a cart ride; it was much too late to be walking alone this late at night. She arrived home just as her Father was closing the shop. "Where have you been so late, he asked, it's becoming a habit." "Just at the hospital, Father, I've been tending the young man who had the accident on Argyle Street." "It seems such a shame that he could wake up and no one would be there." "Has no one asked after him then?" "No, Father, no one, but we found an address in his belongings today." "You did, and where was it?" "It was a woman's name in Perth." "You mustn't get too attached, Abby." "I won't, Father, but he has no one else right now to sit with him." Her Father shook his head, "Come; let's go upstairs, it's getting late." "I should admonish you, Father, for working so late, you know you have to get some rest; you haven't been feeling well lately." "I know, I know, he replied, but the work has to get done."

Next day Abigale headed to the hospital early. She passed the desk and the nurse called, "Abigale." "Yes madam." "If you don't mind, could you send a post to the ladies' address, maybe we'll find out something there." "I will," Abigale said, and she went to find some paper and pen; next she went to Shawn's room and found him lying there as usual. She touched his forehead and pushed his hair back. The cut was healing but it would leave a nasty scar, he would be disfigured now, what a shame. "I'm here, Shawn, maybe you want to wake up today and meet me," she said. She sat in the chair next to his bed and started writing the letter. *Dear Kristine: We are writing to you because a note with your address was found in the pocket of one of our patients, a Mr. Shawn Ferguson, a young man. Shawn is in The Royal Infirmary Hospital in Glasgow, he was struck by a carriage on Argyle Street and has not, as of yet, regained consciousness. He has a badly broken leg, a broken arm, some crushed fingers and a large cut on his face. I don't know what your relationship is with him but we felt compelled to let you know. We* have no other information about him. We're sorry we are the bearers of bad news. Sincerely: Abigale O'Cleary, Nurse, Royal Infirmary Hospital; Glasgow, Scotland. She touched Shawn's hand again and then left to find the nurse so that she could mail the letter. She then began her shift for the day. Periodically throughout the day she checked in on him but there was no change. When her shift ended she rushed to his room and pulled a chair close to the bed and sat there reading to him. She was reading from 2 Corinthians, Verse 4. *We are often troubled, but not crushed; sometimes in doubt, but never in despair, there are many enemies, but we are never without a friend; and though badly hurt at times, we are not destroyed. At all times we carry in our mortal bodies the death of Jesus, so that his life also may be seen in our bodies. Throughout our lives we are always in danger of death for.......*She looked up, a sound was coming from him so she grabbed his hand and leaned in close to his face, "Mary, Mary." His eyes were flickering. "I'm here Shawn, open your eyes and talk to me," she said. He opened his eyes and she touched his face. "It's all right, it's all right; you will be ok now." Immediately he closed his eyes again and was still. She left the room to get the head nurse and told her what had happened. The nurse came and checked him. "His signs are still ok, perhaps he is coming out of it, I will have the night doctor check on him when he comes by." "When you leave tonight, let me know, we will have someone sit with him, he may be frightened when he wakes." "Listen, you need to get your sleep too, you will be no good to him if you get sick." "I know, Abigale replied, you're right." She spent the next few hours holding his hand and talking to him. The words flowed out of her, she told him about her mother, the store, where she went to school, anything she could think of. For a shy lass, she would never have been able to let the words flow from her if he would have been awake; he was becoming her friend and he wasn't even aware of it. It was obvious that he was twitching more, sometimes emitting sounds, but it wasn't clear what he was saying and she hoped he wasn't remembering the accident. He would open his eyes sometimes but it didn't seem as if they were focused. It was getting late and she didn't want to leave but knew she must, her Father would be worried if she didn't come soon and she really needed to make sure he had a good supper. She went to the desk and told the nurse she was leaving and they sent a replacement in to sit with him. She didn't get very much sleep that evening because her thoughts were with him.

Once home again, she scurried to fix supper for her Father. He came in looking more tired than he had before. "Father, you really have to stop working so hard, it's wearing you out." "I'm fine, he said, I suppose it's time to advertise for some help." "I could do it, Father, but you won't let me." "It's not the place for a young lady, but I appreciate the offer, you stick to nursing, it's more appropriate for a young lass."

"How is the lad by the way?" "We think he might be coming out of it, I hope so." "Good, good, he's had a rough go of it," he said. They had their supper after which Abigale cleaned up the kitchen and then got ready for bed. As she lay there, she thought about Shawn. She was sure he had said the name Mary and she wondered who that might be; the name on the address was Kristine. It was unlikely that he would have the name and address of a wife or fiancee'; maybe it was a sister or long lost relative, she supposed it would come out eventually.

In the morning she prepared breakfast and lunch for her Father, did a little cleaning in the flat, and headed to the hospital. She entered the room where a nurse was sitting by Shawn's side. "How is he doing today," she asked. "He's restless and utters words at times, then seems to wake and go back to sleep." "I will sit with him until my shift starts," she said. When the nurse left Abigale rose and touched his cheek, "I'm here, Shawn, could you open your eyes today?" She rubbed his arm and quietly sang an old Irish children's song to him, *I'll tell me ma when I go home the lads won't leave the lasses alone. They'll pull my hair; they stole my comb, well that's alright till I go home. She is handsome, she is pretty she is the belle of Belfast City. She is courtin' one, two, three, please won't you tell me, who is she.* To her credit, she kept up a steady flow of talking, singing, humming; anything that she thought might awaken him. His eyes opened and he blinked a couple of times. "Where am I," he said. She tried to suppress her surprise, "You've had an accident and you're at The Royal Infirmary Hospital in Glasgow." He looked at her for a moment then closed his eyes again. She called to him, "Shawn, Shawn, can you wake up again?" There was no response so she left the room and went to the desk. "He awoke and asked where he was, then went back to sleep," she told the nurse. "The doctor will be in shortly, stay with him please." Abigale went back into the room and continued her vigil, she held his hand and constantly rubbed his arms while continuing to talk and sing to him. He woke and looked at her, "Who are you?" "I'm your nurse, my name is Abigale." "How did I get here?" "You had an accident, it's been almost two weeks; do you remember what happened?" "I remember losing the note." "The note?" she asked. "With the address, I was lost." "You were struck by a carriage in the street, you have some broken bones." He tried to raise his head but was unable. "My arm?" he said. "Yes, it's broken in several places." "And my hand?" he asked. "Your fingers were injured, they're wrapped." "What will Mr. McGregor say?" "Mr. McGregor?" "I promised him." "Just lie still, don't overdo it, everything will be clear in time." He lay back and closed his eyes again, then apparently fell asleep. The doctor came in and she told him what had happened. He checked Shawn's signs, "Keep up the good work and try to get some fluids and broth in him if you can; it will be a slow process."

"Thank you doctor," she said. When he woke again she asked him, "Shawn, can you tell me who Kristine is?" "Kristine?" he said. "We found a note in your suit with her name and address on it." "My suit?" he asked. "Yes, the suit you wore when you had the accident." "Me Mum bought me the suit, she wanted me to look nice, and I wore it to the wedding." "The wedding?" she said. "Yes, Harry and Colleen, Mary and I were in it." "Who is Mary?" "She's my fiancee'." "Can you tell me how we can contact your family?" He dozed off again. It was time for her shift so she had no choice but to leave the room. She went to the head desk and related the conversation. "It sounds like his memory is blocking out the accident, it's a healing process; he will remember in time, it's not unusual." Abigale, somewhat relieved, began her work for the day.

At some point during the day William woke again. He lay there quietly, trying to move his limbs one by one. He realized his arm was bandaged and his leg was up in a sling. His face was itching and he moved his good hand towards his face to try and touch it. "Careful," the nurse on duty said, you don't want to disturb the stitches." "Stitches, have I been cut on the face then?" "Yes, you have quite a nasty cut but it's healing nicely." "I want to see," he said. "There's time for that later, it's too soon now." "Please, he said, it's me face isn't it?" "Yes sir, but I'm not sure, let me ask." She scurried out the door to find the head nurse. "I don't know, she said, tell him we have to wait for the doctor, he'll be along in about an hour." She went back in the room and told him; he seemed satisfied with that. "The doctor said you need to eat something, should we try some broth?" He nodded. "I can raise your bed a little if you like." He nodded again. "I'll be right back with the broth, lie still." He lay there trying to access the damage to his body. It must have been pretty bad but he just couldn't remember exactly what happened. He remembered the note flying out of his hand and him running after it. He would have to get word to Mr. McGregor soon. The nurse came back with the broth and he was able to get most of it down. "Good, good, she said, it will help you, you need nutrition, try to drink as much water as you can; when you want some, just let me know." He was quite alert now but his head was hurting, he wondered if he had bumped it in the accident. He supposed so, otherwise he wouldn't have been unconscious for so long. How long was it, he wondered?

The doctor arrived and sat down in a chair next to his bed. "You're a lucky lad, son, you've had a bad accident and you'll have a long recovery." "Can you tell me what's wrong with me?" "You've broken your arm in two places, the elbow and the wrist." "Three of your fingers were crushed, probably by the carriage wheels, we couldn't do anything for them, let's just hope they heal." "I don't think you'll ever have use of them, I'm sorry." William shook his head. "Your leg was badly broken, we had to make the decision to try and fix it or take it, I hope we made the right one; time will tell." "The bone was sticking out of the skin, if it heals, and I stress if, you will never walk on it fully again, you'll need the use of a cane or crutch." "I'm sorry lad; I know this must be hard on you." "My face?" he asked. "You had a severe cut from your ear to the corner of your mouth, we had to stitch it shut." "We did the best we could but you will be scared." "I want to see it," he said. "Very well then, but keep in mind, it will look somewhat better when it heals, your face is still very swollen right now." They gave him a mirror and he slowly brought it up to his face. When he saw himself, he gave an audible gasp and dropped the mirror. "Oh My God, I look like a monster." "No, please don't think that, said the nurse, you don't look like a monster at all, you're still swollen: it will get better." The doctor stood up, "I'll stop in again, have faith, every day you will heal a little more, but it will take some doing on your part, you must not give up, is there anything the nurse can get for you?" "Could I have ale?" "It's not usual, but in your case, I think we can manage to get you one; you've been through a rough patch." He patted William on the arm, told the nurse to find him an ale even if she had to leave the building, then he exited the room stating he would return again. William had a lot to think about now, as he understood it, he would be a cripple and disfigured from the scar on his face, he couldn't return to Killin like that, he just couldn't; especially to his bonnie Mary. "She deserves much more than that," he thought. Oh, he knew she would make light of it and insist that none of it mattered to her but he couldn't do that to her; no, that dream was over as was the power loom; he was a failure.

Abigale hurried to Shawn's room as soon as she could and she was pleasantly surprised to see him alert. "You're awake then, how are you feeling?" "I know you, he said, I mean, I know the voice." "Yes, I've been here talking to you every night." "Thank you, he said, what's your name?" "Abigale, have you eaten?" "Aye, some broth and I've had some ale too." "You've had ale?" "Where in the world did you get that?" "The doctor told the nurse to get it, I was thirsty for some." "Can you tell me who Kristine is?" "Kristine?" "Why do you ask?" "We found a note in your suit pocket with her address on it and we sent her a post to let her know what happened, it was the only contact we had." "She's just a friend of mine, we met on the coach and her Da gave me a ride to the Inn; she told me to write and let her know how I was doing." "Can we contact Mary for you?" "You said she was your fiancée?" "No, William said, she was my fiancée but when I left to come here she said she couldn't wait that long, you see I was going to be gone for two years." "Have you been a nurse long?" "Only about a year, I wanted to learn my Father's business but he wouldn't have it so I went to nursing school instead." "I see; why didn't he want you to learn the business?" "Because it's a men's emporium and he didn't think it was proper for me to be there." "Did you know I was there, at the scene of the accident?" "I ran over and took your pulse; I had to crawl under the carriage to do it, that's where you ended up." "I was under the carriage?" "Yes, a group of men had to move it off of you." "Was anyone else hurt?" "The driver, but not badly, just a broken arm and some scrapes and bruises, he flew off of the carriage seat." "The horses fell and were frightened, but they're all ok." "I'm sorry I caused it, at least I guess I must have, I'm not used to the city." She smiled, "It's quite dangerous; it seems everyone is always in such a hurry here." "They shouldn't drive the carriages so fast when there are people on the street." "I don't know how I will pay, he said, I have no job and no money." "Don't worry, she said, I understand they have a number of cases like yours; I'm sure it will be taken care of." "Do you have somewhere to go when you're released?" "No, he said, I'll have to figure that out." "They have a new facility on North Frederick Street called The Night Asylum, they just moved there about three years ago from another location." "It's a place for homeless people to go, I'm sure they will take you until you can find something else." She stayed with him another two hours telling him about herself, all the things she had told him when he was unconscious; she thought he was easy to talk to. He didn't really say much about his life or where he was from. "You have a soothing voice," he told her. "Thank you, I wish I could stay longer but I must go home now, my Father will want his supper, I'll stop in tomorrow." "Thank you for everything Abigale." "It's nothing Shawn, I was glad to do it and of course it's my job." When she had gone, he sat there wondering if he had heard her correctly, Shawn?" "Why would she call me that?" He pondered it until he finally fell asleep.

Abigale's mind was racing and she wanted to talk to her Father about it. She was elated that Shawn didn't appear to have a lass in his life any more. He said she had a soothing voice, would she have a chance with him? She didn't know. In any case, he was going to need some assistance and she had an idea but her Father would have to agree to it first. She fixed supper, did some cleaning up in the flat and then sat down and waited for him to appear. Finally, she heard him coming slowly up the stairs. He looked surprised to see her home so early. "You're home early today?" "Yes, Shawn is awake now and his mind seems to be fine." "Good news," he replied. "Yes, we found out that the name on the paper was just a lass he had met in the coach, they traveled together and her Father gave him a ride to the Inn." "He says she wrote down her address so he could send her a post and let her know how he was doing." "Is there anyone else, has he said anything?" "No one Father, that's what

I wanted to talk to you about." "Me, what have I to do with it?" "Possibly that help you need in the shop." "Now before you say anything, just listen to me and then you can make a decision." "All right then, out with it." "He has nowhere to go, we have the flat in the back of the shop just sitting empty, he could stay there until he heals and you could start training him once he's able to get around." "He will be somewhat crippled, but he should be able to handle the work; after all, he'll have to find something to do." "How do you know he would even want to do this?" "I don't, Father, but he'll have to go to The Night Asylum for the homeless because he has nowhere else to go." "How do you know he is reputable?" "Doesn't he have family somewhere?" "I just know Father, I can tell." "Let me think on it dear, I'll let you know tomorrow, perhaps I should take a trip to the hospital and meet this young lad." "Yes, you should, Father." He looked at her, "I hope you're not falling for this lad, you know what they told you in nursing school about getting too involved with the patients." "No Father, I'm not falling for anyone but what's wrong with helping someone out when they need it?" She went to bed that night feeling much more optimistic than she had the last several days.

At breakfast, over porridge, Mr. McCleary asked Abigale what time her shift was over. "At four, why do you ask?" "I think I'll close the shop early and meet you there." "It's high time I meet this mystery man." "I'll wait by the nurse's desk for you," she said. When she saw Shawn that morning she told him that her Father wanted to meet him and would be stopping by later that day. "I wanted to ask you, he said, did you call me Shawn when you left last night?" "Yes, that's your name isn't it?" "It says Shawn Ferguson on your satchel." A light came on in his head then, the satchel, of course. "I forgot about that, I just wondered how you knew, that's all." He felt a sense of relief because he knew that in a matter of time they would be searching for him, no one here knew his real name. He had never been a coward before but he was a proud person and in his mind it would cause everyone more sorrow to see him like this than to assume him dead. His mind was set; he would take on a new identity.

CHAPTER TWENTY-FOUR

In the days since Kristine last saw William at the train station he was on her mind much of the time. She wondered if he was enjoying the work and how he was getting along with his roommates. She imagined that he was quite happy, he was doing what he had come to do. She had no expectations that she would see him again, it was in his hands now; he had her address. "After all, she thought, he does have a fiancée but then again, so did I." She was surprised when the post came from Glasgow but worried because the return said The Royal Infirmary. She read the letter slowly and then re-read it. There was no one she knew by the name of Shawn Ferguson and the only time she could remember writing her name and address was the note she had given William. She didn't know what to make of it so she found her Father to see what he thought. He was also perplexed. He suggested that the note may have been dropped, but no, that wasn't right, they said they found it in his suit pocket. Could he have been murdered, his suit stolen, and then in flight the murderer had an accident? Yes, that must be it. Kristine told him that William said he was going to be training on the power looms but she didn't know where. "It's a booming business right now, dear, he said, it could have been any number of places." "I have to make a trip to Merchant City in Glasgow next month and it's not far from the hospital, you can go with me and see for yourself who this person is." "Thank you Father, she said, I'll send a post back to the nurse and tell her our plans."

She drafted a letter to Abigale that evening and would mail it tomorrow. When the letter arrived at the hospital, Abigale anxiously opened it. "Curious, she thought when she read it, there's no way that he is a murderer, no way at all." Instead of sharing the letter with the head nurse, she folded it up and took it home with her. When the nurse, who had seen the letter come, asked what it said, she told her that they didn't know anyone by that name. Perhaps, she said, he had borrowed the suit from someone else and the note wasn't removed. "That's probably it," the nurse said not giving it another thought. On the contrary, Abigale thought about it all night long; Shawn said that he met Kristine on the coach; why then would she come all this way just to see him? She supposed that Kristine was curious as to why her name and address were found in Shawn's suit pocket.

Each day William felt stronger and each day he asked for the mirror so he could look at his face. He wasn't vain by nature but he didn't want to look like a freak either; he wasn't unaware that he was handsome. The swelling had gone down now but it was clear the injury wasn't going to go away; aye, he would have to stick to the plan he had formed. He felt that Abigale had become a good friend and it was his salvation, he could listen to her talk for hours. He felt it was her who had brought him back to consciousness and he waited for her to appear each day and each night after her shift. As usual, she showed up right on schedule. "My Father wants to meet you today, would that be all right with you?" "He wants to meet the person I've been spending my evenings with." She laughed and he joined in. "That would be ok, I guess; if I don't scare him." "Oh Shawn, other people won't think as much about it as you do, you will have to learn to live with it, look at me, I've lived my whole life being passed over for the way I look, it's about what's on the inside, not what's on the outside." "There's nothing wrong with the way you look Abigale, he replied, I think you're very pretty." Abigale, not used to a compliment, felt herself blush. They talked a while longer until she rose, "I've got to go to work; I'll see you later." ""Later, he said, and then laughed, I'll be right here waiting." He was genuinely sorry to see her go; he knew so much about her and she knew so little about him. For the most part, he had blocked his former life out of his mind and was doing his best to create a new one. Today he would see the doctor again. Eventually the doctor made his way to William's room, "You're doing well, Shawn, we've discussed your case, you'll most likely be here another ten weeks or more." "We're going to try and get you out of bed next week but it will be an ordeal so I want you to muster up." "It's ok, he said, I know you're doing all you can and I appreciate it." "Good, lad, he said, I'll check on you again later this week." The day dragged by, he would have to ask Abigale to bring him a book so he had something to do with his time. He was getting his appetite back now and he thought about the tea cakes Kristine had made him. He wondered what she thought about the letter when she received it; she must have been shocked. Finally the door opened and Abigale came in, her Father behind her. She was smiling, "Father, this is Shawn." William lifted his left hand, "I'm sorry, my other hand is a little out of commission right now." "I can see that, lad, you're having quite a time of it aren't you?" "It seems so, Shawn replied, but they're taking good care of me here, your daughter included." "My daughter seems to be fond of you," Mr. McCleary said. "Aye, he replied, we've become friends; I feel as though she has saved my life in a way." "She told me that you have nowhere to go when you're released, is that correct?" "Unfortunately, that's true." "Where is your family then?" "To America. I should have gone with them but I loved it here so I stayed behind." "Have you sent them a post?" "No, I don't really know where they are, we had a falling out when they left because I didn't want to come with them." "What a shame, I have a proposal for you." "You have a proposal for me, sir?" William asked. "I'm sure that Abby has told you we have a men's shop on High Street." "Yes sir, she has." "The shop has a flat in the back, it's been empty for years; we've been using it for storage." "Abby suggested that we let you have it and I am willing to do that with the hope that in time, if you're interested, I will need some help in my shop." "I am finding it harder and harder to keep up with the shop and I'm willing to train you." "I think with your injuries, you could still do the work, it's not difficult; and of course; I will be there to help." "Goodness, I never expected an offer like that; it's very generous and trusting of you." "I would be open to your offer but, of course, right now I don't know what my abilities will be or even when I might be released from here." "In short, I have nothing to offer you in return right now." "I understand that, we're not asking you for anything, my daughter believes in you and I think she is a good judge of character, you don't have to make a decision right now; it's something to chew on for a while." "Thank you, sir, I'm glad to have met you." "The same here lad, I'll come visit you again." Abigale smiled at him, "I'll go with Father, see you later Shawn," "I'll see you tomorrow, he replied, and then he called, wait." She turned, "Yes?" "Would you have any books lying around, I get a little bored in here." Mr. McCleary piped up, "Goodness, I have a lot of books sitting around; Abby says I'm somewhat of a pack rat." "In fact, they're in that flat I was telling you about, we'll send some over tomorrow." Shawn smiled, "Thank you once again, I appreciate it, don't worry, I'll take good care of them."

When they left, he lay there feeling like a complete fraud, he couldn't believe the lies that had poured out of him so easily. Why had he done it? He could have simply owned up and told the truth but he was afraid they would try to contact his family and he couldn't have that. Not now. What kind of a person was he anyway? Maybe his Da and brothers were right about him all along. He was troubled when he fell asleep, he wasn't sure he liked this new person Shawn.

CHAPTER
TWENTY-FIVE

Everyone was in a flutter because there still had been no post from William. Finally Mr. McGregor had sent a telegram to The Templeton Carpet Factory and the reply came back that William had never shown up. They sent a telegram to the St. Enoch Hotel, again, no show. Did he get to Perth, they wondered. A telegram was sent to The George Inn. Aye, he had been there. Now the question was whether or not he had been on the train; the station confirmed that the ticket had been picked up and was punched so it was assumed it was him that boarded. The conclusion, then, was that something had happened in Glasgow but what could it be? It had to be something which had rendered him incapable of contacting them. They were all filled with a sense of dread.

By this time Mary became ill and took to bed and no amount of cajoling could get her up. They continued the search without her, none of them having the energy to deal with her depression. Telegrams were sent to the police department, the morgue, and all of the hospitals. Each one said they didn't have any records of a William Stevenson or for that matter any unidentified person of his age and description during the time specified. There wasn't a person who believed that he had disappeared on purpose, they all knew him too well; so they once again scratched their heads and pondered what else could have happened. They were out of ideas and no one wanted to say that he may have met with foul play. They all knew that the station wasn't far from The River Clyde, what if he had gotten lost and ended up in there? Perhaps someone had come along and done him in, then thrown him in the river; it wasn't known to be the best part of town. They could spend hours running different scenarios through their minds but at some point they would have to get back to daily living. That was it then, there was nothing more they could think to do. Mr. McGregor felt terrible, feeling it was his fault, he said that he should have never sent him to a city of that size in the first place. They all tried to reassure him that it wasn't his fault; many young lads made their way to the city all the time. Margaret and Douglas, of course, were devastated and they, too, thought the worst had happened.

After a few more days John had enough, he couldn't stand to see his bonnie daughter wasting away so he marched up the stairs and entered Mary's room. "Mary Munro, get out of that bed right now, I understand your pain, I truly do but we have done all we can, it's time to get back to the business of living." "I can't," she cried. "You can, the bakery was your idea and now you're mother is over there working while you're laying up here." "It's not fair we know that, but things happen in life, you have to learn how to deal with it." He turned and left the room feeling terrible but not knowing how else to get her attention. Mary lay there a while longer, the truth was, she was mad at William. "Why did he have to leave anyway?" "Why wasn't it good enough here for him?" "Why did he leave her, he was supposed to be in love with her?" "Why, why, why, she couldn't stand it." She slowly rose from the bed and got dressed, went downstairs and stood in the living room doorway. "I'm ready to go Da." she said in a monotone voice. "Good, he said, that's me lass." He grabbed her around the shoulders and held her close, he couldn't let her see that inside he was crying for her; she was so young to have faced a loss like this one.

It was lunch time before John arrived at the bakery with Mary; most of the work for the day had been completed. Catherine saw them coming and met them at the door. "You two sit down at a table, and I'll bring you lunch." "I'm not hungry," Mary said. "Try to eat something, it will do you good." The door opened and Henry walked in. "Come, John said, sit here with us, we've just arrived." Catherine came over, "Are you here for lunch, Henry?" "Yes, please," he responded. John asked Henry about his parents and they talked. Mary sat with her head down, not contributing to the conversation. Catherine came back with the food, "Here you are, enjoy." They ate in virtual silence, Mary just picking at her food. Henry looked up from his plate, "Mum loved the tea and tea set; she said she was coming in to see the store, maybe she's already been here?" "Haven't seen her," said John. Mary looked up, "I haven't either but then I haven't been here the last couple of days." "Yes, I heard what happened, Mary, I'm so sorry, I truly am." "Thank you, Henry," she said. Once again they were silent, Mary just toying with her food and Henry looking up at her every so often not knowing what to say. John stood up. "I'm going to run over to Richard's for a while and then I'll be back to pick you ladies up." He went to talk to Catherine and then left the store. Henry was finished eating and he sat there not wanting to leave, his heart was breaking for her. He could tell that she was depressed and he supposed it would take a matter of time for her to get over the shock of it. "Mary, I don't want to pry but if you want to talk about it, I'm a pretty good listener." She looked at him, "What's there to talk about, he's gone and that's that." He felt sorry for her, she looked lost. "I understand you couldn't find out what happened?" "No, it's like he just disappeared off the face of the earth." "If you like, I could make some inquiries, I'm not saying I will find anything but I could try, I have to go to Glasgow next week for some books." She gave him a feeble smile, "You would do that?" "Of course I would, I would do anything for you Mary." She looked down at her lap, "I would appreciate it but I don't want to trouble you." "It's no trouble at all, it really isn't, would you like to go for a walk, or a ride?" "Maybe the fresh air will do you good." "I don't know, maybe," she said. He was surprised that she had agreed, "Good, let's just walk over to the square and you can wait for your Da there, I'll tell your Mum." Henry went to pay his bill and tell Catherine they would be in the town square. "Thanks, Henry, she said, you're a good friend." They walked over to the square and sat on the bench, not saying anything to each other for several minutes, then she looked up at him, "It hurts, Henry, I know it's wrong but I almost feel mad at him." "Mad?" he questioned. "Yes, I feel like he didn't care enough about me to stay, I mean I was happy for him and yet I didn't understand how he could leave for such a long time." He touched her arm, "It's not wrong Mary, you're just trying to deal with it, I can understand how you felt, and yet, he was trying to do something that would make a better life for the both of you." She put her head in her hands and bent down, sobbing. "I'm sorry," she cried. He put his arm around her and pulled her to his side. "Don't be sorry, get it out, it will do you good." They sat there like that for some time and then he pulled a handkerchief out of his pocket and gave it to her. He dropped his arm and moved away from her, then said. "It's never good to keep things bottled up, it will destroy you, let me be your friend; I have strong shoulders." She touched his hand, "Thanks Henry, I forgot what good friends we used to be, I could use a friend right now." He looked at her with sympathy, "In a way, Mary, you've lost Colleen too, I mean, I know you are still best friends but now that she's married you must feel you've lost a part of her." For the first time she gave a genuine smile, "I think you're right, I was happy for her, I still am, but I was a little jealous too." "It's ok to be a little jealous, he said, it's a natural instinct, as long as you don't let it eat you up; I know you're not that kind of person." "I've been jealous too, we all have."

They saw John coming with Catherine and Katie so they stood up and walked to meet them. "Goodbye, Henry, and thank you, I feel much better, I'll return your handkerchief clean." "Goodbye Mary," He reached out and gave her a hug and then they both went separate ways.

No one asked Mary what they had talked about, they were just glad that she was seemingly coming out of her depression. John was smiling as he drove the cart. "What are you smiling about," asked Catherine. "Peter won't be home for supper tonight." "No?" "Is he staying at Richard's?" "Nope, not there." he said "What then?" "He has a beau." "No, really, are you serious?" "Who is it?" "Tricia Gallagher, you know her brother, he's always over at Richard's." "Aye, aye, I know the family." Mary leaned forward, "So where is he going tonight?" "They've invited him over for supper," John said. Mary nodded her head, "She's a lucky lass; she won't find a better man." "I agree," said Catherine. "Me too," said John. Mary leaned forward. "Henry is going to Glasgow; he said he would do some checking around and see if he could find out anything." Catherine turned around in her seat, "That was really nice of him Mary, but please don't get your hopes up." "Isn't that all we can have Mum, hope?" "Aye, I suppose your right," she replied.

"Mary, you weren't at the shop this morning when Charles came out." "He's really depressed; Nancy is fading before his eyes, I wish he would let us do more but he's just as stubborn as she is." "Has the doctor been there again?" "He stops in every couple of days, but says there is nothing more he can do." "Shouldn't someone stay there with them?" "He won't have it, I tell you; I have practically begged him." "Did you see her today?" "Yes, several times." "What does she say," "Nothing really, she is in and out of sleep." "I think tomorrow we will have to put our foot down and chase Charles out of there so we can bathe her and change the sheets on the bed." "If she won't get up she'll have to be turned several times a day or she'll develop bed sores." "Whatever you need Mum, I'll help." "Thanks Mary, we'll definitely all have to pitch in just like we did when Ethan was sick."

They were sitting around the kitchen table thinking about going to bed when Peter rolled in. "Look who's here," Rebecca said. "Whoo whoo Peter," laughed Lillian when Peter entered the house, "Shush, you two little ninny's," he said. John laughed, "Well, out with it, how did it go?" "Ok, ok, I'll tell you all the little details if you get me a treat and milk." The lasses ran and got him a snack then sat with their elbows on the table and their chin in their hands waiting to hear the story. Peter smiled and then turned and winked at Mary. "I drove to her house, I stopped the cart, I got out and then I knocked on the door." "Stop, stop, they cried, we don't care about all that, get to the best part." "Oh, you mean the part where we had supper or, the part when I left to come home?" "No, no," the part in between. "Ah, you must mean the part when I kissed her goodnight?" "Yes, that part." He laughed. "I didn't, I'm a gentleman you know." They looked at each other, disappointment in their faces. Lillian stood up and grabbed Rebecca's hand, "Come on, let's go upstairs, he'll never tell." Rebecca ran after her but called out over her shoulder, "Peter, Just remember when our turn comes we won't tell either." "Really, Mary laughed, I thought you hated lads?" "Well I do, sometimes," Rebecca said. Mary stood up, "Oh you, I think I'll go to bed, we've got an early day tomorrow." She touched her mother's shoulder, "I'm sorry I haven't been doing my part lately." Catherine patted her hand, "With good reason, Mary, with good reason, we all understand."

Next morning they left for the bakery and it was good to have Mary back. Of course she wasn't the same old Mary but she was coming along. They opened the door and went to the workroom to get the dough going. Katie usually came in an hour later with Ethan. Mary came out to the front to get a cup and saw Charles sitting on a chair by the table. "Why Charles, whatever is the matter?" "Why are you sitting there like that?" "She's gone." "Gone?" "My God, when?" "Mum, Mum, come here!" "Whatever is going on?" Catherine said. "Charles says she is gone." "No, oh no." "When Charles?" He seemed to be somewhat in shock; she went over to him and hunkered down before him. "When did it happen?" "About an hour ago." he replied. Catherine took charge, "Mary, go and get the doctor, Katie and Ethan should be here soon, we'll take the cart and get Richard to help?" "The shop has to be closed for the rest of the week, get a sign up." "We'll sell what's already on the shelves and bake the dough they bring in but that will be all." "Katie will be able to handle that by herself." She took Charles hands in hers. "Charles, I'm going back there to see to her, you stay here until the doctor comes, there is nothing you can do for her now." "Oh my, oh my, she thought to herself; it's one thing after another lately."

CHAPTER
TWENTY-SIX

The dark haired lass stood impatiently at the nurse's station. She was finally here to get to the bottom of the note with her name on it. "May I help you," said the nurse looking up. "Yes, please, I'm here to see Shawn Ferguson." "Are you a relative?" "No, just a friend, I've received a letter from a nurse by the name of Abigale McCleary." "I see, Abigale is not here at the moment, but in that case, I suppose it's all right." "Come with me." Kristine followed her. The nurse stopped at a door and told her to wait, "Let me see if he's awake, one moment please." She knocked on the door and then peeked in." "Shawn, you have a visitor, would it be all right if I show her in." "A visitor, he answered, who is it?" The nurse turned to Kristine, "Your name please?" "Kristine Oswald." The nurse poked her head in the door again, "It's a Kristine Oswald." He panicked. "Tell her I'm sleeping." "Oh no you don't said Kristine and she pushed past the nurse and entered the room. "Wait a minute, young lady; you can't just barge in there." Kristine turned to her. "I can, and I will, I need to talk to him, I won't be long." The nurse, clearly offended, stomped off. Kristine turned back and walked towards William. If an award could be won for the best acting of the year, Kristine would have taken it home. Shocked though she was at the sight of him one would never have known. "William, I just had this feeling it was you; whatever has happened and why don't you want to see me?" "Sshhh, he said, they think I'm Shawn." "Whatever for," she said. He said to her, "Isn't it obvious Kristine, look at me." "So, you're banged up now, you'll heal in time, I still don't get it, you're the same person." "That's just it, I won't heal, at least not like I was." "Oh William, she said, grabbing his hand, I'll

151

help you." "You can't just go around pretending you're someone you're not; why are you doing that anyway?" "It wasn't intentional, at least I didn't think of it meself, it just happened." "You know the satchel I had with me?" "Yes, I saw it." "Did you notice a name on it?" "No, I never noticed." "Me Mum gave it to me when I left, it had been me Grandda's; it had his name on it, Shawn Ferguson." "When I was unconscious, they saw the satchel and assumed that was me." "I didn't correct them for a reason; Kristine, you have to play along with me on this, please." "Oh dear," she said, let me sit down for this one." "Out with it, and it better be good." "When I realized that I would be crippled and then this, he moved his good hand to his face, I knew I couldn't go home again." "You see, Mary is a bonnie woman, as bonnie as you are; she would have taken me under her wing and cared for me; that's the kind of person she is, but I won't have it." "I knew if they looked for me they would look under my real name so I just went with it, I pretended I was Shawn." "I know it's the coward's way out, but I'm set on this, please, don't let my secret out." She closed her eyes and shook her head, "I think you are wrong but it's your life, not mine, I'm your friend, so yes, I'll help you; maybe in time you'll change your mind." "I won't," he said. "How long will you be here," she asked. "At least another two months." "What happened to you, how did you end up like this?" "It was an accident on Argyle Street, I was struck by a carriage but I still don't remember it." "You know I won't be able to walk normally again or use some of my fingers; I look like a monster." She laughed, "No you don't, you're exaggerating, you still make my stomach flip you're so handsome." "It's kind of you to say, but I know the truth, I've seen it." "Say what you will, William, I mean Shawn, it gives you character." "Listen, will you go home, when you get out that is?" "No, oh no, I couldn't, not like this, a failure." "You're wrong William, why are you thinking that way; no one would consider you a failure, I'm sure they all love you." "What will you do then?" "My nurse's Father has a men's shop, they have an empty flat in back, he said I could stay and learn the business, he's getting too old to do it himself." "Really, I was hoping I could talk you into coming with me, I'm sure we could find you something, in Perth, you'd like it there, it's large but not as large as Glasgow, well you know, you've been there." "We have some cottages behind our main house, you could have one." "Kristine, I can't take advantage of you like that but thank you for offering, you really are a good friend, and by the way, it's wonderful to see you." "Come over here and let me give you a proper hug." She bent down and laid her head on his chest and he held her for some time." "I've missed you," he said. "You'd be surprised how often you're in my thoughts."

The door opened and Abigale came in. She saw Kristine and came to an abrupt stop. William quickly spoke up, "This is my friend Kristine; the one you wrote to, she came after she read your post." Abigale came forward with her hand outstretched. "I'm glad to meet you, have you come all the way from Perth?" "Yes, I came with my Father, he's here on business; he's a tobacconist." She turned to William, "I'll see you tomorrow, we'll still be here in Glasgow another day." "It was nice to meet you Abigale." "Likewise, Abigale replied, perhaps we'll meet again." "I hope so, Kristine said, Shawn told me what a good nurse you are." Abby looked at William and smiled, "I'll be right back Shawn; I have to get you some supper." When she left the room, Kristine grabbed William's hand and leaned over and gave him a kiss on the cheek. "See you later, Shawn," she said winking at him. William smiled at her and watched her leave the room. He had never encountered anyone like her before; she was one of a kind.

Abigale returned with the food to find that Kristine had left. "Your friend left then?" "Aye, she's coming back tomorrow, they're here for another day." "She's very bonnie." "She is, he replied, and a good friend too."

"I don't understand, she said, in her letter she said that she didn't know anyone named Shawn Ferguson and yet she came here to see you and called you by your name." "Oh, he laughed, thinking quickly, I never told you my nickname is Will, that's what she knew me by." "I don't think I ever told her my last name." He offered no more on the subject and she didn't ask. "Tell your Da I'm enjoying the books, it helps pass the time." "I'm almost finished with The Last of the Mohicans; I'm going to read Oliver Twist next." "I'm glad they're helping you pass the time, he has a lot more; I don't think you'll run out." "They always say a book is like a good friend, I believe it now," he replied. "You're a good friend too Abigale, I couldn't have come this far without you." She smiled and looked down. "You've finished all your food, that's good." He laughed, "Good or bad?" "I seem to have a big appetite again I'll be huge before I get out of this bed." "Have you thought about what my Father said?" she asked. "I have actually, why haven't you rented out this flat before?" "I don't know, my Father just never got around to it I guess." "I would be grateful for a place to stay other than The Night Asylum but I'd have to earn my keep somehow until I was able to get around better, do you think I'd be able to price items or do something to help him." "I think there are a number of things you could do if you want, it's not going to be a problem." "If you are sure, and he is sure, then I accept." "Good, I think you'll like it, we'll have everything ready for you it will be fun." "Fun?" he questioned. "Yes, some of the things back there we haven't looked at for years, you see, some of my mother's belongings are there." "I see, he said, I would think that would be hard on you." "It's been a long time, Shawn, it doesn't hurt anymore." "Listen, I have to go to work now; I'll get these dishes out of your way." "Your friend is coming back tomorrow again?" "Aye, once more before she leaves." She gathered up the dishes, "I'll see you tonight." "I'll be waiting," he said and then laughed. She left the room thinking that he seemed to be in a much better mood, she hoped he stayed that way because it was going to be painful to get up on that leg of his. She was still mystified about the relationship between this lass and him; they seemed too close to have just met recently, she hoped that he was being forthright with her.

He picked up his book and started reading again; it was so nice to have something to do. He tried to read but his mind was wandering. He wondered what Mary was doing but he felt sure that she was alright; she had a lot of people surrounding her who would make sure nothing happened to her. His heart ached for her but he still felt he was doing the right thing. That man, Henry, had a good education now, he was sure that he would be in the picture soon; it hurt but what could he do about it? He felt bad for his mother; at least his Da had seemed to be more affectionate now, he knew she would recover from the shock in time. Did they wonder what had happened? Of course, he knew they did. Life sure could be unpredictable; you never knew what might lie around the next corner. Kristine flashed into his mind, what a strange, enchanting lass. She would be back tomorrow and he was looking forward to it. He wondered what outrageous thing she would say or do. He had to suppress a chuckle just thinking about her. Lord knows the man who wed her would have an interesting life, he was sure of it. He wondered why she was so interested in him, just a country boy. He could tell by the way she dressed that she came from money.

The next day, Kristine breezed into the room, her arms full of packages and that black hair of hers flying behind her. He shook his head, "What in the world have you there?" "You'll see Shawn, I've been busy." "I see that." She gathered everything at her feet and sat down. "I thought, because you've had such time of it, you deserved a few presents." "No, no, he said, that's not necessary, not necessary at all; your presence is quite enough for me." "Oh come on now Shawn," she cried, with an emphasis on Shawn. "Don't be a spoil sport and ruin all the fun for me." "Ok then, I won't," he replied, resigned to letting her have her way. She bent down and then came up with a book. "First, we have Pride and Prejudice by Jane Austin; I know you'll like it." He was happily surprised and tried to browse it, which was difficult with one hand. "Thank you, I will enjoy this." Down she went again and came up with a little package. "What's this now?" he asked. "Silly, you won't know unless you open it." She was all smiles and he thought how enchanting and sensuous she was all at the same time. He couldn't get the package open so she stood and assisted him then patiently watched while he peeked inside. "Chocolates, he smiled, now you are spoiling me, I don't have them often." "I found the most delectable chocolate shop on High Street." "Did you know they have the most interesting shops on that street?" "I don't know, he said, I haven't gotten there yet." "Right, she said, of course you haven't, well, I can't wait to show you when you're able." "No matter, I can do all your shopping for you, I love it." He laughed at her. She disappeared again and came up with yet another small package. She clapped her hands together in anticipation then helped him open it. Inside was a small rectangular box. When it was open she told him to pull the tissue paper away. He gasped in surprise; it was a silver engraving of Loch Tay with Ben Lawers towering above it and the name Loch Tay engraved below. It brought tears to his eyes. She took her hand and wiped the tears away. "I didn't mean to make you sad; I thought it would be a reminder of home." "You didn't make me sad, he replied, well it did in a way, but I was touched, it's the nicest gift I've ever received." "Wherever did you find it?" She smiled, "A little shop on High Street." He pulled her to him with his good arm and gave her a kiss on the cheek. "You are so special, he said, I feel lucky to have met you; and not because of the gifts, because you're the most interesting person I've ever met." "She stood up and put her hands on her hips, "I have two proposals for you." "Only two, he laughed. I can't wait to hear." "Ok, first one and don't interrupt me until I've finished." "Promise," he said a smile on his face. "You told me yesterday that I was just as bonnie as Mary, right?" "Right," he agreed. "What you are doing is not fair to her." "When you are able, we will come for you and I will take you home to her." "I believe, with all my heart that these injuries will not matter to her." "You see, William, I too, fell in love with you the first time we met and they don't matter the least to me." "I fell in love with you, not what's on the outside but what's on the inside." "You will hear my second proposal but know that I love you enough to let you go, if you are happy." Once again, he couldn't stop the tears flowing from his eyes. "My second proposal is this; "Come home with me because I want to be with you the rest of my life." "Come here," he said. He pulled her to his chest and ran her hair through his fingers. She lay there and he said, "I've had some feelings for you too, at the train station I thought if it wasn't for Mary, I would be tempted, I still feel that way, more so even today." "For that reason, I have to let you go as well." "Live your life as it should be lived, not stuck at home taking care of an invalid; we'll always be friends, I don't want to lose that, it's so special to me." "I don't know how we became so close in such a short time, but I feel as if I've known you all me life." "Don't say more, me mind is made up, you are the most exciting, wonderful person I've ever encountered, and anyone who can't see that doesn't deserve you." She sat there not moving then lifted her head, nodded at him and sat down, she grabbed his hand and they sat there lost in thought. When the lump in his throat had gone away he turned to her and said, "Will you come to Glasgow and see me again someday?" She smiled, "Of course I will, you couldn't keep me away." "All right then," he smiled too. "Best friends forever?" "Yes, best friends forever; every time I look at my engraving I will think of you, I so love it." "I'm glad," she said. When it was time to go, once again she laid her head on his chest, breathing in the feel and smell of him. She had never encountered a deep feeling like this before and she didn't understand it but there was no denying it either. They were still lying like that when Abigale came in the door. "Oh, I'm so sorry, I didn't mean, I should have knocked." "No, no, come in, smiled Kristine, it's all right, we were just saying our goodbyes; we won't see each other for a while." "You're leaving today?" "Yes, I have to; my Father is finished with his business." "Thank you so much for taking time to send the post, without it I wouldn't have known where he was." "You are an angel; I would have thought he had forgotten all about me." She looked at William, "I'll miss you," he said. He pulled her to him and gave her a soft kiss on the lips. She touched his face and let her fingers linger on his lips, then turned, and said to Abigale, "Take care of him will you?" Abigale nodded, touched and confused by the emotion between them. Kristine left the room without looking back. She walked down the hall and then stood against the wall sobbing. It was so hard to leave him behind.

Abigale walked to the bed and looked at William. She could see the tears in his eyes. "She loves you, it's clear." "She does, I love her too but in a different way, she's an unusual and exciting lass." "She brought presents for you?" "Yes, she has a mind of her own, there's no talking her out of it; do you want to see?" "Yes, yes I do, very much." First he showed her the book. She clapped her hands, "You'll love it, I've read it and it's very good." Next he pointed to the candy, "Can you help?" "I've trouble with these small ones." She took the package in her hand, "Open it and peek inside," he said. "Chocolates!" "Yes, let's have one shall we." "I couldn't, they're for you." "No, I want you to, it's more fun to share, you must, please." He smiled at her, "You first." She took one and put it in her mouth and then he took one too." "Ummm, good," they both said in unison. "She said she got them on High Street, that there were a lot of unique shops there, isn't that where your shop is?" "Yes, I know the chocolate shop, it's very expensive." William shrugged, "She comes from money; I suppose it was not unusual for her to buy something like that." "Do you want to see the last one?" "Yes, yes I do." She picked up the package and laid it on his chest. "Open it," he said. She took out the engraving, "Oh, it's beautiful." "Aye, it's from where I live, Loch Tay and Ben Lawers." "You miss it there?" "Very much, maybe someday we will go there, if you'd like to." "I would, you would take me?" "Of course, why wouldn't I?" In the days to come, William looked at that engraving every day, sometimes holding it in his hand until he fell asleep. If she had wanted to buy him something with meaning, she had found the perfect thing.

CHAPTER
TWENTY-SEVEN

The funeral was over. They had a lovely service at St. Fillian's Episcopal Kirk; then laid Nancy to rest in the cemetery. The attendees were invited to the bakery where they had a luncheon. Charles was sad, but doing alright. Mr. McGregor led him around like a little child and tried to cheer him up as best he could. Ethan didn't attend; he stayed at the bakery with Katie. Walking that much would have been too hard on him, he was still very weak. Most of the villagers attended, Charles and Nancy had been prominent citizens in town for many years. Douglas came with Margaret although it was hard for him to face everyone. No one said anything against him but no one went out of their way to talk to him either. Mary sat with them a while, she felt a bond with Margaret, like holding on to William in a way. They didn't talk about him, it was too painful. "You should come in again some morning and bake with us we had such fun last time." "We did, thank you, I will." "Did I tell you that Michael is getting serious about Nellie?" "No, do you like her?" "Aye, very much, she's a nice lass." "I'm happy for you it must be nice to have some female companionship up there." "It is, she likes to cook too, so she helps me in the kitchen, they'll probably take the cottage behind us, when they get married; it needs some fixing but the men can do the work themselves." "Well, it was nice seeing you again I'd better get back and help Mum," said Mary. "She seems to be doing ok," said Douglas when she left. "Aye, Margaret, replied, she's a strong woman."

Catherine said to Mary, "We'll have to go in and do some serious cleaning for Charles, Nancy wasn't able to do much for some time and although he tried, it needs a woman's touch in there." "I'll have to talk to Mr. McGregor and have him coerce Charles out of the house so we can do it; otherwise he'll poo poo us." I talked to John and he said to ask him if he wanted to stay with us, it's going to get lonely here." Mary nodded her head, "I'm sure he won't, he's too set in his ways, he'll keep busy around here; he always does." "I think I'll go visit Colleen tomorrow, I miss her." Catherine patted her hand, "Good, she would be happy to see you it's been a while, your Da can take you over."

Next day, after work, Mary was waiting for her Da so she could go to Colleens when she saw the couple pull up in front of the store so she ran outside to meet them. They were both all smiles; Harry jumped down and gave her a big hug, "I've brought me wife to spend the day, if that's alright." "Alright, it's better than alright." "You'll never guess; I was sitting here waiting for Da to take me to your house." They laughed just like old times. "We have like minds," Colleen said. "Harry is going to pick up Tom O'Donnell, they're going fishing, he's been depressed, well you know, over William." Mary grabbed Colleen's hand, then called over her shoulder, "Have fun, Harry, we'll see you later." "Come, she said, Mum would like to see you and you must see Ethan's Tea Shop." They entered the shop and Katie and Catherine ran to give Colleen hugs. "How's the newlywed, they asked?" "Just fine, I like it, but Harry says my cooking needs a little work, I should come down here some day for lessons." Catherine laughed, "Oh those men, they're never satisfied." Mary, still holding Colleen's hand, pulled her to the back and they entered Ethan's store. He was sitting at the table marking items. The shop had been so popular and busy that he was ordering more things every week. "Colleen, how nice to see you." He stood up and came around the counter to give her a hug. "How's married life?" "It's good, I'm happy to see you are getting better." "Aye, each day I'm a little stronger." She looked around, "The shop is lovely, I definitely will have to take some tea home with me, when do you close?" "Not for another hour or so, usually when Katie is done cleaning up." "Then I'd best get what I need now." She picked out a couple of teas and a few kitchen items and then took them to the counter. "It's so nice to have a shop like this here in Killin, it was needed." She paid for the items and they decided to leave the shop and go for a walk. "See you later," everyone called. "Just leave your packages here, Colleen, on the table." "We can pick them up later." Colleen put down the packages and then asked, "Can we go and see the wee bairn?" "Bairn?" questioned Mary. "Richard and Sarah's, I haven't seen him for so long." Mary laughed, "Oh, I see, you have baby fever already." "No, I don't, but I do like them." "Sure, let's go," Mary said, Sarah loves company, she doesn't get out that much and Richard is always so busy in the shop.

They walked to the other side of town where Richard and Sarah lived and saw Peter's cart parked in the back. "Oh, I have something to tell you," said Mary. "What is it?" questioned Colleen. "Peter has a beau." "No, who is it?" "Tricia Gallagher." "I know who she is, she's a nice lass." "Yes, I know who she is too, said Mary, I haven't officially met her yet since they've been seeing each other." "Peter was to their house for supper the other night." "Good for him," said Colleen. "She's a lucky lass to get him; he took his time picking someone." They walked to the door of the blacksmith shop and called in, "Hello." Peter looked up and smiled. "Come in," he said. "No, that's ok, we're going to see the bairn, is Sarah home?" "Aye, aye, she's there." "We'll see you later," they called and ran to the house. Sarah answered the door, "Well, look who's here, come in, come in." "Colleen has baby fever and she's come to see Collin." "Oh Mary, stop, I don't have baby fever but I haven't seen him for a while." "He's awake and growing like a weed." "May I hold him?" "Of course, can you stay and join us for dinner?" "Peter and Richard will be in soon." "I've already eaten," said Mary. "We've eaten too, that is Harry and I." "Well you can come and have some tea and a snack then." Richard and Peter came in and of course they had to get all the details about his new beau. They sat at the table and had a snack then played with the bairn some more and left to go and see Harriet. Mary felt like it was old times again; it was good to be with her best friend.

They arrived at Harriet's and knocked on the door. Her sister answered but invited them in, then went to find her. In a few minutes, she came down the stairs, excited to see them. "How's the newlywed," she said. "Fine, answered Colleen, everyone asks me that." They all laughed. "We're just spending time together today and thought maybe you'd like to come along, Harry is fishing with Tom." "He is, she said, I didn't know that." "Aye, aye, I want to come along just give me a minute to get ready." She ran upstairs and then came back down again, ready to go. They had no plan or destination, they were just happy to be together. They went over to the schoolyard and sat for a while talking about their school days and how they wouldn't be returning. "Are you and Tom still seeing each other?" Colleen asked Harriet. "Off and on, not regularly, she replied, I get the feeling that he's not interested in a serious relationship." "That's too bad," said Colleen. "Do you want it to be serious?" "I don't know, she said, I like him but he's a little self-centered I think." "I heard about William, Harriet said, I'm sorry Mary." "It's hard but I'm trying to work through it; the worst part is not knowing what happened; it eats me up." They walked around the fields, collecting wild flowers and heather. "I can dress up the tables in the bakery with these," said Mary. "Oh aye, they cried, let's go and do that, it will be fun." They went to the bakery and decorated, then admired their work when done. "I'll get some milk, we can have a snack, we deserve it," said Mary. They spent the rest of their time sitting at the table talking and gossiping, then Harry came and it was time to go. "Did you catch any fish? Colleen asked. "Aye, we did, can we have them for supper?" "Aye, Colleen replied, can you clean them?" "Aye, Aye, I'll clean them, I know you don't like to" Harry replied. Mary and Harriet gave Colleen a hug and then watched them drive away. "I'll walk you home," Mary said to Harriet. "How will you get home?" "I'll go to Richard's, Peter will still be there." She walked Harriet home, then went to Richards and waited with Sarah. When Peter was finished with work they left together. "Are you liking blacksmith work, Peter," Mary asked. "Aye, I like it very much, I've always wanted to do it." She smiled at him, "I'm sure Richard is glad to have the help, he's been so busy." "I don't know how he did it; we're still busy with the both of us working." "Better than not to be busy at all," Mary replied. "So true, said Peter, "Did you have fun with Colleen?" "Aye, we did, Harriet came along; it sounds like Tom and her aren't that serious." "I couldn't tell you, Mary, Tom never mentioned anything to me about her but he sure asked a lot of questions about you." "Me?" "Whatever for?" "He wanted to know how you were doing since William disappeared and if you were seeing anyone." "Oh for heaven's sake, I'm not running around looking for someone else already." "I know, I know, Mary, but sometimes Tom speaks before he thinks."

Henry was on his way to Glasgow. The students were given the week off and he had been given funds to pick up more books and whatever else he needed to teach the children. He basically took the same route as William, traveling by coach to Perth and then catching the train to Enoch Station at Glasgow. When he arrived at Enoch Station he went to the counter and found the attendant. "May I help you?' he asked. "I know this is a long shot, but I'm looking for a missing person, he would have arrived here five weeks ago on a Wednesday, he was only 19 years old." "We know that he was on the train, at least his ticket was punched." "I'm sorry, sir, there is no checkout here, once the passenger has left the train, he doesn't have to check in with us." "I see. Henry said, of course I should know that as I've just arrived myself." "Thank you anyway." He turned to walk away when he heard, "Sir, sir, one moment please." He stopped and looked up, "Yes," "I remember around that time there was an accident on Argyle Street." "I don't know the details, but I was told it was a young person about the age of the person you are looking for?" "They said he was a young man." "Do you know where he was headed?" the attendant asked. "He was supposed to check in at The St. Enoch Hotel but never showed up." "I see, that probably wouldn't have been him then, unless he had business first on Argyle Street, he wouldn't have gone that way; if I were you, I'd check the hospitals." "I'll do that, have a good day, by the way, can you direct me to Argyle Street." "Yes sir, come with me, I'll write it down." They went back to the counter and the attendant sketched out where the station was; the hotel and Argyle Street. "I see what you mean, Henry said, it was probably someone else or he lost his direction and went the wrong way." "Yes, that could happen but there isn't a lack of people here to ask for directions." No, you're right there it's quite busy isn't it? "Good luck, Sir, I wish I could have been more help." "Thank you; I appreciate the time and the directions all the same."

Henry hailed a carriage and asked to go to Buchanan Street; then he gave them the address for the book store he was going to. He looked at the map on the way. "Aye, he could see how someone would get confused and end up on Argyle Street, perhaps he should take a trip over to The Royal Infirmary, it couldn't hurt; maybe he would find out something new; it wasn't far from here. He would do anything he could for Mary. He entered the book store and was pleasantly surprised that they had everything he would need. He then left and hailed another carriage to take him to The St. Enoch Hotel, the same one William should have come to. He thought he'd better check in and leave his packages; then continue with the investigation. He checked in, realized that he was hungry, and decided to go down to the dining room. He ordered some dinner, watched the traffic out the window and thought how easily one could have an accident, it was so busy out there. For the third time, he hailed a carriage and asked to go to The Royal Infirmary Hospital. He found the main desk, "Excuse me, I wonder if you could help me?" "Yes, sir, what may I do for you?" "I'm looking for someone who may have been taken here five weeks ago on a Wednesday." "He was a tall good looking boy, 19 years of age, his name was William Stevenson." "Let me check the records, sir, I'll be just a minute." She disappeared for a while and then reappeared. "I'm sorry, sir, we have no one by that name registered in the last two months." "There was one young man who had an accident, it was on Argyle Street; but his name was Shawn Ferguson." "I see," said Henry, do you have anyone without a name, someone who was unidentified." "No sir, I'm sorry." "Thank you for your time." "Good day, sir." Henry left thinking, "so it wasn't him on Argyle Street, I don't know if I should be relieved or not." "What could have happened to him?" His mind was racing on the way back to the hotel, he had hoped he could bring Mary some news but he had nothing more to tell and no more ideas. He would catch the train tomorrow morning and be back home in two days. He was anxious to see her again but this time he was going to take it very slowly, he did not want to scare her away. He looked at his packages again and smiled as he opened one of them that he had purchased when he was walking along Buchanan Street looking for the book store. He had passed a window with beautiful hair combs displayed so he stopped in and purchased one for Mary and then some ribbons for his sisters Bethany and Marianne. He was just about to check out when he decided to get more ribbons for Mary's sisters Rebecca and Lillian. He hoped they all liked them; it was fun to treat everyone to something special, he enjoyed it.

CHAPTER
TWENTY-EIGHT

Abigale was busy in the storeroom at home sorting through the mess they had made the last few years and enjoying some of the things that she found; crying over others. It was good that they were going through all of this stuff; it had lain around way too long now. She decided to take a little break and have some tea. As she sat there, she thought about Shawn and the lass. They seemed to have a strong attraction towards each other and yet it was an unusual one. He said he would take her to see Loch Tay, he must mean to stay here for some time then. It wouldn't be long and he would be able to leave the hospital. He was doing remarkably well, more so than they had initially hoped. To be alive was miracle alone. They unwrapped his damaged fingers to look at them however they were still badly bruised; he had no feeling in them, nor could he bend them. The nurses were taught how to massage them several times a day. Whether or not feeling would could back to them, only time would tell. They felt he would be able to bend his arm in time and hopefully his wrist; the leg was another matter. "Well, she thought, enough dilly dallying, better get back to work." She had spent less time in the evenings with him recently. He seemed to be content with the reading, although it was hard to turn the pages with one hand, he seemed to manage. He had therapy several times a day which took a lot of his strength and the doctor said he would develop new muscles in time which would compensate for the ones he couldn't use right now. As she sorted through things, she kept running back and forth to the living room upstairs to ask her Father if they could dispose of something or if she should pack it back up. He, like her, was finally ready to get rid of things they didn't need.

The flat had a nice little kitchen with a table. The window had been boarded up but she planned on removing the boards and putting up a pretty little curtain. The view wasn't much, just a small back yard, the livery and then the back street, but it let in the light. The sitting room was large she would put a chair, couch, desk and end tables in there which should be all he needed. The window in there was also boarded up and faced the front of the building. He might enjoy sitting there looking out at the traffic. She would hang a heavy curtain there so he could have more privacy when he wanted. There were three bedrooms and a bathroom. There was a pump in the kitchen and also in the bathroom and a commode in the bathroom that had to be flushed with pumped water. Abigale found some nice braided rugs for the floor; it was starting to look very cozy. They should have rented it out all these years; she wondered once again why they hadn't. One of the living room walls had shelves from floor to ceiling so she dusted all of the books and put them on the shelves, she was so glad he liked to read, it was a passion of hers too. They would have to get some living room furniture and some beds; she would talk to Father about it later. She found some end tables and kerosene lamps so she dusted them off and arranged them in the room. She made a pile of boxes to throw and another pile of boxes to save. There was a door off of the sitting room that opened into the back of the shop; on both sides of that door were storerooms. One of them they used as inventory for the store. The other was unused so she carried the packed boxes into that room and then finally she was finished. She made a mental note to go through the upstairs kitchen and find unused dishes and bring them down. She went upstairs, worn out from all the work but she was pleased with what she had done.

Her Father was sitting in the living room, looking over his latest order. "Father, you'll have to check out the flat, I've finished with it." "Yes, Abby, I will in the morning." "We'll have to get some living room furniture and a bed, other than that, we should be set." "Yes, go down to the furniture store tomorrow and order what you want." "Have them deliver it and set it up." "Tell them to bill me." "Thank you, Father, I will." "Oh, by the way, did you know there were shelves on the wall in the living room?" "I think I remember that, yes." "I've put all of your books there and they've filled the shelves almost up, it looks like a library." "Good," he said, we should have done that long ago, books are like friends, you should treat them right, not stuff them away in a box." He chuckled and she laughed thinking how true that was. So many times in her lonely life she was entertained by a book or two, a book could be a friend on a lonely night." "Can I get you anything, a snack perhaps?" she asked her Father. "Yes, a snack would be nice; thank you Abby," he smiled at her. She brought him his snack then threw her arms around him and gave him a hug. "I love you Father." "And I love you, Abby lass."

William was pleased with his progress. He was working hard to do what the doctors asked. It hurt but he stood the pain, they had saved his leg and of that he was grateful. It was debatable whether or not they had made the right decision but they had un-wrapped it yesterday and said things were looking very good then wrapped it back up again. They said he wouldn't be able to walk on it. If he couldn't, he'd live with it but maybe with enough work, he would prove them wrong. The scar was another matter. He just couldn't look at himself without cringing; what must other people think. He asked if it would fade and they said some but not entirely. He was looking forward to going home with Abby; he called her that now, just like her Father. He wanted to begin the next chapter of his life, he tried not to think about his past; it hurt too much. He did think about Kristine, quite often in fact. The little engraving was never far from his side. He knew he'd have to talk to Abby, and soon, before he left the hospital. Everyone would be done searching for him now; there was no more danger of being found. He couldn't keep lying to her, it wasn't right. If she rejected him then he would have to go to The Night Asylum until he could find work. Maybe that's what he deserved.

Next day, Abigale entered William's hospital room, excited to tell him all about the flat. He was reading when she entered and looked up with a big smile on his face. Just like everyone else, she melted at that smile. "Hello Abby." She sat in the chair beside him. "I've been busy, I can't wait for you to see the flat; I think you'll like it." "I'm sure I will, anything will be fine, don't go to so much work, you work hard enough already. "It wasn't work it was fun, we should have done it years ago. "Listen, Abby, I have to tell you something that I shouldn't have kept from you, it was wrong of me." She felt like the wind had been knocked out of her. "What is it?" "It can't be that bad, can it?" He took a deep breath. "Remember when I was unconscious." "Yes," she nodded. "When I woke up, everyone was calling me Shawn." "I couldn't figure out why until I found out it was on my satchel, well the satchel I was carrying, it was my Granddas." "When I found out the extent of my injuries, I didn't want to be found, I still don't." "I knew they would be looking for me under the name William Stevenson, my name." "It was perfect." "I know now that it was wrong, and I understand if you hate me for deceiving you." "I can't believe I deceived you of all people who have been so kind to me." She sat there trying to absorb what he had told her. "But Kristine, when she was here she called you

Shawn." "That's only because I talked her into going along with me." "You trusted her but you couldn't trust me?" "I knew her, she would see the excitement and make a game of it; she's very adventurous." "A game, you think lying to people is a game?" "No, of course I don't; I didn't know any other way." "I knew they would find me and talk me into coming home." "I couldn't go back there, not like this." "I just couldn't." She looked at him. "But you don't feel that way with me?" He shook his head, "It's not about that, I made promises I can't keep; to Mary, to Mr. McGregor, to me Mum and Da." "You think so little of them that they wouldn't understand?" "Think how they're feeling now, not knowing what's happened to you." "I do think about it, Abby, every day." "I'm not changing me mind." "I don't expect you to understand and I don't expect you to do anything for me." "I just want you to know the truth, I respect you and I owe you that much." "Oh Shawn, William that is, I can't understand how you can do this to people you love." "You've been through a lot, maybe it has clouded your thinking, you'll have to make it right some day or it will eat you up inside." He shrugged, "I can't make any promises; I won't do that." Abby leaned her head back in her chair, closed her eyes and sat there for a few minutes. "I shouldn't judge you, I wasn't completely honest either." "When Kristine wrote back to us saying she didn't know anyone by the name of Shawn Ferguson, she made a suggestion as to what might have happened." "She said that someone may have murdered you, taken your satchel and suit, and then was struck by the carriage as they were fleeing." "It was a plausible explanation, and I wondered myself if it could be true." "Instead of giving the note to the head nurse like I was supposed to do, I threw it away." "I couldn't see you as a murderer." William threw back his head and laughed harder than he had since he had come to the hospital. Confused, Abby said, "What's so funny?" "Only Kristine would think up a story like that." Abby, couldn't help herself, she had to laugh too. She stood up and patted his hand. "I'll have to talk to my Father about this, it wouldn't be fair not to." "I want you to Abby, no more lies." "I'll see you later, William." She left. He wasn't surprised at her reaction; she was an honest woman and she felt betrayed. Maybe she wouldn't come back, if not, he would understand. It might be The Night Asylum for him after all.

Abigale finished her shift and didn't stop to see William, she left for home. She had to admit she was still perturbed at him for the ruse he had pulled. She had to talk to her Father tonight, it would be hard. She fixed supper, and as usual they ate together. "I've checked out the flat, Abby, it looks good, real good." Thank you, Father, we may have to consider letting it out, we should have done so years ago." "Letting it out?" "Has something happened to Shawn?" "Yes and no." "What do you mean, yes and no, what kind of an answer is that; it makes no sense?" "Shawn isn't Shawn, Father." Surprised he said, "Well then, who is he?" "William, William Stevenson." She explained the whole story to him and then sat back and let him digest it. He too, sat there for some time, thinking. He looked at her. "So, you've found a crack in the lad then?" "I suppose you could say that." He folded his hands together, "This is how I see it." "He's a proud lad, good looking, never had to depend on anyone before." "All of a sudden he wakes up and his world is topsy, turvy." "He sees himself as half a man now." "I can understand that, I really can." Abigale shook her head, "So he settles for me then, is that it Father?" "No, he chooses someone who didn't know him before; someone who isn't going to pity him." "So you think what he did is all right?" "No, I think what he did was out of confusion and fear, he'll reconcile to it someday, I'm sure of it." "Give him some time." "What if I give him too much of myself and he leaves anyway?" "There are no guarantees in life, Abby dear." "If you put a wall around yourself hoping never to get hurt, you'll not experience life either." "Thank you Father, you're the wisest man I know, I'll take your advice." She had a lot to think about, now the ball was in her hands.

Back in the hospital, a post came for William from Kristine. He eagerly opened it; he should have written to her by now but hadn't. It read: *Shawn, I hope all is well, I miss you. As usual, I'm being dragged to all the social events but they bore me. Soon, you will receive something at the hospital. Please tether your pride and use it until it is no longer necessary. I think it will make your life easier, it's the newest one. With love, your best friend forever. Kristine.* William caressed the letter lovingly, "Bye that lass, what has she done now?" He would ask the nurse for some paper, a pen and envelope today and send her a post. He had some money in his satchel, at least last he knew he did, he could use that towards the stamp.

Later that day, when they had helped him sit in a chair, (he always had to have his leg propped up), he asked for the paper and pen. They gave him a small board to use on his lap, and although difficult with his left hand, he managed to scribble a letter to Kristine. *My Dear Kristine: I received your post today. I'm sorry I haven't written sooner and I hope you can read this; it's a little difficult to write clearly. I see you are still the mysterious one. I will be waiting to see what your mystery gift might be. You have to stop buying me things; hearing from you is all I need. You'll never know how much joy I get from the Loch Tay etching, I can't stop looking at it. I have confessed my real name to Abigale, whether or not she forgives me remains to be seen. Your loving friend; William.* He folded the letter as best he could, put it in the envelope and sealed it, then waited for the nurse to come in again. He liked sitting by the window where he could catch some sun. He closed his eyes thinking of Harry and himself fishing, bye, how he missed his good friend. The nurse came in to check on him and he asked if he could have the letter from Kristine which was by his bed. She gave it to him and he asked her if she could copy the address from it onto his envelope. "Yes, I'd be happy to." "I'm sure I'll get the hang of it, but my writing is poor right now." "You will, just give it some time," she said. "Could I bother you for my satchel?" "Yes, of course, it's no bother at all." "Can you wait for a minute, I have some money in here; I wonder if you would send the letter for me?" "I'll send the letter, Shawn, it's the least I can do." "My name is William, he said, the name, Shawn, it's here on the satchel, but that was my Grandda's." "I see," she said, wondering why he hadn't said anything until now. "I'll see to it the records are changed." "I'd appreciate it, he said, I'm sorry I've waited so long to clear things up." "No problem, she replied, you've had quite a time of it, and by the way, the doctor will be in today to check on you."

He dozed off sitting in the chair and soon the doctor arrived. "How are we doing today, William?" "I understand there was a mix-up with your name." "Yes, I should have straightened it out sooner." "Let's take a look and see how things are coming along, we'll start with the arm." He unwrapped the hand and looked at the fingers. "The color is good." He poked at them, one by one. "Can you feel anything?" "No, sir, but sometime I think I feel pain in them." "That's good, it means the nerves are trying to come back, maybe you will be able to use them again, at least partially, that's the best we can hope for." "I think we can leave the bandage off now and let nature do its work." Next, he unwrapped the elbow and he had William bend his arm as best he could, it was stiff but he could move it. "Does it hurt when you move it?" "Aye, a little bit." "That will disappear in time, I'm going to leave it unwrapped as well, I think it has healed." "I want you to exercise it like we've just done, several times a day, but don't lift anything or put a weight strain on it for at least another week." "I won't," he replied. With that, the doctor stood up and stated that he would be back shortly. He returned with some crutches and a nurse. The nurse stood by the chair watching; the doctor unwrapped the leg and looked at it. He touched it here and there asking William if he felt anything or any pain. He bent it slightly; it was still painful but seemed to be healing nicely. "We are going to have to brace this for some time, but I have high hopes, it has good color." "I've brought in crutches but I don't want you to use them unless there are two other people in the room to help you; they will take some getting used to." "We can't have you falling and hurting yourself more." "The crutches will be painful to use, you are a tall boy." "I've ordered some longer one's for you; they will be easier to use." He then demonstrated how to use them keeping all of the weight off of the injured leg. "Do you think you could try?" "Aye, I could try." "Alright then, keeping the weight off your leg, try and stand up on your good leg, use us for support."

Once William was standing on one leg, the doctor tried to put the crutches under his armpits. "You will have to bend down so they are touching your armpits." "Try and maneuver yourself to the bed in the manner I showed you." William managed to get to the bed and sit on it." "I'm sure this has tired you out, it is very difficult right now, don't get discouraged." "When you get taller crutches it will be much easier." He re-bandaged William's leg with the braces and gave him a pat on the arm." "We'll get there son, we'll get there, don't give up." The doctor and nurse left and William lay still on the bed, he felt weak from the effort. Abigale came in and saw the crutches. "So they've had you up then?" "Aye, it was an effort, but I made it to the bed." "What did the doctor say about your progress?" "He said everything was coming along well." "That's good, I'm glad." William reached for the letter from Kristine so Abby could read it. "What in the world would she be talking about?" "That's what I've been laying here thinking about; knowing her, she'll probably have a donkey and cart delivered." They both laughed. She looked at him, "I've talked to my Father." "Was he angry?" "No, not at all, he understood, actually better than I did." He feels like you will have to reconcile with your family in time or you will never have any peace inside" "Maybe, said William, but I don't see how I can do it now, after all this time." "We'll see, Abby said, think on it will you?" "It will only get harder as time goes by." "By the way, my Father saw the flat and was pleased with what I've done to get it ready." "I'm grateful to the both of you, William said, especially after lying to you about meself."

CHAPTER
TWENTY-NINE

They were all sitting outside at home talking about Charles. Mr. McGregor's best efforts to cheer him up weren't working very well; he just wasn't the same person any more. It was almost like a part of him died with Nancy. He barely touched the food they prepared for him. They cleaned his house weekly which wasn't much of a job as barely anything in it was touched. The only semblance of his old self was when he had his daily draughts game (*checkers*) and tea with Ethan. He had formed a bond with him and they would sit and talk periodically throughout the day.

A cart turned into the drive and they saw it was Henry, back from Glasgow. He parked the cart and John yelled, "You're back, come over and sit with us." He walked across the yard carrying packages and stood in front of them, "I come bearing gifts." He took out the ribbons and divided them up giving half to Lillian and half to Rebecca. Squeals of delight were heard, ribbons were hard to come by in Killin. "I bought some for Bethany and Marianne too, he said, and for you Madam," he handed a silk scarf to Catherine. "It's gorgeous Henry, you shouldn't have." "I wanted to," he said. John and Peter were enjoying the delight of the women. Henry handed them each a package of tobacco. "Last, but not least," he said, handing a package to Mary. She opened the box, wherein lay a hair comb with pearl inlay. Mary gasped, "I've never seen anything like it why it's just stunning, thank you Henry." "I saw it in the window on my way to the book store and I just couldn't resist; they tell me it's from India." The shopping was fun for me, a way to pass the time." He sat down next to Mary. "I'm sorry, I was hoping to bring you news of some sort, but I didn't find out anything new at all." "First, I asked at Enoch Station where the man at the counter told me there had been an accident around that time on Argyle Street." "He drew me a crude map of the area but to tell you the truth, I couldn't see what he would be doing there on his way to the hotel, it was in the opposite direction." "In any case, I thought maybe I should check with the hospital perhaps something new had developed." "Yes, they said, they did have a young man who was injured in an accident on Argyle Street but his name was Shawn Ferguson." "And no one else?" I asked. "Maybe there was someone unidentified or someone who didn't make it." "No, they said, no one else." He dropped his head and folded his hands on his lap. Mary touched him on the arm. "It's ok, you tried, and we all appreciate it." To lighten the mood she asked, "Did you find the books you were looking for?" "Oh yes, they had a nice collection, it was worth the trip. "Did you know that Comrie has some of the best schools in the area; they don't mind spending money for education." "Aye, I did know that, she replied, don't be surprised if you feel the ground move under your feet over there." He laughed, "I haven't yet, but it's quite the topic in the area, they are known for their earthquakes." "I wish you and Peter would take a trip over there some day, I'd like to show you around." "I'd like that, what do you think Peter?" "Aye, as soon as Richard and I catch up on the work, we'll come over." "Good, Henry replied, I like it but it gets a little lonely, I yearn for company." "Pretty soon I'll be out there talking to the horses," he said, and they all laughed.

Henry stood up, "I hate to, but I'd better get heading for home before it's too dark out, I'm sorry I didn't come with better news for you." Mary stood up too, "I'll walk to the cart with you." Everyone called goodbye and thanked him for the gifts." Mary asked him about Glasgow, "What's it like there, in Glasgow?" "It's very different from here, Mary." "It's quite dangerous, it's always busy on the streets, everyone drives the carriages so fast and the streets are narrow." "Then too, there seem to be a lot of unsavory characters hanging around everywhere." "I'd like to take you some day, the shops are incredible." "Maybe, some day," she replied. They hugged and Henry headed for home. He could still feel her touch when he left and he thought about her all the way home.

Everyone had gone into the house already where they usually gathered in the kitchen before retiring for bed. Bedtime came early for them; since having the bakery, they always got up at the break of dawn. Catherine was admiring her scarf. "Henry is so thoughtful, I just love the scarf." Mary removed the hairpiece from the box. "Look, Mum, have you ever seen anything like this?" "I'm almost afraid to wear it." "Can I borrow it someday, Mary," asked Rebecca. ""Aye, perhaps," she replied, "but it will have to be a special occasion." "Tricia is coming for supper on Saturday," said Catherine. "Good, then we'll finally get to meet her, said Mary, I mean, I already know who she is; I've seen her around but never talked to her."

Mary undressed and lay in bed finding it hard to fall asleep. Why, she wondered had she actually thought Henry would come home with William. Wouldn't he have found a way to contact her if he was alright? She still felt like she would turn around and he would be standing there with that big smile on his face. She just couldn't get over the fact that he had disappeared without a trace. Not knowing what had happened was something she just couldn't seem to get off of her mind. Whatever had happened, she hoped that it was fast and painless. Tears streamed down her face as she lay there, crying for herself and for him. She prayed. *"God, free me from this pain, fill me with the strength to go on without him. Give me assurance that it's ok to stop worrying about him and that he is now in your loving care."* She finally fell asleep, the tears drying on her cheeks. Henry, on the other hand, was sleepless with thoughts of Mary, oh how he loved her, she was a surprising and intriguing woman.

Summer was quickly ending and life in Killin went on as usual in the community. Henry would come to town every other weekend and stop in the bakery. Sometimes Mary would accompany him to his parents and sometimes he would come to her house and visit. He was very careful not to scare her away; he was content at the moment just to spend time with her. Mary enjoyed Henry's visits, looked forward to them actually. She liked to visit the MacAlduie home and talk with his sisters, they had been friends forever. She had not suggested to him that they go to see Colleen and Harry; perhaps subconsciously not wanting them to know she spent time with him. There was no reason to feel guilty, but somehow she did. She couldn't deny the fact that his sudden appearances lifted her heart a little. He was such a thoughtful and caring man and he treated her like a princess.

Margaret didn't stop by very often and when she did Nellie accompanied her. They had become close friends. She would always love Mary but it was painful to see her, maybe in time that would change. She, like Mary, felt as if she would turn around and see her good looking lanky son coming in the door. There was no closure for either of them because of the unknown way he had disappeared. Like, Mary, she kept as busy as possible to stop the thinking. Michael and Nellie were planning a wedding next month, she was happy for them. Mary was glad to see her when she came, but it always left her with an empty feeling afterward.

It was amazing how busy both the bakery and Ethan's store were, the door was constantly in use with customers coming in and out. Ethan suggested staying open longer in the day but everyone hushed him. No one wanted him to overwork and get sick again. He still had a long way to go before his strength was fully back. John was fed up with the farm, it seemed he worked so hard and couldn't make any money. What was he to do but stick it out; there was no other avenue open to him. They had already paid Charles back his investment as had Ethan. Rebecca and Lillian had been experimenting cooking at home. Feeling left out, they wanted to sell candies in the bakery. They presented a tray of sweets to Mary for tasting. "Good job, lasses, she said. "I'm sure we can find a place to put them but don't overdue, it's a luxury for most people." The candies sold better than expected so Mary added some chocolate to her next order; it was hard to get chocolate and sugar. The lasses packaged the chocolates up in fancy little packages and Ethan sold them in his store. Ethan had expanded his items and was finding that he had no more shelf space. There was nowhere else to expand short of taking out some tables and chairs in the bakery and that was not an option. The lasses had made enough on their candies in a few short weeks to each buy a new dress for the upcoming Village Dance. It was held every year to celebrate the end of the season and the approaching winter. They were excited as could be, this being their first year to attend as young ladies and both of them had secret crushes on a couple of lads in the village.

Henry was in town again; the conversation usually was about his school teaching experiences and hers in the bakery. Peter had finally agreed to go and visit him in Comrie so Mary asked him if next Saturday afternoon would be alright for him. "Yes, of course, every day would be ok with me." She laughed at him.

They left on Saturday and it took them a little over an hour to get there. It wasn't far but the roads were bumpy and rough. Catherine had packed up some treats for Henry, and Mary held them on her lap. Tricia had come along and they talked most of the way, Mary liked her instantly. Peter was in his usual good mood commenting every so often. Henry was waiting for them outside and stood up and smiled when he saw them coming. He looked so happy to see them and she thought how he must get lonely here all by himself. She handed him the package and he peeked inside. "Tell your mother thank you, I will enjoy these." "I'm not the best cook in the world you know." "Nor I," said Peter. Peter introduced Tricia and Henry invited them all in. The cottage was clean and bright, sparsely furnished and needed a woman's touch. Henry had several shelves filled with books; Mary supposed that was how he spent most of his evenings, reading. "It's a nice little cottage, Henry, she said. I wasn't expecting it to be this large." "Well you know some of the past teachers had families so they needed more room than I do." "Come sit at the table, I'll fix us something to drink; I have tea, at which he smiled, from Ethan's store." "There's also ale and milk." Peter asked for ale." "Driving the cart always makes me thirsty, all the dust you know." "Yes, Henry said, I'm exactly the same way." "Mary, if you don't mind, maybe you could find a plate and put the treats on it." "What can I get for you lasses?" "I'll have milk," said Mary. "The same please," Tricia replied. "I'll be right back then." Henry went outside and then over to his root cellar where the milk and ale were kept cool from a stream that ran through it. "Here we go, let's sit, shall we." They sat at the table catching up on all the news." "Charles is getting forgetful," Mary said. "Mr. McGregor came to take him fishing and he had forgotten all about it." "They're good friends then?" asked Henry. "Oh yes, for quite some time as I understand it." "Would you care to see the schoolhouse?" "Aye," they all replied. There was a well-worn path from the cottage to the schoolhouse, fields on both sides. They walked along slowly; Tricia and Mary kept running off the path and picking wildflowers. "I bet we can beat you," she cried. The lasses had a head start and beat the lads to the door. "That wasn't really fair," said Peter. Henry laughed and opened the door. You could see the work he had put into it, there were maps of countries on the walls and pictures that the children had made. There were jars with insects. In one corner stood a stove with a braided rug next to it where the children could sit and read books. On the walls were bookshelves filled with books, it was very cozy. "It's lovely, Henry, said Mary. "How many children have you." asked Tricia. "About twenty; that's when they all come." "They don't always come?" "No, the older lads have to help on the farms; sometimes the older lasses too." They left and went back to the cottage, Peter and Henry stayed outside, talking, Mary said they were going in to put the flowers in the house. "You need a woman's touch, Henry," she laughed. He teased her, "You can move in tomorrow, Mary." It wasn't long before they had to head for home. Peter shook Henry's hand, "Thanks for having us, I enjoyed it." "Anytime, I'm always ready for company." Mary gave him a hug, "We'll see you in a couple of weeks then?" "Actually, next Saturday, I hope." "Alright, til then I guess," she said. They left in the cart and Mary turned around from the back seat and looked behind her as they left; he was standing there watching them. She gave a little wave and he waved back. He entered the cottage and saw the flowers she had put around the house. When he told her she could move in tomorrow he had said it in a joking way but truthfully he would like nothing better than to have her here with him every day. He would marry her in a second.

Midweek, Catherine came out of Charles' side of the house asking when they had seen him last. Katie said, "He was here this morning, had his porridge and said he was going out to the shed and then over to see Mr. McGregor." "That's probably where he is then." "I'm leaving a little early to go with the lasses, they want to pick out their dresses today, and they are so excited." "John should be here with them soon." "I'll have to tell them to make another batch of cinnamon drops and toffee, we're almost out again." John came with the lasses and Catherine hurried out to meet them. Katie and Mary were finishing cleaning up from dinner. "How was your trip to Henry's?" "It was fun, he has a nice little cottage, I really liked it; it was bigger than I thought it would be." "He must get lonely there," Katie said. "Aye, I suppose so, but he has his books." "Ethan's mom wants to go home soon, it's been such a blessing to have her here but of course I don't blame her for wanting to get back home." "I'm not sure what we'll do about the bairns; I may not be able to work." "Sarah says she will watch them but with the wee one, I think it would be too hard." "We could ask Colleen, they'd love it out there where they can run in the fields." "Thanks, Mary," but it's too far to go every day." "At least Ethan's store is doing well, maybe you should take some time off during the week; the lasses can watch them on the weekends." "We'll see," Katie said. "I guess I'll just leave Charles a note that his supper is on the hearth." "Yes," Katie said, they must be busy over there." They gave one last look around and then went to get Ethan. Ethan usually dropped Mary at Richard's and she went home with Peter but today she was meeting Catherine at the clothier where the lasses were picking up their dresses. She entered the shop and Catherine said they were just finishing up and were almost ready to go. "Katie left Charles a note that his supper was on the hearth, said Mary, he's still not home from Mr. McGregor's." "What's that you say," John piped in. "I said Charles is not home from McGregor's yet, so we left the supper on the hearth." "He wasn't there today?" "I saw George earlier and he said Charles must be in a mood, he hadn't come over again." "Well where in the world is he then?" said Catherine, startled. "Oh, no," Mary said, "He told Katie that he was going out back to the shed and then over to George's." "I hope he wasn't climbing on something out there and fell." "You stay here," said John, "I'll go over and see what he's up to."

John entered the store and then went to the back calling Charles name. When he didn't answer, he entered the house and looked around but there was no one to be found. He left the store and walked around to the back and entered the shed. There he lay. John bent down and felt for a pulse, but it was apparent he was gone. He immediately got into his cart and headed to Doctor Traymoor's. The doctor jumped in the cart and they went back to the shed together. "What a shame," he said. "He just went downhill since Nancy passed." "I'll have someone come and lay him out." "Can the women attend to the funeral as they did for Nancy?" "Yes, yes, of course," said John, "Oh, I hate to tell them the news." "It's never easy," said the doctor, doesn't matter, young or old, it's never easy."

Where in the world was John? They told the clothier that if John came look-ing for them they would be at their son Richard's house." "I'll tell him, thank you lasses for the business, you're both going to be the belles of the ball." They giggled at him, "Thank you sir, we love the dresses." They walked to Richards and Sarah was surprised to see them at the door. "Come in, however did you get here?" "We walked from the clothiers; do you want to see our dresses?" "Yes, of course I do." "Where's the bairn?" asked Catherine. "He's sleeping for a change." "Oh, then I won't disturb him, I'll just go peek at him." The lasses monopolized the conversa-tion with talk about the dance and the money they were making on their candy. They were entering the prime of their life and were enjoying it immensely. Finally John came, they could tell by the look on his face that something had happened. "What is it?" Catherine asked. "He's gone, he was in the shed." "Did he fall?" "No, no, I don't think so." "Doctor Traymoor said probably a stroke or heart attack, he's not sure yet." "Dear God, Catherine said; first Nancy and now him." "Oh poor Charles; poor Charles, what will we do without him?" They sat there for over an hour, stunned by what had happened; the joy of the afternoon gone. "Dr. Traymoor asked if you would take care of the funeral again as you did for Nancy?" "Of course, we'll close the shop for the week out of respect for him." John patted his wife's hand, "You all made his life exciting again, he's told me that multiple times." "We'd best be getting home, we'll have to stop at Ethan's to tell them." "I'll do it Da, said Peter, I'm leaving now too." "Thanks son, I'll see you at home." "It will be a busy day tomorrow." On the ride home John said, "We'll have to face the fact that we may be asked to leave." "Leave?" "The bakery you mean?" "We don't own it dear, we only rent it." "Don't get worked up about it, we'll see what happens."

They had a large funeral for Charles. He was so dear to the village that it seemed everyone came to pay tribute to him. They laid him in the cemetery next to his long time wife, Nancy. It was hard to fathom that he wouldn't be coming out of the back with one of his jokes. He was truly a generous and wonderful man; they would miss him greatly. The shop just wouldn't be the same. Mr. McGregor was crushed that his good friend wouldn't be around anymore and he sat at the table looking like he lost his best friend; which of course he did.

Not knowing what to do, they continued to run the bakery and store as they had been doing. One day Mr. McGregor came in and sat down at the table. Mary went over to talk to him; perhaps he knew what might become of Charles property. Did he have long lost relatives somewhere? George didn't know; they had never discussed it; he knew that they had taken several trips to Edinburgh in the past; he assumed it was to see family. "I know he had a sister who was a countess, he told me she had died in childbirth and the bairn hadn't survived either." The bakery was filled, everyone wanting to come in and tell a story about Charles, it was a way of relieving the shock of losing him.

Several weeks later a gentleman in a suit came into the bakery. He was tall and slim and was wearing what looked to be an expensive business suit. He asked for Mary Munro. "That would be me, can I help you?" She felt faint, thinking that there was news of William. "Yes, is there somewhere we can go that would be private?" "Can I bring my mother with me?" "Yes, of course." Mary went to get Catherine, she was shaking. "Let's go back into Charles house; we can sit at the kitchen table." She took off her apron and came from behind the counter with her hand outstretched, "I'm Mary's mother Catherine; may I ask what this is all about?" "I'm sorry, he said, "I should have introduced myself." "My name is Duncan McMann, I am Charles solicitor." "We'll go back here then, follow me." They sat down and waited for him to begin but Mary couldn't stand it, "When will we have to leave?" Duncan looked at her, "Leave?" "Yes, here, we are renting." "I'm well aware of that my dear, I'm the solicitor, remember?" "Yes, of course, I apologize." "No need to apologize young lass, perhaps I will be working for you." "Me?" "I don't understand." "Everything is yours my dear except for a few special requests." "He was quite taken with your entire family; he was touched that you had been so good to his Nancy." "He wants your Father, John Munro to have his horses and carriages." "George McGregor, his best friend, is to have all of his tools and fishing gear." "He has set aside a monthly payment for Ethan and his family; he told me about the illness and what a nice young man he is and how close they had become." "It may surprise you that I know so much about you but Charles and I communicated weekly by telegram." "You are free to hire your own solicitor, if you wish and I will see that everything is transferred to him, however, I would be happy to continue watching over your affairs, I am quite familiar with his assets." "Congratulations, Mary, you are a very wealthy woman now." He reached out and shook her hand. "I had no idea, I mean, Charles financed the bakery and Ethan's tea shop, we've been successful and have paid him back." "Yes, I know, he was very proud of his little investment." "He has other investments, you know." "I don't know; he never talked about it." "Would you like to hear his story, have you time?" "It's quite an interesting one." "Aye, aye, I would, can we get you some tea?" "Yes, that would be nice, thank you." "We'll be right back then." They left him sitting there at the table. "Katie, said Catherine, can you manage on your own?" "This will take some time; I'm going to have Ethan come back with us." "Yes, I can manage, what is this about?" "It's Charles' solicitor." "Is it bad then?" "No, dear, it's quite the contrary." She fixed the tea, chose some scones and told Mary to get Ethan." Mary returned with Ethan and introduced him. Mr. McMann reiterated the details to him" "Now for the story: Charles and Nancy came from Edinburgh." "Their families were both quite wealthy; that's how they met." "They were considered the elite of society." "Charles told me that he always felt more of a common man, that he was uncomfortable living that kind of life." "He said Nancy felt the same way, that's what drew them together." "Charles only had one sibling, a sister." "She married a count and became a countess but she died in childbirth along with the child." "One time she had come to visit him here in Killin." With that he laughed. "I'm sorry, but Charles told me this numerous times with a glint in his eye." "He said she pulled up to the front in her fancy carriage and her carriage man helped her out." "In his words, she was dressed to the gilt in her high faulting gown." "When he opened the door and led her to the back through the Fish Shop, she was horrified." "As he tells it; she said, Charles, why ever are you living in such humble surroundings, when you could have the best there is, and that smelly fish shop; however do you stand it?" "He told me his answer was; Because I enjoy the good people of this village." He says it was beyond her understanding and she never visited again although they saw each other throughout the years until her death when he and Nancy traveled back to Edinburgh to visit their families" "They were always more than happy to return to Killin." "When his parents died, he inherited the family business, The Edinburgh Shipping Company, which is still very successful today." "It is being run by a forward thinking Imperial Administrator who is an honest businessman and it brings in a goodly sum of money; more in fact then you would ever be able to spend." "The family mansion is let by a wealthy family who travels between England, France and Scotland." "There are a number of warehouses storing the goods for the import business." "I have several associates who see to the affairs and make sure nothing is amiss." "Nancy had two brothers who are still running that family business." "They have visited here from time to time in the past but were unable to attend her funeral as they are quite elderly now." "Nancy wanted nothing to do with the business and they paid her quite a large sum of money to buy her out which is just collecting interest and remains in their joint account, which now belongs to you." "What do I do now?" Mary asked, clearly overwhelmed. "Again I would like to continue being your solicitor; I think I know his affairs better than anyone; however, I suggest you hire your own solicitor to go over everything; it will give you peace of mind that I am not trying to pull the wool over your eyes; so to speak." "Here is a cheque, you can deposit in the bank of your choice, and draw from it as you need." "This is nothing more than a document stating you have received the funds, I will need your signature on it." "When you require more funds, contact me, there is much, much, more where that came from." "I will need these other documents signed and returned as soon as possible." "You can send them by post if you wish." "How will I get in touch with you," she said. He handed her a business card. "Call me or visit any time you have more questions, and I'm sure you will." "I can see myself out; this has probably been somewhat of a shock to you." "By the way, I will have to stop by for some more of those scones when I'm in the area; I can see why you are so successful."

Mary sat at the table with Catherine and Ethan when he left. If they doubted anything he had told them, saying they were in shock was an understatement. The second shock came when they looked at the cheque. It was written out for 100,000 pounds! Mary spoke first. "I'll have Peter take me to Comrie, to see a solicitor, I don't want anyone in Killin to know our business; we may be gone overnight, several days even." "Mr. McMann is from Crieff, they may know of him." "If this is all as he says, then we have some decisions to make, and soon, I'll have to see Henry he will know what to do."

When John came into town, he had to take a seat when he was told, it was too much to absorb. Mary made plans to leave the following day; they would take a carriage this time, not knowing what the weather would be. Mary asked her Father to see to the horses, a task he had been doing already anyway. Their first stop would be to see Henry; they pulled up to his house and walked the path to the schoolhouse and knocked on the door. Henry came to the door and was shocked to see them there. "Children, continue as you are, I will return in a moment, no shenanigans please." He stepped outside the door to talk to them. "Henry, Mary said, I know this is an imposition on you, but something has happened and I need your advice." "Of course, Mary, anything you need, whatever has happened?" "It's complicated, she replied, I have some documents for you to look over and then I need your help." "When will school be out today?" "At three," Henry said. "We'll return shortly thereafter if it's ok with you, Peter and I intend to take a room at the inn, we'll go and arrange that now." "Nonsense, Henry said, I'm swimming in all those rooms over there, you must stay with me; I won't have it any other way." "If you're sure it's ok?" Mary replied. "Of course I'm sure, please, go over there and make yourselves comfortable, I will be there as soon as I can." "You must tell me something now or I will be going crazy wondering what is happening." "It's Charles, he's willed everything to me and I don't know what to do." "Oh my, we'll figure it out, don't worry, Mary." "Peter, there's room in the shed, see to your horses there." "Thank you, Henry, I will," he replied. Henry turned and went back into the schoolroom and Mary and Peter walked to the cottage. "Who would have ever thought," Peter said. "Aye, Mary agreed, never in a million years." "I guess Charles is getting the last laugh after all." "Aye, I can picture him up there laughing at all of us."

Peter saw to the horses and Mary brought in the package from the bakery and started the teapot for tea. She got some dishes and laid out the food they had brought along for dinner. She sat at the table thinking how strange it was that Henry was the first one she ran to for help. Then again, maybe not so strange, he was certainly the most educated person she knew. Peter came in and they ate their dinner. "Thanks for bringing me, Peter." "You know I'm always here for you, Mary." "Yes, I know, you always are." "I think I'll go over to the root cellar and see what I can find for supper, the least I can do is have some supper ready for Henry, it was nice of him to let us stay; I hope it's not an imposition" "I'm sure he's thrilled, Mary, you know how lonely he gets here." Mary brought some things from the cellar and started making supper." "You should see the root cellar, Peter, I wish we had one like it, a stream runs through it." "Aye, he's very fortunate; there's not many of those around, not many at all." "Listen, while you're busy in here I think I will go outside for a while and wander around." "Ok, see you later, said Mary, don't get lost, we don't want to send a search party out for you." Peter chuckled, "Funny Mary, funny," and out the door he went.

Mary had a quick mind and she already knew what she wanted to do, that is, if everything she had been told were true. John thought no one knew how he struggled to make ends meet with the farm, but Mary had known for some time how hard he worked, and for so little. He had always wished he had a hardware store, well now he could. The shed behind Charles house was quite large, more than was needed for the horses, carriages and carts. It would be quite easy, with Richard's help, to make a hardware store. There was the money; they would have enough to start an inventory to stock it. Catherine and John weren't getting any younger; the constant running back and forth to town must be wearing on them. They could have Charles house or better yet, Ethan and Katie could take it and Catherine and John could move into theirs. It would be perfect, Ethan wouldn't have to go out once winter came and they could all stop worrying that he would catch another cold. The children would be right in back and Katie would be able to work more. Her Da could finally have his comeuppance with Mr. Stevenson when he came to collect the rent and was told they were leaving. The lasses would be thrilled to live in the village. She would see to it that Richard and Sarah were given some money and Peter too. Oh yes, especially Peter.

She watched him out the window; she loved her dear brother; always there for everyone. Tricia couldn't have found a better man. What in the world was he doing out there, he was picking something; she thought she would have a look. She grabbed a pot from the kitchen and went across the field to the edge where the woods started. "Peter, what have you found?" "Blueberries, lots of them Mary, I wonder if Henry has seen them." "Here, I've brought a pan; if you can pick enough I'll make a tart." "Yes, yes, there will be enough, I'll be in shortly." She went back to the kitchen and started the dough for the tarts; it would be a lovely dinner indeed. Of course, they wouldn't be as good as those made in an oven, but she could manage. Mary had found a slab of Aryshire bacon and some root vegetables so she was making a stew and she was enjoying herself. Henry had such a nice kitchen, with windows on all sides, you could see in every direction. She sat at the table watching Peter picking blueberries; and she could hear the children screaming and laughing, they must be outside for exercise right now. Peter came in with an almost full pan of berries. Mary looked in the pot, "Oh my, they must be plentiful." "I could have picked three more pans; if we were going right home I'd take some to Mum." "What are you cooking?" "It smells wonderful." "Oh, it's an Aryshire stew." "Peter, are you set on becoming a smithy, then?" "Aye, I like it." "Will you marry Tricia?" "It's too soon to tell, but I like being with her." "I; well all of us, like her a lot too." "Thanks Mary, that means a lot to me, coming from you." Mary finished the tarts and Peter stole one. "It's too hot, Peter, you have to let it cool." "Fine, he said, let's wait outside, it's such a nice day, and I'll take me tart with me." "I'll be out in a minute, I have to clean up the kitchen and make sure the stew won't burn." She finished up and joined him outside to wait for Henry.

"I saw Bethany the other day when Tricia and I were in the square." "She told me that several young ladies in Comrie would like nothing better than if Henry would give them some attention." "Did you know that in Glasgow, he was invited to quite a few social events?" "No, I didn't know that," Mary said, feigning disinterest. Peter continued, and there was a purpose to his conversation, "It seems a few of the social elite young women, requested his presence at social events." "You don't say," replied Mary. They heard a commotion, a few carts were pulling up and the children were running here and there. School was out for the day. Mary and Peter laughed, just watching them. When all the children seemed to have left, they saw Henry walking down the path toward them. Mary thought, "Bye, he looks handsome, why haven't I noticed that before?" "I guess I have." She felt nervous and excited at the sight of him. He wasn't tall and lanky with boyish good looks like William, he was dark and mysterious looking, with black hair that was wavy and just touched the collar of his shirt. He was a little taller than she and had a slim build. He didn't have that infectious smile that

William did but when he looked at her, she could feel the intensity. She realized she had never looked at him that way before, the way other women must see him. He looked up and saw them and a smile came over his face. She had to smile herself, and like a school lass she felt a blush creeping over her face. "What in the world have you been up to Mary?" "I can smell the food from here, it smells delicious." "You'll never guess, Peter found some wild blueberries, I made some tarts, and I was surprised to see that you had flour." "My Mother taught me how to make biscuits a few weeks ago, they don't taste like hers by any means, but they are edible." He laughed, "Yes, I knew the blueberries were ripe, I was going to bring some home the next time I go, if the birds don't get them all first." "I have a lot of time to roam around the area." "I hope you don't mind, Henry, I found some Ayrshire bacon and made a stew for supper." "Mind, of course not, I'm delighted, you have no idea how nice it is to have a well cooked meal." "Sometimes the parents send over food for me, but most times I do for myself." "How long before supper, he asked?" "The stew will have to cook a while yet, maybe an hour or so, why?" "I thought we might have a look at those papers of yours."

She gave him the papers and he spent quite a while looking at them, flipping back and forth between the pages. He looked up, "My God, Mary, have you any idea the extent of this? I am stunned!" "They said it was a goodly sum, the cheque they gave me was for 100,000 pounds and they said to ask for more when I needed it." "What have you done with the cheque?" "I have it here in my bag." "You'll need to find a bank and deposit it, do you know what solicitor you want to see in Crieff." "No, do you know of any?" "I know that Miller's is reputed to be a good firm." "They've done some work for the school." "Well, I suppose we should start there then." "You'll need an appointment; tomorrow, go to town right away and send a telegram to them; tell them that you have inherited some property and you need an appointment as soon as possible, tell them to send the reply to The Crieff Hotel." "I'll go with you tomorrow; that's if you want me to?" "I couldn't ask you to, the school and all, you can't just leave." "No, I can't just leave, there's a substitute; we'll drive over there and tell him to come for the next few days." "Are you sure?" "Yes, Mary, I'm sure." Mary stood up, "I'd better see to supper then, she patted his hand, thank you Henry!" Peter and Henry went out to hitch up the cart so they could drive over to the substitute teacher's after supper. When they came in, Mary had everything ready." They ate until they could eat no more. Henry said, "I don't think I can get up, I've eaten too much, this was really a treat for me; I've enjoyed the food and most of all the company." "We had best leave right away Peter; I don't want to get over there too late." "I'll stay here and clean up the dishes," Mary said. They drove to the substitute's cottage and he was more than happy to oblige, always wanting to make a little extra money. On the way home, Henry said, "If I could have picked one person in Killin who had money, it would never have been Mr. McPhee." "We're not talking about a little money here, Peter, this is a fortune." "If anyone deserves it, she does," said Peter. "Oh I agree completely, replied Henry; how often does something like that happen in life?"

Mary had everything tidied up by the time they were back. She watched the two of them out the window, they were talking and laughing. Peter seemed to like Henry and Peter was a good judge of character. Then again, Peter liked everyone. She was comfortable here, she felt at home. They came in with milk from the root cellar and immediately went after more blueberry tarts. She teased them, "I thought you were full from supper." "Oh, we were, Henry laughed, but the tart's kept calling to us." They sat around talking the rest of the evening; Mary would look up to see Henry looking at her and he would do the same. Eventually they became tired at which time Henry told them to each pick a room. "Good night Henry, she said, I really appreciate all you're doing for me and I love this cottage it's so cozy and comforting." "Good night, see you tomorrow," he replied.

If thoughts could talk they would have been bouncing off the walls in that little cottage the night. Mary was thinking about Henry; how he talked, walked, smiled. Likewise, he was thinking of her, as he had done the last several years every night. With her being in the room next to him, he could almost imagine them sharing a bed; and oh, how he would like nothing more than to hold her all night in his arms. When Mary awoke in the morning and came into the kitchen she found Henry already sitting at the table. He looked at her and smiled and she blushed. "I'm sorry I'm up so late, she said, I slept like a bairn here." "You should have awoken me, what would you like for breakfast?" "You don't have to make breakfast for me Mary; I don't want to trouble you." "It's no trouble at all Henry, do you want porridge?" "Yes, porridge would be fine, sit here by me for a while." "Where's Peter?" she asked. "He's out hitching up the horses, he'll be in soon." "It's nice having you here Mary," he said. She smiled at him, "I didn't know where to turn and the first thing that came into my mind was you," she said, looking down shyly. He looked at her, "I'm glad Mary, I'll always be here for you, I hope you know that." She looked down at the table not knowing what to say but feeling a little flip in her stomach from the nearness of him.

They left after eating porridge and yet more blueberry tarts. "I'll be riding with two blue people," she laughed. Their first stop was the telegram office. Henry asked Mary if she wanted to deposit her cheque in Comrie or Crieff. "Comrie if

I can, she said, it will be closer." They found a bank and presented the cheque for deposit. The surprised teller said, "This is quite a large cheque, please follow me." They followed her to an enclosed office with quite expensive furniture and waited. A gentleman, briskly walking, came forward smiling with his hand outstretched. "Good Morning, my name is Mason Gordon and I will be assisting you today." "I understand you have a rather large cheque that you would like deposited?" Mary shook his hand. "Aye, sir, it's from an inheritance." "My, my, you seem to be quite the lucky lass?" "Yes, sir, I'd like you to meet my brother Peter and my friend Henry." "Henry is a schoolteacher here in Comrie." "Yes, yes, I've heard of you, the community is lucky to have you." "It's nice to meet you as well Peter." "Mary, have you any documents to substantiate this cheque?" Mary turned and looked at Henry who nodded towards the papers in his lap. "Yes, sir, here they are." She handed them to him. He sat behind the desk looking at the documents flipping the pages back and forth. He looked up from under his glasses. "Have you any idea, the value of this inheritance?" "Some," said Mary. "I am familiar with Duncan McMann, you have a good solicitor in him." "We are going to see another solicitor in Crieff, to verify everything in the document." "For your piece of mind, that is a good move, I assure you though, that Duncan will not take advantage of you." "You must be careful with a fortune such as this." "Why, may I ask, are you depositing into our bank?" "I live in Killin, and as I said, my good friend Henry, teaches in Comrie, I wanted a bank close to home." "We appreciate your business, if you need anything in the future, I will be happy to assist you." "Will you be depositing the entire cheque?" "I would like to keep 100 pounds, please. "As you wish, Madam, I will return shortly." He left the room and Mary turned to hand the documents back to Henry. The man returned with her 100 pounds. "The rest of your money will be safe with us and once again, it was nice to meet all of you." He shook their hands and they left.

Once out on the street again as they walked to the carriage a lovely young lady was walking down the street and she stopped and said, "Hello Henry, how are you?" "Oh, hello Amanda, I'm just fine, it's nice to see you; these are my good friends; Mary and Peter." She extended her hand to each of them, "It's so nice to meet you," she said. "We all love Henry here in Comrie, we are lucky to have him as a teacher." "Nice to meet you too," each of them replied. "Well I must be off," she said and she hurried on her way. Henry made no further comment and neither Peter nor Mary asked him about her.

Mary rode inside the carriage. Henry and Peter up top. They were on their way to Crieff. Mary thought about the lady on the street and wondered if Henry had been seeing her; she certainly was bonnie. The jostling of the carriage and the voices of the men lulled her into sleep. She woke to a sound and realized they had stopped. "We're here, Mary, you fell asleep." said Peter. "So I did, and I wasn't even tired because I slept well last night." They found the Creiff Hotel and stopped in front; an attendant came out and asked if they would be spending the night. "Aye, said Peter, perhaps several." "Shall I take your carriage to the livery then?" "Aye, thank you." Mary gave Peter the money. "Can you get the rooms for us?" Peter got them two rooms, one for him and Henry to share and one for Mary. He checked with the desk and found they had a telegram waiting from the solicitor, Lewis Miller. "It says they will see us today at 1:00." "We'll have lunch in the dining room then, and after go and see him," said Mary. They found their rooms; Henry took the keys and opened Mary's door so she could go in. She looked at him and he looked at her; once again, she felt a small tingle in her stomach just to be so near him. "See you in a little while," he said softly, we'll knock on the door." "Ok, I'll see you later," she said. She sat at the little table for quite a while and then went and washed her face in the bathroom. Traveling was dusty and dirty. She felt refreshed and soon she heard a knock and opened the door to see Peter and Henry standing there. She looked at Henry and felt a blush cross over her face. "What in the world is wrong with me, she thought; every time he looks at me I feel myself blush." The blush on her face did not go unnoticed by Henry; he thought perhaps she was looking at him in a different light than she had before.

They waited in the solicitor's office for Lewis Miller to come. He walked toward them, a short, chubby man who seemed to smile from ear to ear. "Hello, hello." He shook all of their hands. "I understand from your telegram that you've received an inheritance?" "Yes, here are the documents." "They were presented to me by Duncan McMann; we wanted a second opinion to make sure they are authentic and we are not signing something we shouldn't." "Duncan McMann, you say?" "Good man, good man, you'll have no troubles there." He opened the documents and looked at them for quite some time, occasionally emitting a hummm or ahhh. Then, suddenly, he closed the documents and sat there looking at them with his hands folded on his desk. "Young lady, it is very rare, in this life, to come into something as you have." "I can tell you that the Edinburgh Shipping Company has been, and still is, one of the most prosperous in Edinburgh." "They are very futuristic and a force to be reckoned with." "I'm not familiar with the mansion, I could check into it further if you like but it will only cost you more money." "The warehouses, of course, must remain with the Edinburgh Shipping Company if you were to sell it." "The property in Killin appears to be in order, and of course, if your business is located there, then you would want to keep it." "I understand you have received 100,000 pounds, you don't have to be frugal with it, I can assure you there is more, much more where that came from." "Now, all that being said, I would be thrilled to be solicitor of all this wealth, but I must be honest and tell you that you are in good hands with Duncan McMann" "If you follow his advice, you will be set for life, he has an excellent reputation." He stood up and Mary shook his hand. "Thank you, I feel better knowing that this isn't all a fraud." "Will you send a bill or shall I pay now." "No, no, give the secretary your address and they will send a bill by post." "I wish I had known your benefactor, he was an unusual man." "Maybe, said Mary, but as we knew him, he was a lovely, kind man, one we were sorry to lose.""

When they were outside, again Mary said, "I guess I may as well sign the documents then, what do you think, Henry." "From all appearances everything is as it should be, I don't know what more you could do to protect yourself." "Let's go over there and see if Duncan McMann is in." At the desk the secretary told them he was out for the afternoon. "He'll be in tomorrow morning I can pencil you in for then." "Aye, said Mary, that will be fine, what time shall we be here?" "Let's say 10:30, will that work for you?" "Aye, that time will be just fine, thank you."

They walked down the sidewalk and Mary grabbed both of their hands, "Let's window shop, we've worked hard enough today, it's time to enjoy ourselves and spend some of that money." They spent the remainder of the day going in and out of shops and by the time they were done, all of them were loaded with packages. There was no talking Mary out of anything, she insisted that Henry get something for his Mum and two sisters, Peter was coerced into buying a beautiful pendant for Tricia. Sarah got toilet water. Rebecca, Lillian, Bethany and Marianne got books, bracelets and little oriental boxes. Catherine, Katie and Alicia got new dresses. All of the men got new shaving brushes and stands. Collin got a wooden truck. Gretchen and Carolyn got dolls. Peter picked out Donald's present, a wooden wagon. They piled their packages in the wagon and rolled it down the street. Laughing and joking all afternoon like children at Christmas, it reminded Mary of when they were children and all played together. Finally they headed back to the hotel; they couldn't buy more as there was no way to carry anything else. "My God Mary, said Peter, you've gone overboard this time." "Don't worry, Peter, it's a one-time shopping trip, I don't plan to do it again, I just want to share it with everyone." Then, "Oh no, we have to go back." "Why?" said Henry. "I forgot something for Harry and Colleen." "Tomorrow, Mary, tomorrow." they both said in unison. "We can't carry more," nor did they want to.

They went up to their rooms. Henry put his packages down by the door and hurried to help Mary open her door before she dropped hers. "Put them on the bed, Henry, I want to look at them all again." He entered the room and dropped them on the bed." She sat down on the bed and looked at him. "Is this a dream, Henry, or is it really happening?" "It's really happening, Mary." She asked him, "Did you have fun today, I wanted you to, I'm so glad you came along." "I always have fun with you, Mary." She smiled, "Let's go somewhere else for supper tonight, you pick." "I can't," he replied. "Why not Henry?" she asked. "Because I don't know Crieff that well, I have no idea what there is to offer." Mary laughed, "Ok, we'll walk down the street until we find something we like." "No shopping?" "No, no more shopping, I promise." She stood up and gave him a hug. "Thank you, I'll find a way to repay you, I promise." "He broke away from her and took her face in his hands and it was all he could do not to kiss her. "Listen, little lass, don't say that, you don't owe me a thing." He dropped his hands and looked at her and she felt the intensity in his eyes; then he said, "Peter and I will be back later, get some rest." Mary undressed and washed up, then put on a shift and sat on the bed looking over her presents. It made her feel good to give them all something. She picked up a little box; inside was a pocket watch. The cover was silver and it had gold etchings all around the sides. On the back she had the letters *H. M.* inscribed. The chain was solid gold and had a trouser clip; it was quite expensive and was magnificent; it came in a little velvet bag with a drawstring. She hoped he would like it; she had secretly purchased it for him without either of them seeing her.

They walked down the street, all three of them hand in hand, stopping pedestrians and asking where they could get a good meal at an inn. Several people mentioned The Barley Inn, so they decided to go there. It was a festive atmosphere and they all ordered ale. "Only one for you Mary," Peter teased. "One will be quite enough," she laughed. They had a good meal, ate too much again and just relaxed while Peter and Henry had yet another ale. When Henry went up to get the ale, Mary noticed a woman looking at him and despite herself she felt a twinge of jealousy.

They went back to the hotel and retired for the night. Once again Henry opened the door for her and she stepped inside the room then turned to look at him. "What?" he asked softly. She took her hand and brushed back his hair at the side of his face, "Nothing I guess, she said, thank you for being my friend." He took her hand in his then lifted it and kissed it, "You're welcome Madam, see you tomorrow." She closed the door than stood with her back against it, "I'm falling in love with him and it's too soon," she thought. Next morning they had breakfast at the hotel, then left to see Duncan McMann. "Nice to see you again," he said. "And you, replied Mary, I have everything ready for signature." "I have some questions for you," she said. "Go ahead, Duncan replied. "If I decide to transfer ownership of the properties, what will I need to do?" "You contact me, I will draw up the documents, and you sign." "There's no need for you to travel all the way here again, I can come to you, as before." "You should know that we did obtain a second opinion and you have quite a favorable reputation." "Good to know," he said. "We deposited most of the 100,000 pounds in the bank at Comrie." "I'm familiar with that bank, good choice, if you need more money, just let me know and we will arrange it directly with the bank." "How much is there, money that is?" "It's hard to put a number on it because it is accumulating on a daily basis." "Unless you are planning on spending one hundred times the amount you have received, you will not run out." Mary's face went white. "One more thing, he said, as you know, Charles took care of the ordering for your bakery and tea shop" "That will be your responsibility now, this is the contact." He handed her a piece of paper. "Send him a telegram and he will get you what you need; don't forget; you are now in the import/export business so you will get the best price on everything." "We will send a list of new items to you by post monthly, there's no need to pay for anything; there is a special account set up for each of the businesses." Mary signed all the documents and they thanked Duncan and left the building. It had been a revealing visit, the enormity of it all was hard to fathom.

Once back at Henry's it was late and they decided to spend the night again. They were bone tired; the trip, the shopping and the mental stress of the past two days had taken a toll on them Peter and Henry went outside to care for the horses. Peter stood by the carriage with his arm on the door and said, "You're in love with her aren't you." Henry turned toward him, and replied, "I have been for years but she sees me as a friend, I can't get past that." Peter felt for him and nodded his head, "She had a blow, there's no closure, if there had been a body or at the least something." "Aye, said Henry, I can't go on much longer though, it's killing me." Peter walked over to Henry and patted him on the back. "It's understandable; I wish I knew the answer." They all retired early, it had been a long day.

Mary made breakfast the next morning; then sent Peter out with a bucket to get some more blueberries; she told Henry they would drop some off for his Mum on their way home. She cleaned up the kitchen and sat at the table waiting for Peter to finish; Henry was getting ready to go back to school; he came out and sat down by her. "I hate to leave, she said, I just love it here, I slept like a bairn again" "You could stay," he said. "Tempting, but I can't," she smiled. Peter loaded the blueberries and then peeked in the door stating he was ready to go. Henry shook his hand and they hugged, then Peter went to pull the carriage up to the door. Henry turned to Mary and she reached up, and hugged him around the neck; then brushed her lips against his cheek. He turned his head and they locked lips for the first time. She broke away and laid her head on his chest. "Will you go with me to the dance on Saturday?" he asked, stroking her head. She pursed her lips and looked up at him, "I'm sorry, I can't?" "But why?" he asked. "I don't know, she replied, it's too soon, people will think, we're friends, I'm sorry." He broke away and turned his back to her. "I'm sorry too, Mary, you won't find anyone else who would treat you like I would." "I love you."

Mary turned to him, "Goodbye, Henry, thank you for everything, you have no idea how much I appreciate it." He didn't reply, but went out the door by Peter and told him to have a good trip home. Mary pulled the package out of her pocket and left it on the kitchen table then she closed the door and left. No more words passed between them. Henry watched them drive down the road until he could see them no more, then turned and went back into the cottage. He saw the package on the table and opened it. "My God, he said, this must have cost a fortune." He put his head in his hands and cried, something he couldn't remember doing since he was a wee bairn.

They stopped at MacAlduie's and dropped off the blueberries. "Oh, said Mrs. MacAlduie, I do so love blueberries, you say you got them at Henry's? "Aye, "Mary said, he was kind enough to go to Crieff with Peter and myself to see the solicitor." "The solicitor?" she asked. "Oh, you haven't heard then, Mr. McPhee left me some property." "No, no, I hadn't heard, how kind of him." "Aye, said Mary, but I'd much rather he were still here with us." "Can you come in for a while?" "No thank you, we have to get back to work, we've been gone two days already, maybe next time." Finally they arrived back at the bakery. "You're back," everyone cried. "Aye, finally," said Mary. "How did it go?" asked Catherine. "It went well, we saw a second solicitor for another opinion and he highly recommended Duncan McMann." "Everything seems to be in order." "We need to talk about things tonight; I have to make some decisions." "Oh, I almost forgot, I'll be right back." Mary ran out to the carriage and brought in the blueberries. "You wouldn't believe all the wild blueberries Henry has behind the cottage; Peter found them when he went for a walk." "We stayed at Henry's cottage, it's lovely, the kitchen has windows on all sides; it's very relaxing there." The rest of the day, Mary was subdued; everyone assumed she was tired from the trip, but the truth was, she just couldn't get Henry off her mind.

She knew Henry had been hurt and she felt badly about it but the kiss had evoked emotion in her and she was scared of it.

When lunch was complete and they had cleaned up, Mary asked Ethan and Katie to join her at the table. "What's up?" Katie said. "I have to make some decisions and they will be dependent upon your answers." "Would you and Ethan move in here?" "It would solve the problem of watching the children and there certainly is enough room." She continued, "Ethan could expand his shop it wouldn't be hard to do with Richard's help." "Mum and Da are getting older, the farm isn't making any money, and I thought they could move into your house." "Now, before you say anything, there would be nothing for you to do except sign the deed." "One other thing, Da has always talked about a hardware store, there is a lot of room in the shed; he could easily convert it." "I don't know what to say, Mary," Ethan said. "Why would you do this, the money is yours and Charles has already provided me a monthly allotment?" "The house is yours for the taking, Ethun, I don't want the house or anything else," she replied. "Think about it, will you?" "Peter and I will stop over on our way home; we have some gifts for the children."

That evening, at home, Mary talked to her Mum and Da about the move. "They, like Ethan, were hesitant, but agreed to at least consider it." John though the hardware store was a good idea, something needed in the village and what he had dreamed about, but wanted Mary to know that he would return her investment when he could." "I don't need it, Da, I have more than I will ever use." "Shall we, Peter?" she said. They produced the presents for everyone which of course caused a lot of excitement. She would have to go to Richard's tomorrow so they could have their presents too. That night, she dreamt about the little kitchen with all the windows and a man with intense black eyes sitting at the table waiting for her.

The dance was coming on Saturday. Mary wondered if Henry might show up after all. He didn't know that the kiss he had given her had terrified her, she was sure she had feelings for him. He was a gentle, educated, handsome man, she would be lucky to have him. The lasses were all a flitter getting ready for the dance and Mary decided that she would go; maybe he would be there. She dressed and then fixed her hair with the hairpiece he had given her. They left, with their baked goods in hand. It was customary for all the women to bring something to eat. They heard the Piper playing before they reached the square. Peter and Tricia were already there as were Richard and Sarah who wouldn't stay long with the bairn, but it was a lovely evening and the fresh air would do him good. For once the lasses acted like young women, they looked bonnie in their new dresses and didn't bicker at all; in fact they were getting along splendidly. Mary saw Colleen and Harry and waved; they were sitting with Tom and Harriet. MacAlduie's stopped by to say hello; Henry wasn't with them and Mary's heart sank. Mrs. MacAlduie told Mary that she had brought a blueberry pie and Mary laughed and said that she had made tarts again. The evening wore on and it seemed that everyone was having a good time. Mary watched John and Catherine dance; he seemed to be in a jolly mood. Soon, everyone was packing up for home. Mary saw Rebecca talking to a young lad. "Ah, she chuckled to herself; I thought she hated lads" It was a merry ride home, everyone talking about who they had seen, what they were wearing, and so on, and so on. Mary nodded and smiled but added nothing to the conversation.

The following weeks were busy for all. They started work on the hardware store and Mary sent a telegram to the Shipping Agent asking for a list of items they could buy for inventory. She talked to Richard and Sarah, telling them they could have money if they wished, or property, they just needed to tell her so she could arrange it. John and Catherine decided to move into Ethan and Katie's home and they, in turn, would move into Charles house Weekend after weekend went by and still no sign of Henry. Finally, just before winter set in, Mary went to Peter. "I know I've asked you for a lot of favors, but I need to go to Henry's on Saturday afternoon." "Henry's?" he asked. "Yes, I must see him." "Ok, Mary, as you wish, should Tricia come along?" "No, not this time, Peter, it's a rather private matter." She left Peter wondering what in the world she was up to now. One never knew with Mary.

On Saturday, they headed for Henry's all bundled up in blankets; it was starting to get cold. When they arrived, Mary saw him outside by the shed and her heart leapt at the sight of him. When the cart stopped, she asked Peter if he would go inside, she wanted to talk to Henry alone. Peter did as he was asked. Henry looked up at her and said with no emotion, "Whatever are you doing here today?" "I've come to see if you are alright, we haven't seen you for a long time." "I'm surprised you noticed," he said. She walked up to him and took his hands. "I owe you an apology, I've been trying to fight it but I can't anymore, I love you." He touched her hair and wondered if he had heard correctly. Then, in unison, they grabbed each other and kissed for a long time." He pushed her up against the side of the shed and they leaned into each other until he emitted a groan, "Oh Mary, Oh Mary, I thought this day would never come." "I'd given up." She put her arms around the back of his head and pulled him to her and they kissed again, neither wanting to be the first one to let go." Mary felt a passion that was new to her; there was no longer any doubt in her mind that she was in love with him. He took her hand, "Let's go inside where it's warm or we'll both catch our death of cold." Peter saw them coming, hand in hand. He let out a long sigh; finally she had come around, the absence must have gotten to her. He was happy for both of them. They spent the afternoon in the sitting room, Mary snuggled up to Henry. Finally, Peter said, I hate to say it but we should go, Mary, it gets pretty cold when the sun goes down." "You're right, she said, we should go." They embraced and kissed again, both glad that Peter was in the room; something had ignited between them and it was hard to draw away. "I'll see you on Saturday, weather permitting," he said. "Don't come if the weather is bad, I don't want to worry." "I won't, I promise," he said.

That evening, Mary announced to the family, "Henry and I are seeing each other, I thought you should know." She offered no further explanation.

CHAPTER THIRTY

William was hobbling around pretty well on his crutches until he couldn't stand the pain in his armpits. They were going to let him go home soon; maybe even the end of the week. He was getting some feeling back in the fingers but he couldn't straighten them yet; nor his leg. He avoided looking in the mirror because he still couldn't stand the sight of the scar. He sat in the chair, waiting for Abby when he heard a clanking noise. The noise stopped, and the door opened; in came the nurse with a wheelchair, on the wheelchair was a big bow. Immediately he thought, "Kristine, that's what she was up to." The nurse showed him how to put on the brake and suggested that he not try to use it without assistance. "Make sure you call someone to help when you are ready to sit in it." The nurse left and he took his crutch, released the brake and pushed it back and forth until finally he had it right next to his chair. He took his crutches, stood up and then plopped down in the chair, forgetting the brake wasn't set. Luckily for him, he didn't fall. He fiddled with the door handle then opened it and rolled himself out to the hallway. Immediately, a nurse came after him, "What do you think you are doing?" "Didn't I tell you to wait for someone to help?" "Aye, he replied, but I managed on me own." "Where do you think you're going then?" "Nowhere, he said, I've been looking at these four walls for weeks now; I just wanted to see something different." "I want to make sure you ladies are really working out here," he said with a big grin on his face. The nurse couldn't help but smile herself and she shook her head, "Go ahead then, I can see you're determined, if you need assistance, let me know and I will come and help; and please, for all of our sakes, stay away from the stairway." He winked at her, and off he went. She thought what a shame this had happened to him; "My God, she said, he is so handsome and his smile makes you melt." "You have to count your blessings, she thought, "He's still alive and able to get around." She thought about his friendship with Abigale and wondered if it could be more than just friendship.

William knew Abby would be coming soon so he wheeled his chair all the way down the hall to see what she would do when she found the room empty. The nurses put up with his behavior, only because they knew what he had been through the last few months and also because he had captured their hearts. He saw her coming in her usual manner of looking down as she walked. Soon, she came back out of the room and headed to the nurse's station. He wheeled his chair down the hall toward her; she looked up and saw him. "William?" "Where in the world did you get the chair?" "Kristine, it came with a big bow on it." She shook her head, "That's what she was talking about in the post, I guess now we know." "Aye," I guess so. "What a wonderful gift, and an expensive one." "I agree; I'll have to send her back a post and thank her; would you be able to get me paper, pen and an envelope?" "Yes, I'll find some, are you ready to go back into your room yet?" "Aye, can you push the chair, me arms are all worn out." She scolded him, "You always overdue, remember what the doctor said." "He says I can go home next week." She smiled, thinking that he had called it home. "Good, everything is ready and waiting for you." She wheeled him into the room; then insisted that he climb into bed and she helped him elevate his leg. "How long have you been out there running around in the chair; you still have to keep your leg elevated part of the day like the doctor has asked you to do." She brought the satchel to the bed and asked him what clothes he wanted to wear home, she would take the rest of his things to the flat. "I'll see you later, she said, I've got to go to work now." "Come here a minute, Miss Flighty Whitey," he said in his teasing voice. She stood over his bed. "Yes?" "No, he said, come here," and he touched her shoulder and pulled her toward him. He wrapped his arms around her. "I love you, Abby." She lifted her head and looked at him. He touched her hair for a moment, then pulled her to him and kissed her. She was so shocked that she pulled her head away and emitted an "oh," then touched her hand to her lips. She walked to the door, then turned and looked at him. "I love you too, she said, I have for some time now." "Aye I know, Abby, I know." She felt as if her lips were burning; it was the first kiss she had ever received, although, like any lass, she had dreamed of the moment. Now that it had come, it scared her. William chuckled to himself, Abby was such a timid little thing but she had the heart and soul of a million men. How he had come to love her, he wasn't sure himself but love her he did.

He picked up the pen and paper and began his letter to Kristine. He was finally able to write again with his good hand, although he had to hold the pen differently because of his fingers, it was much more legible now. He began: *My Dearest Kristine: I have lain here these past weeks trying to figure out your cryptic post but never would have expected such a generous and thoughtful gift, and yet, that's you isn't it, always generous and thoughtful. I look at the chair as freedom after lying here in this room so long. I'm not sure the nurses feel the same; I have driven them crazy with my trips up and down the hallway. I'll never know why you continue to bestow upon me these gifts when I have nothing to give you in return except my friendship. I hope that someday, I will be able to make it up to you. I am told that this will be my last week here. Hooray, I can't wait to see life outside these walls again. That is not to take lightly that I owe them me life; everyone here has been so kind to a penniless country boy like me. When you come to Glasgow, and I hope you do, please come and visit me. You will find my flat attached to McCleary's Cigars, Tobacco & General Men's Emporium at 536 High Street. I will so be looking forward to seeing you again; I miss you! And as always I still have my most treasured possession beside me at all times, the Loch Tay engraving you gave to me; Your dearest friend William.* He folded the letter and placed it in the envelope but didn't seal it as he didn't want Abby to think he had secrets from her.

All week, William was excited to begin his new life, such as it would be. At times, he was haunted by memories of Mary, Killin, his mother, Harry and the good times they had. He pushed the thoughts aside because they brought feelings of guilt that he could not deal with. Abby told her Father about the wheelchair, he had a hard time understanding what the connection between this lass and William was and he hoped it wouldn't cause a problem for Abby in the future. This time he would have to trust his daughters' instincts and hope for the best. He told her he would send a carriage with an extra hand to help William in and out of it.

Finally the day of release was here and William sat in the chair, his few belongings by his side. No one would have guessed that he was scared inside, he had never feared for his future until now. To calm his nerves, he wheeled his chair out to the nurse's station and then one by one thanked everyone for all they had done for him. Some of them had to turn their heads to the side to hide the tears; they all felt for the lad and what he had been through. "I'll bring you all flowers when I'm able," he said. The doctor came by and shook his hand, wished him luck and warned him not to overdue so as to injure himself. He gave him an appointment card for his next visit. Abby came to pick him up and all the nurses stood in line patting him on the shoulder as he left. They would miss this outgoing, teasing lad.

Abby had taken the day off. She explained to everyone at work that her Father had a vacant flat and had offered it to William in return for some work. This alleviated any of the gossip she felt was brewing about herself and William. William was able to get into the carriage with minimum assistance. This was the first time he had been back on the streets of Glasgow in many months. Abby rode inside with William and it was only a matter of minutes before they pulled up behind the flat. "It isn't far from the hospital then," said William. "Oh no, not far at all," she said. "When it's light out, I like to walk to work; when it's dark he sends the carriage for me or I catch one myself." Abby jumped out and ran to open the back gate. The gentlemen carried the wheelchair to the walk and helped William in; then pushed him to the door where he had to stand up with crutches because of the step. The gentlemen rushed to assist him but Abby held up her hand, "he can do this himself, he needs to get used to it." It was hard to watch, but through sheer determination, William was able to get up the step and through the door where he found himself in his new kitchen." "He immediately took a crutch and pulled a kitchen chair forward and sat down, pleased with himself but spent with the energy it took." He raised his hand in greeting to the men and breathlessly yelled, "thank you." They nodded at him and left. Abby brought the packages in and then pulled up a chair and sat by him. "The front door will be much easier, there is no step, but you'll have to fight the pedestrians, it's quite busy most hours of the day." She opened the icebox and took out a bottle of ale and gave it to him, "I think you deserve this one," she said. He nodded his head and chugged it down, it tasted good to him. "The iceman comes on Tuesdays, Thursdays and Saturdays around ten in the morning." "If you unlock the door for him, he will bring it in for you; otherwise he will leave it on the step." "Mind you keep the doors locked at all times, there are many pick pockets and thieves in the area." William noticed the windows were all barred; this would be quite different from Killin where you could leave home for days without locking anything. "I will, Abby," he said. Now that he had gotten his wind back, he sat there looking around. He touched her arm, "I like the kitchen, it's so bright and cheery; did you make the curtains?" She nodded. "Perfect," he said. She opened the door and brought in the wheelchair, "I'll set up the chair and you can look at everything else if you want." He sat down and moved the chair to the bedroom off the kitchen and peeked in. Next he peeked into the bath and was surprised to see a pump, tub and latrine. "You have to flush with a pail of water," she said. "When you are ready for a bath, let me know, don't try to carry the hot water from the hearth, it's too dangerous right now." He nodded. He moved to the edge of the sitting room and saw yet another bedroom. He turned to her, "Another bedroom?"

"Yes, she said, there are three but one is very small." He continued into the sitting room and passed by the shelves of books astounded by the number of them; he reached out and touched them. He saw the book he had been reading next to the chair on an end table with a kerosene lamp. "Wasn't that just like her he thought; always thinking about the little details?" There was a couch against the other wall with an end table on each end. He rolled the chair to the couch and maneuvered himself onto it. "You did all of this yourself?" he asked. She nodded. Come here and sit by me." She sat next to him as requested and he took her hands. "I could not have imagined in a million years anything to the extent of this, what you have done, it's incredible." He put his arm around her and pulled her to him. "The flat is so homey and inviting and yet, somehow still masculine." "Abigale McCleary, I think you have a knack for decorating, I couldn't have made it more suitable for me, if I'd done it meself." He tickled her and then kissed her; this time she didn't resist. She pointed to the inside door of the sitting room and told him that outside of it was the staircase to the upstairs and yet another door to the store. "I can't imagine why you haven't let this before, he said, I just love it, I mean that." "When my Mother died, Father took everything of hers and brought it down here and through the years it became a storeroom for what we weren't using as well as for inventory." "You won't be able to use the chair in there or in the store, I'm afraid there's not enough room." "It's ok, I'll manage," he said. "What direction is the hospital from here?" She pointed, "Why do you ask?" "I dunno," he said. "If you think you're going to be able to wheel yourself all the way there, don't even try, it's too far and you would have to cross a busy street." "I'll leave you now so you can get adjusted to your surroundings, remember to keep your leg elevated every couple of hours and at night; I've set pillows around for you to use." "We'll talk about your kitchen supplies later, for now I'll be down with your meals; you'll find milk and ale in the icebox." He mustered a feeble grin, "Ok Abby, see you later." This was the first time he had been alone since the accident; he could do this. It took all of her strength to leave him alone but she knew that if she watched his every move he would never become self-sufficient. She opened the door to the hallway. "We don't usually keep this one locked, but it's up to you, you can if you want." He watched her disappear up the stairs then he made his way over to the bookcase and marveled at the collection.

He was feeling tired so he made his way to the chair and sat down, then took the crutch and parted the drapes. He was surprised when he saw all the traffic on the street and sidewalk. He could see a steady stream of men coming and going in and out of the shop; it must be quite popular. He remembered Abby's warning about keeping his leg elevated so he pulled the hassock over with the crutch and reached to the side of the chair for the pillows. He was quite comfortable and actually dozed off when he heard a gentle tapping on the door; he looked up and could see through the glass that it was her. "Come in, come in," he yelled. She was pleasantly surprised to see that he was sitting in the chair with his leg elevated. "You don't have to knock, Abby, just come in when you want; I was so comfortable that I fell asleep here in the chair." "The shop seems quite busy, I was watching through the drapes; I can see why your Father needs assistance; I must learn soon." "In time, in time," she said. "Speaking of Father, he would like to welcome you and visit this evening if you feel up to it; if not, it can wait." "Aye, tell him to come, of course." "If you like, again, it's entirely up to you, we could all have supper down here to-night." "That would be great for me, Abby, I hate eating alone." This would start a tradition, the three of them eating downstairs in the future

"Abby, I need to use the bathroom, would you mind waiting down here for me, you know, first time and all?" "Of course I don't mind, silly." He navigated to the bathroom, this time forgoing use of the chair. "Don't help me; I have to do this meself." She waited in the sitting room for him; it took some time and she heard the crutches drop several times but resisted the urge to run over and knock on the door. She heard him banging the pot and then the flush of the toilet and the clink clink of the basin. Finally he opened the door and stood there, looking pale and exhausted, then said, "I've done it." "Each time will be easier," she said. "There are scones in the tin if you get hungry." "I'll wait for supper, thanks," he said, sitting at the table.

She entered the bathroom and refilled the pot with water and set it next to the latrine, pumped clean water into the basin and then came out stating she was going upstairs and would be back down later. "You don't need to tap, tap at the door when you come, your welcome in here anytime, you know that." He grabbed her hand and kissed it. "Are you sure this isn't going to be too much for you, you can change your mind and I won't think less of you for it." "Of course it's not too much, don't think that way." She bent down and kissed him on the cheek, then tousled his hair and left. Once again he found himself alone; he would have to find ways to keep busy until he could start his training. He decided the chair was more of a hindrance in the flat; he would use the crutches for inside as it was much easier to navigate that way. He spent the next half hour manipulating the chair to an unused corner of the room. He would use the chair for longer distances when he planned to venture outside at some point. He went to the doorway of each bedroom, trying to decide which one to use. All three were inviting and he had a hard time deciding but finally chose the one closer to the kitchen and bathroom. He sat on the edge of the bed and found it so comfy that he lie down and soon fell into a deep sleep.

Several hours later, Abby was busy in the kitchen getting supper ready. She peeked in and saw him asleep; it would be hard for her to go back to work tomorrow knowing that he was here all alone. Her Father stated that he would look in on him periodically, when he could. William awoke to the smell of food and lay there looking around him; then he rose up and could see her flitting around the kitchen. This was a domestic side of her that he hadn't seen before; he went to the doorway and stood there watching her. "You look good in the kitchen, Abby." She smiled at him and he thought what a bonny smile she had; it was something he hadn't see from her very often. "Sit down, she said, you're making me nervous." He sat down on the kitchen chair. "When will your Da come?" he asked. "It will be at least another hour, would you like something to drink?" "No thanks, but I have something picking me on the neck, it's driving me crazy." "Where?" she asked, pulling his shirt collar back. He reached out and grabbed her around the waist, pulling her onto his lap. "Fooled you," he laughed." "You, she said, I think you've had too much sleep." She turned to push him in the chest but instead, he tipped her in his arms and bent down to kiss her. She threw her arms around him to keep from falling and they remained locked in a kiss for some time. This time she wasn't afraid, a fire had been ignited within her. Why he would pick her over the other two bonnie women, she no longer pondered or cared.

"You are my angel, you saved me," he said. "I helped, she replied, it was in God's hands." "I guess you are my knight in shining armor then." She felt good, really good. While she cooked, he kept up a steady stream of chatter about the hospital, Kristine, the flat. He never mentioned anything directly about his former life; it was as though his life had just begun after the accident.

"Let me help you, he asked, there must be something I can do." "Do you think you can use a knife yet?" "Don't know but I'll try," he said. She put a bowl of potatoes and a knife in front of him. "Try peeling these, it's ok if you can't." It took him a while to figure out with his stiff fingers but he finally managed to finish. "All done," he said proudly.

The food was ready, the table was set, and they sat there waiting for Abby's Father to come; sometimes touching hands and smiling at each other. Abby was finding out that William was a tease; he was quite captivating. They heard a knock on the inside door. "That's probably him, I'll go," said Abby. She came back with her Father walking behind her. He stretched out his hand to William, "Welcome home, lad." William grabbed his hand and held it, "Thank you sir, it feels like home, I never expected this, it's just beyond words." "I told Abby if it isn't working out for you, just let me know, I will certainly understand; I'm a bit of a mess right now." "You give me a hard day's work and I will give you my respect, I ask nothing more." "Fair enough, and as soon as you have something for me, I will welcome the work." "Another thing, no formalities please call me Liam." He pulled a chair to the table and sat down. The talk flowed easily at the table and the food was good. "Abby, you're a great cook; this is wonderful", said William. "A nurse, decorator and cook all rolled into one." They all chuckled. "My Abby has had the burden of cooking for me since she was a bairn, I couldn't have asked for a more dedicated daughter." William shook his head, "It must have been hard for the both of you." "We leaned on each other that's how we survived," Liam said. "I can testify that she's a remarkable nurse, she has a caring and selfless nature, and I don't want to see her hurt, said Liam." "You don't have to worry about that with me, I wouldn't dream of hurting her in any way, not after all she's done for me; well, the both of you." "We'll have you in the store soon, lad, for now, if you like, you can start pricing inventory." "Aye, anything will be welcome, anything at all." Abby tidied up the kitchen as they talked, enjoying just listening. "I wonder, Liam said, do you play Maw or Chess at all?" Abby turned toward the table, "Here it comes now, William." Liam gave a ho, ho, ho, that erupted from his stomach. "I tried to teach Abby to play but she hated it." William smiled, "I can't say as I've ever played but I'd like to give it a go, anything to occupy me mind." "Chess will definitely occupy your mind, it's quite complicated, that's just what I wanted to hear, I'll be back in a few minutes." "Liam," William said. Liam turned, "I've told Abby, neither of you need feel you have to knock, I'm perfectly fine with your coming and going at will." "As you wish, lad, as you wish, we'll just give a little tappy tap to let you know we're here." He rose from the table and hurried out the door, Abby was sure that he had a new spring to his step.

"You have no idea what you are in for William, she said, guess I'd better get the ale out for this." Down he came with his hands full; a chess board, the pieces and cards. William rose to assist him. "Stay seated everyone, Liam said, I've got it under control." Abby just shook her head. William sat back down, amused. Thus began the chess lesson which already had become confusing. William raised his hand, "Stop, I need to write some of this down so I can study it later, Abby is there pen and paper here somewhere?" "Yes, I'll get some for you; they are all in the desk by the wall in the sitting room, even envelopes and stamps." She came back with the pen and paper and William wrote down the moves of all the pieces.

CHAPTER THIRTY

Once all the moves were explained Liam sat there quiet. "Ok, said William, let's give this try, shall we?' Liam asked what color William wanted, "I dunno, how about black?" "Black it is then." Liam took the white pieces one by one and set them down on his side of the board telling William to do the same on his side. "Ok, young lad, here we go.' You could tell by his manner that he was excited to have found someone at least trying to play chess. Abby opened more ale. William kept looking back and forth between his notes and the board; it wasn't long before he lost the first game. "Another?" he asked. This continued for several hours, it was like they had both become transfixed by the game. Finally William said, "I like this game, Liam, let me do some studying on it tomorrow and we'll go another round if you want." "You don't have to ask me twice, lad, I've thoroughly enjoyed myself tonight." He stood, "What do you say, Abby, we leave the lad alone for a while," he stood up and they went into the sitting room while Abby picked up the kitchen and then joined them.

"I don't know your preference, William said, but if it's easier for you, I'd welcome the company for supper every night." They said goodnight, and he was left alone once again. He felt relaxed and happy; Abby's Da was easy to get along with; he enjoyed him. He saw the desk in the corner; funny he hadn't noticed it before. She said she had put paper pen and stamps in there; he couldn't get over her thoughtfulness. There was a tap on the door and Abby was back. "I forgot to ask, did you want bath water, it will only take me a minute." "Mind you won't be able to get into the tub for quite some time but you can sit on the chair by the basin and wash up." "Thanks, Abby, if you don't mind, aye, I would like some warm water." She fixed the water for him and then came to the couch and sat down. "I hope you didn't mind the chess lesson, sometimes he can get carried away." "Mind, no, quite the contrary, I enjoyed it." "You wait, Abby, I'm going to beat him at it one day." He pulled her close and stroked her hair and thought how soft it was. "Your hair smells good," he nuzzled her ear. She brought her lips to his and threw her arms around his neck. "I love you William Stevenson," she said. "And I love you, my little angel."

Abby left and William made his way to the bathroom, undressed, and washed himself as best he could, even washing his hair. He picked up his clothes and hung them on the hooks in the room and went into the bedroom where he put on his nightshit and lay down for the night. He fell asleep thinking about how much fun he had that evening and trying to remember all of the chess moves he had been taught.

CHAPTER
THIRTY-ONE

Kristine was in Glasgow, shopping again as usual and about to surprise William with a visit. They pulled up in front of O'Cleary's Cigar Shop on High Street and she told the driver to come back for her around six in the afternoon. She entered the shop and browsed around, gently touching some of the items as she passed them. Liam watched her and thought what a bonnie lass she was; even at his age, her beauty did not pass him by. He walked up to her, "May I assist you Madam?" She looked up and smiled, "Yes sir, are you the owner of this shop?" "I am," he smiled. "It's lovely I'll have to pick up some things on my way home." "Home?" he asked. "I'm sorry, she said, offering her hand, I'm Kristine, I've come to see William." "So you are Kristine, he shook her hand, I'm very glad to meet you, follow me please." He took out his keys and unlocked the door to the hallway, then held the door for her and she passed through. He followed her, and knocked on the glass door. William was in the kitchen when he heard the knock so he grabbed his crutches and made his way to the door. He couldn't have been more surprised to see the both of them standing there. "Come in, come in," he said. Kristine immediately flew through the door, dropped her packages on the floor and ran towards William, arms outstretched. "Oh William, I have missed you so much, you won't believe everything I have to tell you." With that, she threw herself at him and nearly knocked them both to the floor except that William was able to catch himself on the wall. Liam watched, astonished, he had never seen a young lady act this way before. William saw the look on Liam's face and laughingly said, "As you can see, Liam, this is my very good friend, Kristine, she's always enthusiastic."

He bent down and gave her a kiss. Suddenly, seeming to remember her entrance, Kristine stood up straight, brushed herself off, then turned towards Liam, and in a very prim and proper way, said, "I'm very sorry to have gotten carried away." "My mother always tells me, and in her usual way of imitating her mother she pursed her lips and raised the tone of her voice as she said, Kristine, you must always remember your manners first and act like a lady." With that, Liam emitted a belly laugh and said, "I'll see you later, I have to tend the shop, it was very nice to meet you, Kristine." He turned, went out the door, entered the shop and locked the door behind him. He was still chuckling to himself, "My, what a bonnie, but unusual lass she is, she reminds me of a gypsy lass I met one time years ago." One of his customers, a regular, asked him, "Liam, whatever are you chuckling about?" "I'm sorry, he replied, I've just met the strangest, yet hauntingly bonnie lass." Throughout the day he was to ponder at the relationship between William and the lass, they didn't seem to have any bounds of decorum between them.

William made his way to the couch and sat down. Kristine dropped her gloves and jacket, leaving a trail across the floor. He patted the couch and she sat down beside him. He pulled her close to him and wrapped his arm around her. "Now, tell me what you have been doing with yourself." She pushed herself even closer into the crook of his arm, "As usual, Mother has been dragging me to social event after social event and you know how bored I am with those." "However, William, since you won't have me, I've met someone." "No, he said, who? "His name is Gavin VanWart, he's British but his ancestry is Dutch and he's very, very, wealthy." "He is fifteen years older than I am but he spoils me dreadfully and Mother is all agog about him." "He's handsome, but not nearly as handsome as you William." She reached up and touched him on the face, running her fingers down the scar. He grabbed her hand and kissed it. "That's nice of you to say dear, now go on, what else?" "First of all, he knows all about you, I told him that there would be nothing between us unless I had free will to come and see you whenever I wanted." She laughed, "He agreed," and now she deepened her voice, "Anything for you, just name it, my dearest Kristine." William was worried. He took his hand and grabbed her face, looking at her. "That's all well and good, but do you love him?" She sat up straight, in her defensive way, and said, "Of course I do, what's love really anyway?" "You love someone and they dally with you for a while and then let you go." "There's only one, I truly love, and you know who that is." They spent another hour or so cuddled up on the couch talking and laughing. "When will Abigale be home?" she asked. "Around four-thirty, I think, she gets done at four but she likes to walk home when it's light out." "Have you been out since you came home?" "I mean out front?" "No, actually, I wanted to take the chair and go out but there are so many people, I just didn't." "Let's do it then, she said, you must see all of the lovely shops on High Street." "Where is your jacket?" she asked. "I'm not sure, he replied, maybe in the bedroom closet." He watched her running this was and that, looking at everything and finally she came back, jacket in hand. "I've found it, on a hook by the kitchen door." "I must say, William, this is a lovely flat, I could easily live here myself." "I was shocked when I saw it, he said, I expected a one room dismal flat, obviously I was pleasantly surprised." "They didn't have a tenant here then?" "No, they've never let it before, Abby says it was a storeroom." "You say it was a storeroom, oh my goodness; who fixed it up for you?" "She did, Abby, she's quite talented." "I agree, said Kristine, she could be hired, she has a knack for it." "Are you ready?" "As ready as I ever will be," he laughed. She brought the wheelchair to the door and he handed her the key from a little box on the end table. "Abby says to lock the door at all times because there are lots of pickpockets and thugs in the area." She unlocked the door and pushed the chair over the stoop and put on the brake. He rose and with the aide of the crutches he made it to the chair and sat down. She put the crutches inside the door, locked it, put the key in her bag, unlocked the brake and off they went to explore the streets. Liam saw them go by the window and thought, "Dear Lord, hopefully she won't get excited again and accidently push him out into the street." It felt good to be outside again, he marveled at the number of stores, the traffic, and all the people. He had a moment of panic thinking about what had happened to him on the street although he still couldn't remember the details. She tucked her bag beside him in the chair. They took their time, stopping to look in the shop windows, sometimes resting when they found a bench. William noticed that some people looked at them curiously. "Probably thinking the beauty and the monster," he thought. High Street was quite long and they came to a little restaurant of sorts with tables outside. She pushed the chair near a table, grabbed her bag and stated she would return. She came back with haggis and milk for them. They watched people come and go as they ate, thoroughly enjoying themselves. "Best we be heading back soon, said William, I've got to elevate me leg today or Abby will be at me about it." "Yes, she replied, the carriage will be coming for me at six and I want to buy Father something at the shop, they have some very nice things in there, have you seen it?" "Not yet, replied William, but I've been marking the items for Liam."

Once back at the flat, William sat in the chair and Kristine helped him prop up his leg, she told him she was going next door to the shop and would return shortly. She unlocked the door and entered the shop from the street side. "Hello again," she said to Liam. "Hello, young lady, I see you had an outing with William." "Yes, she said but he had to get back and elevate his leg so we came home, I was telling him what a lovely flat he had and he told me that Abigale decorated it all by herself." "Yes, yes she did, I thought the same, that she had done a fine job." "Of course, I'm not surprised, she has the upstairs, where we live, quite nice indeed." "I'm here to buy something for my Father, what would you recommend?" "How much are you looking to spend?" "I'm not sure, she replied, something quite nice and elegant." "We have a good line of pocket watches in a range of prices, would you like to take a look at those?" "Yes, please." He showed her the watches and immediately she spied the railroad watches. "Oh, she cried, delighted, I think he would like one of those, he so loves the railroad." He took several of them out and laid them on the counter so she could look them over. She picked one and he put it in its little velvet bag, then in a box, and wrapped it for her. "Good choice, thank you for the business, will I see you later?" "No, I'm afraid the carriage is due soon." "You take care, young lass perhaps we'll meet again." She left the shop and went back to the flat to find that William had fallen asleep in the chair so she locked the door and made her way to the kitchen to look for some tea. She sat there thinking about him sleeping in the chair and she walked to the doorway and watched him. Oh how she loved him, it was deep inside her and she knew it would remain with her as long as she was alive. Why he rejected her she wasn't sure but just to be near him was better than nothing at all. Was she in love with her soon to be new husband; probably not, but she enjoyed his company and it would keep her mother from constantly trying to find someone for her.

She was still sitting there drinking the tea when she heard a tap, tap on the door. She went to answer it and in came Abby who stopped short when she saw her. "Kristine, you're here, how nice." She reached out to give her a hug. Kristine nodded her head towards William who was still sleeping. "Come, have some tea with me, I've had him out on the street all afternoon." "Oh, Abby laughed, it must have tired him; my Father has taken to keeping him up at night playing chess." "You must stay and have supper with us." "I can't, the carriage is coming at six." "You're leaving Glasgow today then?" "No, we're leaving the day after tomorrow." "Well, it's settled then, that's if you want to, stay here with us, we have more than enough room." Kristine grabbed Abby's hands, "If you're sure, Abigale, I would love it." "Of course I'm sure, and William will be thrilled." William woke to the sound of voices. He could tell it was Abby and then he remembered Kristine was here. He listened to them chattering away in the kitchen, talking and laughing. It was good for Abby to have a female friend. He smiled and closed his eyes again. Soon the lasses came and sat on the couch, still busy chattering away. William quietly slipped out of his chair and crawled over to the back of the couch on his knees, he emitted a loud shriek popped up his head, and grabbed both of them on the back of the neck. There were loud screams and then lots of laughing. He managed to pull himself up and squeezed himself on the couch between the two lasses, putting his arms around both. Much to her surprise, he kissed Abby on the lips, "I'm glad you're home, he said, I bet you were surprised to see Kristine here, we've had a grand time today, but she tired me out and I fell asleep." "What did you get at the shop?" "Do you want to see, she said, aye, we do," he replied. He explained to Abby, "She bought something for her Da at the shop." Kristine brought the package and handed it to William. He opened it carefully and exclaimed, "It's a pocket watch; bye it's lovely." "Yes, she said, "It's a railroad watch, my Father is crazy about the railroad, he'll love it." She looked at Abby. "You have a lot of nice items in the shop." "Thank you, Abby replied, they say my Father has a knack for ordering what people like." "Goodness, said Abby with a start, I'd better be seeing to supper, it's getting late." "I've asked Kristine to stay here with us tonight, and she agreed." "Wonderful, said William, I'm glad." Abby got up from the couch and Kristine asked; "Can I help with supper Abby, I love to cook." "By all means, follow me," Abby replied. Kristine asked William to watch for the carriage and let her know when it arrived so she could tell them she was staying the night. He arose from the couch and drew open the drapes enough to see out. The lasses were busy running up and down the stairs and in and out of the kitchen getting everything ready for supper; soon the carriage came and they both ran out to talk to the driver. "He'll return at two tomorrow afternoon," she said to William as they breezed through the sitting room.

Liam was done for the day and he headed upstairs to clean up and then return downstairs for supper. He too, watched the coming and going of the lasses. "Kristine is staying the night, Father." "Good, good, replied Liam, she can have the spare room upstairs and I'll take the spare room downstairs, if William doesn't mind." "Just don't keep him up all night playing chess," she laughed.

They had a nice animated supper during which time Liam was in stitches laughing at Kristine most of the time. He now understood how William could have bonded with this wild beauty who had a bigger than life personality. It was apparent that she didn't give much thought to what she said or did. The lasses cleared the table of dishes and William asked if Liam was going to get the chessboard. "Oh no, not tonight lad, you have company." "No, it's ok, said Kristine; I have a few plans of my own." She walked over behind Liam's chair and grabbed him around the neck and gave him a kiss on top of the head which greatly shocked him but also brought a smile to his face. "Thank you for opening your home and hearts to William, you know he refused to come and live with me, don't you?" "Kristine, it wasn't like that," William said. "Of course it was William, admit it, you rejected me, I'm a broken woman now." She stood there with her lower lip pushed out pouting. "Come on, Kristine, quit the play acting now, will you," said William. She laughed, which caused them all to roar with laughter again. "Seriously, she said, "it feels good knowing he's here with the both of you."

The chessboard came out, ale was opened and the games began while the women worked cleaning up the kitchen. When they were done Kristine announced that they were going upstairs and would be back down shortly. Abigale was left with nothing to do but follow. William smiled at her patience with Kristine. Kristine was busy gathering up all the packages she had brought in with her. Abby couldn't help but notice the string of gloves, hat and jacket, that Kristine had left behind her; seemingly dropping them wherever they landed. Abby was a neat person but not to offend, she left them lay where they fell thinking that like Kristine's whirlwind personality, her belongings followed the same breeze. "Can you carry these for me?" asked Kristine. Abby took the bags and they both went upstairs. Abby showed Kristine where she would sleep and Kristine peeked in. When she saw the vanity with mirror she looked at Abby and said, "Perfect this will do just fine." Abby sat on the bed wondering what in the world Kristine needed with all the bags she had brought with her. More presents for William, she supposed.

"I'll leave you alone now, said Abby, when you need the bath its right down the hall to your left." "No, Kristine said, you have to stay here with me I've something planned for us." Abby stopped in the middle of the floor. "Take off your clothes, everything except your shift and undergarments," said Kristine. "Whatever for?" asked Abby. "You'll see, you'll see, it's a surprise." Abby did as she asked, because to refuse Kristine anything when her mind was set was near impossible. "Close your eyes until I tell you to open them," she instructed. Feeling foolish, Abby stood in the middle of the room with her eyes closed. She could hear Kristine rattling around in the bags. Then, "Ok, now open your eyes." She opened her eyes and Kristine was standing in front of her holding a beautiful blue gingham dress with a silk pinafore in the front. The sleeves were elbow length and had little silk bows attached. "It's beautiful, said Abby, put it on," instructed Kristine. "I guessed your size; it may need a little altering." "I couldn't, protested Abby, it's too much." "You must, or I will be offended," said Kristine. Abby slipped the dress over her head and Kristine clapped her hands together in obvious delight. "Come look in the mirror, Abby." She pulled Abby to the mirror and Abby put her hands to her mouth. "I've never had anything like this before." "It looks so good on you, sit down in the chair." Abby sat in the chair and Kristine proceeded to take the pins out of Abby's hair until it fell in light brown waves over her shoulders. She lifted the hair and ran her hands through it, then took the brush and brushed it. "You have soft, gorgeous hair, Abby, its lovely. "Thank you," Abby replied. Once more, rustle, rustle, rustle, you could hear Kristine digging in her bags. She reappeared and took the side of Abby's hair and braided it; likewise she did the same with the other side. She produced a very pretty blue hairpiece and clasped the two braids together at the back of Abby's head. Next, dig, dig, dig, in the bags some more. Out she came with some dusting powder, lip color and blush which she applied to Abby's face. When she was done, Abby was looking in the mirror at someone she did not know. She, herself, had to admit she looked pretty, not the dowdy lass who had been passed over so many times. She stood up and hugged Kristine. "Thank you, I don't know what else to say, I love it; all of it." "You don't have to say anything, Abby, can I call you that, Abby, I mean?" "Of course you can, I consider you my friend." "Sit on the bed," Kristine said. Abby sat on the bed and Kristine produced two more dresses, each one as pretty as the last and there were hairpieces to match both. "You are too generous, Kristine, I've never worn anything like this before." "You are a very bonnie lass, Abby you just never had anyone show you how to bring it out before." "Wear those bright colors, let your hair down and enjoy your life more." "I will," Abby said. "Good, let's go down and see the king and bishop of chess shall we?" They both laughed and skipped down the stairs hand in hand.

When they entered the kitchen and stood by the counter neither man looked up at first, they were too busy trying to figure out what the next move would be. Kristine got more ale from the icebox, opened the bottles and set them down on the table. The men looked up, "Thanks, Kristine, said Liam, and then, Wow, Abby, my God, you're bonnie." William then looked up and saw a transformed lass standing before him. Knowing that Kristine had something to do with this, he winked at her, then rose and grabbed Abby's hand. "Madam, I must say you are stunning tonight, may I have this dance?" He kissed her hand then held it above her head indicating she should turn around, which she did. Then he said, "You are always bonnie, Abigale McCleary, but I must say you've outdone yourself tonight." Abby blushed. Not wanting Kristine to feel left out he took her hand and kissed it as well. "Miss Kristine, you are quite the little wizard yourself tonight, looking bonnie as ever." Kristine, taking the cue, put her hand across her stomach and stretched her leg behind her and bowed as she had seen in plays. "Thank you, kind sir, but flattery will get you nowhere?" At that, they all laughed. The men finished up their chess game while the women retired to the sitting room to wait. When the men came into the sitting room, Liam said, "What say, we all take a stroll, the evening is young yet, and the ladies look too fine to be sitting here at home, I know a nice little shop where we can have a sarsaparilla and ice cream." "Oh, fun," cried Kristine. They strolled down the street, Abby pushing William in the chair. Kristine hooked her arm around Liam's and they walked together, side by side, Liam obviously enjoying being seen with a bonnie woman on his arm. The men ordered the sarsaparilla and ice cream and they sat at an outside table and ate it watching the people on the street and talking. On the walk home Liam suggested that next time Kristine was in town, they all go and see a play, he would buy the tickets and they agreed it would be fun. Once home again, Liam announced he was retiring for the evening and would see them on the morrow. They talked for another hour or so, Kristine telling them about her plans for the future, which were sketchy at best. "Just make sure we know where to send our posts, we don't want to lose track of you," William said. The lasses went up to bed so alone once again William washed up and went to the bedroom. Liam was already settled in the spare bedroom downstairs. Everything was becoming easier for William, although he still had little use of the fingers, and the leg wouldn't bear his weight, he was getting around much better every day. It was just learning how to do it with the least amount of effort that was the trick. He thought about Kristine and hoped that her future would be wonderful, she deserved it. She had a way of making everything exciting, even Liam seemed to be a new man tonight. It was so generous of her to open her heart to Abby, bye, how she had transformed her. William always knew Abby was bonnie inside and now Kristine had brought out the exterior beauty. He had to admit he felt a little jealous about the new man in her life because she really did have a piece of his heart.

Liam lay in bed, no longer worried about William's strange association with the dark haired beauty. Kristine was truly a gem who touched everyone around her. He was happy that Abby finally had a female companion to share secrets with and he hoped that Kristine would visit again. Oh yes, she would be welcome, welcome indeed. He regretted they had lived such a solitary life up until now.

The next day Kristine was getting her things ready to leave. She asked if William and Abby would attend her wedding. They thanked her for the invitation but, as William said, "Our hearts will be with you the day but me bones still won't be able to make a trip like that." He hugged her tightly to his chest, "Be happy Kristine, as you always make me happy." Holding back her tears, Kristine turned and hugged Abby. "Thank you for making me a new woman, Abby said; I will miss you, my friend." Kristine threw her arms around Liam and then gave him a kiss on the cheek. "I will tell everyone about your store, she said, thank you for letting me stay I've had the most wonderful time." "Don't wait too long to come back, he said, you've brightened the last couple of days, I hope your Father enjoys the watch." Soon, the carriage rolled up in front of the flat and Kristine once again threw her arms around William and showered him with kisses; on his nose, his forehead, his cheeks and then smack on the lips." She gave a little wave with her hand and quickly opened the door and went out. Liam carried her bags and Abby stood next to the carriage outside. William stood in the door frame and there were tears in his eyes. They all watched until the carriage was out of sight and they were subdued the rest of the evening; Kristine brought a chaotic vibe to the house that was now missing. William sat on the couch and patted the seat next to him, indicating to Abby that she should sit by him; he wrapped his arm around her and they stayed that way for some time, not talking. "I hope she knows what's she's doing," he said. "Doesn't matter, Abby replied, there's no talking her out of something, once her mind is made up, I think she'll be ok."

CHAPTER
THIRTY-TWO

Henry didn't come on Saturday, and Mary understood why, they had gotten quite a bit of snow. Things were getting done at the bakery; a wall was moved in the house and Ethan was able to extend his store to add quite a few more shelves. Mary was grateful that Richard and her Da were such good carpenters it saved them from having to find someone else to do it. She wanted to do something for Richard too but she didn't know what and he hadn't suggested anything to her as she asked so she finally decided that on her next trip to Henry's she would open an account under his name and he could do as he pleased with the money. They had hired some outside help to reconstruct half of the livery into a hardware store and it was coming along nicely, but there was still much to be done. Mary had received the newest item list from the Edinburgh Shipping Company and her Da poured over it each evening, trying to decide how best to stock the store. Once the renovation to Ethan's shop had been completed, the family was going to move into the house; likewise Catherine and John would soon be moving into Ethan's house. Catherine insisted on an oven, so they were going to hire the same mason that Charles had for the bakery ovens. Not knowing when the hardware store would be ready, John had not told the tacksman, Douglas Stevenson, he was leaving yet.

Mary had one more mission, she wanted to do something for Mr. McGregor. He had put his hopes and financing on William and seen them disappear. "I'll be back later, she said, I'm going over to have a chat with Mr. McGregor." Katie and Catherine looked at each other, "I wonder what she's up to now," Katie said. "You never know with Mary," Catherine replied. She entered the shop and found him sitting behind the counter. "Hi, Mr. McGregor, how are you today?" she asked. "Mary, how nice to see you, what brings you here?" "I just came for a little visit, oh, and here are some bannocks for you." "Thanks Mary, come on in, let's go in back and have some tea, a bannock would taste mighty good right now." He lumbered over to get the teapot and cups and poured them some tea. "I so love Ethan's tea shop, I don't know how the village survived without it before." "Aye, he's quite busy all the time, I'm happy for him." "We've had quite a loss, the two of us," she said. "Aye, I was thinking about that just before you came in, I so miss Charles, I look across the street now and can't believe he's gone." "I know, Mary said, the place has lost a little of the cheerfulness it had before." "How are you doing otherwise Mary, he asked, I'm doing well now although I still would like to know what happened to him; it's hard not knowing." "I've been seeing Henry MacAlduie, we grew up together, and I think we'll be getting married soon." "I'm glad Mary you can't live in the past." "No, you can't, she replied, but the reason I came over was to talk to you about something regarding your business." "My business?" he questioned. "Aye, I think Charles would be clapping his hands right now if he knew what I was going to propose to you." "Well, I must say, I'm intrigued," he replied. Mary continued, "I'm not sure if you know the extent of Charles' fortune but it was quite massive, I want you to order those power looms and go ahead with the expansion as you planned, perhaps you could contact The Templeton Carpet Factory, I'm sure there is someone else who could come here and train everyone." She put up her hand, "Before you say no, think about the benefit to the village, more villagers would have employment." "I want you to give all of the bills to me and I will take care of them." "Oh my, said Mr. McGregor, do you have any idea of the cost involved?" "I think so, Mary said, I've given it a lot of thought." "Why Mary, would you do this?" "Let's just call it a continuation of William and your dream, shall we?" "It's a little something to honor the both of you." "I believe that Charles intention was for me to spread his wealth around." "He loved this village, as do I." "Mary, you're a remarkable lass, come here and give me a hug." Mary rose and hugged Mr. McGregor, "I know Charles will be watching over the business and smiling," she said. Mr. McGregor had to turn and wipe a tear from his eye. "Thank you lass, I don't know what else to say." She patted him on the arm, "You don't have to say anything, I'm happy to do it, just remember to give me all the bills." "I might be moving to Henry's in Comrie soon so leave them with me Mum and I'll get them from her." "Oh, and by the way, here is a contact at The Edinburgh Shipping Company I have authorized you to order what you need." She left the store feeling good about what she had done, she felt like Charles' money should be shared with everyone.

Mary had a sit down with her Mum. "Mum, I'm not quite sure how it happened so quickly, but I've fallen in love with Henry, it feels right." "I can't explain it to you, but when I'm there, at his house, I feel like I belong there, in a way, it feels like home to me and when I'm not there, I miss it; and Henry too" "If Henry asks me to marry him, and I think he will, that would leave you with the bakery, would you be able to manage it on your own; there's always the option to lease it out." "I would like to keep the bakery, Mary, I enjoy it, if need be, we can always hire a hand or two." "Good," replied Mary. "You know Mary, Catherine said, I think you may have had feelings for Henry quite a while, you just couldn't see it." "Maybe Mum, Mary replied, I'm glad I've seen it now before it was too late, he's a good man." "That he is, that he is," Catherine replied.

Finally, one day, the door opened and Henry entered the bakery. Mary looked up and let out a scream, then dropped everything and ran to him and threw her arms around his neck. "I've missed you so much," she said. "God, I've thought about you night and day," he replied, holding her tight. She grabbed his hand, "You're half frozen, come, stand by the hearth for a while and get warm, I'll see to the horses." Before he could protest, she donned a coat and hat and left the bakery. She took the reins and led the horses around back to the livery and opened the door. John and Richard were working on the store and they came to assist her. "It's Henry's horses and carriage." "He's here then?" "Aye, Da, he's here." She went back to the bakery to where he was standing, rubbing his hands by the hearth and talking to Catherine. "Da and Richard saw to the horses, they are working out there, you will have to take a look at the progress later." "I'll make you some tea, are you hungry?" "A little he said; he grabbed her hand and whispered, for you." Her stomach immediately felt funny, the attraction between them was electric. "Go sit at the table, I'll be there in a minute." She brought him the tea, left, and then returned with a steaming bowl of broth. "Here, this will warm you up," she said, smiling at him. "I couldn't stand it wondering when you were coming." He looked at her with those intense black eyes of his. "Just seeing you again Mary has warmed me up, I was so afraid you had changed your mind about me." She threw her arms around his neck, "Never Henry, I'm never letting you go now that I've found you." "Oh Mary, the weather just wouldn't let up, it's not the same without you there." She could barely look at him because the want to touch him was almost overwhelming. "I told me Mum how much I loved the cottage and missed it." "She knows about us then?" "Aye, they all do." When he was finished eating, she cleaned up the table and then said, "I want to show you what Ethan has done with his shop." She grabbed his hand and pulled him up and they walked to the entrance. Ethan looked up, "Henry, you're back?" "Yes, finally," he said. Henry looked around at the expansion. "Looks good, Ethan," "Aye, I've got more room now, seems my goods are in demand." "Listen, Henry, if you're staying a few days, you're more than welcome to stay in back, there's plenty of room; we're not moved in yet." "Thanks, Ethan, I just might take you up on that." "Come Henry, said Mary taking his hand, I'll show you the house." They entered the house and she showed him the wall they had moved to make more room for the shop. "They still have a large sitting room left," said Henry, "Aye, it's a big house, they will have more room here than in the old house." "Here, she said pointing to the bedroom; you can use this room tonight; how long can you stay?" "Only two days, then I have to return," his voice was husky with emotion. It was too much, he couldn't hold back any longer and he grabbed her and almost roughly pushed her against the wall and brought his lips down to hers. She threw her arms around him and pressed her body to his. For a few moments they were lost in each other. He ran his hands up her back and his hands wanted to feel every inch of her. She, in turn, touched his face, his eyes, and his hair. "It's unbearable, being without you now, he said. "I know, she gasped, I've been miserable waiting for you to come." He fell to his knees in front of her; marry me, I want you to be my wife; I know I haven't asked your Da yet, but I will, as soon as I can." "Aye," she said. "Now, marry me tomorrow." "Tomorrow?" he repeated. "Aye, I can't see you leave again, let's get married tomorrow." "I have nothing to wear, the wedding, don't you want a big wedding?" "No," she said, no, I don't Henry, I want you." "I want to be with you in that little cottage I love so much." "I want to see you when I wake up in the morning and go to bed at night, you're all I need, or want; I've never been so sure about anything in my life." He threw his arms around her once again and hugged her, he could barely hold back his passion, "I have dreamed of you every night for the last three years of my life or more, I thought I'd lost you, and now, there you are standing in front of me agreeing to be my wife." "I will marry you right now, tomorrow, next week, next year, whenever you want; but first, I must make it right and ask your Da." "He's still out back in the livery," she laughed. "I'll go see him then, I don't know what he's going to say about getting married tomorrow." He grabbed her face in his hands and kissed her not wanting to break apart. "Soon you will be Mrs. MacAlduie, I can't wait." "Me either, she said, I won't be able to stand another long absence from you."

Mary went to tell her mother and Katie that she was getting married tomorrow; needless to say they were shocked. "Tomorrow, repeated Catherine, are you out of your mind?" "I know, I know Mum but me mind is set, I'll not have him leave again without me." "He's gone to ask Da; then we are going to the church to find the pastor." Catherine touched Mary's arm, "Don't you want a big wedding dear." She looked at her mother, determination written all over her face. "No Mum; I don't care about all that; all I know is that I must be with him." "We'll just have family and we can have a dinner here afterwards." "I can see your mind is set, I'll mix up a cake then," Catherine said. "I don't need one, Mum, it's ok; we'll be fine without one." "Nonsense, Mary, it won't take that long, we'll get some bannocks and broth going this afternoon." "You can have your way about getting married tomorrow, but I'll have me way about the dinner." Katie touched Mary's arm, "You can wear my dress, if you want." "Thanks, Katie but I'll just wear the dress I wore to Colleen's wedding, besides Henry doesn't have good clothes with him." "He can borrow Richard's suit, they're about the same size and you can wear my dress, you must." Mary gave Katie a hug, "You're both always there for me, thanks for understanding."

Catherine thought she understood her daughter's insistence on this immediate wedding. William had been snatched from her and she was not going to let it happen with Henry. She had resisted Henry for so long but now the spark was kindled and it seemed to have grown fiercely and quickly.

Henry approached the livery with a sense of apprehension. He was thrilled that Mary wanted to wed immediately, but he wasn't sure about everyone else. What about his family, they would have to be told today and the pastor as well. He felt like he was walking in a dream, that Mary would be his wife was almost too good to be true. Bye, he loved that woman but was he being fair to Mary? Should he have asked to wait a while? Was his need for her so great that he would deny her the wedding she should have? No, it was her idea to wed immediately and she said she couldn't see him leave again likewise, he couldn't bear to go without her. He opened the door and went inside. John saw him and yelled, "Henry, good to see you again." "Good to see you too, I wonder if I might have a word with you." "Aye, of course, step into my office." With that remark, he laughed, as the so-called office was nothing more than a few boards with walls at the present time. "This is looking good, said Henry, you've made quite a bit of progress." "It was Mary's idea, that daughter of mine is always thinking" "Speaking of your daughter, sir, that's what I've come to talk to you about." "You've come to talk about Mary?" "Yes Sir, I would like your permission to wed her." John slapped Henry on the shoulder. "I've wished for that some years, son, of course you have my permission." "Thank you sir, there's something else." "Something else, what is it?" "She, Mary that is, wants to wed tomorrow." John threw back his head and laughed. "Good one, Henry, good one." "No, sir, I'm serious, she, well we both want to wed tomorrow; you see, we miss each other too much." John put his chin in his hand and looked up at the ceiling for a few seconds then he looked straight at Henry. "You haven't disgraced my daughter on that little trip to Crieff, have you?" "No, absolutely not, sir, I can assure you that." "Hmmm, you say this is what Mary wants, to wed tomorrow?" "Yes sir, it was her idea." "I have no objection if you think you can pull it off, I'm not big on those fancy to do's anyway." He stretched out his hand, "Congratulations, I couldn't ask for a better man for me Mary." "Thank you John, I'll treat her right, you can be sure of that, I've waited a long time for her to notice me; in fact I thought I'd lost her." "I thought so too, son, I surely did." John watched Henry leave the livery and thought how strange life could be, he had resigned to Mary and William becoming a couple but fate stepped in and brought Henry back into the picture. "Well, if he could have picked someone for his daughter, it would have been Henry, yes indeed, it would have been Henry."

Henry returned to the bakery, a smile on his face. "He said yes, Mary" Mary clapped her hands with delight, "We've so much to do, Henry, we'll have to go and tell your family, but first, we'll go and see the pastor, I hope he can do it tomorrow, if not, I don't know what we'll do." They scurried off, leaving Catherine and Katie to shake their heads in wonder. They stopped in front of St. Fillian's Episcopal Kirk and went inside. "Hello, Mary called, is anyone here?" They heard the click, click of steps and then the pastor emerged from a doorway. Henry walked forward, his hand outstretched, "Hello pastor, I'm Henry MacAlduie, and this is my fiancée, Mary Munro, we'd like to ask a favor of you." The pastor shook his head and nodded, "Follow me." They sat down in his office and he peered down his glasses at them for what seemed like forever. "What can I do for you?" he asked. Henry replied, "We'd like to be wed tomorrow." "Tomorrow, the pastor said with surprise, that's quite unusual." "Yes, said Henry, you see I live in Comrie and Mary, here in Killin; we don't get to see each other very often in this cold weather." "I see, said the pastor; is there anything else you would like to tell me?" Mary and Henry looked at each other. "I'm not sure what you mean?" Henry asked. The pastor stared at both of them. "Have you been together, is she with child?" Mary blushed and Henry stammered, "No, of course not, I respect her too much to take advantage of her like that." "Very well then, I think tomorrow can be arranged, say two o'clock?" "Yes, thank you that would be just fine." Henry grabbed Mary's hand and was smiles from ear to ear. Mary said, "Pastor, I've come into some money lately, I suppose you may have heard about it by now." "No, I can't say that I have," the pastor replied. "I'd like to make a contribution to the kirk of three hundred pounds if you will accept it." "Oh my, the pastor said, that's quite generous of you, of course we will accept, the church is always in some state of disrepair." "Good, she said, I'll have a cheque drawn up and sent to you via post next week." "We'll see you tomorrow then; thank you for doing this on such short notice we appreciate it."

When they reached outside, Henry grabbed Mary around the waist and turned her around and around, then kissed her. "We'd best head to my parents then," he said. "Aye, and I'd like to stop and tell Colleen and Harry too." She sat on the carriage as close to him as possible, wrapped up in a blanket to keep warm. They arrived at MacAlduies and knocked on the door. Mrs. MacAlduie was surprised to see them and gave them hugs, then motioned for them to come in. "Henry, we were wondering when you'd get back here again." "Mary, it's nice to see you." "We come bearing news," Henry said. "News?" she asked. "Yes, we're getting married tomorrow at two o'clock, can you come?" She looked at them as if they'd gone mad. "Tomorrow, did I hear you correctly?" "Yes, repeated Henry, tomorrow, we never get to see each other in this abominable weather and we don't want to be separated any longer." "Aye, aye, very unusual, but of course we will be there, St. Fillians is it?" "Aye", Mary replied, we'll have a dinner at the bakery afterwards." Mrs. MacAlduie grabbed Mary around the shoulders and looked at her, "I guess I almost have another daughter. please, take care of my son, he's very special." "I will, you can be sure of that," Mary replied. "Come in and sit down," she said. "I wish we could Mother, but we have to let everyone else know so we can't stay." "Alright then, we'll see you at the kirk son," she said. When they left she had to go and sit at the kitchen table to absorb the shock of the news. Mary and Henry left to tell Colleen and Harry. Mrs. MacAlduie couldn't help but wonder if there was something else behind the sudden wedding, had there been an indiscretion. She hoped not but she knew that Henry had pined for Mary all these years and there was that little trip to Crieff not long ago. She hoped that Mary wasn't marrying Henry on the rebound; she knew about William. Time would tell; there was nothing she could do but hope for the best.

Mary and Henry pulled up in the yard and saw Harry coming with a load of wood in his arms. "Mary, he called, whatever are you doing out in this cold weather?" "I've come to bring some news to you," she yelled. "Come in, come in, he said, Colleen's in the house." They walked in with Harry and Colleen gave a scream with her hands outstretched. They threw their arms around each other and hugged. "I've missed you so much, I never see you anymore," she said. "I know, Mary said, I miss you too, what have you been doing out here?" "I don't know, Colleen replied, it seems there is always something to do." "Come, sit down and have some tea with us." "We can't stay long, Mary said, I'll explain why in a minute." They went into the kitchen and left the men in the sitting room; the conversation between Harry and Henry was awkward as they didn't really know each other. Harry's mind was spinning wondering why they had come together; he still had periods of depression over losing his best friend, William. In the kitchen Mary said, "I suppose you wonder why I've come here with Henry?" "Aye, I did," said Colleen, he's very handsome isn't he?" Mary smiled, "Aye, I think so, I, that is, we, have come to love each other." "Good, Mary, I'm happy for you." "He teaches in Comrie, we don't get to see each other very often; it's been difficult." She grabbed Colleen's hands, "Oh, Colleen, we're getting married tomorrow, and I want you to come if you can." "Married, tomorrow?" "Aye, I know, I know, it's sudden but I need to be there, with him, I miss him so." "I don't want to lose him, you know, like William." Colleen threw her arms around her and held her. "I'll be there, don't you worry; I wouldn't miss it for anything Mary." Mary gave her a kiss on the cheek. "Thank you, it would mean the world to me, I know its sudden notice, but would you stand beside me." "Aye, I'll stand beside you, what time is it?" "Oh, laughed Mary, two o'clock at St. Fillians, we've having a dinner afterward in the bakery." They fixed the tea and brought it into the sitting room where the men were waiting. "Guess what, Colleen said, Mary's brought some news." "Aye, I heard, Henry was just telling me." said Harry. "We can't stay but a minute, Mary said, there's so much we need to do to get ready for tomorrow." "Both of you must come to Comrie and stay with us some time, we have plenty of room; you'll love it there, I do." "Aye, I'd like that, we'll come, won't we Harry?" Harry just nodded but made no further comment. It crossed Mary's mind that Harry wasn't his usual jovial self and she wondered what was wrong with him. Mary stood, "Thanks for the tea, we'd best be on our way, we'll see you tomorrow." Henry grabbed Mary's elbow to assist her in the carriage and she turned to Colleen. "Next week I'm sending Harry and you a cheque for two hundred pounds, don't say anything, I want to do it, and I'm able." She turned back to Henry; he smiled at her and helped her into the carriage. Mary blew kisses at Colleen as they left. Colleen and Harry walked back into the house. "Two hundred pounds, said Colleen, I can't believe it." "He's after her money," Harry said. "No Colleen replied, he's wanted her for a long time, before the money; she's always rejected him." "Why would she do it?" "Do what?" "Why would she marry him, not knowing if he's still alive out there?" Colleen turned all of her fury on him. "Harry Rutherford, what do you expect her do, spend the rest of her life pining away for a ghost?" "You'd better reconcile yourself to it as well, he's not coming back." He looked at her, "You don't know that Colleen, I can feel him, every day." "Oh for heaven's sake, she said, be happy for her will you?" "I miss him too, we all do, but life has to go on." "Think about what you're saying, if he were alive he'd contact someone."

When they returned to the bakery, Mary told Henry to bring in his things as he was staying the night. He helped her down and then returned to the carriage to take it to the livery. When he entered the livery there was a lot of hammering and sawing going on. He walked over to Richard. "Can you use a hand, can't say that I'm a master carpenter but there must be something I can do." "Aye, said Richard, we won't turn down the help." "Good, I'll just change my clothes and be right back," Henry said. He found Mary and she walked with him to put his clothes in the bedroom. "Do you have anything that needs to be hung," she asked. "Yes, he said, my shirts." "Hand them to me and I'll hang them." He handed them to her, careful not to get too close, he was afraid to touch her. "I'll hang them now, but they will need ironing, I'll do that later." He couldn't stand it anymore; he came behind her as she was hanging the shirts and grabbed her around the waist. She could feel his breath on her neck and almost felt like she could faint, then she turned and fell upon him; they were ravenous for each other. Finally, they broke apart and he was clearly shaken, she could tell from his voice; she felt the same way. "Oh Mary, it's a good thing we're getting married tomorrow." He sat on the bed and she walked over to him and touched his hair, then bent and kissed him on the cheek. "I'm changing clothes and going over to the livery to help Richard and your Da." She sat down beside him, "That was nice of you to offer; we'll have supper ready when you are done." He nodded, afraid to touch her again, it was too much for him. She left the room and he changed his clothes and then went out to the livery.

Richard and John were busy getting everything framed in and walls put up; it was going to be a very large shop. Henry pitched in with anything they needed. Richard offered his suit to Henry for tomorrow. "Thanks, I would appreciate it," Henry said. It was good to do some physical labor; it kept his mind off of Mary. "Peter is finishing up some work at the blacksmith shop and then he'll be over to help," Richard said. "You've made a lot of progress, Henry said, it shouldn't take too much longer to get done, I suppose you're excited to open it." John stood and looked at him, "Aye, I am, Mary has done so much for all of us; some would have kept the money for themselves." "I suppose, said Henry, she told me that she felt she hadn't earned it in any way and that the Village should benefit from Charles' generosity." "She said maybe Charles knew she would spread it around and that's why he picked her to receive it."

Colleen was busy trying to fashion a couple of bouquets from what she could find; there was no scouring the fields for flowers at this time of the year. She had some dried thistle flowers and managed to find enough dried heather which she tied together with a bow made from a piece of silk on an old dress. When she finished, she was satisfied with the work. That Mary had given them two hundred pounds was not at all surprising to Colleen; Mary had always been a generous lass. She hoped Harry would come around; he had been so moody and depressed since William had disappeared, almost surly to her at times. She almost wished they would have found him dead somewhere, at least there would have been some closure. She didn't mean to get irritated at Harry but he would have to face facts, after all she was here in the land of the living and it did no one any good to dwell on the past. She didn't distrust Henry, as Harry did because Mary had told her more than once that she knew Henry liked her. Mary had confessed that if she weren't in love with William she would look at Henry differently; she said that she felt something strange when she was in his presence and she tried to avoid him because of it. Colleen had wondered at the time why she didn't have those same feelings for William; if she did, she didn't talk about it. How it had come to pass that she had a change of heart, Colleen didn't know, but she was sure it would not have happened if William had still been here. She could see why Mary would fall for him, he was dark, good looking and educated. She hoped that whatever brought them together would keep them that way for many years to come. Mary certainly seemed happy now.

Back at the bakery the women were scrambling to get everything ready for the dinner tomorrow. They put a sign on the front that they would be closed for a private party. The cake was out of the oven and cooling for decorating. Mary ordered more ale and ice and Katie had gone home for a while, she wanted to get the wedding dress and bring it back to see if it would fit Mary. There were no customers at the present time; so Catherine took the opportunity to have a few words with her daughter. "Mary, you know what your duties towards your husband are, don't you." Mary smiled, "Aye Mum, Colleen and I talked about it; all the lasses do." "A man has needs, she continued, sometimes you won't feel like complying, but it's your duty as a wife." Mary blushed, "Mum, you're embarrassing me." "I just want you to understand that if a man doesn't get what he needs at home, he will find it elsewhere." Mary touched her mother's arm, "I understand, Mum, I have those same feelings towards him." This time her mother was surprised, "You do?" "Yes Mum, I do, that's another reason we wanted to get married now, the absences have increased the passion in both of us and Henry doesn't want anything to happen." "He's an honorable man, your Da saw that in him years ago," Catherine said. Mary smiled, "Aye, maybe that's why I was so resistant to him, because I knew Da liked him so much." "You're not just settling for him then, I mean, because of what has happened?" "No, Mum, maybe I was finally able to see him after what happened, but I'm definitely not settling, I love him." "When I'm not with him I ache inside, he's a good man, and I realized he's always been there for me." She smiled at her mother, "Even when I wasn't exactly nice to him." Catherine hugged her daughter, "I'm glad we had this talk, I feel so much better."

Katie returned with the dress and the lasses headed back to the bedroom to try it on. It fit almost perfectly. "Oh Mary, you're going to be the most bonnie bride, Katie exclaimed, I'm so happy for you!" Mary hugged her sister. "I can't explain it, Katie, but something happened between the two of us; something unspoken, I felt weak when he looked at me, it happened during the trip to Crieff." "It's called a spark, Mary, maybe you finally saw him for the man he is." "Maybe, said Mary." If Peter could have been a fly on the wall he might have attributed it to the conversation he'd had with Mary when he told her that a number of other lasses were interested in Henry. There's nothing like a little prick of jealousy to ignite a flame; persistence doesn't hurt either and Henry certainly had plenty of that.

The men came in at supper and the woman had food ready and waiting along with cold bottles of ale. They had accomplished quite a lot that afternoon and were ready to start putting up shelves, painting and all the small details that still needed to be done. John had ordered the inventory and it would be arriving sometime in the near future. Richard was going to build a desk in John's office along with more shelves. The women cleared the dishes and the men continued to talk and drink ale throughout the evening; finally Catherine said they would take the cart and go home, John and Richard could come later with Peter. Henry, of course, was staying at the bakery. "Ok, dear, we'll be home later, John said, this will have to be Henry's stag night as he didn't give us time to plan a proper one." "Don't worry Mary, we won't tar and feather him and leave him tied to the lamp post all night." With that, all of the men laughed. It was a chilly night but they always had plenty of horsehair blankets in the carriages and carts this time of year. Normally, the women didn't drive the carts but most of them knew how in case of emergencies so they left; they dropped Katie off at her home. Katie said she would see them at the kirk tomorrow; hopefully shortly before the service. Mary would get dressed in a room at the kirk; she didn't know that Catherine had contacted the Piper and he was available to play the Highland March at the wedding and greet the guests. The lasses were already in bed when they arrived home and they didn't wake them to tell them about the wedding. Mary and her mother had some milk and a snack and then went to bed as well; it would be a long day tomorrow. Peter and John arrived much later that evening, something that was unusual for John. Peter would have to find Tricia tomorrow morning to see if she would be able to come to the wedding. Mary had a hard time falling asleep; she pictured Henry sleeping only a few miles away and she wondered how it would feel to be snuggled up beside him in bed.

They all slept well that night, even Henry, in his new surroundings. Late next morning, they all headed to the bakery to finish up last minute details. Colleen was going to meet Mary there; Harry would drop her off later. Catherine finished decorating the cake; other than that, everything was ready. It wasn't long before Henry wandered out into the shop, looking sleepy and disheveled. Mary had to smile at the sight of him; it must have been quite the evening. She thought he looked adorable, all sleepy with his hair messed up. She couldn't wait to wake up next to him tomorrow morning. "What would you like to eat this morning," she asked him. He pulled her to him and gave her a kiss. "I don't know, maybe some porridge and tea?" "Have a seat then, I'll get it for you." "Are you sure the bride is supposed to be working today?" he teased. "This isn't work, Henry; it's practice," she said laughing. "Judging from all the empty ale bottles, you men had quite the time last night." "And feeling it this morning, Mary, my head is killing me." She fixed the breakfast and then sat by him as he ate. "You haven't changed your mind have you, at the sight of me this morning?" "No, she said, I think you look cute." "Cute?" he asked. "Aye, cute, she repeated, did you want some ale to go with the porridge?" "No, I've had quite enough Mary," he said. "I love you, Henry MacAlduie," she replied then rose, gave him a kiss on the forehead and went back to the kitchen. He finished breakfast, wandered into the kitchen and announced he was going to clean up and try on the suit that Richard had brought over. "Did you want to see it?" he asked on the pretense of getting her alone. She played along with him. "Aye, I would." She followed him to the house and as soon as they turned the corner, he grabbed her by the shoulders and held her in a long kiss. "This might be the last kiss you receive as a single woman," he teased. "Unless I change me mind." "You wouldn't dare, not now," he said. "I guess you'll just have to wait and see if I come down the aisle." "In that case, maybe I should just kidnap you." "I'll scream for help." He tickled her and then once again they were locked together. It was hard to break away but she gently pushed away from his chest and breathlessly said, "I'll see you later." "Later Mary, I love you," he replied. Mary went back into the shop and resumed cleaning up in the kitchen, smiling the whole time.

Henry tried on the suit and it fit almost perfectly if perhaps just a shade too long. No matter, all eyes would be on the bride anyway, he was just glad to have something nice to wear. He lay on the bed and before he knew it, he was fast asleep again. Mrs. MacAlduie came into the shop and everyone came to greet her with smiles and hugs. She told them that the rest of the family had gone to her daughter's house but that she had come to see Henry for a moment. "He's right in back, in the house, Catherine said, just go ahead in." She entered the house and called for him, "Henry, are you in here?" He woke to the sound of his mother calling him and lay there trying to get his bearings. "I'm in here, he called; I've fallen asleep." He sat on the edge of the bed and his mother entered the room. "Well, I guess today is a big day for you then?" "Yes, he said, one that's been a long time coming." "Listen, Henry, I know the wedding was a sudden decision and I wondered if you had thought about a ring?" Shock registered on Henry's face, "A ring, oh no, I have none, what will I do." She smiled at him. "That's why I'm here, I thought as much." She reached in her pocket and pulled out a little box. "This was your grandmother's ring that was given to me; it's lain in the drawer for all these years, now I think it's time to pass it along." "Whether it will fit remains to be seen but it can be adjusted at a jewelry shop later if need be." She handed him the little gold band. "Thank you Mother, you've saved me." She took his hands in hers. "I'm so happy for you Henry; I know how you've wanted this for so long" "I was at the end, Mother, I really had given up and I had decided to try and move on with my life, perhaps find someone else, if that was possible." "It was killing me, but I knew it was something I had to do." "Then, I looked up one day, and there she was in my arms, I couldn't believe that she had come to me, I thought I was dreaming." "Sometimes, Henry, you can't see what's right in front of you." "As they say, absence makes the heart grow fonder." "I think she will make you a good wife, she sees you for who you are now, any lass would be lucky to have you." He hugged her. "I love you Mum." "And I you, son"

Mrs. MacAlduie returned to the shop and Catherine brought tea and sat down with her. Mary had gone with Katie to her house to get ready. "Well, our children will be wed in just a few hours." "Henry is a fine young man, we will be happy to have him as a son-in-law." "John has hoped for this reunion for years." "Thank you, Catherine; we feel the same about Mary." "Mary says she fell in love with the cottage in Comrie, and that she felt at home there, Henry has asked us to visit him there and we just have never gotten around to it." "He likes it there too but I'm afraid he's been pretty lonely." "I'm glad he found the position so near to Killin, it's a good fit for him; you know Comrie is very forward thinking in their education." "Mary said he had the schoolroom decorated with the children's pictures and maps, she was very impressed." Just then Richard and John arrived with Peter. "Where's Henry," asked Richard. "He's in the back." "Oh, ok I'll just go back and see if the suit fits," he said. He walked to the back and called, "Henry, are you up, it's Richard." "Yes, come in," Henry said. Henry came out dressed in the suit. "Not bad, said Richard, just a tad long, but no one will notice." Henry laughed, "That's what I thought, all eyes will be on the bride, and I appreciate you letting me use it." "Well after all, we're almost brother-in-laws," Richard said, slapping Henry on the back. "Listen Richard, I wonder if you would stand with me, in the kirk, that is." "I'd be honored," Richard replied. Henry handed him the ring, "You will need this then, it was foolish of me, I hadn't given the ring a thought, and then Mother came this morning with my grandmother's ring, I hope it fits well enough." "You can always count on your mother to save the day, Richard said, mine has gotten me out of a few jams too." "What say, we go have a spot of tea, maybe it will wear off the rest of the ale in my system." "I'm ready as I ever will be," Henry replied, following him.

Here comes the bridegroom said John when they entered the store. "You look good, son." Henry smiled, and sat down. Catherine brought them tea and a plate of breads. "Does anyone prefer milk?" she asked. Everyone agreed tea was fine. The wedding meal was ready, there was nothing left to do but wait. Soon Colleen came into the shop, her arms loaded with bouquets. John ran to help her. "Where's Mary?" she asked. "She's at Katie's getting ready, they will be heading to the kirk soon with Peter, you can ride along with him," Catherine said. Colleen went to the flowers and produced a corsage for Catherine and Mrs. MacAlduie which she proceeded to pin on their dresses. "These are lovely, Colleen," said Mrs. MacAlduie. Colleen smiled, "Thank you, I had to make do with dried flowers, there's nothing to be found this time of year." "And this is for you Henry?" "Who is your best man?" she asked. Henry pointed to Richard. She pinned a single cluster of heather, tied with a ribbon, on both of their lapels. "And one for you sir", she said to John as she pinned the same on his lapel. "Where is your Father, Henry?" "He'll be coming in a little while to pick up mother." She handed him the last corsage, "This will be for him." "Sit down with us Colleen; that was so nice of you to make these." "It's the least I could do, not being able to give Mary a bridal shower or anything; after all the things she did for me." "Your presence alone will make her very happy," Catherine said, patting her hand. "Where is Harry?" Colleen looked down, "He couldn't come today, I'm sorry." "Don't be sorry, it's ok, we understand, it's not like we gave anyone much notice." Colleen didn't elaborate further but Harry had refused to come; in his mind, it was a betrayal to William. She didn't understand his thinking but to avoid an argument, she dropped the subject and let him have his way. Soon Peter was ready to go and Colleen and Catherine went with him. They arrived at Katie's house and found Mary was seated waiting to go to the kirk looking bonnie as always. Katie had fixed her hair with the beautiful hairpiece that Henry had given her and she would put on the wedding gown at the kirk. She was thrilled to see that Colleen was here and Colleen took Mary's hands, "I can see that Henry adores you, I am so happy that you found someone after all you've been through." "He's always been there for me, Colleen it just took me some time to see it." "I'll always miss William, but he's part of the past, I'm reconciled to it now." "Good, Colleen said thinking to herself, I wish Harry could do the same." Colleen told Mary she had been to the shop. "I brought corsages for the men and mothers, ours are still in the carriage." "Henry looks very happy, he's so nice; I can see why you've fallen for him." Mary smiled, "He is handsome, but he's a good person too, that's what I fell in love with." Then she laughed, "Well maybe I fell in love with his eyes too, they're quite intense, they make me melt." "Colleen, I never felt that with William." Colleen didn't know what to say so she hugged her friend. "Thank you for making the flowers, you didn't have to do that." "Of course I did," Colleen laughed. Before long, it was time to go to the kirk and this time they were transported by carriage. When they drew close, they heard the Piper, just as they had for Colleen's wedding. Mary was surprised, "A Piper, I didn't know we were having one; I'm thrilled." There he stood in front of the door to the kirk in full Highland dress, playing his music as the few guests were entering the building just as he had done for Colleen's wedding. They parked by the side door and entered a room where Mary could finish getting dressed. Catherine and Colleen helped Mary into the dress and fussed with her for quite some time. Catherine peeked out the door to see how things were progressing, "I'll be right back, she said, I want to make sure John knows where we are. The men had just arrived; Henry and Richard were sent to a room just outside of the front of the kirk where they would wait. John went with Catherine to escort Mary down the aisle. Everything was almost ready, everyone had arrived.

The Piper stood inside the kirk and began the Highland March. Henry and Richard, along with the pastor, entered and stood in the front of the kirk. Henry was about as proud as he had ever been; still not believing it was really happening. Soon Colleen came down the aisle and then, on John's arm, came Mary. There was an audible gasp from the guests, if an angel would have come down the aisle, she could not have been more bonnie. Henry nearly collapsed at the sight of her and he didn't take his eyes from her as she approached. John gave her a kiss on the cheek and Henry stepped up to take her arm and the ceremony began. If looks alone could speak, it was clear from the look between Henry and Mary that they were truly in love. The vows were said and pastor called for the exchange of rings. Richard stepped forward and gave the ring to Henry.

Henry placed the ring on Mary's finger and with a visibly shaking voice said, *"I give you this ring as a symbol of my love and faithfulness. As I place it on your finger, I commit my heart and soul to you. Let it be a reminder to you of the vows we have spoken here today in front of God and these witnesses.* They stood there, hand in hand as the pastor recited I Corinthians to them: *If I speak in the tongue of men or of angels, but do not have love, I am only a resounding gong or a clanging cymbal. If I have the gift of prophecy and can fathom all mysteries and all knowledge, and if I have a faith that can move mountains, but do not have love, I am nothing. If I give all I possess to the poor and give over my body to hardship that I may boast, but do not have love, I gain nothing. Love is patient, love is kind. It does not envy, it does not boast, it is not proud. It does not dishonor others, it is not self-seeking, and it is not easily angered. It keeps no record of wrongs. Love does not delight in evil but rejoices with the truth. It always protects, always trusts, always hopes and always perseveres. Love never fails.* The pastor then placed his hands on the heads of Henry and Mary, "As God is my witness and before these people, I now pronounce you husband and wife." Let us now bow in prayer: *Lord, help us to remember when we first met and the strong friendship that grew between us through the years and developed into love. Let nothing divide us from each other. We ask that our words, always be kind and loving and hearts always ready to ask forgiveness, as well as to forgive. Dear Lord, we put this marriage into your hands.* He then said to Henry, "You may kiss the bride." Colleen moved the veil and Henry took Mary's face into his hands and they kissed for the first time as husband and wife. The pastor raised his hands and said: *Let us go in peace.* Everyone joined in singing: *Praise God from whom all blessings flow. Praise him all people here below. Praise him above all heavenly host; praise Father, Son and Holy Ghost. Amen.*

The Piper led the couples down the aisle and because it was cold outside, they stayed inside shaking the hands of their guests. The pastor and the Piper were invited to attend the wedding dinner. Mary was the happiest she could ever remember and she was proud to be standing there next to her new husband. Henry bent down and whispered to her, "You are the most bonnie bride I've ever seen, I am so lucky to be your husband." She kissed him, "I'm the lucky one, Henry." It was a small wedding but there could not have been more joy and happiness in that kirk than if one thousand people had been there. They had hired a couple of the village ladies to have things ready and to serve the food so it would be ready and waiting when they came back to the shop. Mary announced that she was going to change into another dress and she went into the house with Henry. Henry removed the suit jacket and pants and put on a shirt and pants of his own so that he could return the suit to Richard. Mary sat on the edge of the bed and watched him; she was not embarrassed; it felt natural to her to see him like that. Henry smiled at her sitting there and she said, "I'm going to need some help with this dress, Henry." She stood up and turned her back to him. "Oh my, these are little buttons," he said. With shaking fingers he undid the buttons, one by one. "There, all finished," he said. She pulled her arms out of the sleeves and let the dress drop to the floor, then bent down and picked it up and put it on the bed. She turned toward him in nothing but her slip and threw her arms around his neck. He ran his hands up and down her sides and then reached around and pulled her to him; she leaned her body into his and could feel the hardness of him. He pulled the straps of her slip until the top fell away from her body. He kissed her neck and his hands caressed her breasts. They both audibly groaned, then broke apart, shaken. His voice husky with emotion, "We'd best get back to the guests." He reached down and pulled her slip back onto her, then tenderly kissed her again. She smiled shyly at him and slipped her dress over her head then turned her back to him. He reached around and fastened the clasp for her, and whispered "I love you," then went into the bath and rinsed his face with cold water. He grabbed her hand and they made their entrance to the front where everyone was beginning to arrive and sit at the tables.

They sat close as possible together, neither very hungry but eating something nonetheless; both of their minds were on the evening to come. Mary noticed Colleen sitting with Sarah and Richard and wondered why Harry hadn't come. The other day when they had stopped at Harry's she thought he was a little cold to her. Maybe something was up between them that Colleen didn't want to talk about; she hoped not. Henry grabbed her hand, "I wanted to tell you about the ring, it was my grandmother's." "It fits perfectly, how did you manage that?" "Luck, he said, pure luck." Everyone had finished eating and it was time to cut the cake. They went to the table and Henry guided Mary's hand as she cut the first piece. They fed a piece to each other and then the cake was passed out to the guests and more refreshments were passed around. Soon came the usual click, click, click of glasses and John stood up. "To the newlyweds, "We're going to miss our Mary, but I feel that she will be well taken care of by our new son-in-law Henry." "We've known Henry since he was a wee bairn and we now welcome him to our family." Richard stood up, "Henry, we've played together since we were little, I can only reiterate what my Father has said, welcome to the family." Next Mr. MacAlduie stood. "Mary, our Henry has adored you forever and we think he has made a perfect choice for a wife." "Love each other, take care of each other and have lots of grandbabies for us." Everyone laughed and the newlyweds blushed; Henry squeezed Mary's knee under the table which brought a shock throughout her body. Colleen was next, "Mary, I am thrilled that you have found someone but not so thrilled that you are moving away." "Henry, you are lucky to have her, she is the best." Clink, clink, went the bottles again. Finally, Henry stood, "Today, I stand before you feeling like the luckiest man on this great earth; most of you know that I've never had eyes for any other lass." "Mary, I will love and cherish you until the end of my days, thank you for becoming my wife; I don't know what else to say except that this is the happiest day of my life." With that he choked up and had to sit down. Mary grabbed his hand and squeezed it. The last one to stand up was Mary and it was very moving, bringing tears to everyone's eyes. "Today, I married my soul mate; even though it took me some time to realize it." "Some of you may wonder why the rush to get married?" "The simple truth is because we couldn't live another day apart." "When the snow fell day after day, and Henry couldn't come, I realized very quickly that I belonged with him and he couldn't leave again without taking me along." "I love Killin with all my heart but it is nothing compared to the love I have for Henry." "Thank you for your persistence, Henry, when I finally saw you for the person you are, I found life's true meaning." "Everyone must come and visit we have more than enough room and would welcome the company, you must see the cottage, it's very lovely."

By early evening, one by one everyone started to leave. Mary and Henry would spend the night at the house and leave for Comrie in the morning. When the last of the guests had left and they were finally alone, they went hand in hand to the back. "We're finally alone," Henry said. "Aye and I want to take a bath but if you want to, you can go first, I have to brush out my hair." "Yes, I want to," he said. She went into the bath and pumped water into the tub and then went out to the hearth to bring the pot of warm water. "I'll do that Mary," he said. He carried the water and poured it into the bath, then undressed and climbed into the tub. She sat at the dressing table brushing her hair; she could hear him splashing in the water and then the drain. He cleaned the tub, pumped fresh water into it, then opened the door and came out. She saw that he only had a drying cloth wrapped around his waist and she felt her stomach do a couple of flip flops. He came behind her and wrapped his fingers in her hair, "If you're ready, I'll put some hot water in for you." "Aye, I'm ready," she said in a shaky voice. He bent down and kissed the top of her head and ran his fingers through her hair, "You have soft hair, Mary," he said quietly, then went to get the water. She rose and walked to the bathroom and stood watching him pour the water into the tub, he refilled the pot and then went to hang it back on the hearth. Without closing the door, she removed her dress and stood in her shift. He came to the doorway and they looked at each other, passion in each of their eyes. He smiled at her and then turned and went into the bedroom. Mary removed her shift and entered the tub. She lay back in the water for a few moments relishing the warmth and thinking about the day. She was a little anxious but not afraid, she knew Henry would be gentle with her. When she finished, she put her shift back on, cleaned the tub and entered the bedroom. Henry was sitting on the edge of the bed, the drying cloth still wrapped around his waist. He looked up as she approached and she stood before him not sure what to do. He reached out and pulled her to him, his hands on her hips. She knelt down and wrapped her arms around his neck and ran her fingers through his hair then they locked lips. He ran his hands up and down her back and then with the shift in his hands he slowly brought it up and over her head. She groaned, and he pulled her to him and then onto the bed; his drying cloth falling to the floor. As gently as he could in the height of passion he explored her body and she gingerly explored his until finally, he took her. They lay there spent not moving, arms and legs entwined for several minutes. "I'm sorry if I hurt you Mary." "You didn't she said, reaching out to touch his face: I love you, Henry." "I cherish you, he said, every inch of you."

It was still early and they were not tired so they sat up talking about the wedding and their plans for the future. "I can't wait to go home," she said. He smiled at her, she was even more bonnie with her hair all messy and tousled, if that was possible. She was not modest around him, something that he had not expected but it pleased him. "Are you hungry," she asked. "No, thirsty maybe," he said. "Let's go find something then," she replied. They sat on the edge of the bed and he picked up her shift and put it on her, then wrapped the cloth around himself and they went to the store to find something to drink. They laughed at their state of undress wondering what someone would think if they were seen like that. Mary questioned why she had ever thought that Henry was stuffy and uninteresting; now he seemed carefree, fun and sensuous. In the past, it seemed the conversation between them was stilted, now they were talkative and open with each other. She supposed it was her and not him who had changed.

He went to the icebox and looked in, "Do you want to have ale, Mary?" Sure," she said. He reached in to get the ale and his cloth fell off. Mary laughed and handed it to him, then got the ale and took it to the table while he wrapped himself again. They sat at the table and he asked, "Why didn't Colleen's husband come today?" "I wondered that meself,' she replied. "I don't really know, Colleen didn't say anything." Henry shook his head, "My mother asked if we could stop for dinner tomorrow before we go home. I told her yes but I should have asked you first." She smiled, "Of course it's ok with me to stop." He looked at her with those dark eyes of his, "Are you going to miss the bakery?" "I'll miss everyone but I'm looking forward to a new life with you, that's all I want or need." He touched her hand,

"I've been so lonely there, I yearned for you every night; when you were there, you and Peter, it was the happiest I'd been since living there, but when you left again, I felt lost and alone even more so than before." He was so handsome sitting there that she felt passion rising in her again. "Come, she said, let's go to bed." He followed her into the bedroom and once again they came together, this time Mary knowing what to expect. They lay, satisfied, in spoon like fashion, Mary relished the feel of his arms around her; they both fell asleep curled up together, not waking until morning.

Mary woke first and smiled to herself; Henry's arms were still around her. She snuggled against his body, loving the feel of him next to her. He groaned and she felt his arms tighten around her; she moved her leg against his and he nuzzled her neck, starting to wake. He pushed against her and she could feel him. They moved together and yet once again consummated their passion. Henry pushed her hair from her face and said, "You're going to wear me out." She smiled, "I can't get enough of you." They lay there not wanting to get up but soon heard the activity in the shop so decided they had best begin the day. They rose from the bed and Mary put her shift back on then bustled around, stripping the bed sheets and tidying up the house. Henry dressed and helped her put clean sheets on the bed. He got his bag and repacked all of his things. "We'll have to go out to the farm so I can get my things," she said. She found her dress and he helped her button it, kissed her on the neck, and then sat on the edge of the bed watching her fix her hair. He loved everything about her; the way she talked, moved, made love to him, smiled, and laughed. When she was ready, they went into the shop together; he carrying his bag with him. "Good morning, Catherine said, what can I get you for breakfast?" "I can do it Mum, Mary said, come and sit with us." "Katie's not here yet?" "No, not yet," Catherine replied. Mary fixed porridge and tea and they sat together talking. "Remember Mum, if you need anything at all, just send a telegram to the bank in Comrie, Henry and I will check there a couple times a week." "We should be fine, dear, but if something comes up, I'll let you know." Mary asked, "When will Ethan and Katie move?" "I think this week, as soon as Richard and John have time to help." Mary blushed, "I changed the linens and left the others in the wash room I hope that's ok." "That's just fine, dear," Catherine replied. Soon Katie came in and Catherine went back to work. Mary cleared the dishes and took them in back to wash them; Henry gave Mary a long kiss and then left to get the horses and carriage ready. Mary told her mother, "We have to stop at home so I can get my things and then Henry's Mum wants us to have dinner with them before we leave." Katie and Catherine hugged Mary goodbye. She told them she would see them as soon as the weather was better; then went to see Ethan. She left the bakery and turned one last time to look at it before she closed the door. It was time to begin her new life and she was ready. Oh yes, she was ready.

Catherine watched her leave and felt satisfied that it would be alright, she knew her daughter pretty well and could see that she was quite relaxed and affectionate with Henry; apparently their first night together had gone well.

CHAPTER
THIRTY-THREE

William began marking inventory and spending an hour or two a day in the shop. He was amazed at the quality and variety of items the shop carried. When the shop was absent of customers; which happened rarely, Liam explained in detail what he would need to know to run it efficiently. Although this wasn't the work William had initially hoped to do, he found that he enjoyed it very much. He liked talking to people and people were attracted to him. He had abandoned the crutches after his visit to the doctor, and was now able to hobble around using a cane which gave him more flexibility. Some evenings they would go out and he still used the chair for long distances.

Kristine had gotten married and they would receive posts from her in various locations including Paris, Spain and Portugal. William missed her terribly but was glad that she was seemingly enjoying her new life. He studied chess with a passion and even beat Liam several times; most of his evenings were spent at the kitchen table playing. Abby was content to watch them or else she kept busy in the house.

One day Liam announced that he had some business to conduct and he was leaving the shop to William for the afternoon. In reality, he didn't have any outside business but he wanted to see how the lad would do on his own. He was pleasantly surprised when he returned to find William in a conversation with a customer about the various types of cigars they had in stock. Without saying anything he listened and realized that William had a knack with people and he had absorbed everything that Liam taught him. It wasn't long before Liam was leaving many of the details solely to William and he finally felt less stress and was able to get more rest.

He had secretly gone to the doctor not telling Abby lest she worry; he was finding himself breathless more often than he liked.

Then, one evening after returning from a stroll down High Street to get ice cream, Liam fell to the ground. He was taken to the hospital and doctors determined that he had a mild stroke; they kept him for several days and then sent him home with instructions to get lots of bed rest. He was fortunate that he was not paralyzed but he tired easily and seemed a little befuddled most of the time. When William was devoid of customers he would run over and talk to him, telling him who had been in the shop and asking him questions about the inventory, William felt it would help entertain him during the day. Liam was pleased that things were running so smoothly and that William still came to him for advice; they had moved his bedroom downstairs with some hired help so that he wouldn't have to go up and down the stairs. William offered to move upstairs, but Liam said no need, he enjoyed the company. They still attempted to play chess in the evenings but Liam had lost some of the zest for the game; chess took a lot of thinking and he just didn't have that ability anymore. Abby was like a waif in the house, barely noticed by either of the men.

One evening Abby finished up the dishes after supper and then went upstairs and didn't come back down as usual. William made his way up the stairs and knocked on the door. Abby opened it and stood there looking at him. "Why haven't you come downstairs tonight? Aren't you feeling well?" he said. "I feel fine," was all she replied. "Well what's wrong then, it's something?" "It's nothing," "Let me in," he said. She opened the door and he came in and looked at her. "Come," he said, and led her to the sitting room where they sat on the couch. He put his arm around her and kissed her on the lips. "Out with it, what's bothering you?" "Is it your Da?" She looked down at her lap, "I'm worried about him of course but it's you, you never talk to me anymore." "That's it?" "That's what's bothering you?" "What would you have me do, Abby, close the shop?" "I've got a lot on me mind." "No, of course not I don't want that at all, just never mind." He laughed at her, "Ok, Miss Crabby, I get the point, you're right, I have been distracted." He grabbed her and tickled her until she laughed and screamed at him to stop. It was hard to stay mad at William because he had a way of brushing everything off in his usual manner of lightheartedness. "Listen, I promise, every night to give you at least one full hour of my attention, come, let's go downstairs and stop all this worry wort pouting."

They checked in on Liam who was sleeping comfortably. "He'll be all right for a while, Abby, what do you say we take a little walk down for ice cream, we'll come right back." All smiles now, she agreed. They got their ice cream and came back to the flat where they sat together on the couch, talking and eating. "He seems a little under the weather lately; more so than usual, William said, maybe he should have another visit with the doctor. "No, she replied, it's to be expected at his age, he might never get back to the way he was."

As promised, William made it a point to spend time with Abby every evening and she seemed happier again. Liam passed away several months later in his sleep; Abby took it as well as could be expected. William did his best to help her with the funeral at a nearby kirk. They closed the shop for the day and posted a sign on the front door letting customers know where the funeral and reception would be held. William had moments of nostalgia wondering if his family was ok but he quickly brushed the thoughts aside and put them out of his mind as only he could do. Abby spent a couple of weeks in mild depression; she was close to her Father and missed him so much. They reopened the shop and it was now totally up to William to make it or lose it, Abby had the utmost confidence in him and helped him as much as she could. She thought it was a shame that her Father hadn't let her become involved in the business; she could have been so much more help if he had. Customers seemed to like William he had the gift of gab and treated everyone like he had known them forever.

One night at supper, William said, "It's not appropriate for the two of us to be living together in the same house." She looked up and stared at him, "What, you're moving out now?" "No, I'm not, did I say I was?" "Then what, you want me to move, you can't be serious." "No, I didn't say that either, now did I?" Once again, you're taking in riddles William. "Oh, riddle's now is it?" "Here's a riddle for you." "What's round and shiny and fits on a finger?" She answered, "A ring of course." "A ring you say?" "Is that the best you can do?" "Yes, that's the best I can do." "I can do one better than that," he said. "Of course, as always William," she replied dryly. "Close your eyes, he said, and don't open them until I tell you to." She closed her eyes and he reached in his pocket and pulled out a box, then set it on the table in front of her. "Open your eyes now." "What's this?" she asked. He took her hands in his. "Abigale McCleary, will you marry me, I love you?" He opened the box and showed her the wedding band. She let out a shriek and threw her arms around his neck. "Yes, I will marry you." "Good," he said, then pulled her to him and kissed her.

They planned the wedding for a Saturday in three weeks at St. George's Kirk on Queen Street. It would be only the two of them they had no close friends in the city. Abby went shopping for a dress but it wouldn't be the traditional wedding dress, merely a white silk dress with lace; very simple, but elegant. William had no suit, the fine one his Mum bought him had been damaged beyond repair; Abby arranged for a tailor to come and fit him at the house. They closed the shop for the day and were married in a very simple ceremony, then went to a fine restaurant to eat and later to The Theatre Royal on Dunlop Street. William cared deeply for Abby, he owed her a lot, but the passion was missing between them. That evening, she slid into bed beside him in her shift, ready to accept her duty as wife but not knowing what to expect. William was gentle with her, knowing that she was afraid and timid; afterwards there was nothing more than a sweet kiss goodnight. As far as Abby was concerned, this was normal for everyone; she had never had those kinds of discussions with her mother or any close friends. William barely noticed, his needs were met and he was otherwise too busy to think about it. It was ironic that both William and Mary were wed, and not to each other.

They sat one evening talking about the business and the house. "We really should do something with the flat, Abby, as much as I love it, we don't need all of this room upstairs and downstairs, we could be letting it out." "Yes, I suppose you're right, she said, there's more room upstairs but it would be harder for you to get up and down the steps." "That's nothing, he said, I can get around pretty well now." "There's another option we could do." "What's that?" she asked. "You always said you wanted to run the business but your Da wouldn't let you; you could quit the hospital and open a ladies shop or something else in the flat." "It already has the street entrance and the big window and we have the connections we need for inventory." "I like that idea," Abby said. Although she was satisfied being a nurse, it hadn't been her first choice. Carpenters were contacted and plans were made for renovation. Abby had decided to carry a line of ladies dresses, undergarments, hats, scarves, gloves, shoes, hatpins and brooches. "What will we call it?" she asked. "I don't know, Abby, it's your shop, you name it." "I can't," she said. "All right then, think about it, the men's shop has a good reputation, why not call it McCleary's Women's Emporium. "You wouldn't mind, using me Da's name." "Of course not, why would I?" "Well, because I'm not a McCleary any more, I'm a Stevenson." "I know, but what a tribute to your Da, he would have liked the name." "Ok, that's what we'll call it, I'll have to contact the sign maker, there's so much to do and I still have to give notice at the hospital." "Don't get yourself all worked up, take it one step at a time; things usually work out." "I'm not worked up, but decisions have to be made," she said, irritated with him.

They decided to keep two bedrooms, the bath and kitchen downstairs. The smaller bedroom could be used for a changing room so that ladies could try on the dresses; Abby would have to order some long mirrors. Now they faced the dilemma of what to do with all the furniture; the storeroom was already full as was the upstairs. "Either you can sell it or we can build a shed in the back to store it but I want to keep the books and bookshelves," he said. Abby moved all the books and shelves upstairs for William then she put a sign on the door: *Furniture for sale, see next door at McCleary's Men's Emporium for details; coming soon 'McCleary's Women's Emporium.'* During the next few weeks they were able to sell all of the furniture and William had a lot of people ask about the new shop and if he were affiliated with it. "Aye, he replied, my wife is opening it."

Abby gave her notice at the hospital and they were sad to see the tiny, quiet lass leave them. She mentioned that she had recently been married and was starting a shop. The nurses had a little bridal shower for her and were surprised when they found out that she had married William, the lad who had been injured so badly in the carriage accident. "We'll be sure to check out your shop," they told her. "Yes, please do, she said, I'll give all the nurses a discount." With lots of hugs, they wished her good luck and said goodbye.

William contacted their supplier, Edinburgh Shipping Company for a list of items available for Women's shops including mannequins, racks, cash register, counters, tags and shelves. It wasn't long before the list arrived with a note that a representative would stop by shortly to meet the new owner; pick up the order, and determine what the future needs of the business might be. Abby and William spent many hours laying out the shop on paper trying to determine how they could get the most use of the space. When they finally had what they believed to be a good floor plan, they first decided on the counter, racks and shelves that needed to be ordered and then built the inventory from the plan. Abby wanted a two station sitting table with mirrors so women could try on the hats. She ordered several full length mirrors; one for the changing room; four mannequins, a small jewelry counter, hat stands and various other items. The carpenter built a wall across the back leaving an opening to enter the back bedroom, kitchen and bath. On the back side of the wall he installed shelves and closet doors so they could store inventory; on the front side he installed more shelving. They removed the heavy drapes from the large window and built a platform so they could set the dressed mannequins in the window. It was starting to look like a store. They were not the typical newlyweds full of passion and desire for each other but were busy with work from sun up until sun down, usually falling into bed at night with not much more than a good night kiss. On occasion William would turn to her to meet his needs but there was no excitement attached to the act and Abby secretly detested it.

All the work was done and the shop was finally ready for inventory; Abby was excited and William was happy for her. The initial cost would be expensive but Liam had left a good sum of money behind, never spending much of what he made. One day, a rep from the shipping company entered the men's shop looking for Abby. William called her down from upstairs to meet with him. She escorted him to the kitchen table in the flat and asked if he cared for refreshments of any kind. "I'll have a tea if it isn't too much trouble." While Abby made the tea, he strolled around the shop referring back to the order form as he assessed the space. He returned to the kitchen and sat down with his paper, making pencil marks here and there. Abby brought the tea and sat down with him. "I think this will be a profitable little shop for you, I've made a few minor changes in what I believe you will need, let me explain." He turned the paper around and made his suggestions; Abby, having had no experience, agreed with him. He opened his case and showed her snatches of material, asking her to pick what she wanted for the dresses. "I'm not a fashionable person, she said, perhaps you could decide for me, at least on the first order until I can get some feedback from the customers." "I'd be happy to," he said, and he began jotting down on paper what he believed to be the best selling items. It took them most of the afternoon and finally they were finished; he tallied up the cost and it was shockingly more than she had anticipated; this coming after having just paid the carpenter for all his work. "Do you require payment now?" she asked. "No, when the shipment arrives, we will collect the cheque." "The total will be somewhat less as the shipping company gives a 20% discount to all new shop owners; you will receive a final invoice in the post, prior to the shipment." "Recently, ownership of the company has changed so we didn't know if the policies would stay the same but it appears as though nothing has changed, at least not yet." "I see, she said, why was the company sold?" "It wasn't sold, the former owner passed away and from what I understand everything was inherited by a young woman we have yet to meet." "Will the cheque be made out to The Edinburgh Shipping Company then?" "Yes." "We'll have it ready for you; do you know when we might expect the shipment?" "My best guess would be in two weeks but it's only an estimate, we always suggest that you place your orders three or four weeks ahead of time." "Good enough then, thank you for your time." "It was nice to meet you Mrs. McCleary." She smiled, "Actually, it's Mrs. Stevenson; we just used my maiden name for the shop to tie it in with the men's shop next door." "Good thinking, he said, the men's shop is very popular, is it your Father who runs it." "Yes, but he passed away recently, my husband has taken over." "I'm sorry to hear that, I hope you have a very successful business; good day, Madam." "Good day to you, sir and thank you for all your help."

That night Abby told William how much the shipment was going to be. "I never dreamed it would be so much," she said. "Aye, he agreed, I'm sure your Da spent as much starting his shop." "I suppose so, she said. I just hope that I've ordered what people will like." "I'm sure you did, have you forgotten how lovely the flat looked after you decorated it, I told you then you have a knack for decorating." "This isn't decorating, William; it's the way people dress." "I know, he said, but it shows you have taste; why are you always so defensive?" "Kristine said I dress too drably." "You dress just fine, Kristine is a flamboyant person, and she dresses differently." "You said you liked the dresses she picked out for me." "I did, Abby, for heaven's sake, I like anything you wear." "Stop second guessing yourself I'm sure the order will be fine as is." She fixed them supper and then they played a few games of Maw. William missed his chess buddy; in fact he missed male companionship in general. He loved Abby but she was always worrying about one thing or another, driving him crazy. "You know what we should do Abby," he said. "No, what?" she asked. "Take the carriage down Buchanan Street where all the shops are." "We could look in the shop windows and you could see what they're offering for sale, get some ideas." "Maybe we could stop in a pub and have a couple of ales." "A pub, she said in shock, you must be kidding?" "Aye, what's wrong with that?" "Women don't go into pubs." "They do, Abby, it's not like you'd be going in alone, lots of women accompany their husbands." "I swear, sometimes you're such a fuddy duddy; there's a world outside of these four walls you know." "Now you're calling me a fuddy duddy?" "All I'm saying is that we should do something different once in a while, meet other people, go somewhere new; enjoy our life." "I do enjoy my life but if you want, I'll go with you." "I'm going to bed, he said, are you coming?" "Not now, she said, I have a few things to do first." He kissed her on the head, "I'll see you later then don't stay up too long." William lay in bed thinking about Kristine and wondering where she was, they hadn't heard from her in such a long time; apparently her husband was keeping her busy. He guessed that she wouldn't think twice about entering a pub with him, she would probably relish the excitement of it. He was happy with his work in the shop but he yearned for some friends; Abby was a wonderful person and he loved her but she had a tendency to be glum and at times it brought him down. Maybe he would just go to the pub by himself if she was going to stress about it.

The next few days William asked some of the customers if there were a pub where they played chess near the shop. No, there were a few pubs close but none where they played chess. One young gentleman said, "I used to play chess in Edinburgh, but since moving to Glasgow, I haven't found anyone who plays, do you?" "Aye, William said, my Father-in-law taught me how, but he recently passed away, I miss the game, not that I'm an expert at it or anything." "What say we get together once or twice a week for a game; I'm Ryan; I live just down the street." "Nice to meet you, William said; I'd enjoy that very much, should we meet at one of the nearby pubs." "Yes, that would work, how about McNamers, it's between here and my place, just about two blocks down." "I'll be there," said William. "Would Thursday, around seven be ok?" "Yes, I'll see you then, I'll be looking forward to it," he said. "Shall I bring the set or will you?" "It's difficult for me to get around if you could bring yours, it would be easier for me." "Not a problem, see you then." William was elated, finally something to do, he hoped Abby would understand, he wasn't trying to hurt her feelings but he needed to get out, he couldn't understand why she didn't. That evening he paid special attention to her and did not say anything more about going out. It seemed easier to spend time in the house when he lived downstairs, upstairs seemed more claustrophobic or maybe it was just because he was able to move around now. "On Sunday, she said, maybe we should go down to Buchanan Street, like you said, and window shop, we could stop somewhere for lunch." "That would be nice, Abby, I'd like that." "Did I tell you the shipping company has a new owner?" "No what happened to the other one?" "He said they died and a young woman inherited it." "Hummm, he said, she's a lucky one." "My sign should be done early next week so we'll have to get someone to hang it." "Just hire the same carpenter again maybe he'll give us a break for all the work we've given him, I wish I were able to do it." "I don't expect you to," she said. He pondered how he was going to get to the pub, he didn't really want to take his wheelchair; if it weren't far, maybe he could walk; after all he was getting around pretty well in the house. "Abby, let's take a walk down the street, we haven't been out for a while." "Ok," she agreed. They went down the steps and she said, "I'll get the wheelchair." "No, he said, I want to walk." "If you're sure," she replied. William had an ulterior motive he wanted to see where the pub was. "Let's go this way for a change," he said. They walked slowly but William was doing ok and he kept looking at the names on the signs. "What do you keep looking at?" she asked. "Just trying to see what places we are passing, that's all." They walked another block and a half and then he saw it. "Ok, he thought, I can do this on me own." There was a bench outside one of the stores. "Let's sit and rest a bit, and then go back," he said. They sat there for a few minutes watching the people go by and then, indicating he was ready, they turned and went back home. He sat on the inside steps for a few minutes before going upstairs, to rest himself. "I'll be up in a minute," he said. "Did you overdue?"

she asked. "No, just a little out of breath," he replied. He was quite pleased with himself.

On Thursday at supper William announced that he was going to play chess at seven. "Play chess, where?" she asked. "Just down the street, at McNamers." She looked at him, "McNamers; what do you know about McNamers?" "I don't know anything about it, that's where I'm meeting Ryan to play chess." "Ryan?" "Who is Ryan?" "He's one of our customers, I don't know his last name, he said he moved here from Edinburgh and didn't know anyone here to play chess with." "We agreed to meet at McNamers on Thursday." She shook her head, "You're just full of surprises aren't you?" "I don't know why it should come as such a surprise to you, I already told you I have to get out once in a while." "You're welcome to come along with me, in fact I'd enjoy it if you would." "No, you go I would feel out of place." "You'll only feel out of place if you want to feel that way." She stood up, "Right, Mr. Know It All." She flounced out of the room saying, "Now I know what you were up to the other day when we went for a walk, you were trying to figure out where McNamers was." William had to chuckle to himself, she always got worked up about everything; well, she would get over it, he was going and that was that. He gave himself a half hour to get there and peeked into the sitting room where Abby was reading a book. "Bye, Abby, I'll see you later, are you sure you don't want to come along?" "Yes, I'm sure," she said. He left the house and made his way down the street; it didn't take him as long as he thought it would and he entered the pub. He stood, looking around, but didn't see Ryan anywhere; he found a table and sat down. A young waitress came to the table; she smiled at him and asked if she could get him anything. "Aye, I'll have ale, please," he said. She came back with the ale and stood by the table, "I haven't seen you in here before." He laughed, "That's because this is my first visit, I'm meeting someone here; we're going to play chess." "Chess?" she said, that's unusual although a lot of people play cards here." "I learned the game not long ago and really liked it," he said. "Do you live near here?" she asked. William thought to himself, "She's flirting with me?" "Yes, just down the street." She held out her hand, "I'm Maggie it's nice to meet you." William shook her hand, "Nice to meet you too, I'm William." "If you need anything William, let me know," she said. "Thanks, I will," he replied. He sat there a few minutes enjoying his ale when he saw Ryan come in the door. He raised his arm and Ryan spotted him and came over to the table. "Am I late he asked, how long have you been here?" "Only a few minutes, and I'm early." The lass stood at the table again, smiling at William, "I see your friend has come, can I get something for either of you?" "I'm good right now, said William, get my friend whatever he would like." He laid some money on the table. "I'll have an ale too," said Ryan, then he looked at William, "Thanks, I'll get the next one, are we ready to play?" William laughed, "Remember I'm not an expert at this, I've just learned not long ago." "That's ok, Ryan replied, you have to start somewhere." He laid the board on the table and asked William to choose his color; they placed the pieces on the board and began the game. There wasn't much conversation between the two of them as the chess game took most of their concentration. Periodically the waitress came by and brought them another bottle of ale. Around nine-thirty Ryan called checkmate and the game was over. William shook his hand, "Good one, I didn't see that coming, how about one more ale, William asked, then I have to go home or the wife won't be too happy with me." "You're married then?" Ryan asked, "Aye, only a few months now." "I haven't found the one yet, Ryan said, I was seeing a lass in Edinburgh." "What kind of work do you do?" asked William. "Railroad, I work at the station." "Which one do you work at?" "I work at Enoch Station." "That's the one I arrived to Glasgow on," William said. "My wife is starting a ladies shop next to the men's shop; she's just about ready to open the doors." "You don't say; I hope it goes well for her." "I think it will, at least I hope so because we could have let the flat but decided to start a shop instead." "Too bad, Ryan laughed, I looked for a nice flat for quite a while until I finally found one." William smiled, "It was a nice flat, I lived there after the accident, that's how I met my wife, she was a nurse at The Royal Infirmary and they offered the flat to me." "What happened to you?" "I was struck by a carriage on Argyle Street, I'm lucky to be alive." William stood, "I guess I'd better go, did you want to meet again next Thursday?" "Yes, yes, Ryan said; wait up for me, I'll walk with you." "Why did you come to Glasgow," asked William. "I was offered the job and thought why not go somewhere different for a while, I didn't think about the loneliness, I haven't met many people yet." "Well, here we are, William said, I've enjoyed the evening, would you like to come in for a while?" "No, no thank you, it's much too late, maybe another time." "You'll have to come to supper one night, my wife, Abby, is a good cook; stop by this week and I'll let you know what night to come." "Thank you, that's kind, I'll be looking forward to meeting her." William entered the house and made his way up the stairs to the flat, he felt a little tipsy but it was good to have gone out and done something for a change and he liked Ryan, he thought they might become good friends.

Abby was already in bed so he washed up and crawled in next to her. He threw his arms around her and held her. "Did you have a good time?" she asked. "I did, but I got beat." he said. "You smell like ale." "Aye, maybe I had a couple too many, listen, Abby, Ryan is new in town, he works for the railroad, I told him what a good cook you were and invited him to supper one night." "What night?" she asked. "I didn't say; I wanted to ask you first." "I don't care, she said, how about Thursday, that's your chess night now anyway." "What would I make?" "Make anything you want, everything you cook is good." He rubbed her arms, "I missed you." "You did?" she said. "Aye, I did," he pulled her around and kissed her, then made love to her after which they turned opposite from each other and fell asleep in their usual way.

That week Ryan came to the shop as usual and William asked if he could come to supper on Thursday. "Yes, he said, what time." "I close here at five thirty, can you come then?" "Yes, or shortly thereafter, I'm done work at five." "The entrance is at the back of the house, if you want to go to the pub after, bring your chessboard." William waited at the bottom of the steps for him on Thursday and when he knocked, let him in the door and led him upstairs. "When will you open the ladies shop?" he asked. 'Hopefully the goods will arrive next week Abby quit her work at the hospital so we're counting on it." Just then Abby came out of the kitchen wiping her hands on her apron. "This is my wife, Abby." "Abby, this is Ryan." Abby smiled and offered her hand, "It's nice to meet you, come in and have a seat; I'll have dinner ready in a few minutes." "This is a nice flat, Ryan said, you have a lot of room; mine is quite small, but large enough for me I suppose." "Aye, we had to decide if we wanted to keep the downstairs flat or move up here, so we chose this one but now I think I liked the lower one better." Abby glared at him wondering why he hadn't said anything to her about not liking the upper flat as much; soon she announced that dinner was ready and they all sat down around the table. Ryan ate with gusto, enjoying home cooked food; he looked up, "I'm sorry, I must look like a sod; everything is so delicious I forgot my manners." "It's been a long time since I've had a home cooked meal, you're a wonderful cook Abby." Abby smiled, "Thank you, I've cooked for my Father for years, my Mother died when I was young, is your family in Edinburgh?" "Yes, well my Father is, my Mother died a few years ago; I have two brothers in Edinburgh and a sister in Stirling." "What does your Father do?" she asked. "He's an accountant, he works for the University; he wanted me to follow in his footsteps but I found the work dull and boring, I like it at the railroad, I get to move around." "If I'm not too forward, may I ask who decorated your flat, it's very lovely." William looked at Abby, "Abby did, I told her she has a knack for decorating, you should have seen my flat downstairs." "You should do well in the shop, obviously you have an eye for fashion, Ryan said, maybe you could give me some pointers with my flat someday?" Abby looked down and said, "Thank you, that's very kind of you to say, I'd be happy to help you." They sat around the table talking while Abby cleared the dishes and then to their delight offered them tea and oat cookies. "Now you are spoiling me, Ryan said, I haven't had oat cookies since I was a wee bairn and my mother made them." Abby smiled, she liked Ryan; he was easy to be around. "You're welcome to come every Thursday night if you like; William and I enjoy having company." William smiled at her she was trying very hard to be sociable.

They sat around the table talking until it was almost seven, Abby included. "I guess we'd better go before it gets too late." said William. "Yes, Ryan agreed, Abby, why don't you come with us?" "Thank you, but no, she said, I have some mending to do." "Here, she said, and handed Ryan a little package, it's some oak cookies for you to take home." "Thank you Abby, that was kind." He looked at William, "Can I give her a hug?" "Aye," smiled William. Ryan gave her a hug, "I'm so glad to have met you, I'll see you next Thursday then, if you're sure?" "Yes, I'm sure, it was fun," she said. William gave Abby a kiss and they were off to the pub. "She's nice, your wife," said Ryan. "Aye, I owe her my life, she's a wonderful nurse, I was in a coma for a long time and she sat by my side throughout." I wish she had some female companionship, she's alone most of the time." "I have a good friend, Kristine, they took to each other, but Kristine got married a while ago and we don't see her much now." "Is Abby from Glasgow?" "Aye, right where the shop is now, she was raised there, her mother died when she was a wee bairn and her Da raised her."

When they entered the pub Maggie, the waitress, saw them and came to the table with a big smile. She looked at William, "You've returned again; what can I get for you today?" "I'll have the usual, a bottle of ale; Ryan what would you like?" "Yes ale for me too, please." She left and Ryan whispered to William, "I think she's flirting with you." "Me, with a face like mine," he laughed. "That's nothing, does it bother you?" "Aye, that's why I've never returned home." Then, for some reason, he told Ryan his story, something he never talked or even thought about that much anymore. "I was going to marry a bonnie lass from Killin, but I came here to learn a trade first; then the accident happened." "When I saw that I was crippled, and this, he pointed to his face, I couldn't go home again." "You see, Mary, with that he choked on the name, my lass, was so kind and bonnie, I couldn't have her taking care of me, they didn't even know if I would walk again." "I didn't want them, the people in my village, feeling sorry for me." "What a shame, William, it really doesn't look bad, not at all." William nodded his head, "It's in the past now, I've made a new life for meself." The waitress brought the ale and Ryan said, "Well, shall we begin the game?" They played the game for several hours and several of the other customers wandered over to the table to watch. Ryan beat William again. "I'm not giving up, one of these days I'm going to beat you," William laughed. They ordered more ale and a couple of lasses came over to the table. "Can we join you?" they asked. William looked at Ryan then turned to the lasses, "I'm married, he said, it wouldn't be appropriate." "I won't tell, if you don't," Maggie commented. "Maybe another time," he said, quite abruptly. "I understand," the other waitress said and left. William looked at Ryan, "Perhaps you would have liked some female company." "No, it's quite alright" said Ryan. William had a revelation, could it be true that he didn't look like a monster. When he looked in the mirror, all he could see was the scar; maybe it wasn't as bad as he thought. Ryan looked at William, "There's a nice lass I work with, well, she likes me, I like her too, but only as a friend, I think she would make a great companion for your wife, I wonder if we could arrange for them to meet sometime, you see, she doesn't have any family here, I think she may be lonely too." "That's a great idea, let me give it some thought," said William.

The freight arrived on Monday morning and William asked Abby to see if the carpenter could come back to help. They couldn't come that day but arrived early on the next day. The first item of business was to get all of the shelves and counters in place. It took all day, well into the early evening hours but they finally had everything where it belonged including hanging the sign out in front. "Now comes the fun part, said Abby, putting everything out on the shelves." "If you need some help, Ryan says he works with a nice lass maybe we could hire her for a few days." "Yes, if she wants to, that would be fine." Coincidentally Ryan stopped into the men's store next day. "Come, have a look," William said, taking him over to the shop. Abby looked up, she was busy opening boxes and stocking the shelves. "You have your hands full," he said to her. "Yes, William said you know a young lady that might want some extra work, I could hire her for a few days, if she's willing." "I'll ask her later," he said. "We'll be here until at least nine tonight, if she wants to come by, I can arrange a carriage to take her home." "Ok then, if she agrees, I'll see you both later." "Thanks Ryan," Abby said.

Abby put a sign on the door, "Open Soon." She dressed two of the mannequins with dresses, hats, shoes and boots, even a purse and brooch and set them in the window. She went outside to look at her work and decided the window needed something. She removed the mannequins, went into the storeroom and brought out the drapes she had removed from the window. She draped them on the floor of the window and then brought out a small vanity with mirror which she placed on top of the drapes. She found a hairbrush and some hairpieces and laid them on the vanity top, then took some strands of jewelry and draped them over the edge. She placed the mannequins back in the window and then went into the storeroom and brought out a bamboo divider and placed it on one side behind them. Once more she went out the door to see how it looked from the outside. Several women had stopped and were looking in the window. "Lovely, they said, is this your shop?" "Yes, she said, I should be open in a few days." "We love the dresses, we'll stop back." "Please do," she replied. She stood there a few more minutes admiring her work; she had managed to create what looked like a cozy boudoir. She nodded her head and returned inside; as she worked, throughout the day she saw people stop and stand by the window; she was pleased.

William waited for his shop to clear of customers and then rushed over to Abby's because he wanted to tell her something. "Abby, I've had so many people stop and ask when your shop was going to be open." "They tell me they love the window, I'll have to take a peek meself." He hobbled over to the door and opened it, then went outside and stood there. "Bye, the window looked lovely." He came back in, "I knew you had a knack for this, Abby, it's magnificent; however did you think of it?" "I don't know, she said, it just came to me." "Maybe you'd like to take a try at my window sometime, I don't have the imagination." "I'd love to, if you'd let me." "Listen, he said, don't worry about supper tonight you've worked too hard all day." "We'll go down to the pub and get something to eat it smells like they have pretty good food there." "To the pub, really, she said, and then; ok, if you want to I'll go." He turned and smiled at her surprised that she agreed.

William closed the shop around five thirty as usual and went over to see how Abby was doing. She had made a lot of progress, but there was still a pile of un-opened boxes. "It's the pricing that takes time," she said. "Don't forget, the inventory for your shop is here too, I've set it off to the side over there." "I'll take care of it in the morning," he replied with a sigh. Just then they heard a knock on the front door and looked up to see Ryan standing there with someone. "That must be the lass he told us about," William said. Abby opened the door and they entered the shop and for just a slight moment, William felt lightheaded, the lass was thin and on the tall side, she had long flowing auburn hair, and he thought it was Mary until she turned her head. "Come in, said Abby, motioning with her hand, I apologize for the mess, I'm buried in boxes right now." The lass extended her hand, "I'm Bella, she said, Ryan told me you might need some help for a few days, I'd be happy to assist you." "Yes, as you can see, I do need help," laughed Abby. William stepped forward, "I'm William, I'm glad you could come; listen, Abby and I were just about to go down to the pub for a bite to eat, we'd like it if you would come along, the work will wait, it always does." Ryan looked at Bella and they both shook their heads, "Yes, we haven't eaten yet either, we'll go." The men walked behind the women. "I love what you've done with the window, the dresses are beautiful," Bella said to Abby. "Thank you, Abby said, to tell you the truth, I don't know what I'm doing, I just kept putting things in it until it seemed to look ok." Bella smiled, "I think it's better than ok, it could rival others that I've seen." William tells me I should go window shopping someday, just to see what others are doing, he's probably right. "Oh, I love window shopping; I could go with you sometime; that's if you want me to." "I'd like that very much," Abby said. William was observing the women and was glad to see that they seemed to be hitting it off, he thought that was just what Abby needed; she had been so sullen and snippy lately.

They entered the pub and sat down. The men ordered ale and the lasses tea; the waitress left a menu for them. "Order what you like, William said, it's on us to-night." The food was good and the company better, even Abby thoroughly enjoying herself. "Anyone care for dessert?" William asked. Everyone said no, they were too full. "I'm still enjoying my oat cookies," said Ryan, explaining to Bella that Abby had sent a package of them home with him. "Bella, suggested Abby, you should come to supper on Thursday nights, it's kind of a tradition with us now; the men go to the pub and play chess after." "Thank you, it sounds like fun, I will," said Bella, then she looked at Ryan, that's if Ryan doesn't mind." "No, of course not, he said, why would I mind?" "Shall I bring anything?" she asked. "No, Abby said smiling; just yourself and your appetite." The men had one more bottle of ale and then they decided to go back to the flat and have a game of chess while the women worked on the inventory. They entered the shop and William told Ryan to follow him, "We left the kitchen back here, it comes in handy." They set up the game and William got some more ale out of the icebox. Bella and Abby got right to work on the inventory and Abby could see some progress now that the two of them were working on it. Around nine-thirty Abby said, "Let's call it a night, we've completed a lot of work tonight." "I think this is going to be a big success for you, Bella said, I like the things you have ordered, you have good taste." "Thank you, Bella, can you come tomorrow night again." "Yes, I can come, she said. They walked to the kitchen to find that the men had just finished their game. "I finally won one," William said proudly. "We'll get the cart out and give you a ride home, said William, it's too late to be on the streets alone but I might need a little assistance, Ryan." They exited the back door to the shed where they had a couple of horses, a cart and a carriage." "Abby has had them out since Liam died; but I haven't tried yet so I guess it's about time," said William. "We have a man who comes every day to feed and exercise them." They harnessed the horse and Ryan went in to tell them they were ready to go. "I'll come along, said Abby; this is William's first time driving the cart since the accident."

William was nervous but figured he had to do it sometime, the streets weren't nearly as busy at night as they were during the day; it was quite different than driving the country roads he was used to, but he managed just fine. They left Ryan off first and then Bella. "We'll wait until you get in safe and sound," Abby said. "Thank you, she said, I know it's not that safe in this area but it's the only flat I could afford." "I like her, said Abby on the way home, she was a lot of help; she shouldn't be living down here by herself, it's quite dangerous." "I wonder, I know there wouldn't be a sitting room but the bedroom is large and she would have the bath and kitchen, perhaps we could ask her if she'd like to live in the back flat." "That's my lass, he said, reaching over to kiss her, always thinking about everybody else, it's up to you whatever you want to do is fine with me."

The next evening, Bella showed up around six to help and Abby offered her the flat. "I know it's not much, there's no sitting room anymore, but the bedroom is large. "To tell you the truth, Bella said, I'm scared all the time; and I have to share the bath with three other tenants; the only reason I haven't gone back home yet is pride, they didn't want me to come to Glasgow." "It's wonderful of you to offer, but I wouldn't be able to afford it." "But you would, Abby said, I'd just deduct something from your wages, that is, if it's ok with you." Bella threw her arms around Abby, "Oh, thank you, thank you, I accept before you change your mind." "Good, said Abby, on Sunday we will take the cart and get your things, it's settled then." They were getting a lot done in the store and Abby thought they may be able to open next week. "Have you known Ryan long," Abby asked. "No, only since I've started work at the railroad, maybe three months now." "What do you do there?" "The counter, I wait on people." "William is thrilled to have found a new chess partner." "Ryan was pleased too, he likes William." "Yes, said Abby, everybody likes him; he seems to have a way with people." William came down to see how they were doing, "Did I hear my name?" he asked. "Yes, I was telling Bella that you were happy to have found a chess partner." "Aye, I am," he said. "Bella has agreed to move in here, I told her we would bring the cart on Sunday to load her things." "Good, I think you'll like it here, he said, it's much safer at least." "I think we're going to wrap it up for tonight, said Abby, can you get the carriage ready?" "Aye, I'll go right now," he said. He was quite pleased with himself now that he was able to manage the cart by himself; it gave him a sense of freedom from the house.

On Sunday, mid-morning, they took the cart to Bella's and loaded all of her belongings and Ryan came along to help. She moved into the now much smaller flat but seemed quite satisfied. On Wednesday she asked Ryan, William and Abby to come for supper and they found that she was also a good cook.

It was a good week. Abby opened the store on Monday; customers flocked in and the sales were excellent; the women gushed over the dresses and accessories and already Bella and Abby poured over the purchase order, finding it necessary to place another order again.

A letter finally came from Kristine: *Dearest Abby and William, I'm returning home to Perth in another week. It turns out that my husband has an eye for many other young ladies and he has grown tired of me. No matter, life goes on, I've gotten to travel and see new places. My heart is always with you in Glasgow of course and I hope to see you soon. Don't be surprised if I show up on your doorstep for a visit; I need to get away, mother is once again on the hunt for another man for me. Love Kristine.*

William immediately sent a post back to her. *Dearest Kristine: We have been anx-iously awaiting some word from you but supposed that you were traveling from one country to another. I am sorry to hear about your marriage. I regret to tell you that Liam passed away several months ago; he went peaceably and we miss him every day; he often talked about you and how much he enjoyed your visit. Things have changed here but I'm not going to tell you, you'll just have to come and see for yourself. Come as soon as you can, we will be waiting; and please, just bring yourself, not the usual carriage full of gifts. Love As Always; Abby and William.* William addressed the envelope, folded the letter and then gave it to Abby to send, not sealing it in case she wanted to read it as was his usual custom.

CHAPTER
THIRTY-FOUR

Abby found it a blessing to have Bella in the house, it gave her some free time to catch up with the housework and finances; things she was finding it hard to do before. The bulk of the inventory had already been taken care of and William asked Bella if she would help him with his and she spent her time running back and forth between the two stores. Abby rearranged Williams store window and he received quite a few compliments from his customers; in fact, it brought in some new ones. Abby and Bella made plans to go window shopping on Sunday and William was glad he didn't have to go; it wasn't something that interested him very much. He asked Ryan to come over for the day and play chess and they sat in the upstairs kitchen instead of going to the pub. "I think Bella has her eye on you, William said. "Yes, I wish I felt the same way, she's a nice lass," said Ryan. "She is a nice lass and bonnie too; what are you looking for?" "I don't know, Ryan replied, a spark I guess." The comment brought memories back to William and for a moment he was lost in the past. "A spark, aye, he could understand that, oh he could." He tried to push back the memory because it almost physically hurt him inside, "Oh Mary, he thought, "what have I done?" He loved Abby, in a different way, she was good for him and he felt he owed her so much but a spark? No, there was no spark. He thought about Kristine, "Aye, there was more than a spark there, if ignited, it would become a fire."

"William?" "William?" William snapped his head, "Aye?" "Are you all right, Ryan asked, I was talking to you and you didn't hear me." William smiled, "I'm all right, just daydreaming I guess, if you're looking for a spark, I have one for you,"

William said. Ryan threw his head back and with a grin said, "You do, who would that be?" William explained, "I have a very close friend, Kristine, she may be coming to visit soon, I think you would like her; she definitely is full of excitement." "Where does she live?" he asked. "She just moved back to Perth, she was married to a very rich man but apparently he has eyes for a lot of other young women as well; she's very bonnie but quite forward, I'm sure you have never met anyone like her before" "Interesting, Ryan said, how did you meet." "Like I said, she's a very unusual lass; we met on the coach when I came to Glasgow." "She thinks she's in love with me." Ryan looked shocked, "And your wife, Abby, she doesn't mind?" "No, she likes her, you'll understand once you meet her." Ryan shook his head, "She sounds very intriguing I'll be looking forward to meeting her."

The next several months went by uneventfully, both stores were doing extremely well and Bella considered quitting her job at the railroad because Abby had asked if she wanted to work full time in the shop. They were fast friends now and their window dressings were becoming the talk of the town. They spent hours poring over magazines and walking various streets on Sundays looking at other store windows. Thursday evenings were set aside for supper with William, Abby, Ryan and Bella all joining in. Later, the men would play chess, sometimes going to the pub and other times staying home. It was apparent to Bella that Ryan wasn't interested in her and one day while stocking William's shop she met a young man from Glasgow who asked her if she'd like to have dinner some evening. She agreed to go and they started seeing each other weekly; sometimes going out to eat or to a play and sometimes just strolling around Glasgow. It wasn't long before she was cooking supper for him at least once a week and eventually she bowed out of the Thursday suppers.

Abby hadn't been feeling well in the mornings and William asked her about it. "Are you sick again, Abby?" "It's nothing, must be something I ate, that's all." "Come on Abby, you've been sick in the morning for over a week now, are you pregnant?" She stared at him, "Pregnant?" "Is that what you think?" "Aye, that's what I think, I want you to go to the doctor tomorrow; Bella can tend the shop." "I suppose if that's what you want, but I tell you it's nothing." "Just go Abby, please." The next day Abby came back from the doctor's office and went straight up the stairs, talking to no one. At five-thirty, William closed the shop and peeked in next door where Bella was standing at the counter. "Have you seen Abby?" "No," she said, I haven't seen her all day." "Hmmm, he replied, I'll see if she's upstairs, maybe she's still not feeling well." He found her sitting on the couch and it looked like she had been crying; he sat down beside her and took her hands in his. "What's wrong, why are you crying?" "I'm not." "Abby, I can see that you were crying, now out with it, what's wrong?" "Did you see the Doctor?" "Yes, I saw the doctor and I'm pregnant, just like you said." "That's good; wonderful, I'm going to be a Da." She sat there and stared at him, "My mother died in childbirth you know." He pulled her to him, "Oh, Abby, that doesn't mean it's going to happen to you, thousands of bairns are born just fine every day." "I suppose you're right she said, but still I can't help but worry." "You're always worrying about everything, why can't you be happy for once?" "I don't know, she said, maybe because you have a surplus to go around." "What's wrong with that, he replied, are you suggesting that I shouldn't be happy about it?" "Of course I want you to be happy but just once it would be nice if you would see my side of it too." "Look, Abby, don't ask for problems before you have them, you're a nurse for heaven's sake, you'll know what to do." He pulled her to him and she laid her head on his chest, they sat like that for quite some time. She looked up, "I guess I'd better see to supper." "I'll come with you, he said, let's just have leftovers, I'm not that hungry." They played a couple games of Maw after supper and then Abby announced she was tired and going to bed." "Are you coming?" she said. "No, I'm not tired yet, I'll be in later," he replied. He scanned the bookshelf for a book to read, "It's going to be a long nine months," he thought. It was a good thing that Bella had quit her other job, he had a feeling they were really going to depend on her now. The weeks flew by and soon Abby was showing a baby bump; for the most part the morning sickness had passed and she seemed more relaxed about having the baby. She left a majority of the work in the shop to Bella who had been a blessing; she was a hard worker and never complained.

One day a carriage pulled up out front and Kristine got out. She stood on the street looking at what was once the door to the flat and realized that this must be the surprise William had been referring to. She opened the door and saw a young lass behind the counter so she went over and introduced herself. "Hi, I'm Kristine, William and Abby's friend, are either of them here today?" "Yes, William is next door and Abby is probably upstairs, I haven't seen her since this morning." "The shop is nice, real nice," Kristine said, looking around. "Thank you, by the way, my name is Bella." "Nice to meet you, Bella, I guess I'll peek in next door and surprise William, is it ok if I go out the side door." "Yes, it should be unlocked," Bella said. Kristine left her bags in the hallway by the steps and entered the shop where she saw William waiting on a customer.

She stood there watching him; she loved how he looked, talked, moved, the little piece of hair that always escaped above his eyebrow; she loved everything about him. If he only knew how much she thought about him when they were apart; even when she was married. Why did he have to pick Abby? She had practically thrown herself at him but he looked at her only as a friend, she couldn't understand why. No matter, just to be near him, if only for a few days now and again would have to suffice; she would never hurt Abby, not in a million years. He looked up and saw her standing there and a huge grin spread across his face; he winked at her and she blew him a kiss. He kept looking at her hoping the customer would finally decide what he wanted, "Bye, he thought, she's more bonnie than ever." He checked out the customer and they were finally alone in the shop. "You're here," he said, and he grabbed her around the waist and threw his arms around her. "I've missed you so much." She reached up and touched his face, running her hands over his nose, his eyes and then lingering on his mouth. He felt weak in the knees and physically groaned. "I missed you more," she laughed. "No, I don't think so, he replied, have you seen the changes?" "Yes, the shop is very nice I want to look around later can I stay for a few days?" "Aye, he said, kissing her hair, you can stay for a few years and more." "I'm sorry the marriage didn't work out for you." "It's ok she said looking at him, my heart wasn't in it anyway." Just then a customer came into the shop, "Go upstairs, Kristine; Abby will be happy to see you," he said. "Ok, I'll see you later," she replied.

All afternoon he couldn't wait for five-thirty so he could see her again. What in the world was the matter with him? Sure, he was always happy and excited when she came; but now he felt differently; something had changed. He had to stop thinking like this, he was a married man now, hadn't she begged him to come with him before and he had made his choice. Now he had told Ryan about her, thinking at the time maybe they would hit it off; but he wasn't so sure he wanted that to happen. He closed the shop and peeked into the women's store on his way upstairs. He saw that Abby, Kristine and Bella were all in the women's shop, laughing and talking; he didn't go in, but continued upstairs where he went into the bathroom and cleaned up, then stood looking at himself in the mirror, something he tried to avoid. He turned his head this way and that, trying to assess how others would now perceive the scar on his face; to him it was still grotesque. He was a common man and it was beyond his understanding what a woman would see in him, even before the accident; he didn't realize how good looking he was in a boyish sort of way; coupled with his good natured personality and tall, lanky frame. Everyone liked William when they met him, in fact, people were naturally attracted to him; even the nurses in the hospital still thought about him from time to time. He sat at the kitchen table drinking ale and thinking about his life; it was good but he missed Killin and the country. Here, everything was buildings and streets; he longed to go fishing again; he missed Harry; he missed his Mum. He pushed the thought of Mary out of his mind it was too hard to think about her. He left a note on the kitchen table, *Gone to meet Ryan, go ahead and eat without me, I'll be home a little later, William.* He exited the house and headed down the street; he would stop at Ryan's flat and see if he wanted to go to the pub for supper. He looked up and saw him just going into the building so he yelled, "Ryan, wait up a minute." Ryan smiled and stood by the door waiting, "Hey William, what's up?" "Nothing really, Abby has company so I thought I'd go to the pub for supper, do you want to join me?" "Sure, just let me change my shirt; you can come up if you like." "No, I'll wait here, William said, one set of steps an evening is enough for me." "Ok, I'll be just a minute, Ryan replied, should I bring the chessboard?" "No, William said, I can't stay out that long tonight." They entered the pub and took a table, the waitress came over. "What can I get you gentlemen tonight?" she asked. "For starters, I'll have ale, said William then we'd like to have supper." "I'll have the same," said Ryan. He looked at William, "So, why are you out tonight, it's not Thursday?" "To tell you the truth, William replied, the four walls are driving me insane, I miss the country and now that I can get around better I'm noticing it more." "There are a number of plays in the area, you should take Abby." "I yearn for something to do outdoors; it's being inside all the time that I'm not used to." "You have a small yard why don't you start a little garden." "That's not a bad idea, maybe I'll do that." They ate their supper, had a few more bottles of ale, and then went home. "Glad I ran into you, said William, I hate eating alone." "Same here, Ryan replied, see you Thursday." "Thursday it is," William said. Ryan went up to his flat thinking that something seemed to be off with William, he wondered if he and Abby had a falling out.

William entered the back gate and looked at the yard, "Hmmm, he thought, I just might start a little garden, at least I'd be outside." He entered the hallway, heaved a sigh, and went upstairs where he found Abby and Kristine at the kitchen table. "Hello," he said, sitting down. Abby looked at him, "Why in the world did you go out before supper, you've never done that before?" William looked at her and then put his head down, "I don't know, I thought you were all busy in the shop and I just wanted to get out for a while." "I love, love, love the shop," said Kristine. He smiled, "Aye, Abby has a flair for decorating; we've had a lot of compliments." "Deservedly so," she replied. She reached out and touched his arm, "I heard about the baby, congratulations!" "Thanks, we're happy about it," he replied trying to absorb the shock of her touch. "We've already eaten, did you want something?" Abby asked. "No, Ryan and I ate at the pub," he said. She looked at him, "You went to the pub with Ryan?" "Aye, what's wrong with that?" "I was walking down there and I saw him just coming home and asked if he wanted to go along." "I see," was her only comment. "Who's Ryan?" asked Kristine. "Just a customer, he works at the railroad and lives down the street, we all have supper together on Thursday nights, Ryan, William and I, it's become a habit." "Bella used to join us but she has a man in her life now so she spends most of her time with him." "That sounds like fun, said Kristine, good friends all enjoying a meal together." "Well, we'll see what happens this week, he said, Ryan might not be available." Abby squeezed her eyes together in a questioning look, "That's the first of heard of this," she said. "I guess I forgot to mention it," he replied. Kristine wondered what was wrong with the two of them, they almost seemed to be sparring with each other; the usual cheeriness of the house was missing; William seemed almost sullen. They sat at the table a while longer and then Abby said, "Let's go into the sitting room where it's more comfortable." Normally William would sit in the middle of the couch with Abby on one side and Kristine on the other but tonight he almost pushed them aside and sat down in the chair. "You're the quiet one, aren't you feeling well?" Kristine asked. "I feel fine, William replied, just tired that's all." "Maybe it's all the ale you had at the pub," Abby said. "Could be," replied William. The women talked about this and that in the shop, trying on occasion to include William, but he had little comment on any subject. Sometimes Kristine looked up and found him staring at her; Abby didn't seem to notice. It wasn't long before William stated he was going to bed for the evening; he bent over and gave Abby a kiss and then kissed Kristine on the top of her head, "See you tomorrow," he said. He went to the bath and cleaned up, then into the bedroom and lay in bed not able to sleep.

Kristine looked at Abby, "What's wrong with William, is he upset that I'm here?" "No, oh no, never that Kristine, he adores you." "Well he seems different, more subdued." "I don't know, Abby replied, he hasn't said anything specific to me." She rubbed her hand across her baby belly, "Maybe he's worried about the baby; you know my mother died in childbirth." "Oh, I'm sure that won't happen to you Abby, you must stay positive; just think, soon you will have a bairn" "Yes, you're right," Abby replied. Kristine was thinking to herself that if she were to have William's child it would be the happiest time of her life, she wondered why Abby didn't seem to feel the same. Maybe it was her fear of childbirth that had affected her mood; good thing they had Bella now, otherwise it would be too much for her. "I guess I'm getting a little tired now too, Kristine said, maybe I'll go to bed." She bent down and gave Abby a kiss on the forehead. "Don't worry so much dear, everything will be alright, I'm sure of it."

Kristine went into the bath to wash up and then to the far bedroom to retire for the evening. William watched her walk back and forth and he lay there wondering if she had crawled into bed yet; he could picture her undressing for the night and he closed his eyes wondering what it would feel like to be lying next to her. He imagined that she would lie curled up next to him not turning away like Abby did. He drifted off to sleep and then woke when he heard Abby come to bed. He turned and pulled her to him, kissing her and rubbing her back. She kissed him back but then turned away from him and lay on her side of the bed. Frustrated, he lay there until she fell asleep, then rose, put his pants back on and went to the kitchen for yet another bottle of ale which he took into the living room. He stood by the window watching what little traffic there was at this time of the night and thinking about Kristine just one door away. He had to get his mind straight and stop thinking like this; he was confused as to why he was having these thoughts now after all this time. He sat on the chair for several more hours, drifting in and out of sleep, then finally rose and went back to bed. What he didn't know was that Kristine was also having a hard time falling asleep; she had sensed a distance from him and was hurt, not understanding why he wasn't his old self and happier to see her. She wondered if he was miffed because she had gotten married but he had seemed happy about it at the time. Maybe it was the bairn he was worried about like Abby had suggested.

In the morning William woke to the sound of dishes in the kitchen and the two women talking and laughing. He rose from the bed and went straight into the bath, simply nodding his head at them when they called good morning. He took longer than usual in the bath, not wanting to come out into the kitchen but finally he could delay it no longer and he opened the door and walked to the table and sat down. Abby was busy at the hearth and he looked up and found Kristine staring at him. He looked back at her and then bent his head down and ate the breakfast that Abby had in front of him. "Kristine is going to help us with a new window in the shop today," Abby said. "Good, he replied, that sounds like fun, you'll have to let me know when you're done so I can go out and look at it." "Bye the way, we need to telegram our new order to the shipping company today, have you got yours ready?" "Almost, Abby said, I wanted to get Kristine's input on a couple of new items since she's been traveling abroad." "Aye, William replied, staring at Kristine again, let me know when it's ready." Abby rose to clear off the dishes and then went into the bath leaving William and Kristine alone at the table. "I'll just do these dishes up for Abby," Kristine said, rising from the table. William rose too and said, "Guess I'll be getting down to the shop, I'll see you later." They both turned at the same time and looked at each other. "What's the matter?" she whispered. He pulled her to him, "It's nothing with you, Kristine." He buried his head in her hair and in a shaky voice said, "I love you." He was feeling much too much passion so he pushed her away from him and nearly fell in his rush to leave the kitchen. She was clearly shaken, perhaps for the first time in her life and she stood there frozen in place. Yes, he had said I love you to her many times before, but this was different, she could sense the intensity in the words. Should she leave and go home, she didn't want to cause any problems between Abby and William, she loved them both; and Abby pregnant now. No, she couldn't leave, just to be around him for a few days, that's all she needed, nothing more. Kristine was finishing up the dishes when Abby came out of the bath. "All done," she said. "Thanks Kristine, you didn't have to do that." "I wanted to," she said. "Where's William?" "He said he was going down to the shop." "That's funny usually he has a cup of tea and goes down later." "Oh well, he's a little strange lately, I never know what he's going to do." Normally Kristine would have laughed at that comment, today she said nothing.

The women were busy all morning redoing the window; they kept running in and out of the store to look at their work; finally they were satisfied. They finished up their order between customers; Bella and Abby appreciated Kristine's advice. Abby asked Kristine if she would mind running the order over to William as she wanted to help Bella get some more inventory out of storage. Kristine entered the shop and waited while William finished up with a customer. She held out her hand with the order and William walked over to take it from her, "The windows done if you want to look at it," she said. "Aye, I'll have to do that," he replied, but kept standing there in front of her. "Ok then, she said; I just wanted to bring the order to you." She turned to go and he grabbed her by the arm. "Wait a minute, Kristine, I know it's wrong but I can't help it, I think about you all the time." She turned toward him, about to reply, when the door opened and a customer came in so she turned and left the shop. The afternoon flew by and he was just about to close when Ryan came in. "Hi William, closing up?" "Aye, you're done with work today?" "Yes, just on my way home and wanted to stop and see if we're on for tomorrow night." Abby walked in the door and answered, "Of course we are, and we have a guest for you to meet." "You do, he said, who?" Abby turned and motioned for Kristine to come in, "Kristine, this is Ryan, a good friend of William and I, he will be join- ing us for supper tomorrow night." Kristine walked past William and held out her hand, "Nice to meet you Ryan, I hear you're a chess player, right William?" William just stood there, staring at Kristine not answering. "William, Kristine asked you a question," Abby said. He kept staring at her and replied, "That's right, we play chess together and drink ale." Ryan laughed, "We don't drink that much ale, just a few bottles a week, it's something to do." "Well, I must go and let you get on with your plans for the evening." "When you go by, you'll have to check out our new shop window on your way," Abby said. "I'll go with you, Kristine said, I wanted to take another peek myself." "Lead the way Madam, Ryan said, holding open the door for her." William locked the door behind them and then stood there not moving, "Come on William, what are you standing there for?" asked Abby. William turned and without a word he marched past her and straight up the stairs. Abby was perplexed at his attitude but shrugged it off and followed him to the flat. "I'll see to supper," she said. He stood behind her with his hands on her shoulders, "I can help if you tell me what to do." "Just go in the sitting room and relax, I'll see to it," she said dismissively. He walked to the sitting room window and looked out on the street below. He could see Kristine and Ryan standing there talking, "What could they possibly be talking about, he thought to himself, she doesn't even know him." He sat in the chair, closed his eyes and tried to picture himself back home fishing with Harry at Lake Dochart pushing Kristine out of his mind.

He heard her come in the back door and watched her go into the bedroom; she looked at him and he just stared at her. "What's wrong with you?" she said. "Nothing," he replied. "Your friend is nice he said he lives just down the street." William nodded his head, but made no comment. She shrugged and continued into the bedroom then came out, looked at him, and went into the kitchen. She thought to herself, "He's jealous." "Supper's ready," Abby called. William didn't go to the table immediately but sat in the chair for a few more minutes, then slowly rose and sat down at the table. Kristine looked up, "Ryan says that he works at the railroad station and Bella worked there too, that's how they met." "I guess," said William. Abby looked at him, "Why do you say that?" "Say what?" he answered. "You said, I guess, when you know that's where they met." "I don't know, aye, aye, that's where they met at the railroad," he practically shouted. Kristine and Abby looked at each other and shrugged. "Ryan said he was originally from Edinburgh, that's where his family still lives, I've been there a few times," Kristine continued. "That's where the shipping company we do business with is located," Abby said. "Ryan said he could take me to the station on Friday morning when I leave," Kristine commented. William looked up and said sarcastically, "My, my, Ryan has a lot to say, doesn't he?" He drank the rest of his milk and set the glass down rather loudly, "I have to go," he announced. He left the kitchen and went down the stairs to the shop. "I'm sorry, Kristine, I don't know what's wrong with him," Abby said. Kristine touched Abby's hands holding back her tears, "It's not your fault dear, maybe it was a bad time for me to come." "Nonsense, said Abby, I'm sure it's not you, he loves it when you come, something is bothering him but I don't know what it is." "Maybe I'll have a talk with him today, that is if you don't mind," Kristine said. "No, not at all,

I'd appreciate it, Abby replied, he's so close to you that he might get it out, to tell you the truth, we used to be able to talk things out but lately we seem to be at each other's throats all the time." "That's too bad, replied Kristine; it should be a happy time for both of you now, the bairn coming and all."

Kristine thought that she would have to put a stop to this before it got out of hand; she would try and have a talk with him later; she couldn't leave with things so strained between them. Late morning she asked Abby if Bella could tend the men's shop for a little while so that she could talk to William upstairs. Abby agreed and went to tell William, "William, Bella is going to watch the shop for a while, Kristine needs you upstairs." "I haven't got time for that now," he said. "Yes, you do, she said, you have been rude and surly the entire time she has been here, now, please, go and talk to her." "As you wish Madam," he said sarcastically, and went upstairs.

She was seated on the couch when he came in. "What's this about?" he said. "Come and sit here by me, we have to get this fixed." "Fixed?" he said, that will be a little difficult, don't you think?" "Sit," she said. He sat next to her looking straight ahead with his arms folded across his chest. "You know that I love you and have since we met, I never hid that from you" she said. "You made a choice and turned me away, that doesn't change how I feel about you; it never will." "For me, still having your friendship keeps me going, day after day, whether we are near or far from each other." "I feel like we've lost that friendship and it's tearing me apart." "What happened, William?" "What's changed?"

He sat there with his head in his hands. "You may think me a sod, because I do; I made a mistake to turn you away; I felt grateful to Abby, for all she's done for me, she saved me life." "Night after night, when I was in a coma, she sat there with me." "I felt like I wasn't good enough for you, all crippled up like I was, and you so bonnie." "I care for Abby deeply, but there is no passion, she can barely stand for me to make love to her; she's scared of it." "She's pregnant, what do you expect?" "You don't understand, even before, it was the same, she only wants to mother me, she doesn't like to be intimate with me; I feel like I'm attacking her, but I have needs Kristine, you understand don't you?" She touched his arm, "Aye, I understand, she probably can't help it, she didn't have a mother to teach her about men." There were tears in his eyes, "I've messed everything up; first I lost Mary and now you." She bent over and grabbed his hands, "No, no, you're wrong, you didn't lose me, I'll always be here whenever you need me because I need you too." "I thought I could find love elsewhere but it's not possible, I found that out." "Abby is a wonderful lass and she adores you in the only way she knows how; she is pregnant and you must stand behind her, it's the right thing to do; if you don't, you will hate yourself."

He turned to her and pulled her to him on the couch, "Oh Kristine, I know you're right, I do, but it won't stop me mind from thinking about you every night, you're the best thing that's ever happened to me, I was a dunderhead not to know it." He held her as tightly to his chest as he could. "You're wrong, William, the best thing to happen to you will be your bairn, you must think about that." She touched his face and leaned towards him to give him a kiss on the cheek and instead he turned his head and their lips met." He touched her hair and ran his hands down her back and then over her breasts, he just couldn't stop himself. It took all the strength she had to push away from him because she wanted him too; she cupped his face in her hands and kissed his eyes, nose and lips. "I would give myself to you in a second, William, married or unmarried, but I care too much for Abby and it would ruin us." "This is just as hard on me as it is on you; please tell me that we can be best friends again." "Aye, best friends and more, he said, I can't live my life without you in it." Trying to make light of the situation, she grabbed his hand and said, "Come, we'd best get back downstairs or they will begin to wonder what we are doing." For the first time, he laughed at her, "Don't give up on me." "Never," she said. "Oh, and by the way, don't be jealous, I'm not interested in Ryan, I just think he's nice." "Me jealous, never," he said, and winked at her.

Many times in the future both of them would wonder whether their friendship with each other had ever been just a friendship as they tried to convince themselves; or something more that they had been unable or unwilling to communicate to each other. Obviously there had always been a strong attraction between them; they couldn't seem to keep their hands off of each other; always touching and kissing. Why Abby never questioned this was strange; she just seemed to have accepted it; perhaps she hadn't wanted to see it. Whatever happened, the spark was lit now and there would be no turning it off; they would live a lie going forward, neither could resist any longer.

William returned to the shop and Kristine went to find Abby who was in back digging through the inventory. "There you are, she said, is everything ok," Abby asked, a worried look on her face. "I think so, Kristine said, men are like little boys, they need a lot of attention and affection, maybe he's feeling left out lately." Abby looked at her, "Left out?" "I always have his food ready, his clothes clean and anything else he needs done." "I know you do, Abby, it was just a suggestion, sometimes men need a lot of loving, you know, intimacy." She looked shocked, "That's what he told you?" "No, of course not, I'm just speaking from my own experience I have no idea what's in his mind." "Obviously, by the state of my condition, we have been intimate." "Of course, Kristine said, it must be something else then, I'm sorry, I don't know what it is." Kristine was alarmed that she may have triggered some hostility in Abby and she certainly had not meant to; sometimes things were better left alone; she was not helping the situation. "He did say one thing," Kristine offered. "What was that?" asked Abby. "That he was looking forward to being a Father." Abby smiled, "Thank you for trying, I'm sure whatever it is will pass." "I'm sure you're right, Kristine said, things usually do in time."

Ryan came in the morning to pick up Kristine but William got up early and announced that Bella would have to watch the shop because he was driving Kristine to the station and Ryan could ride along if he wanted and show him the way. Ryan was disappointed, he thought maybe he would have a chance to talk with Kristine alone; he liked her. It seemed that William was quite protective of her; last night he hovered around any time they had a chance to talk together. Kristine hugged Abby good-bye, patted her belly and told her to send a telegram if she needed her to come for any reason. Ryan took her bag before William had a chance to grab it and the three of them went out back to the cart. William practically pushed Ryan aside to help Kristine up into the cart. When they reached the station Ryan said, "We'll just get out here I can show Kristine to the platform, will you find your way back alright?" "No, just show me where to park the cart, I want to wait with her until the train comes; you never know about the pickpockets down here." "Just drive the cart down over there then where you can park it; we'll get out here and wait for you." William had no recourse but to do as Ryan suggested and Kristine had to suppress a smile when she saw the look on his face as Ryan took her hand and assisted her off the cart. "Look, said Ryan, when William drove off, I was wondering, well if you want to, I've written my address down, maybe you could send a post once in a while and let me know how you're doing." "Thank you Ryan, she said, taking the piece of paper, I'll do that, I'm sure we'll meet again on my next trip back." "Do you come often?" "No, at least while I was married I didn't, now I'm not sure, it depends on whether Abby will need some help or not." William came up beside them, "Did you find out what platform?" he asked. "I'll go check," said Ryan. Ryan left and William muttered, "Are we ever going to be alone Kristine?" "He's just trying to be nice, my goodness, I saw the look on your face," she laughed. "Can't you understand I'm dying inside, I don't know when I'll see you again." "What else can we do, I can't live with you can I?" "Here he comes now," said Kristine. "It's platform four; right over there, Ryan said, I'm sorry, I've got to go to work now." He turned to Kristine, "Can I give you a hug goodbye?" She reached out and gave him a hug, "It was nice meeting you Ryan." "Likewise," he said, and then turned and walked away disappointed that he didn't get to spend more time with her.

"Come on Kristine, let's find a bench and sit down." William said, grabbing her bags. They found a bench and sat there not saying anything for a few minutes; lost in the agony of their separation. "Don't get all grumpy about it but Ryan gave me his address and asked me to write to him once in a while," she said. "Are you going to?" he asked. "It would be rude not to, don't you think?" "I suppose so," he said. He put his arms around her waist and nuzzled her ear, "I don't want you to leave?" "I don't want to leave either, but if I stay something is going to happen that we'll be sorry for." They cuddled as close as possible without drawing attention to themselves, occasionally kissing each other and touching. Anyone passing by would have thought they were newlyweds but unknown to them someone else was watching. Ryan, going about his work had business to attend to at the end of the terminal and was going to make a quick detour over to talk to them when he came to a dead stop and stood transfixed watching them; instead, he turned and went on his way, thinking to himself that there was more than met the eye between those two. What he had seen was much more than a close friendship, it was intimate, almost seductive. "Well, he thought, time usually brings things into the open." Now he understood why William had acted the way he did, he was obviously jealous. He thought about Abby and how she was at home pregnant with his child.

"The train will be here soon," Kristine said. William choked up and there were tears in his eyes, "I'm so sorry, I should let you go, you deserve to be with someone who can give you what you need." "I've tried that, remember, it didn't work, my heart is with you whether you see me again or you don't, I can't help it." In her favorite pose, she pursed her lips and sat up straight, "Mother will be dragging me around again, hoping to find a rich man for me." William laughed, "I wonder what she would think of a country lad like me." "She's a snob, what can I say, but it matters little to me what she thinks." They saw the train coming and stood up holding each other tightly as long as they could until she had to board the train. He reluctantly let her go. She took a window seat and put her hand against the window, looking at him as the train left the station. Instead of leaving, William sat on the bench holding his head in his hands wondering how his simple life had become so complicated. With heavy tread he found the cart and made his way home. When he arrived, he peeked into the shop to let Abby know he was back. "I was hoping you hadn't got lost, she said, you were gone a long time." "Aye, I sat with her until the train came, it was the least I could do." She nodded in agreement and he went to relieve Bella from the men's shop. Ryan stopped in after work, "I see you made it home safe." "Aye, William replied, I did." "I guess Abby will miss having Kristine around now." "Aye, that she will, I think we need to find a housekeeper soon, it's too much for her running the shop and trying to keep up the house in her condition." "Yes, Ryan said, you could put an ad in the Glasgow Herald on Mitchell Street; I could show you where it is, it's not far." William nodded, "Let me talk to her about it first and I'll let you know." "Listen, William, you don't mind if I write to Kristine once in a while, do you?" "Mind, no, why should I, William replied, she is free to do as she wishes." "Well, best be getting home, see you later." "Later," William replied.

That evening William said to Abby, "Look, you're going to need some help with the bairn coming and all, it's too much for you, I'm going to put an ad for a housekeeper in the paper." He thought she would refuse but instead she said, "Maybe you're right, once the bairn is here it's going to be hard to spend as much time in the shop." "Good, maybe Bella can watch the men's shop on Saturday Ryan offered to show me where the paper is." "Yes, yes, I'll tell her," she said. She turned and looked at him. "Can I ask you a question?" "Of course, he said, what is it?" "Why were you so rude to Kristine, didn't you want her to come?" "She can come any time she wants to, I don't have a problem with it." Abby looked at him, "I think you hurt her feelings." "Just drop it Abby, you're always dredging something up, let it lie will you." He turned and walked away from her leaving her to wonder if he had some kind of spat with Kristine that he didn't want to talk about. It never occurred to her that it was quite the opposite.

Ryan and William went to the paper on Saturday and put in an ad; the paper was in the Charles Rennie Macintosh Building in the area near Enoch Station. "What do you say we have lunch as long as we're here," William said. They found a little place to eat and had a nice lunch with ale; neither in a hurry to get back home. "If you don't mind my asking, Ryan said, how did you and Kristine get to be such good friends?" "I don't know, William replied, we hit it off the minute we met." Ryan looked at him, "She's quite bonnie isn't she, I've never see anyone quite like her." William picked up the ale and took a drink, choosing not to comment.

The next week, several women stopped to inquire about the position; one of them was a woman named Agnes who was in her late forties. She lived on Ingram Street, not far away and was willing to come every day except Sunday. "That's me kirk day, she laughed, when I go to account for all me sins." She stated that she would cook, clean, do laundry and look after the bairn. She had been a nurses' assistant at one time and made it clear that she was an honest woman. "Ye won't be needin to check me pockets, I'm honest as the day is long." William and Abby both took to her instantly and so she was hired. William told her that if it was rainy or slippery out, she should wait at home for him and he would pick her up.

The days flew by and William had hoped with Agnes' help Abby would become more relaxed and affectionate but that didn't happen. Many nights he fell asleep reading in his chair in the sitting room; sometimes he would lay in the spare room on the bed that Kristine had slept in wishing that he could be with her; he was lonely and Abby didn't seem to notice; in her mind, as long as his daily needs were taken care of, she was being a good wife. The bairn grew inside of her and it would be only a couple more months before it was born. "I think we better go shopping for the bairn," he told her one day. "I suppose you're right, she said, but we can't let the men's shop go unattended and Bella can't watch both of them." They were making a lot of money on both shops and decided that William should hire an assistant so he could get other things done; now he was basically tied to the shop every day. Once again he made the trip to the Herald Advertiser and placed an ad in the paper; he also placed a sign in his window. One of his long-time customers inquired about it; "I'm looking for part-time work, he said, I have a small accounting business out of my home but I wouldn't mind picking up a little extra pocket money." He was an elderly man, perhaps in his early fifties and was quite personable, William had talked with him many times when the shop wasn't too busy. "Why don't we give it a try and see how you like it, William said, come in whenever you can and I will show you what needs to be done." In the meantime, Agnes offered to go shopping for the bairn with Abby stating that she was proficient in driving a cart, "I'm from the country, we grew up driving the cart to town; when me man died, I gave up the horses, it was too much for me to take care of." William was relieved because he wasn't one for shopping anyway. That evening Abby showed William the bedroom next to theirs which had now been turned into a nursery; she seemed happy and excited, Agnes was good for her.

One day William wrote a letter to Kristine: *My dearest Kristine: I hope this letter finds you well. I think of you constantly and yearn to be near you. It's only the thought of you that keeps me going, day after day. We hired a housekeeper for Abby, a lovely lady named Agnes; I don't know how we did without her before. I have also hired an assistant for my shop so that I can get away when I need to. It's hard to believe the bairn will be here soon, I am looking forward to it. I remain, as always; your loving friend. William.* This time he addressed the envelope and sealed it; he would mail it himself.

Nathaniel showed up the next morning, ready to work. William was pleasantly surprised because he required very little training and the customers liked him. He felt free, like he wasn't tied down to the shop every minute of the day so he went out on his own to mail his letter. This would be the beginning of his secret life. He passed a little jewelry shop on his way to the post office and looked in the window where he saw a necklace; he went inside and asked the clerk if he could show it to him; it was a gold heart on a golden chain, very delicate and expensive. William asked the clerk if he could engrave on it and the clerk said yes, so William asked him to engrave, *Love Always, William* on the back. He had the clerk wrap the package for the mail and he took it with him to the post office where he addressed it and sent it to Kristine. He was quite pleased with himself and his good mood carried into the evening so he asked Abby if she wanted to play a few games of Maw. "I must say you're in a good mood this evening," she said. "Aye, it's nice to have some help in the shop." They finished their game and sat on the couch for a while before bed. William rubbed Abby's stomach and she let him feel the bairn move. "Let's go to bed," he said, kissing her on the cheek. They donned their night clothes and crawled into bed; he reached over and put his arms around her and slowly caressed her back and arms, then nuzzled her neck and pulled her to him. He kissed her on the mouth and began to fondle her breasts but she broke away saying, "Stop, William, mind the bairn." She turned her back to him and once again he was frustrated. That was the last time he tried to touch her before the bairn was born, there was no more intimate affection between them which was a relief to Abby.

Kristine had received William's letter and gift and had cried herself to sleep that night, holding the necklace and letter to her chest. She knew that any letter she sent to him would have to be addressed to both of them even though there was so much she wanted to say only to William. The letter came one day and Abby brought it over to William in the shop. "A letter came from Kristine, she's doing well." Not wanting to seem too excited, William said, "Just lay it on the counter, I'll read it in a little while." As soon as she was out of sight, William opened the letter and read it. *Dearest Abby and William: Everything is well in Perth but my heart is with both of you in Glasgow. I am anxiously awaiting news that you have a bairn, I hope you are not getting too uncomfortable. I have been busy helping mother with a social tea she is having next week; with her, everything has to be perfect. I had a little golden surprise that I cherish, it's with me day and night; I'll tell you about it when I see you. Tell Bella hello for me, I will write a note to Ryan and let him know what I've been doing, which isn't much. Love Always, Kristine.* William smiled at her cryptic remark, oh how he missed her!

CHAPTER THIRTY-FIVE

The months flew by and one day Abby announced that she needed to go to the hospital, she was having labor pains. William got the carriage out and took her, leaving instructions for Bella to see if she could get ahold of Nathaniel to run the shop; if not, then to put up a closed sign. It was two days later when Daniel Stevenson came into the world, a beautiful healthy bairn, weighing seven pounds. Abby had a rough go of it and she was exhausted; to William's credit, he stayed by her side through it all, except when the nurses kicked him out of the room. He couldn't stop looking at the bairn who was now his pride and joy. On the third day, he kissed Abby and told her that he needed to go home and let everyone know that all was well. "I'll come back tonight," he said. He arrived home to find that Nathaniel had come in every day and all was running smoothly; next he went upstairs to let Agnes know that the baby and mother were doing fine and would probably be home on the weekend. Agnes was excited, "Oh, I just can't wait to get me hands on the wee bairn." William smiled at her, grateful that they had found such a wonderful housekeeper. "Mr. Stevenson, she yelled, as he was going back down the stairs, what have you named the bairn?" "Daniel, he replied, Daniel Stevenson." He went into the women's shop and told Bella the news, then once again returned upstairs to bathe and take a long needed rest. He fell asleep almost immediately and woke in the late afternoon feeling refreshed again. He took time to write a letter to Kristine while he ate the supper that Agnes had left for him. *My Dearest Love: I have missed you more than you can imagine but I have news, I am now the Da of Daniel Douglas Stevenson, a beautiful healthy boy. Words cannot describe the joy I feel when I look at him. Abby is doing well although she had a hard time with delivery; they should come home on the weekend. You are always in my thoughts. I love you, William.*

William went back to the hospital, he stood looking at the bairn for some time it was such a miracle to him. He found Abby sleeping and he sat by the bed watching her; she was such a frail little thing, maybe things would change in a few months between them; he hoped so. If not, he didn't know how much longer he could go on. She opened her eyes and he grabbed her hand, "Hi, how are you feeling?" "A little better, have you seen him today?" "Aye, he looks like me." She smiled, "What did Agnes say?" "She said she couldn't wait until he came home so she could get her hands on him." "Are the shops ok?" "Aye, don't even think about that right now, just rest, everything is ok." "Go home and rest, she said, it won't do either of us any good if you get worn out too." "Are you sure," he asked. Yes, I'm sure." He kissed her on the forehead, "I love you." "I love you too," she said. He stopped to look at Daniel again before he left; such a little person. On the way home he pondered his double life. "Was it possible to love two, even three women?" He didn't know; he still loved Mary and always would, he loved Abby feeling the need to take care of her as she had done for him, and he was passionately in love with Kristine."

Abby came home on the weekend and a new routine was set in motion; William was happy to help out with the bairn, even changing dirty diapers; Daniel was his pride and joy. Abby recovered quickly with Agnes' help; in fact, she could hardly get the bairn away from Agnes who adored him. The Thursday night suppers had stopped when Abby was in the hospital and now, with the bairn, they had not resumed. Bella was busy with her new beau most of the time and Ryan stopped by now and again, even bringing over a baby present; William promised to go to the pub with him for a game of chess soon.

One day Nathaniel told William that the imperial administrator from the shipping company would be by tomorrow morning and would like to meet with the owner and introduce himself. William said he would be there when he came. As promised, the administrator arrived in the morning. "I'm Dennis Ingham, The Imperial Administrator from The Edinburgh Shipping Company, I'm making my rounds to meet our customers and you have been one of our best for many years." William shook his hand, "Nice to meet you, I'm William Stevenson, would you care to come back and have a cup of tea?" Thank you, but that's not necessary, he said, I have a lot of visits to make yet today." "I just wanted to leave my business card with you and make sure that we are meeting your expectations." "We have a new owner now but it appears that things will remain much the same." "Aye, I heard something about that, the former owner passed away?" "Yes," he said, a Mr.

McPhee from Killin, his solicitor handled much of the business." "Mr. McPhee from Killin, you say, William asked, did I hear you correctly?" "Yes, that's correct," replied the administrator. "I know him; I grew up in Killin, that can't be right, he had a fish shop until recently when he leased it out as a bakery." "Yes, that's correct, he has quite a story." "He was a very wealthy man but didn't like that kind of life so he more or less left it to the solicitor to run the business and moved to the country." "He had no children so when he passed the lucky lady inherited everything from him." "I see, said William; was she from Edinburgh then?" "Oh no, we've yet to meet her, she was recently married, she's from Killin, a Mrs. Henry MacAlduie." William turned pale and had to sit down, "Excuse me," he said. "Are you all right sir?" "Aye, I'm all right, I've just had a shock, you see, I think I may know the young lady; we were almost engaged to be married at one time." "Did she run a bakery do you know?" "Yes, I believe the solicitor said she did have a bakery but left it for her relatives to run when she married." "You say she's married to Henry MacAlduie?" "Yes sir, from what I understand, he's a teacher, they live in Comrie." "Aye, that would be him," William said. "I don't know what her financial status was before, but I can tell you that she won't have to worry for the rest of her life, she's very wealthy now." "Well, I must be on my way, it was very nice to meet you." "If I happen to see Mrs. MacAlduie I will tell her that I've met you." "Mary, William said, her first name is Mary." "Perhaps you had better not mention our conversation it might come as a shock to her." "As you wish, sir, as you wish, Good day." "Good day," William replied.

William went upstairs and sat on the couch, he couldn't believe what he had just heard; what a small world it was. So Henry finally got his wish and married Mary; he was happy for her and yet sad that he had let her down. He was far less crippled now than what he imagined he was going to be; perhaps he shouldn't have tried to hide his identity. "Well, you can't go back, he thought, what's done is done." There was a time when he thought he wouldn't be able to live without her but now it seemed so long ago; another time really; and he had fallen in love with Kristine. So she lives in Comrie, Henry must have taken a position near Killin so that he could court her; from what he understood, Henry was a good man, he hoped she would have a happy and fulfilled life. He was surprised she had left the bakery; maybe he should have asked her to come to Glasgow with him after all.

"What's wrong with you, why are you sitting there like that?" Abby asked. "No reason, he said, I just felt a little under the weather." "Best you stay away from the bairn today then, she said, no need to make him sick." She hurried off without another look at him and he shook his head wondering if she even cared that he might not feel well; probably not. Maybe he would just write another letter to Kristine, at least she was interested in what he had to say. He got out his paper and pen and began: *My Dearest Love: I've been hoping that you would come soon, I miss you so. Daniel is growing like a weed already, you must see him. Every day without you is like a day without sunshine, you bring light into my life; without Daniel, I would be in a black hole. I lie awake at night wishing you were beside me and I could wake up next to you in the morning. I close my eyes and imagine that you are right here, but I haven't seen you for so long the vision is fading from my memory. If you can't come, please write. I love you so much. William.* He left the house to mail his letter without telling anyone where he was going; they would barely notice anyway; perhaps he would stop at the pub for ale on his way home, it was becoming a habit of his.

William went into the pub and sat down; the waitress came over immediately, "I haven't seen you in here for quite a while," she said. He smiled at her, "I've been pretty busy lately," he replied. "Where's your friend with his chessboard?" "Working I guess; I haven't seen him." "Where do you work?" she asked. "I work just down the street but I had an errand to run so stopped in for a drink." "I get off in about an hour, maybe we could meet somewhere," she said. "No offense, he replied, but I'm a married man and I have a newborn bairn." "That's too bad, she said, I like you." He finished his ale and then left for home hoping that the lass didn't follow him and find out where he lived.

One day a package arrived with a letter from Kristine: *Dearest Abby and William: Congratulations on the bairn, I can't wait to see him. I have been busy, helping mother as usual. I miss you all. Hopefully you will like the baby things, I thought they were cute. As Always: Kristine.* Abby was thrilled with the gifts for the bairn; as usual Kristine had outdone herself. William was distraught that she had not come in person it had been such a long time since he had seen her. He spent his days imagining that she had found someone else and no longer cared for him; he had put her in an awkward position; she was a bonnie lass and he expected her to spend the rest of her life pining for a married man. Was he really that selfish? Perhaps he was?

Month after month went by and Daniel was already six months old; Abby did not let William touch her, she was afraid of getting pregnant again. "For heaven's sake, Abby, I'm a man, I have needs, what do you expect me to do?" "This marriage is a joke, you don't care for me, not in the way a wife should." She turned to him, "I do care for you, haven't I cared for you since the accident?" She put her arms around his neck and kissed him, he touched her but she was stiff as a board; he had his way with her as gently as he could but there was no joy in it; she turned her back on him afterwards making him feel like she was disgusted with him and the next day she was sullen and distant. Thereafter he would sit in his chair until late into the night and then crawl into the vacant bedroom to sleep. If this bothered Abby, he couldn't tell, she soon resumed her usual self.

William decided that he had enough of Kristine's absence and he was going to find out why she had not come for a visit. He told Abby that he would be out of town for a couple of days on business. She looked at him, "Out of town on business, what kind of business would you have out of town?" "Shops, he said, I want to check out a couple of shops I heard about." "Where," she asked. "Edinburgh," he replied, Bella can watch the shop in the morning, I'll have Nathaniel give me a ride to the station." "When will you be back?" she asked. He replied, "Soon, a couple of days at the most." "I don't understand you, she said, this is the first I've heard any mention of looking at shops, aren't there enough shops right here in Glasgow?" She looked at him, "I don't believe you; you're up to something." He shrugged his shoulders and then said, "What difference would it make to you whether I'm here or not, you barely know I'm around." She flounced out of the room saying, "Tell that to the food I make, the clothes I wash, and everything else I do for you." "There you go, there you go, making a mountain out of a molehill again," he said.

In the morning he picked up Daniel and held him, "Da will be back in a couple of days, son, you be a good boy, I love you." Nathaniel dropped him off at the station and he went to the counter to purchase a ticket. "One ticket to Perth," he said. The attendant asked, "One way or round trip Sir?" "One way please." "It will arrive at Station three, the clerk said, over there; it will be about 30 minutes." "Thank you," William said. He found a bench and sat to wait for the train. When the train arrived in Perth he walked to The George Inn which wasn't far but with his cane it was wearing on him. He asked for a pen, pencil and envelope and took it to his room with him. He sat at the table writing a note. *Dearest Kristine: This may come as a surprise to you but I'm here in Perth at The George Inn, I must see you. Please come, William.* He put the address on the front of the envelope, sealed it, and went back downstairs to the counter. "Does the Inn have a service that could deliver this envelope for me?" he asked. "Yes, sir, we do, shall we put the charge on your bill?" "Please do, William said, how long before it's delivered?" "I think we have someone who can go immediately." "Thank you," William said. He returned to his room and lay on the bed.

Kristine was home when she heard a knock on the door; she opened it and was asked if a Kristine lived there. "That would be me," she said. "I believe this is for you then," the driver said, and handed her the envelope. What in the world, she thought, and opened the envelope. If William thought she would be surprised, he was understating it, she was shocked. Why was he here? Her mother came around the corner, "Who was at the door?" she asked. "I don't know mother, she said, stuffing the envelope into her pocket, they had the wrong house." She went up to her room and sat there. "What should I do, she thought, I have been trying so hard to stay away so that their marriage might work." "How can I stay away now, with him here so close to me?" She sat there for a couple of hours and then went back downstairs to find her mother. "Mother, I have to go out shopping, I'll be back later." "All right dear, see you when you get home," her Mother replied.

Kristine asked the family livery man to give her a ride to town and she had him drop her off at the station. "Shall I wait for you madam?" he asked. "No thank you, she said, please tell Mother that I may not be home until tomorrow, I'm meeting a friend." She walked from the station to The George Inn and asked for William's room; she knocked on the door and in seconds it opened and there he was; at that moment all her resistance was gone; she melted into him. "My God, you've come, he said, I was so afraid you wouldn't." There was no talking, or thinking for that matter; for the first time since they had known each other, they were truly alone. The spent up passion they had held back for so many years erupted like a volcano and they were ravenous for each other, there was no stopping them; the fire was kindled. They lie there spent for the moment and William finally knew true passion from a woman; one who didn't turn away from him afterwards. They talked for hours, both avoiding the conversation that would have to come later. "Will you stay with me tonight, he asked, I've waited so long." "I couldn't leave you, not yet," she said. He touched the golden heart between her breasts, "You have it on," he said. "I never take it off, except when I bathe," she replied. "I thought maybe you had found someone else." "No, although Mother has been trying, she says I'm difficult." "Let's go down and have some supper," he said. They dressed and he helped her with her clothes; something Abby would never have let him do; they went to the dining room downstairs and had supper, then sat there listening to the music; his arm around her as they sat there. They drank several bottles of ale and enjoyed each other's company feeling quite alone although they were in a roomful of people. Arms around each other, they went back to the room and immediately all the clothes came off again and they made love. They were so familiar with each other; neither having any modesty. He lay there taking in every inch of her and she felt as close to him as she ever had. He wondered why he had ever turned her away; she was everything to him now. They lay cuddled up together, his arms around her, until both fell asleep. Sometime during the early morning hours she felt his leg moving against hers so she turned and embraced him; once again they came together; perhaps for the last time ever. Molded together they both fell back asleep; when they woke, Kristine said, "I should get dressed, when is your train leaving?" "I don't know, he said, I haven't gotten a ticket yet." "I'll go with you, she said, I had the driver drop me off there yesterday." "You did?" Yes, in case Mother asked the livery man where I went, it wouldn't do for him to say the Inn" They dressed and then left the room; William turned in his key and paid the bill. Hand in hand they walked to the station, now not having much to say to each other. William bought a ticket and they had about an hour before the train arrived. He looked at her, "If it wasn't for Daniel, I wouldn't go home again." She didn't comment. "This is the second time I've waited at this station with you," she said. He looked at her, "I'll come back when I can." "I won't come next time," she said. He looked at her again, "You won't come, why?" "It has to end now, William, neither of us can go on like this, we will be found out it's only a matter of time." "I don't care, it doesn't matter to me," he said. "It matters to me, she said, Abby considers me a friend, and look what I'm doing to her." "I tell you she wouldn't care either, she would be happy someone is taking care of my needs." "Is that what I'm doing William, taking care of your needs?" "No, of course not, you know better than that, I love you, that's not what I meant" "I'll get a divorce and marry you, just say the word." "No, I won't marry you, go home to your son and your wife and don't look back." "I thought you loved me?" he said. "I do, that's why I'm asking this of you; set me free." He looked down at his hands, defeated, "Don't do this to me, I beg you, I love you." She looked at him and with all her will said, "It's over William." He nodded his head; "And so it shall be, will you write?" "Yes, she said, from time to time I will write." She stood up, kissed him on the forehead and walked away. When she was out of sight she stood against the wall, tears flooding her face, it was the hardest thing she had ever done. William didn't watch her go, he didn't ask her to stay, he sat motionless until the train came and when it did he boarded it without looking behind him to see if she still might be there. From that day forward the old William was gone and a quieter, more brooding one was born, the only emotion he showed was for his son, Daniel.

No one had questioned him about the trip again or asked any questions, it was as if he had never been gone. A few months later he noticed that Abby had been sick in the mornings again so he asked her about it. "Are you sick Abby?" She turned on him, "What do you think?" "Yes, I'm pregnant again, that must make you happy?" "Pregnant again, that's hard to believe, there was only the one time, are you sure that's what it is?" "Yes, I'm sure," she said and walked away from him.

True to her word, Kristine sent a post every several months but never a hint that she might come to visit. Abby mentioned to William one day, "Kristine never visits anymore; I suppose it was because you were so rude to her last time she was here." "She has her own life to live, her Mum keeps her quite busy from what I understand," he said. "I guess, Abby commented, still I would have thought she might come to see Daniel, I miss her." "You don't write to her anymore, why?" "I guess I don't have anything to say, feel free to write to her yourself if you like." William couldn't stand to talk about her so he got up and went out the back door and walked down to the pub. Abby would often ponder what had happened between William and Kristine; she felt there had to have been something that she didn't know that caused a rift between them. She decided to take William's sarcastic advice and write to her. *Dear Kristine: We miss you it's been such a long time since you've visited us. It is nice to hear from you once in a while just so we know that you are ok. Daniel is growing up so fast before our eyes, I wish you would come to see him; he's just starting to crawl so we have to keep an ever watchful eye on him. I don't know what I'd do without Agnes; she is such a blessing to us. I'm pregnant again, the bairn will be due in about seven months, I think this will be the last one; I certainly hope so. The shops are increasingly busy, we could use more room but there is nowhere else to expand; we will have to make do. We hardly ever see Ryan; he has a beau; I'm happy for him. William is quiet and moody, I haven't been able to figure out why; he so loves Daniel and is a good Father. Take Care, Abby.* Abby sealed her letter and asked Agnes if she could drop it off on her way home.

Kristine read the letter with sadness and a tear trickled down the side of her face. Like William, she was quiet and moody, a shell of her former self. Her mother no longer prodded at her to meet someone new, she wondered what had happened to her daughter but no amount of questioning would produce any answers.

Abby grew even larger with this baby than she had with Daniel, if that was possible for such a small lass. It was difficult for her to get around during the last couple of months; her back bothered her and William had to tend for Daniel when Agnes was gone; which he didn't mind. William tried to do as much as he could for her, even offering to bathe her which of course she refused; she did let him assist washing her hair. He felt sorry for her, she was so tiny to be carrying all that weight but the doctor didn't seem too concerned about it. William asked Agnes if she knew of anyone who could work at night after she left; someone who would be good with Daniel and could stay the night and share a room with the child. "Aye, she said, there's me daughter, she's looking for something and she loves bairns but she doesn't have any of her own, she's a little on the plain side, if ye know what I mean." William asked her to bring the lass by on the morrow which she did. "Gabrielle, this is Mr. Stevenson," Agnes said. "Please, call me William, he said, I understand you might be able to help us out?" "Aye sir, I'm very good with the wee ones, I love them and I can cook too." "Let me get Daniel and see how you two get along," William said. "He brought Daniel into the room and Gabrielle immediately got down on the floor to play with him; they seemed to hit it off fine. "You'll have to mind the steps and of course he likes to put things into his mouth if he finds them." "Aye, I know, Mr. Stevenson, I won't take me eyes off of him, I promise." "Very well then, when can you start, he asked her. "Tonight if you would like me to?" "Good, I'll send Abby up to talk with you and if she agrees, tonight will be fine." "Thank you," said Agnes, following behind him. William turned to Agnes and gave her a kiss on the forehead, "If it wasn't for you, my dear, I don't know what we would have done all these months, you are a gem, you truly are." He winked at her, "I might have to take you to a play one of these days." Agnes blushed, "Oh go along now, you, and stop fussing over an old fool like me." William laughed and went downstairs. Abby slowly made her way up the stairs to meet Gabrielle; everything lately took all the energy she had. She liked Gabrielle and hired her, relieved that there would be yet another person to help out.

That evening William made Abby sit on the couch and he rubbed her legs and feet; they were becoming so swollen that it was almost alarming. "What did the doctor say about all the swelling, Abby?" "He told me to keep my feet up and stay off of them as much as possible." "Then it's settled, from now on you stay upstairs, I'll tell Bella she will have to manage the shop on her own, I'll help her with inventory." "You don't need to do any more cooking, we will manage and Gabrielle said she was a good cook." "Find yourself a book and just enjoy yourself for once; you work too hard." He gave her a kiss on the cheek and sat with her, holding her hand; he still loved and cared about her; after all she had given him his son and was about to bear him another bairn. William was about as attentive as any husband could be during these last months of Abby's pregnancy; he watched over her as she had once done with him. Now that Gabrielle was staying with them at night, William sat up until Abby had fallen asleep and then as quietly as he could he crawled into bed next to her, careful not to touch her. One night she sat up in bed and poked him in the back, "William, I'm having labor pains, I think we need to go." He got up, dressed and knocked on Gabrielle's door to tell her they were going to the hospital. "You'll be alright until your Mum comes in the morning, mind that you keep the door to the stairway closed." "Aye, Mr. Stevenson, I will, don't worry," she said. He hurried downstairs and out the back door to get the carriage ready, then came back up and helped Abby down the stairs. The bairn didn't come that night or the next, William spent hours holding a cold rag on Abby's forehead, holding her hand and talking to her. The doctor opened the door and motioned for William to come into the hallway. "I'm sorry to have to tell you this but things are not progressing well, we are starting to see some bleeding and may have to consider a Caesarean Section." "Your wife is a small woman and the bairn may be too large for her to deliver, why don't you go home and get some rest and we will make a decision in the morning." "I can't go home and sleep, not with her like that," he said, I'll go home long enough to see to my other bairn but I will be back soon." "As you wish, the doctor said, but it won't do you any good to get worn out." William drove home, fearful that he wouldn't get back before the bairn came. Agnes came out to meet him when he entered the kitchen thinking that he was bringing her news of the birth. He sat at the table, "The doctor said the baby is too big for a small woman like her to have, he said she is getting weak and has started bleeding, they might have to do a Caesarean." "She will hate me Agnes, she didn't want another, she was afraid that something like this might happen, you see, her Mum died in childbirth." "No, no, don't blame yourself William, it's not your fault, you couldn't know, no one could." "Here, you sit and I'll make you some tea." She sat down with him, "Listen William, Caesarean's have become more common now, everything should be alright you have to look on the positive side." He buried his head in his hands and couldn't stop the flow of tears. Agnes stood behind him and patted him on the back, "Now, now, you're overtired and need some rest, why don't you go lie on the bed and have a little nap, there's nothing you can do, it's in the doctor's hands now." "No, I couldn't sleep, I just want to see Daniel and then I'm going back; she needs me there." "Did you know when I had my accident she sat by my side night after night." "No, I didn't know that, but I can see she's a caring woman." "I don't deserve her," he cried. "Now, now, you don't know what you're saying, drink your tea and then come and see your son he's in the sitting room trying to pull himself up onto the couch." As tired as he was, William had to chuckle at the effort Daniel, was making, "I see you're going to be a nosey one," he said. He sat there playing with the lad about an hour and then stated he was leaving again. "Thank you, both of you, remind me to write you your cheques when I come back home, in case I forget." "If its dark Agnes, hire a cart to take you home, I will leave some money on the table for you; I don't want you out there walking in the dark." "Aye, Mr. Stevenson, don't worry about us, we will be fine."

He arrived back at the hospital to find a flurry of activity in Abby's room. "What is going on?" he asked the nurse. "She's started to hemorrhage, we have to get her in the operating room right away, there's no time to waste." He was whisked out of the room and into the waiting room. "We will come and talk to you as soon as we know something," they said. He sat in the chair for hours, sometimes drifting in and out of sleep. He awoke to the doctor's voice, "Mr. Stevenson," He shook his head and sat up straight, "Yes, sir?" The doctor looked at him and then took a seat beside him. "Mr. Stevenson, we did all we could, I'm sorry but your wife is gone." "You have a healthy baby boy we were able to save the child." "Gone, he asked, how is that possible, what happened?" "It's very rare, but sometimes a hemorrhage will occur, we just couldn't stop the bleeding." "It's my fault then, William said, her mother died in childbirth, she told me she didn't want any more children." "You mustn't blame yourself, I am aware that her mother died in childbirth, but it was very different, that was a strangulation; the baby was breach." "You need to focus on the child now do you have someone who can help care for him?" "Aye, I have a housekeeper and her daughter, they will help me." "Do you have a pastor or priest who can help you make the arrangements?" "Aye, I will see the pastor who helped with her Da; he passed away a while ago." "The bairn should stay at the hospital until the weekend, that will give you time to get everything in order; again, I'm so sorry, these cases are extremely rare." William nodded and sat there in the waiting room another hour, not moving.

He was in shock; no matter what their marriage had been, he owed his life to Abby and now she was gone. He went home to a quiet house; Gabrielle and Daniel were both sleeping. He didn't go to the bedroom but sat up in the chair and that's where Agnes found him in the morning. She went about the house as quietly as she could without waking him, Abby must have had the bairn for him to be home, she was anxious to find out if it was a lad or lass. She heard him cough and went in to find him sitting in the chair staring straight ahead, "William, have you news?" she said. He turned his head and looked at her. Without emotion he said, "She's gone, Agnes, the hemorrhage, they couldn't stop it." Shocked she said, "Gone, no, and the bairn?" "A boy, he will stay until the weekend." She bent down and touched his hands, "You've had a shock is there anything I can do for you?" "I'm all right, I have to go to the kirk and see the pastor about arrangements." "Would you like me to go with you?" He looked at her, "Could you?" "I hate to ask, would it be an imposition?" "No lad, none at all." She cradled his head in her hands and he buried his face in her apron and cried like a baby." "We'll get through it together, lad, we have the bairns to think of now, Abby is in the Lord's hands." "You'll need to get cleaned up, you haven't had a bath in days, I'll fix the hot water it will do you good." "Go find some clean clothes to put on." He did as she asked, and once she had the water ready he went in and laid in the tub trying to focus on what he needed to do.

He was barely able to function, but with Agnes' help they closed the shop and had a small service at the kirk. William sat next to Agnes and Gabrielle with his children and when he went up front to say a final goodbye to her he broke down and fell to his knees; Nathaniel and the pastor helped him back to his seat. He couldn't reconcile himself to what had happened, thinking, "She gave me life with her love and I took hers with my lust." Whatever had passed between them, there was no doubt that she would have been a marvelous mother and now he would have to be both a Mum and Da to his children. It didn't seem fair that she was taken so young. He thought it was her curse to have met him.

He heard the words of the pastor: *For everything there is a season, and a time for every matter under heaven; a time to be born, and a time to die; a time to plant, and a time to pluck up what is planted; a time to kill, and a time to heal; a time to break down, and a time to build up; a time to weep, and a time to laugh; a time to mourn, and a time to dance.* Let us pray: *Dear Lord, we commit the soul of Abigale Marie McCleary Stevenson into your hands. Please bring comfort and healing to those who mourn; for she is now in the loving care of God. We ask that you shower her young children with your love and protection; and now, Abigale, may your spirit soar on the breeze and find peace everlasting in the heart of God.* He raised his hand; *May the Lord bless you and keep you in his care; may he show his face to you and give you peace.*

At William's request, the Piper walked down the aisle and led the casket out of the church to the tune of Ode to Joy. At the cemetery they laid her in the ground next to her Father and the pastor read: *Let not your heart be troubled; ye believe in God, believe also in me. In my Father's house are many mansions; if it were not so, I would have told you. I go to prepare a place for you; and if I go and prepare a place for you, I will come again and receive you unto myself; that where I am, there ye may be also. I am the way, the truth, and the life; no man cometh unto the Father, but by me. If ye had known me, ye should have known my Father also, and from henceforth ye know him and have seen him. Go in peace.*

The Piper began to play Amazing Grace and one by one everyone took a handful of dirt and threw it on the casket, then followed the Piper to the road where William stood beside him. The few in attendance left until only William, Daniel, Agnes, Gabrielle and the Piper remained with the pastor. The pastor took William's hand in his, "I know you are grieving son, but you must be strong for your lads, the grief will pass in time; you are fortunate to have an amazing woman here to help you." With that he gave Agnes a hug. "I would like to see you in the kirk on Sunday mornings; I think it will comfort you, God Bless." William nodded his head and shook his hand, "Thank you for everything." He then turned to the Piper and handed him an envelope. "Thank you for coming, this should cover the cost." He assisted Agnes and Gabrielle into the carriage, then handed over Daniel and they left the cemetery and went home.

CHAPTER
THIRTY-SIX

In the next few months, William did what he had to do; he went to the shop, making what decisions he needed to and then went back upstairs to spend time with his lads. He barely ate anything and was visibly pale; his eyes black underneath from lack of sleep. He never went to the bedroom but spent his evenings falling in and out of sleep in a chair. No amount of cajoling from Agnes could get him to change his habits. He instructed Agnes to go through Abby's things and take what they wanted; then get rid of everything else. Agnes did as instructed but kept a box of things she thought the lads might like to have someday. As she went through everything, she noticed the letters from Kristine. Abby had mentioned that Kristine was a very close friend of William's; he had known her before the accident and how Kristine had come to be her friend as well; visiting on occasion. Lately, she had gone on to say, Kristine had not come, not even when Daniel was born, although she still sent a post every so often. Unsure what William would think, she took it upon herself to write Kristine a letter; perhaps she didn't know what had happened. *Kristine: You don't know me; I am a housekeeper for William Stevenson. I am of the understanding that you are a good friend of Abby and William and I am unsure whether you had received the news of Abby's passing. William does not know that I am writing to you, he has not been doing well since her death, blaming himself because she died in childbirth. I believe the only thing that is keeping him going are the two lads, Daniel and Samuel; he barely eats enough to survive and spends his evenings in a chair; sitting up all night. This would be understandable at first but it has been going on for several months now. I don't mean to alarm you and certainly don't expect you to do anything about it, but I thought you should know. Sincerely: Agnes Moorland.* She mailed the letter on her way home, hoping that William would not be angry at her if he found out she sent it.

When Kristine received the post she was stunned, Abby was gone, she couldn't believe it. Why hadn't William written to let her know? Well, as the housekeeper had said, he wasn't doing well. It didn't take her long to decide that she had to go to him and she packed her bags then went downstairs to tell her Mother. "I'm going to Glasgow, Mother, and it may be some time before I return. "What in the world for?" "My friend William, his wife Abby died; they have two small children, he will need help?" "For heaven's sake Kristine, you can't just move into a married man's house, it wouldn't be proper." "He's not married any more Mother, she's gone and he will need help, I'm going there's no talking me out of it; I don't know when or if I will return." "Kristine, listen to reason, think about what you are doing." Kristine turned to her mother, "I've loved him for years, Mother ever since the day we met on the coach, married or unmarried." "It might surprise you to know that we've had an affair." She left the house without looking back; her Mother stood in shock watching her go.

The carriage let her off at the front of the shop and she entered with her bags and found Bella behind the counter. "You're here, Bella said; I suppose you've heard what happened then?" "Yes, I'm so sorry, how is he doing?" "I don't see much of him, he's a different person, that's for sure." "I'm here to help, if he'll let me, is it ok if I go through this way." "Of course, Bella said, I'll help you with your bags." She knocked on the door at the top of the steps and Agnes answered it, "I'm Kristine, you sent me a post." Agnes was momentarily taken aback by the beauty of the lass; she was tall and slim with black eyes and curly black hair that fell past her shoulder, certainly not what she expected. "Aye, aye, come in, come in." "Is he here?" Kristine whispered. "Aye, he's in the sitting room where he always is, with the lads." Kristine reached out and gave Agnes a hug, "Thank you Agnes, for letting me know." "You're welcome, dear, I'm sorry I was the bearer of bad news; can I get you anything?" "No thank you, Kristine replied; nothing at all."

He was sitting on the couch, the bairn asleep beside him and Daniel on the floor playing with a toy. Daniel looked up at her and she knelt beside him, "You must be Daniel, what a handsome lad you are; a miniature of your Father." He nodded his head and repeated, "Daniel," she thought how like William he looked with blue eyes and blonde hair. She looked up and saw him staring at her, his hands at his sides; the sight of him alarmed her, his eyes were black beneath and he looked gaunt and pale." She touched his hand, but he let it lay there, not moving. She looked at him and said simply, "I'm so sorry, William, truly I am." He closed his eyes and nodded his head, not able to talk. "Look," Daniel said. She turned toward the lad and saw that he was holding out a toy toward her; "I see, she said, is that your toy?" He nodded his head. She sat on the floor at William's feet exchanging toys with Daniel as he handed them to her when she felt his hand touch her hair. Instinctively she knew that the healing process had to come from him; she could not push him, so she sat there as if she hadn't noticed. Agnes came into the sitting room and said, "This young lad has dinner waiting for him and I will put the bairn in his cradle." She continued to sit at his feet, laying her head against his legs and not moving; she could hear the sounds from the kitchen and Agnes' soothing voice talking to the lad. William was fortunate to have found her, she instantly liked the woman. It must have been another hour or more when she heard him say, "Why did you come?" She got up from the floor and sat close beside him on the couch, not touching him. "I thought you might need a friend." "You're not married then?" "No, of course not, I couldn't well, you know." "He touched the gold chain around her neck, "You still have it?" "Forever," was all she said. They sat there side by side, not touching for several more hours. He drifted in and out of sleep and Kristine watched Agnes bustle around from room to room; she could smell supper cooking on the hearth. "It was my fault you know, I killed her." Kristine sat up and looked at him, "No, that's not true, why would you say that?" "I knew she didn't want me, not that way, but one time, only one time, and she got pregnant; I didn't know, Kristine, I didn't know it would kill her; I thought it was in her head." She pulled his head to her chest, "Of course, you couldn't know, no one could have, it wasn't your fault, any man would have done the same and more; she wouldn't blame you." "Aye, but she did, he said, every time she looked at me, I could see it in her eyes." She touched his face, "Whatever happened is done, you have lads who need you now, all of you, you must stop punishing yourself, you've done enough of that already." He looked at her and tears started flowing out of his eyes so once again she pulled him to her and rocked him back and forth like a little child. Great sobs burst out of him, emotion that he had been holding back for months. She wanted to kiss the tears away but knew she couldn't so she continued to hold him like a mother until he was spent. Agnes could hear him from the kitchen where she sat drinking tea and she said to herself, "That's it, lad, get it out, finally get it all out." She was glad she had sent the post, perhaps this bonnie lass could bring him back into the world of the living. William fell asleep in her arms and she carefully let his head fall to her lap where she sat quietly so as not to wake him. Agnes came and told her that she had left supper on the hearth; put her bags in the spare bedroom, and that Gabrielle would be there soon to watch after the bairns. Kristine mouthed the words, "Thank you," to her.

After some time, Kristine heard Gabrielle coming into the house and sounds from the kitchen. William stirred in her lap and when he opened his eyes he was disoriented for a moment. He sat up, "I fell asleep, I'm sorry," he said. She smiled at him, "I'm not, I think you needed it." "The bairns are still sleeping?" "Yes, Gabrielle has just come in, listen William, if I fixed something, do you think you could come out and eat." "I'll try," he said and he grabbed her hand in his. "I'm glad you've come, will you stay long?" "As long as you let me," she replied and then rose to get supper ready. She went into the kitchen and introduced herself, "Hi Gabrielle, I'm Kristine, William's longtime friend." Gabrielle smiled at her, she had never seen anyone so bonnie, "Nice to meet you, me Mum told me you were here." Kristine laughed, "I like your Mother, William is lucky to have her here." Gabrielle nodded, "I've got to see to the wash before the bairns wake up, if you want me to help with anything, just let me know don't be afraid to ask." Kristine said, "I'm going to fix us a little something for supper, your mother left it on the hearth, would you like some too?" "No thank you, I ate at home," Gabrielle said smiling shyly at her.

Kristine fixed supper and called William to come and eat. He was still sitting there on the couch as he had done for hours since she arrived, no wonder Agnes was worried about him, it appeared that this must be what he does, all day long. She stood before him, "William, supper is ready, what would you like to drink, tea or milk?" "It doesn't matter, anything," he said. She poured a glass of milk and set it on the table. He came into the kitchen and stood there, she could see that he had lost a lot of weight, it was alarming. "Sit, she said, I'll eat with you." They ate together, William doing his best to eat as much as he could, he didn't talk and she didn't know what to say. He finished most of his food then sat there. "Drink your milk, she said, it will do you good." He finished the milk. "Do you still read, she asked, maybe a good book will take your mind off of things?" "I haven't," he said.

She cleared off the table and put the dishes away; he sat at the table and when she turned she saw that he was looking at her, "Is there anything else I can get for you?" she asked, sitting down by him. "I don't know, he said, my head won't stop thinking about it." She held his hands, "You've had quite a shock it's going to take time to get over." "I'll help you, but sitting around thinking about it isn't going to solve the problem; you have to keep busy, it will clear your mind." "Why are you doing this for me?" "You don't get it, do you William?" "I still love you, I've never stopped." "Go in by your son, I think he's awake again, I'll be there in a little while." She went into the bedroom and sat there wondering how she could get through to him; clearly he blamed himself for Abby's death, it seemed she had made him feel guilty about the pregnancy. She put her head in her hands and cried for him; then she prayed, something she hadn't done in a long time. Why she loved this man so much she didn't know, but love him she did and would continue to the end of her days; good and bad. She rose from the bed and went into the bathroom and held a cold rag to her face, then entered the sitting room with a smile on her face.

William was playing with Daniel who looked at her when she sat down. "Hi," he said. "Hello, do you remember me?" He nodded his head and gave her a toy. Gabrielle brought the bairn in and Kristine held him for the first time; "they both look like you," she said to William. He smiled at her, "Aye, they do." Agnes had told her that the pastor had asked William to come to the kirk on Sundays with the bairns but he hadn't gone. She laid the bairn on the couch next to William and once again she sat on the floor by Daniel playing with him. She looked at William and said, "Let's take them to the kirk on Sunday; it would be good if they got used to it while they are young." "You would go with me?" "If you want me to, yes, I will go." They sat there for several more hours, she playing with Daniel and William speaking a few words every so often." Finally Gabrielle came and got the children for bed which left Kristine and William alone in the sitting room. "Let's go out for ice cream, she said, or to the pub for ale, it will do you good to get out." "Ok," he said, and she told Gabrielle they would be back soon.

They left the house through the back gate and went around front to the sidewalk. She didn't take his hand, avoiding any contact with him until he was ready. "So, where are we going?" she asked. "How about the pub, he said, I could use ale." "The pub it is," she said. They walked along, looking in the shop windows and Kristine commenting, William nodding, or making only small comments. He took her hand in his; she noticed that he seemed to be limping on his leg more than usual; she supposed it was from all the months of sitting and not moving around. They entered the pub and sat down at a table. William noticed Maggie, the waitress, who was always flirting with him in the back. "Oh, I hope she doesn't come over here," he said. "Who," Kristine asked. "Maggie, the waitress, she likes me." Kristine laughed, "I can see why, she said, you're quite likeable." A different waitress came over and they both ordered ale. "Have you been in the shop much lately?" Kristine asked William. "No only to place the orders and check on things." "What about Bella, is she handling it ok?" "I guess, he said, she doesn't say anything." "Would you mind if I check and she if she needs any help?" "If you don't want me to, it's ok." He put his hand on his forehead and rubbed it, "I guess I've asked too much of them, I've only been thinking about meself as usual." "I'm sure they didn't mind, but perhaps it's time to give them a little break." He nodded, "You're right, it is time, I'll go down tomorrow." "Kristine?" She looked at him, "Yes?" "You've brought a glimmer of light back into me life; I want you here, as long as you want to be." "I've always been here with you, she said, even when we were miles apart." She couldn't help but notice him turn his head and wipe away a tear; her heart broke for him, his feelings were still all pent up inside. They sat there for a while and then left for home; immediately he took her hand again and she began to think that things might finally be coming around. "Thank you Lord," she said to herself.

"I think I'll wash up and get ready for bed, she told him, you should do the same, that's enough sleeping in the chair, it's not doing your leg any good I noticed it has been hurting you." "I can't sleep in there I just lie awake all night." "Then move into the other bedroom, we'll switch rooms and I'll sit with you until you fall asleep." She went into the spare bedroom and moved her things to the bedroom that William and Abby had shared; she could understand his hesitancy to be there; some of her things were still in the room. When she was finished in the bath she told him that there was warm water waiting for him, he should take a bath and she would wait up for him. "You will sleep better after the relaxing water." She folded the bed down for him and pulled the shades; when he came out she led him to the bedroom. "Take your pants off, you can't get a good sleep with them on she said, don't worry, I've seen you naked before." He dropped his trousers and got into bed like she asked; she picked them up and folded them over a chair. She brought another chair over to the bed and said, "I'll sit here with you until you fall asleep." She kissed him on the forehead and touched his hair, then sat down and took his hand. He looked at her. "I love you Kristine." Periodically he would doze off and then open his eyes to see her next to him, now with her head lying against the side of the bed; occasionally nodding off herself. He took his hand and laid it in her hair. When she thought he had finally gone into a deep sleep, she rose and went into the other bedroom, undressed and crawled into bed. She lay there thinking that she finally had made some progress; she felt he was coming out of the depression; maybe he just needed to know that someone still loved him. She fell asleep and didn't wake until she heard sounds from the kitchen in the morning, Agnes must already be here.

She opened the door and peeked out to see Daniel at the table and Agnes cooking at the stove. "Will you have porridge with us this morning," she asked Kristine. "Yes, anything you are making will be fine; I'll be out in a few minutes." Agnes thought she was a lovely lass and she didn't seem to have any airs for all of her beauty. Kristine looked in her bags for some of her things and then sat down to brush out her hair when she looked up and saw him standing in the doorway. "Good morning, she said, you're up, how did you sleep?" He smiled, looking a little more like the William she remembered, "I slept good, are you coming for breakfast?" "Yes, I'll be right there. I have a few things to do first." She walked to the door meaning to close it but he was still standing there, partially blocking it. He looked behind him and saw that Agnes had gone into the back room so he bent down and gave her a kiss on the cheek, "Ok," he said, then went and sat down at the table. She stood there and when he looked up again she smiled at him, then closed the door and got ready for the day. The spark had begun to rekindle.

They had their breakfast, both laughing at Daniel as his face and hair were covered with porridge from trying to use the spoon himself. "Were you that messy when you were a bairn?" Kristine asked. "I don't remember, William said, maybe." Agnes piped in, "All me bairns were, they wanted to do it themselves." "Is there anything you need today, William asked, I was thinking about going down to the shop for most of the day, I've left things go long enough." "I'm good for now, Agnes said, we'll have to get a few groceries by the weekend." "We'll go on Saturday morning if that works for you," said William. "Aye, that will work out just fine," Agnes replied. When he left, Agnes turned to Kristine with a smile, "I don't know what you've done or said, but he is like a different person today." "Yes, it's wonderful," Kristine said. "He couldn't sleep in that bed," she nodded toward the bedroom they had shared. "I made him go into the other one and I sat with him until he fell asleep." "I'm so glad you've come," said Agnes. "Let me help with the dishes," Kristine said. "There's no need, that's what I'm here for dear," replied Agnes. Kristine carried the dishes over to the sink, "Two hands can get it done faster." They worked together cleaning up the kitchen. Kristine wiped her hands on her apron and looked at Agnes, "Can I tell you something private?" "Yes dear, what is it?" Agnes said. "I've loved him for years, since the first time I saw him." Agnes touched her arm, "Anyone can see that, even an old fool like me, and he loves you, I can see that too." Kristine hugged her, "You're far from being an old fool you're the wisest woman I know." "Between us, Agnes said, Abby was a wonderful woman, a good mother to Daniel and a good wife except when it came to meeting his needs." "I've had six bairns of me own, I know a good wife has to please her man or he will look elsewhere." Kristine put her head down, "I never told anyone this before but we had an affair one time, but that's the only time it happened; I felt guilty after because I liked Abby, I really did, she was my friend." "Don't dwell on it, dear, what's past is past; you can't stuff your feelings in a box, sometimes they escape." "Thanks, Agnes, for understanding." Kristine kissed her on the cheek. "I thought I'd go down and see if Bella needs any help, I'll see you later." "What a lovely lass, Agnes thought, so bonnie there's just nothing pretentious about her; you don't find many like that in this world."

Kristine entered the shop and found Bella marking inventory. "Bella, I'm here to help you if you need it." "I'd certainly appreciate it; I'm getting a little behind." "Whatever you need, just tell me what to do." Bella had Kristine sit down and start putting prices on the new inventory so they could get it up on the shelves. The shop was so popular that items flew off the shelves about as fast as they went on. With customers coming and going, it was hard to work on the inventory. Kristine helped all afternoon and periodically peeked into the men's shop to see if William was still there; he was. Bella invited Kristine in back for lunch; they got along well together; neither of them mentioned Abby's passing or William's depression. Bella told her about Benjamin, her beau. "I met him in the men's shop when I was filling in for William, we hit it off and have been seeing each other ever since." "Where does he work?" Kristine asked. "At the livery, down near the station, he grew up just outside of Glasgow; I'm going to meet his family on Sunday." "He must be getting serious about you then," Kristine replied. "Aye, I think so," said Bella.

Kristine was back upstairs playing with Daniel; she was lying on her stomach with him on the floor. When William came up he heard the giggling and laughing and peeked into the sitting room; there she was playing with his son and thoroughly enjoying it. He thought, "This is what a house is supposed to sound like; happiness and joy; my God how I've missed it!" He stood there watching them for some time until Daniel looked up and said, "Da." Kristine sat up, "You're home, come and sit by us, right Daniel." Daniel nodded his head, "Sit." William laughed, "Ok, son, come here." He picked him up and put him on his lap. Daniel looked at Kristine, "Sit," he said. She came off the floor and sat beside them. "Bella and I got a lot done today," she told him. "Nathaniel said he was glad to see me back, he needed help." He reached over and touched her arm, "Thanks, Kristine." "Tank Kisse," said Daniel. Kristine reached over and kissed him, "You're welcome Daniel." "He should eat with us at night, Agnes and Gabrielle too," Kristine said. "I agree, replied William, I'll tell her."

Agnes and Gabrielle joined them in the evening for supper after protesting, "Aw, you're spoiling me too much, I'm supposed to be working for ye, not dilly dallying." "Another thing, Kristine said, we want to know if you'll come to the kirk with us on Sunday, Gabrielle too." "Oh go on now, the both of you, it's too much, cavorting around with an old used up hag like me." Kristine laughed, "Good, it's settled then, you'll come, we'll pick you up"

CHAPTER THIRTY-SIX

The days and months flew by and they began to feel like a family, Samuel was sleeping all night now and Agnes said that it wasn't necessary for Gabrielle to stay all night any longer; she could still come on wash day and help with the laundry. "Will she find other employment," Kristine asked? "Aye, she'll find something in time,"Agnes replied. Kristine continued, "Bella could really use some help in the shop, if she's interested." "I'll ask her, you're such a thoughtful person Kristine." "We, William and I, like Gabrielle and we need help in the shop so she'd be doing us a favor." Gabrielle took the job leaving William and Kristine to tend the bairns at night but they didn't mind, in fact, they enjoyed it. When the bairns were finally asleep at night the electricity in the house changed, they were both very aware of each other; long gone was the easy kidding and touching they used to have between them; they both knew that it would now lead to more. Kristine was ready, but she knew that William still had not healed completely.

They picked up Agnes and Gabrielle on Sunday and had to smile because they were dressed in their best frocks and hats. They had dinner at a restaurant after the service. Agnes was always enjoyable because she was full of stories and had a natural way of telling them. The pastor was curious, but didn't ask about the raven haired beauty that came to the kirk with them, he thought perhaps it was a relative; in any case, he was glad to see them there on Sundays. One night they were sitting on the couch after the bairns had gone to bed and William pulled her to him, "Kristine, I can't go on like this anymore, I want to sleep beside you, not have separate bed-rooms; I need you and I want you to marry me." She threw her arms around his neck, "William Stevenson, I have waited years to hear those words." He brought his lips gently to hers and then he pulled her head to his chest, "I won't mess it up this time, I promise, he said, I think maybe it's you I've been waiting for my whole life." "Oh William, you haven't messed up anything you just had more than your share of bad luck; that's all."

They had a simple ceremony at the kirk. Kristine took Agnes and Gabrielle down to the shop and insisted they be outfitted from head to toe and they were be-side themselves, never having had that kind of luxury before. William and Kristine picked out some fancy clothes for the bairns; William got a new suit and Kristine a simple but expensive wedding dress. Her parents came from Perth and her Father walked her down the aisle. Kristine was a bonnie bride and William couldn't stop the tears running down his cheeks as she approached; it had been a long road for both of them but he knew, without a doubt, that this marriage was meant to be. As much as she tried, her mother couldn't resist William's smile and charm; she adored the bairns and said she had more grandchildren now. Agnes cried tears of happiness

293

the entire time saying, "Oh my, I'll have to wring out my handkerchief now," they all laughed at her. Ryan and Bella both came with their beaus, Nathaniel with his wife, and everyone was invited to The Grand Central Hotel on Gordon Street for dinner where they enjoyed the evening and drank a lot of ale.

That evening, the bairns fell asleep early from all the day's activity. The secrets were over, William and Kristine spent their first night of married life cuddled together in bed and William finally knew what it was like to have a wife who welcomed his lovemaking and didn't turn away from him when it was over. They came together several times that night and they both fell asleep knowing they would wake in the morning still in love and still desiring each other for many years to come; their relationship, strange as it was, had weathered the worst and best times throughout the years.

Kristine's parents were staying at the hotel for a few days and they came to the flat to visit before they went home. Leslie, Kristine's Father, took a tour of the men and women's shop and purchased a few items commenting on how fashionable it was. Ruth, her mother, came upstairs with several bags of things she had found in the women's shop, she was quite taken with it. Agnes had left some scones for them to serve and they sat in the sitting room talking. "You know, Leslie said to William, the lads are going to want to be outside when they get a little bigger; Glasgow is a dangerous city and they don't have much room to play outside here." "Aye, William replied, I grew up in Killin, it was lovely there, and I miss the country." "This is just a suggestion, William; I was looking at your shop, it's as progressive as I've seen anywhere and the tobacco is top grade." "I don't know if Kristine has told you I'm a tobacco merchant." "Aye, she did tell me that, we get our goods from the Edinburgh Shipping Company." "Then you probably have some of my tobacco in your store, we deal with them; they're one of the best shipping companies around; they have a new owner you know." "I know her, she's from Killin," said William. "Small world isn't it," replied Leslie. "Anyway, what I was getting at, Crieff is an up and coming town and not too large; a perfect place to raise your lads. The town has a reputation for being fashionable and a lot of wealthy businessmen frequent it; I think your business would do well there, and it's midway between Perth and Killin." "They have railroad service there now which means more people will be visiting." "I like the idea," William said, but Agnes, Bella and Nathaniel depend on me now." "Does Agnes own her own home?" Leslie asked. "No, she rents a flat, it's just her daughter Gabrielle and herself who live there now; the other children are married and have their own homes." "There you go then, Leslie said, let her have the flat or bring her with you, perhaps she would like to get out of the city too." "You could still keep the shops open here and offer Bella and Nathaniel more money to take on added responsibility; with the railroad open in Crieff, you can travel to Glasgow in no time at all once a month or so to check on things." "If you want to do this, and again, I'm only making a suggestion, I will help you obtain a building in Crieff; I do a little dabbling in property you see." "It sure would be nice to go fishing again, I'd like to take me lads," William said. "Let me see what Kristine thinks and we'll let you know, it would take some planning but I'm ready to leave the city, that's for sure, these four walls are not my cup of tea if you know what I mean." "Why don't you think about it and make a visit to Perth one of these day, we'd welcome the company and Lord knows we have enough room for you to stay." "I'd like that, said William, it's very kind of you to offer." "Nonsense lad, we're family now," he said, and patted him on the arm.

Ruth watched Kristine with the bairns and was surprised how she took to them and they took to her; it was apparent that she was a natural mother. For all the years of trying to find her daughter a suitable husband, it appeared she had misjudged her daughter; she could see that Kristine was glowing and yes, she could see how anyone would be attracted to this man, he was very charming and quite handsome. Yes, he might be a little crude for her taste but he seemed so genuine that it was easy to overlook his lack of social graces. His smile was infectious, Kristine told her that he was subconscious about the scar and couldn't look at himself anymore; she thought it was a shame because it really didn't look that bad. She was sorry that he still had the limp but she supposed he was lucky he didn't lose the leg altogether. It certainly didn't seem to hinder him that much, he got around pretty well. She had to admit that she liked him. She would always wonder how the love between them had occurred. Kristine said it had gone on for years and yet she never let on to them. She knew that Kristine had made several trips to see the couple throughout the years but she had just assumed she enjoyed spending time with them. Her daughter was certainly a complicated and mysterious woman but she had always said Kristine had a mind of her own.

Leslie and Ruth left with lots of tears and hugs; William promised they would come for a visit as soon as they could. Once alone again, Kristine took the bairns one by one and bathed them, then put their nightclothes on; she handed Samuel to William so she could get a bottle ready for him and then came and took him in her arms. "You're a great mother," William said. "You think?" Kristine replied, I like bairns, I hope we have one." "Only one, that's all," he teased. "I like your parents, your Da talked to me about something, we'll have to discuss it tomorrow." "That's my Father, always a business deal up his sleeve," Kristine laughed. Samuel fell asleep after Kristine burped him and she laid him in the cradle; he would most likely sleep all night now. Daniel was beginning to nod off and William carried him to bed.

In the morning, William said to Agnes, "You rent your flat don't you Agnes?" "Aye, I rent it," she said; when me husband got sick we lost our home." He went into the sitting room where Kristine was on the couch feeding Samuel. "Your Da thinks we should move to Crieff and start a shop there, he said it would be a better place for the children to grow up, what do you think?" "I'm happy anywhere as long as you're with me, she said, but there really isn't anywhere outside for them to play here, the back yard is so small and we wouldn't want them to get out into the street." "I do miss the country and fishing," he said.

First William approached Nathaniel. "We'd like to move to the country but don't want to leave you without a job, we've talked about it and decided we can leave the shop open and pay you more to run it and of course you can hire more help." "I appreciate the offer, Nathaniel said, but I really was going to talk to you about cutting back my hours, my other business is suffering." "I understand, William said, it's a lot of work; can you stay long enough for us to make a decision?" "Of course, I wouldn't leave you empty handed." "I appreciate it, William said, thanks for everything you've done, especially when I wasn't helping." "It wasn't a problem, really, Nathaniel said, I was glad I could be of assistance." William went over to the women's shop and posed the same question. "My plans are so up in the air right now, she said, we'll probably get married soon and he wants to move to Stirling." "Don't even worry about the shop I'll stay until you've made a decision." "I appreciate you letting me live here it was a Godsend to get out of the other flat." William gave her a hug, "Thank you for your honesty, I'll keep you updated." "Well, he thought, I guess this will be easier, we'll just sell the place and won't have to worry about coming back to check on things every couple months." He went back up and found Kristine, "I've talked to both of them and neither of them wants to stay long term; I think we should just put the place up for sale." "We can buy Agnes a little house here, or better yet maybe they would come with us." "I think we're doing the right thing for the bairns, Kristine said, we'll have to go tomorrow and see a property management firm, Agnes can watch the bairns or have Gabrielle take a break from the shop and come upstairs." "Oh, by the way, I love you William Stevenson, I've never been so happy my entire life," she gave him a kiss and he held her close.

They talked to property management and he agreed to come the next day to do an assessment. "It's in a prime area, he said, you should have no trouble selling." The property went on the market and William and Kristine took a trip to Perth; William and Leslie were going to Crieff to check out property and Kristine and the bairns would stay with Ruth. This would be the closest to Killin that William had been since he left all those years ago. They took the coach from Perth to Crieff and William said, "This is where Kristine and I met, except the coach was going the other direction." It felt strange but wonderful to him to be out of the city. Leslie had called ahead so the property agent was waiting for them when they arrived in Crieff. "I have a shop for you to look at it's in the district that is frequented by some of the wealthy businessmen who like to come to Crieff." They entered the shop and it had more room than the one in Glasgow, the shelves and counters were already there and it had a good sized storage room; they stepped outside and discussed it, then came back in and told the agent William would purchase it contingent on finding a home here and selling his property in Glasgow. "You've told me what you were looking for in a home and I believe I've found something you would like, would you be interested in looking at it today, I can't guarantee how long it will be on the market?" "Yes, of course." Leslie said. It was a cute little cottage just a short drive from the town with a big yard, large livery, lots of trees and two other small cottages on the property. "Can we have a look inside," William asked. "Yes, come along," the agent said. There were four bedrooms, a large sitting room with a fireplace, a modern bath, kitchen with a hearth and oven, a laundry room and large built in porch in the back with lots of closets and storage space. It was perfect, all they had to do now was sell what they had and see if Agnes would be willing to come along. "Can we see the little cottages, please," William asked. The cottages were small but nicely arranged and each one had two bedrooms; they also had a small porch on the back and a laundry room between them to share. "We'll be in touch with you early next week," Leslie told the agent. "Very well sir, I can hold the property until the end of next week, after that I won't be able to guarantee its availability." "Fair enough, Leslie said, we'll get back to you as soon as possible."

"Looks like we had a good days' work son," said Leslie, "Aye, sir, I'm excited just to be here, in the country it has been a long time." "The store and houses are just perfect; exactly what we need." "Thank you for the suggestion; I would never have arranged it on me own." "Thank you William," Leslie replied. "What say you we head for home, I think we have time for lunch before the coach comes." "Aye, William said, I could use something to eat." "I think we are going to be good friends, William, Leslie replied, we have something else in common too." "What's that sir?" "We both adore Kristine." William laughed, "She's certainly one of a kind, there's no one else like her." "Say, by the way, you don't play chess do you?" "As a matter of fact I do," Leslie replied. "I tinker with it meself, William laughed, we'll have to have a go of it." They had lunch at the inn and then made their way to the livery where they would catch the coach. "I was here before, William said, it's amazing how many horses they have." "Yes but it's a dying business, Leslie replied, the train is here now and there are more and more steamboats on the river." They were the only passengers on the trip to Perth so they stretched out and relaxed in their seats. "Does your leg hurt a lot," Leslie asked? "Aye, but I have no choice but to put up with it." "Kristine tells me you were lucky to even walk again, is that true?" "Aye, the doctor was amazed I could walk, they almost took it." "That must have been hard, you had all your plans made and didn't get to fulfill them." "The hardest part was that I let everybody down." "Well, Leslie said, sometimes you can't predict what's going to happen in life." It had been a long day and both men dozed off and didn't wake until they were at Perth.

It was a busy time for all of them, they spent every moment they could packing what they wanted to take with them which would be loaded on a cart and transported to Crieff via railway, making several changes along the way. Kristine asked Agnes if she and Gabrielle would come with them; she explained that there were two cottages on the property they were buying. "Oh, Good Lord, she cried, I don't know what to say." "Say yes then, Kristine laughed, if you'd like to see it first, I can take you there to look at it." "It wouldn't be far for your other children to come, with the train service there now." "I don't need to see it dear, I trust your judgment." "You can even have your own garden if you like, Kristine said." "No, now I've lost me senses, Agnes cried, me own garden?" "Kristine, you and William are too good to me." "I think it's the other way around, Kristine replied, we don't know what we'd do without the two of you." "So you'll do it then, come with us?" "Aye, we'll do it, thank you Kristine" "No thanks are necessary, you are family now and it would have been so hard to leave you behind." "Besides, Kristine said giving her a hug, William and I wouldn't be together today if it hadn't been for you."

The building was sold quicker than they thought it would be and they worked hard from morning until night trying to get everything done. They had decided not to open a ladies shop in Crieff, Kristine wanted to devote all of her time to the bairns. They had a huge sale and sold what they could, the new owners purchased the counters, shelves and register along with the furniture in both flats. The men's shop was packed up, ready to be transported to the new one in Crieff. They had accomplished a lot of work in a short period of time and the toll was showing on William's leg. Worn out from all the work, they spent the last night in a barren sitting room. William was fondling the engraving of Loch Tay that Kristine had given him in the hospital; it was still one of his favorite possessions. Likewise, Kristine never forgot to put on her little golden heart. "I'm not going to miss Glasgow," he said. "I agree, replied Kristine, it's a fun place to visit but not to live." "I'm so glad Agnes and Gabrielle are coming with us, I'm sure they will like being out of the city." "Aye, the bairns would have missed them, they are so close now." "I'll miss Bella, Ryan, and Nathaniel, it's hard to start over, there's always someone you leave behind." His voice husky with emotion he said, "I'd like to get some flowers and go to the cemetery before we leave, would you come with me?" She nodded; Of course I'll come with you I'd like to say good-bye too."

They had a tearful farewell with Nathaniel and Bella who promised to get on the train and visit them. "You must come to my wedding, I'll send you an invitation," Bella said. "We'll be there, Kristine promised; we wouldn't miss it for the world." "Thank you for everything," William and Kristine shouted in unison. They met Ryan and his beau at the pub while Gabrielle watched the bairns. "Let me introduce my beau, Nancy," Ryan said. Kristine and William both shook her hand, "It's nice to finally meet you," Kristine said. "You'll both have to come and visit us in Crieff, it doesn't take long on the train and we have a little cottage behind the house." "We never got in a last chess game," laughed Ryan. "I know, said William, I'm sorry for my attitude after, well you know, after Abby died." "Don't apologize, Ryan said, it was understandable." William nodded, a lump in his throat, "By the time we play again, I'll have forgotten how." "Naw, you won't forget, it sticks with you; if you need any help moving, just let me know." "We hired some men to load everything and take it to the station but I appreciate the offer." They stayed for an hour or so and then decided they'd best get home to the bairns. "Keep in touch, William said, I've enjoyed getting to know you." "Same here," Ryan replied, giving William a hug. They left and walked down the sidewalk, hand in hand. "Nice people," William said. "Yes, and you were so jealous of him," Kristine laughed. "I was, grinned William, I admit it."

The bairns were still up when they got home and Kristine told William to give Gabrielle a ride, "She shouldn't be out on the street by herself at night." Gabrielle came lumbering into the kitchen, "It's not a problem, I've been out late on the street afore now." "Well what do you say if we go in the cart tonight, you must be tired," William said. "Yes sir," she replied. Kristine asked if they were all packed and ready to go. "Aye we're ready," she said. "If you have anything that needs to go by train, we need to pick it up early morning before the movers come." "No, there's nothing, me Mum says ain't nothing worth anything more than a kick." Kristine laughed, "You tell your Mother she can have anything she wants for the new house, now off with you before it gets too late."

When they had left, Kristine thought how generous and giving these common people were, never complaining even though they had very little in this world. Samuel was asleep on the couch so Kristine carried him in the bedroom and laid him in the cradle, then stood looking at him. She loved these bairns as if they had come from her own loins; Daniel was going to be the spitting image of William, already he had the little wisp of hair that liked to escape to his forehead and the big grin that made William irresistible. She sat on the couch by him, "We're moving to the country where you will have lots of room to play outside." He crawled up on the couch beside her, "Side?" She nodded her head, "Yes, outside where there are lots of trees and grass and birds." He pushed himself on the couch until he was snuggled next to her and she put her arm around him and bent down, whispering in his ear. "I love you, Daniel Stevenson." She kissed him on the cheek. He grabbed her hair in his fingers, "Love," he said. With his fingers still entwined in her hair he fell asleep. They sat that way until William came in the house, "Let me carry him to bed," he said, picking him up. Kristine followed, undressed him and put his night clothes on. William covered him up and he briefly opened his eyes and said, "Da". William kissed him on the head and they both left the room. In a playful mood William grabbed her around the waist and pulled her to him, "I love my bairns and I love my wife, life is good again." She ran her hands up his chest and threw her arms around his neck. "And I love my life with all of you." They kissed and William said, "Let's get ready for bed; it's been a long day." They crawled into bed, their last night in Glasgow and made love, then slept curled up together until morning.

They barely had time to get themselves and the bairns fed for breakfast before the men came to start loading things into the cart. Kristine had the bairns dressed and had packed a few extra clothes for them that they would carry along with bottles and diapers for Samuel. 'This is it love, she said to William, are you ready?" "Aye, I'm ready." They would take the horse and carriage to the cemetery and one of the men would be waiting at the station to bring it back to the flat as the livery had been sold with everything else. They were assured that someone would tend to the horses daily. Kristine left William with the children and hurried into the flower shop to get flowers for the cemetery. They pulled the carriage into the cemetery and Kristine kissed William on the cheek, "Go ahead and say your good-byes, dear, we will come in a minute." He walked slowly to the grave sites and kneeled down and laid the flowers. "I'm so sorry, Abby, he said, I promise to take good care of your bairns, thank you for taking care of me, I will always love you." He couldn't stop the flow of tears for the caring, selfless lass whose heart was bigger than her small petite body. Kristine felt for her husband, she knew that he still carried the guilt of her death by childbirth and, like her, the secret of their affair with each other. She exited the carriage with the bairn in her arms and then helped Daniel down. "Let's go and say goodbye to your Mother and Grandda." William turned and came to help them; Daniel still wasn't steady on his feet. They stood in silence at the grave and then slowly walked back to the carriage and went to pick up Agnes and Gabrielle. They were ready and waiting looking like two homeless people who had nowhere to go. Kristine smiled when she saw that they were all dressed up in the clothes they had received for the wedding. William got down and tried his best to help them into the cart. "Well here we go, are you ready?" Kristine asked, looking behind her. "Ready as we ever will be," Agnes replied.

As promised, the man was waiting for the carriage. William handed over the reins, patted the horse on the back and they went to find out where they needed to wait for the train. Daniel was quite fascinated with all the activity at the station and sat on the bench swinging his legs back and forth. Samuel lay in Kristine's arms, still asleep. "It's been a long, hard road since I left Killin, certainly not what I expected, but God's been good to me and I have me bairns and you." "I can't say that I deserve it, I don't, but God willing I will have time to make up for all my mistakes." "I would have stayed here if you wanted me to, but I'm excited to be starting over in our own home," Kristine replied. "I hope you like it, it's not fancy," William said. "You should know me by now, dear, fancy doesn't impress me, that's not what I need." "Did you know Crieff used to be a rather violent town?" "I heard that, William replied, wasn't it something to do with cattle rustlers?" "Yes, I think they still have the original hanging post in the town square." "They used to drive cattle herds through the town, also Comrie." "It will be interesting getting to know our way around but at least it will be safer and we can get away from the four walls." "I'm going to regret one thing," William said. "What's that?" she asked. "With my leg, I won't be able to carry you over the threshold." "If that's the biggest problem we have, she laughed, I think we'll be ok."

The estate agent had purchased a carriage and horses for them; arrangements were already made at the railroad to deliver the freight; the boxes were all marked for the house or the shop and they had the keys to get in if William and Kristine were delayed. William had his work cut out for him getting the new shop ready for business and he momentarily had a feeling of panic; there was so much to do, he didn't know where to start and he felt hindered by his leg." "They drove to the house on the outside of town and William jumped out to assist Kristine with the bairn; and then he lifted Daniel out of the carriage. "It's cute, Kristine said smiling at him; I can't wait to see the inside." "It's furnished, William said, but we can replace what you don't like." "Come along, he said to Agnes and Gabrielle, I'll show you your cottage next." "He unlocked the door and gave Kristine a kiss, "This will have to do as I can't carry you, welcome home Mrs. Stevenson." She took the bairn from him and handed it to Agnes then threw her arms around her husband and planted a long kiss on him. "Thank you for making me your wife, she said, I love you William." Agnes and Gabrielle looked at each other and smiled.

Kristine took Samuel from Agnes, "Go and see your new home, she said, I'll come over in a few minutes." "Come, William said, there are two, you can have either one you want." They went in back and Agnes let out a gasp when she saw them. "Oh my, she said, they are both so adorable, how will we choose." "You'll have to figure that one out on your own, he laughed. I'll leave you to decide; if you need anything, come and get me, our belongings should arrive soon." He went back to the house and saw that Kristine was moving from room to room looking at everything. She spotted him and came towards him, a huge smile on her face. "Oh William, you couldn't have found a more perfect cottage, I just love it." "I'm glad, he said, but your Da deserves the credit, he had a lot to do with it." William was relieved that Kristine was happy. "I can't believe you even remembered to have a crib delivered, she said, what bedroom will we take?" "That's entirely up to you, he replied, whatever my wife wants, she can have."

It wasn't long before Agnes and Gabrielle came into the house, obviously happy as they were all smiles. "We decided on the one by the livery, Agnes said, there's a nice place for a garden behind it." "Good, said William, do you like it?" "Like it? Agnes cried, we more than like it, we love it." "What would you like us to do, she said, we're ready to go to work." "There's nothing today, William said, let's all just get familiar with the place, tomorrow I'll have Gabrielle come with me to the shop if that's alright." "Yes sir, Agnes said, what time shall she come?" "I'll knock when I have the cart ready," he said. "Listen, we're all hungry, let's go to town in a little while and have something to eat, Kristine's Da and I ate there the other day, they have good food." "Oh that's not necessary, Agnes said, Gabrielle and I can make do." "No, you're coming with us, we're a family," William said. "You're too good to us, Mr. Stevenson, we'll be ready when you are," Agnes replied. Kristine showed her their cottage and then left so that she could see theirs. She was pleasantly surprised at how roomy and cozy it was, it looked much smaller from the outside. "I like my cottage, how about you?" Kristine asked. "Words couldn't express how much we like it, dear," Agnes said, wiping a tear from her eye. "Come here, you're supposed to be happy, not sad, let me give you a hug." She wrapped her arms around the woman and then motioned for Gabrielle to get in the middle. "I think we're going to be one big happy family from now on." "I for one am more than happy to leave the city behind." "Aye, aye," they both nodded.

They set off for their first visit to town for supper. William found the eatery and they enjoyed a good supper, all of them hungry and tired from the long trip. Daniel was a perfect little gentleman and Samuel slept through the meal. They returned home; Kristine readied the bairns for bed and William put the carriage away. William was busy out in the livery tending to his horses, they had a pasture behind the house and he was told the fences were intact so he let them out to run for a while. He found the food that had been left for them and put fresh water in the trough. He made a mental note to find out where he could order more food for them. He managed to rake some fresh hay and clean up the area without too much effort but his leg was beginning to tire and he had to sit on the bench and rest. It might be too much for him once the shop was open so he wanted to talk it over with Kristine and see if they could hire someone to do the yard work and take care of the livery. He hoped the horses would return to the livery to eat at which time he would close the gate to the pasture for the night; he would come out and check later. He went outside and looked around at his land, just the smell of the countryside made him feel like a new man and to think that Killin was only a few miles away.

He returned to the house to find Kristine on the couch feeding the bairn. Both children had been bathed and were in their night clothes. Daniel was going from window to window looking outside. William smiled, "Looks like he'll have his walking down soon, he's got a lot to explore." "I know, Kristine replied, and we don't have to worry about the stairs." "Are you tired?" she asked. "I am, bone tired and mind tired from thinking about what to do next." "Just take it one day at a time, everything will work out." "I've let the horses out to pasture, I hope they return to eat so I can shut the gate for the night." "I was thinking that once the shop is open, I might need some help with the yard and the livery." "When you're in town tomorrow, she said, ask around, I'm sure someone will know who might be interested in part time work."

Daniel realized William was back in the house and he toddled over to him, "Da," he said, a big smile on his face. William picked him up and gave him a kiss. "How does my little man like his new home?" "Home," Daniel said. Kristine laughed, "Pretty soon he will be talking so much we will wish he were quiet." William, with Daniel still in his arms, sat down next to her. "We'll have to go to town tomorrow, she said, I have nothing in the house to cook with." "Right, William said, when they deliver the rest of our things tomorrow, why don't you and Agnes catch a ride back to the shop with them and Agnes can take the cart; she says she knows how to drive one." "I guess I'll have to have some lessons too," Kristine said. They relaxed in the house playing with Daniel until he became tired and William carried him off to bed. He came back and announced he would check on the horses, "I hope they're back so I don't have to chase them in," he said. He went out the back door and over to the livery and was happy to see that they had indeed come in to eat. He quickly shut the gate, gave a last look around and went back into the house. Kristine was in the bathroom getting ready for bed so William sat and waited for her. She came out in her shift with wet hair and William's heart skipped a beat at the sight of her. How lucky he was to have found a woman like her and to wait for him all these years, he wondered if he deserved it. "I'll fix your bath water, she said, it felt good to bathe, I was so dusty and sweaty from all the traveling." She flitted around from room to room looking like she had been living there her entire life. Soon she appeared, "all ready, dear," she said. William rose and went into the bathroom. He undressed and got into the tub. She came to the door and said, "I'll wash your back, give me the towel." He handed it to her and she lathered it with suds and washed his back. He turned and looked at her and they kissed. "Let me wash your hair for you," she said. She ran and got a cup and then returned; her shift half wet from washing his back. "You're all wet," he said. "It doesn't matter, she replied, we won't be dressed that long." He laughed. She washed his hair, then ran and got fresh water and rinsed it. He pulled the plug on the tub and rose in all his glory. She took a dry towel and wiped his back, then kneeled down and cleaned out the tub and wiped the floor. She hung all the towels to dry and then returned to find him standing in the kitchen. "What bedroom are we going to have?" he asked. "Oh, this one, she said, it's closer to the bairns." They walked to the bedroom together and he sat on the edge of the bed. She stood before him and he lifted her shift and handed it to her. "Best you hang this up to dry," he said smiling at her. She draped it on a chair and then crawled into bed beside him. "Welcome home, Mrs. Stevenson," he said in a husky voice. She threw her arms around his neck, "Don't keep me up all night now, she said, we have a lot to do tomorrow." He chuckled, "We'll see, you looked pretty inviting in that wet shift of yours." "You should talk, she laughed, you looked inviting when you came out of the water."

Early next morning William and Kristine woke to voice of Daniel who was standing next to their bed. William reached down and put him into bed beside them. "What are you doing up already son," he said. "Mum," he said, his arms outstretched toward Kristine. Kristine looked at William, "Its ok, he said, you are his mother now." Relieved, she reached out to him and gave him a kiss, at the same time trying to keep the sheet pulled up over her body. William scrambled to get his pants on and then he took Daniel into the kitchen so Kristine could get dressed. She came into the kitchen and they smiled at each other thinking how they had been caught. She got them both milk and then started fixing porridge, one of the few things they had in the house to eat." Halfway through the meal, Samuel started crying so she rose to get him a bottle and then brought him into the kitchen too. "Who knew I would be surrounded by three lads in the morning," she laughed. "You sound like me Mum, he said, she always wanted a daughter but just had us four lads." Kristine didn't say anything but it didn't pass her notice that this was the first time he had ever mentioned anything about his family.

"Guess it's time to get to work," he said. "William, she asked, could you get a blanket from the bedroom and lay it on the sitting room floor so I can lay Samuel down?" He got the blanket, kissed Kristine, patted Daniel on the head and said, "Goodbye, I'll see you later." "Bye," said Daniel. "Don't overdue William, it will all get done in time," cautioned Kristine. He went to get the cart and horse and then let the other horse out into the pasture. To be fair, he thought he would rotate them every day so they both got exercise. He knocked on the door and Gabrielle answered. "Did you sleep ok?" he asked. "Like a bairn," she said, I'm ready to go if you are." "I'm ready, he said, is your Mum up?" "Aye, she's been up for a while, come in." Agnes came around the corner and he told her that Kristine wanted her to go to town later for supplies. "I'll be ready, she said, I was just on me way over there to help with the bairns."

They were on their way. "I don't know what to expect but I'm sure we will be busy today," he said to Gabrielle. "It's ok, sir, I'm a hard worker." "Aye, I know you are; I appreciate you helping." "Oh Mr. Stevenson, we want to work, me Mum says we're not here for a free ride." "Call me William," he said. "Oh, I couldn't sir, it wouldn't be proper." He laughed, "Its ok, really, I don't mind, I'll call you Gabby if you call me William, do we have a deal?" Gabrielle laughed, "Deal," she said.

They pulled up in front of the shop and went inside. There were boxes everywhere and it was hard to know where to start. William found paper and a pen and made a sign for the front door. *Stevenson & Sons Men's Emporium: Opening Soon.* "Gabrielle, maybe you can find a way to fix this to the front door," he handed her the sign. She found a hammer and some nails and went to put the sign on the door when she heard some carriages coming down the street. They all pulled up in front of the store. She went in and found William, then pointed towards the door. "What in the world are all these carriages doing here," he said. He opened the door and went outside. "Are you William," one of the men asked him. "Aye, he said, are you looking for me?" "Aye, the man said, we are all here to help you; Leslie Oswald hired us for the week." William smiled, "Come in gentlemen, I can certainly use the help." "One more thing, the man said, we've been instructed to take all of this food to your home." William looked out at the cart which was piled high with food and ice; it appeared that Kristine's Da was just as surprising as she was. "Gabrielle, he said, can you show the gentlemen the way to the cottage." "Yes sir," she said. "Hop up here lass," the man with the food said, and they left.

Kristine and Agnes were working on the belongings that had just recently arrived when they heard a cart coming. They walked outside to look and saw Gabrielle in the seat. "What are you doing up there?" Agnes yelled. "Kristine's Da sent a cart with ice and food so William told me to show them the way." Kristine smiled, "Bless his heart, he always thinks of everything." The man asked where they would like him to put the food; Kristine instructed him to divide it up between this cottage and the one behind." "Agnes, she asked, would you be kind enough to show the gentleman where the root cellar is." 'Of course, Kristine," she replied. "That's not the only surprise," said Gabrielle. They both looked at her, "It's not, what else?" asked Kristine. "He sent six men to help with the shop." "No, really, said Kristine, that's my Father." When the groceries had all been unloaded the man asked if there were anything else they needed. "I don't think so, Kristine said, thank you for coming, do you live here in Crieff." "Aye, Madam, just down the road from here; when I heard they were hiring I offered right away." "I have a farm but with three bairns, it's hard to make a living, I'm always looking for extra work." "You don't say, Kristine replied, it just so happens that we are looking for someone to attend to the livery and yard work, part time of course." "I would offer the job to you right now but I don't know if William, my husband, may have already found someone." "It would be perfect for me, Mrs. Stevenson, being just down the road and all, do you mind if I ask him about it, I'm going back to the shop to work." "By all means, Kristine replied, I hope he hires you, may I ask your name?" "Martin, he said, Martin Feldman." "Maybe you could bring your wife over sometime, we are anxious to meet people from Crieff, we don't know anyone yet." "I'll do that, he said, she'd like to meet you." He left and was thinking about her on the way back to the shop, "What a nice lass she is, so bonnie and yet so friendly."

The shop was coming along nicely; William had never expected so much to get done this quickly. Everyone seemed to work in unison; at this rate he would be able to open the shop by the end of the week. He asked if anyone knew who made signs. "Yes, over on Burrell Street, one of the men said, I could drop the request off for you if you like, I have to go over to the tannery later today and it's not far from there." "That would be wonderful, let me get a measuring stick and I'll write down what I need." He went outside and measured the size he needed for the sign and wrote down what he wanted it to say then gave the paper to the gentleman.

Everything was coming together, the cottages had been stocked with food, the shop was coming along well and it appeared people in the town were friendly and helpful. When everyone had left for the day William stood and surveyed the work that had been done then locked the door and left for home; he couldn't wait to see his bonnie wife and children.

CHAPTER
THIRTY-SEVEN

Henry and Mary made one last stop at Henry's parents on their way back to Comrie. Bethany and Marianne saw them and came running outside. "You're here, they cried, Mum has been busy cooking all morning, we're having a feast." "We are?" Mary laughed and looked at Henry, then said, "I won't have to cook meself when we get home, Henry will be spared my cooking another day." "Oh come now, Henry said, I've had your cooking and lived to tell about it." The lasses laughed and they all went into the house. Alicia came from the kitchen, wiping her hands on her apron, "The newlyweds are here," she said, first hugging Mary and then Henry. "Where's Father?" Henry asked. "I don't know, she said, somewhere outside I suppose." "I'll go find him, Henry said giving Mary a kiss. "Let's go in the kitchen, said Alicia, I've got a few things to do yet." "Can I help?" Mary asked. "Not right now, I've had the lasses busy all morning, they're sick of me." Mary laughed, "I know exactly what you mean, Rebecca and Lillian are the same; I guess I was too at one time." "So, how do you like being married?" Alicia asked. "I love it, hopefully the weather will hold out and you can come and visit us soon, there's plenty of room for the lasses too." Mary laughed, "They won't get out of school though; Henry will have them down the hill with the other students." "Don't tell them that, smiled Alicia, or we won't get them to come." "No need to give us any notice, I'm sure we will be there; in any case there is a key just inside the root cellar." "The house is perfect but I'm going to ask Henry if I can have an oven, it's the only thing lacking." "I'm sure he will give you whatever you wish, dear, he totally adores you." "I know, Mary replied, I adore him too." "What say you we ring the dinner bell, everything is ready," Alicia said.

They talked while cleaning up the dishes, "I meant to thank you for the wedding band, it was very thoughtful of you to give to Henry, he told me it was your mothers." "I was glad to do it, said Alicia, you see I couldn't choose who would have it between the lasses, it wouldn't have been fair; Henry's wife was the perfect choice." "Hopefully we will have bairns so we can pass it on." "You'd better have some, Alicia said, I've been waiting to spoil them."

Henry came in and stated that they should be on their way soon, before it got dark or the weather changed. He gave his Mother a kiss on the cheek and a hug, "We'll see you as soon as we can, I love you." "I love you too son," she said. Henry went out to get the cart and Alicia turned to Mary, "Take care of him, I love him so." "I know you do, and I can see why." "Don't worry, I know you must wonder about my true feelings for him but I assure you, if William..."and she choked up on the word, if he were here now; I would still choose Henry, that's how much I love him." Alicia threw her arms around Mary and held her. "I believe you," she said and then gave her a kiss on the cheek.

On the way home Mary cuddled up under a blanket as close to Henry as she could get. "I want to do something for them, she said, we've done for everyone else, your sisters too." "That's not necessary Mary, they wouldn't want it." "Still, I think I'll send them a cheque, they can do with it whatever they want, it's always nice to have a little extra and we certainly don't need it." "I want something though." He looked at her and smiled, "Sorry, not now, I'm a little tied up." "Oh Henry," she laughed, not that, at least not right now." "Anything for you, what is it?" "I'd like an oven." "Ah, an oven, I think we can see to it, after all, I want some of those baked goods too." She snuggled closer to him, "I love you so much Henry." He turned to kiss her, "I know I had to wait a long time for you to see me but the wait was worth it, I promise to take care of you forever." She smiled and pushed herself even closer to him.

They arrived home and Henry told Mary to go in the house and he would see to everything else. "I want to get the horse sheltered, right away, I'll be in soon." Mary took the key and entered the house, "I'm home, she thought, and how I've missed it!" She hung up her outer clothes and then scurried around getting both of the hearths lit and the fire going. She pumped fresh water for the kettle and put it on for tea, then checked to make sure the pots for bath water were filled. She sat down at the table and waited for Henry. He opened the door and called that he was going down to the schoolhouse to get the hearth going there. She grabbed her jacket and ran out the door after him. "What are you doing out here again?" he laughed. "I wanted to come with you," she said. He put his arm around her and they went down the hill together. "I've lit the hearths in the house, she said, it should start to warm up soon." They entered the schoolhouse and Mary wandered around the room looking at the children's pictures on the wall while Henry saw to the fire. "Do you like it?' she asked. "Like what?" "Teaching, the children," she replied. "I do, he said, sometimes it's frustrating when they don't come." "They'll want to meet my new wife," he said. "I'll come down with a treat one day this week and meet them." "Good, he replied, they'll like that, I think the fire is stable now, let's go home." When they reached the door he said, "Stop, Mary, don't go in yet." Alarmed she asked, "Why not." "Because I have to carry you over the threshold, that's why." He picked her up and carried her through the door. "Welcome home, Mrs. MacAlduie." With her arms still around his neck, she pulled him to her and kissed him.

They spent the rest of the afternoon putting away their things and finding room for the few belongings that Mary had brought along. Then they sat and had tea together after which Mary began fixing the food that Henry's mother had sent along for them; when finished Mary cleaned up the dishes and Henry went to the sitting room to prepare his papers for tomorrow's school day. "The water is warm, I'm taking a bath now," she told Henry. "I'll prepare yours when I'm done. "Ok, I'll be ready," he called from the sitting room. She lay in the warm water for some time relaxing until the water was no longer warm; she took the basin and washed her hair, exited the tub, dried off and donned only her shift. She cleaned the tub and then poured in more warm water for Henry, calling, "It's ready; come now before the water cools." He watched her running back and forth in only her shift and his heart pounded with anticipation for what would come later. He went into the bathroom, undressed and crawled into the tub and she went to the bedroom and brushed out her long flowing hair. When he finished, he cleaned the tub, filled the pots with more water and hung them in the hearth, then came into the bedroom with only a towel wrapped around him. He stood behind her, picked up her hair and let it slowly run through his fingers, then bent down and kissed her on the back of the neck. They spent the first night of their married life at home with no one around but the outside world, lost in the feel and touch of each other. Life was good.

CHAPTER
THIRTY-EIGHT

The shop was finished, William contacted The Edinburgh Shipping Company and gave them the new address then placed another order. He needed more inventory as the shop was much larger. He crossed his fingers and hoped that it would be successful; they had spent a lot of money. Kristine and Agnes invited everyone who helped out over to the cottage for a picnic and along with the food they had prepared, more dishes were brought from the guests. It was a great way to meet the townsfolk. Martin Feldman took on the livery and yard work which allowed William to spend more time in the shop and with his family. Kristine had several friends now, all of them initially surprised that someone as bonnie as she would be down to earth and friendly. Agnes and Gabrielle took to the town like they were born there. Agnes found several new friends in a short period of time and Gabby associated with a group of lasses her age, even a young lad who had been giving her a lot of attention. "Oh me word, Agnes said, I might get to see me youngest married yet." They both couldn't have been happier in the little cottage behind the house.

As predicted, the shop was a success, Kristine's Father had been correct; Crieff attracted a lot of wealthy businessmen who didn't mind spending their money. With Leslie's help, William became proficient in knowing what to order based on the latest trends. Kristine's parents came to visit at least once a month and sometimes took Daniel home with them for a few days; they were already attached to the likeable lad. The children thrived in their new environment, growing like weeds.

If living in the country again was healing, it certainly had helped William; except for the use of a cane and his stiff fingers, he was back to the good natured, carefree lad he had once been, even with all of his added responsibilities. He took Daniel fishing when he could and the lad adapted to it just like his Father had so many years ago. One day they were fishing together and William said, "Someday Daniel, you will have a best friend to go fishing with, just like I did, his name was Harry, I miss him even today." "Where does he live Da?" "In Killin, it's not far from here." "Why don't you go and see him then?" "It's complicated, but maybe I will tell you about it someday." "You're my best friend Da?" "I am, at least right now, but someday when you go to school you will have other friends too and it won't be long until you do" "Maybe, Daniel said, but you will always be the best one."

William couldn't believe the years had flown by so quickly, it was like he had been married to Kristine forever. He still thought about Abby now and then, Kristine and he had decided that they would make sure the children knew all about their mother when they were old enough. They were committed to making an annual trop to Glasgow to visit the graves. There had been some bad times and some good times in his life but Kristine had helped him see that it did no good to live with regrets, he had to reconcile with the past and should not let it cloud what was in the present. God, he loved that woman. He thought about Mary and realized that it was now with a fondness for a good friend, no longer with a sense of having lost love along the way. He couldn't imagine ever having loved anyone as much as he did Kristine.

One night, after they made love, Kristine took William's hand and laid it on her stomach. "Feel," she said. William touched her stomach and grinned, "Are you trying to tell me something dear?" "Maybe," she said. He drew her too him, "Oh Kristine, I hope it's a lass and she looks just like you." "Now, now, Kristine said, we'll love the bairn whether it's a lass or lad and no matter whom it looks like." "Of course, he said, but a lass would be nice." There was no morning sickness, moodiness or apprehension with the pregnancy, Kristine blossomed and William thought she never looked more bonnie. Little Anna Marie Stevenson was born on a warm spring day in July, black hair and eyes just like her mother. William radiated with happiness and wouldn't let Kristine do anything for weeks afterward until she grew tired of the attention and told him she was perfectly fine. Unlike Abby, she welcomed William at night, never once thinking about turning him away; often it was her who initiated it.

Years flew by and Daniel was in school now, Samuel not far behind. Anna was walking and always one step behind her Mother, looking like a miniature of her.

The lads worshipped her except when she wouldn't leave them alone and then they went outside and found something else to do or over to Agnes' where they knew a treat and glass of milk would be waiting. One evening Kristine said to William, "It's time, William." "Time for what, he said, to have another bairn?" "No, time to go home, I want the bairns to meet their grandparents." "No, Kristine, not that, they already have grandparents." "They have one set of grandparents they need to meet the other side." "I can't do it." "You must, I'm going to write them, let's see how they feel." "Don't do it Kristine, I've never been angry at you but I'm warning you not to do this." "My mind is set, I'm doing it," she replied. William rose from the couch and went outside not wanting an argument to ensue in front of the children. What he did know was that Kristine would have her way and write the letters, he knew his wife and when her mind was set on something, there was no changing it. He came back in for supper and although still a little miffed, he didn't bring up the subject again. Maybe she would forget about it or maybe she would still write, either way he didn't want to discuss it further. That night she watched him sitting in the living room holding the silver engraving of Loch Tay that she had given him years ago. He still longed to see Killin again no matter what he said, of that she was sure. How he stayed away, she didn't know, it would be so easy to slip over there; it was only a few miles away.

Next day when William was gone she sat down and wrote the letters; first to his parents. *Mr. & Mrs. Stevenson. I'm sure this letter will come as a shock to you but I feel it is time to bring everything out into the open. Years ago, I met a young lad on the coach to Perth and we became friends; my Father giving him a ride to The George Inn when we arrived in Perth. He seemed so alone that I sat with him at the train station to Glasgow the next day and saw him off. I gave him my address and told him to write and let me know how he was doing. Alas, I didn't hear from him again but I received a letter from a nurse, Miss Abigale McCleary at The Royal Infirmary Hospital in Glasgow. She told me that a note had been found in a Mr. Shawn Ferguson's suit jacket and asked if I knew him. I pondered how a note with my address would be found in this man's suit jacket as I didn't know anyone by that name. I talked to my Father about it and told him that the only note with my address had been given to my friend, William Stevenson. My Father didn't know what to make of it either other than that something had happened to William and his jacket was stolen; he told me he was going to Glasgow in a few weeks on business, I should come along and see who this person was. Imagine my surprise when I went to the hospital and found William; my heart broke when I saw him. You see, William had been horribly injured in an accident as soon as he came to Glasgow. He had a badly broken leg, a broken arm, broken wrist, crushed fingers and a large scar from his ear to the corner of his mouth. The doctors couldn't assure him he would ever be able to walk again; in fact they almost took the leg. He was in a coma for several weeks which led to the mistaken identity. As you've probably surmised by now, he was carrying a satchel with his Grandda's name on it, Shawn Ferguson. When William finally awoke, he perceived himself to be a crippled monster and didn't want anyone to know his real identity, he felt like everyone would feel sorry for him and he didn't want that. The lovely nurse, Abigale, took care of him in the hospital and subsequently fell in love with him; her Father rented him a flat and hired him when he was able to work. Abigale and William were married but I'm sorry to say that she passed away in childbirth bearing their second son. You have three grandchildren, Daniel, Samuel and Anna Marie; I would like you to meet them. William and I were married, we moved to Crieff where William runs a men's store, Stevenson and Sons Men's Emporium. We have a daughter together. He forbade me to write the letter but my conscience tells me it isn't right to keep this from you any longer; he is only afraid that you will reject him now and he knows what he did is wrong. I can tell you that he is a good man and a wonderful husband and Father. Please find it in your hearts to forgive him, I know he would want you to meet the children. Sincerely, Kristine Stevenson*

Kristine wrote three other similar letters. One was sent to Mary Munro, c/o Killin Bakery, one to Harry Rutherford, and another to Mr. McGregor, Clothier; Killin. She asked Agnes to take her to town and she mailed the letters hoping that this wouldn't cause a rift between her and her husband. She made no mention of it to William she would wait and see what happened. They stopped at the shop to see William but he was so busy they just waved at him and continued on their way.

Douglas returned from town with a letter in his pocket. He pondered who it was from on the way home but hadn't bothered to open it yet. He tried to remember any relatives he might have by the name of Kristine but he just couldn't think of anyone. He reached home and took care of the horses, then sat in the shed to read the letter. He remained sitting there when he was done, tears running down his face, when Michael came into the shed. "Da, Da, what's wrong; are you ok?" Douglas couldn't speak, he handed over the letter saying only, "Don't tell your Mum, not yet." Michael read the letter and then had to take a seat by his Da. "Oh my God, he said, after all these years, he's alive."

Douglas pondered what to do, he couldn't just go in there and hand her the letter it would be too much; all those years she had suffered wondering what had happened to him, how could he have done it. She said in the letter that he had been in pretty bad shape, he supposed his thinking must have been clouded, but when he recovered why didn't he come home then. Well he never did understand the lad's thinking, so why should he be surprised that he didn't understand now. No, he'd have to break it to her gently this would be a shock to her. Three children, she said

316

he had; aye, of course they would want to meet them. He had seven grandchildren now, Michael had two lads, Patrick had a bonnie lass and now William had two lads and a lass. Joseph had remained unmarried hopefully with no unknown children running around.

"What are you going to do Da?" Michael asked. "I don't know yet, of course we want him to come home but telling your Mum is another matter altogether." "Keep it to yourself for now and don't tell anyone, I'll break it to her tonight." That night at supper Margaret said to Douglas, "Are you feeling alright, you look positively pale." "I'm fine dear," he said looking at Michael. The families always had supper together as they lived next to each other. "Tomorrow I want to go into town, I thought I'd stop in the tea shop and get some more tea and then talk to Catherine for a while," said Margaret. "We'll see, dear," Douglas replied. That night when they were in bed he said to her, "I've received a letter today." "A letter, from who?" she asked. "Well, I want you to brace yourself for this, it's from Kristine Stevenson." "I don't think I know anyone by that name, who is she?" "Oh God, he said reaching over and putting his arms around her, I don't know how to tell you this, she's William's wife." She shot up in bed like someone had given her an electric shock. "William's wife, I don't understand." He got out of bed, sat beside her and put his arm around her waist. "It's a long story; you'll just have to read the letter." "It seems he met with an accident when he arrived in Glasgow and was injured badly; he was in a coma for some time and then he was mistaken for another person." She put her head in her hands, "Is he alright now, I must see him, where is he?" "Aye, he's alright, he lives in Crieff and has three children." "Crieff, she said, then why hasn't he contacted us before now?" "I don't know dear, it seems that he was ashamed because he was crippled and disfigured." She put her head on his chest and he gathered her to him and held her. "He wants to see us but he's afraid, it's been so long." "Tomorrow, she said, I want to go tomorrow." "We can't dear, we'll have to find out where he lives first, we can send a post tomorrow and wait for a reply." She looked up at him like a lost child, "All those years, all those years I wondered and he's in Crieff, just a few miles away?" "I know, I know, he said, it'll be alright, he's ok, we finally know he's ok."

A letter arrived at the bakery addressed to Mary Munro and it was from Kristine Stevenson. "Hmmm I wonder who that is?" said Catherine. "Should we open it Mum," asked Katie. "No, Peter says he's going over there this week to deliver some boards to Henry so he can make more shelves in the school; he can take it with him then." All day Catherine thought about the letter, Margaret's last name was Stevenson, it must be a coincidence. Things were going well for them, the bakery and Ethan had steady business but the hardware store was booming; John had to hire a couple of lads to help. Catherine thought he was the happiest he'd ever been even though he worked from morn until night. Ethan and Katie loved living in back of the shop and no one seemed to miss the farm, it gave John great pleasure to give notice when the Stevenson boys came collecting rent. Margaret still stopped in every so often and seemed happier now that she had some grandchildren to tend to.

Mr. McGregor had stopped over and told her what Mary had done and they all shook their heads at the generosity of their daughter. Catherine felt that it was her way of saying good bye to William. In any case he had found someone to train workers on the power loom and had hired workers from Killin. His business was doing well and keeping busy alleviated the loss of his friend Charles and the guilt he felt over the disappearance of William.

Peter headed over to Henry's with the boards in his cart and the letter in his pocket. Tricia had plans so she didn't come along; he had finally asked her to marry him and they had bought a small house with the money from Mary. It wasn't far from Richards so he could walk to work. Henry saw him coming and went outside to help unload the boards and they carried them down to the school and put them inside. They came into the kitchen where Mary was seated at the table and Peter gave her the letter. "I wonder who that could be, she stated, I don't know this person." "Maybe you should open it and find out dear, Henry said, we'll be right back, I want to show Peter something in the livery." He bent down and gave her a kiss and then went out the door. Mary opened the letter and read it. She laid the letter on the table and sat there stunned, almost in shock and was still sitting there when they came back into the house. Henry knew immediately from the look on her face that something was wrong. "What's wrong, why do you look like that?" he asked. She pushed the letter at him and he picked it up and read it, then grabbed the table and sat down. "What is it?" Peter asked. When no one answered him, he picked up the letter and read it himself. They all sat there speechless for a few moments. "What are you going to do?" Henry asked. Mary looked at him, tears in her eyes, "That's just like him, not to think about the rest of us pining away for him." Henry looked at Peter then said, "Is that what you're doing Mary, pining for him." "No, oh no Henry, not anymore," she cried grabbing his hands. "You know, everyone was beside themselves not knowing what had happened; even you, you tried to find him." "I did, he said, I wish I had known at the time." "Known?" Mary questioned. "When I went there, to the hospital, they told me the only young man they had from an accident was Shawn Ferguson." He put his head in his hands, "I'm sorry Mary, I didn't know, I didn't even consider that it might have been him." Mary leaped up from her chair and ran to Henry and threw her arms around him, "Don't blame yourself, you couldn't have known, none of us except his parents would have known that." "It really was a selfish thing to do, letting everyone think he was gone," Peter said. "He was right and wrong," Mary said; he was right to think that it wouldn't have made any difference to me but he was wrong to think it was because of pity." "I wouldn't have pitied him." Henry was afraid but he had to ask, "Are you going to meet him?" "I have to, she said, I never had closure, now it can end." Henry nodded his head, he knew she was right but he was afraid something would rekindle the flame they had once had. None of them could get it off their minds that night.

Peter stayed the night and left early in the morning. He hugged Mary and told her that he understood her need to meet with William but she needed to reassure Henry that everything was fine between them. "He knows that, Peter," she said. "I'm not so sure, Mary, I think he's a little scared." "I'll talk to him again, he has nothing to worry about." "Thanks Peter, I love you." "I love you too Mary, we'll see you soon." Henry had already left to work and Mary sat down to write a letter back to Kristine: *Kristine: I must say that your letter came as a shock to me as I was finally reconciled to William's disappearance. I am angry at him for not realizing how agonizing it was for all of us, not knowing what had happened to him. At the same time, I can put myself in his shoes and see how, in his mind, he was avoiding the pity he felt we would bestow upon him. For a long time I couldn't see why he would have left me behind, I felt that if he had loved me enough he would have taken me along. Everything worked out well, I am happily married and his leaving let me finally see the one who had been there for me all along. In answer to your question, aye, I would like to see him again, a small part of me will always love him, but now it is only the love of a good friend. I have found my true love in Henry and I can't imagine living one day without him ever again. I am happy that William has found you for I can sense that you truly care for him. If he would like to meet with me I will be in Comrie at The White Kirk on the last Sunday of the month at one in the afternoon. It is easy to find, just take Comrie Road out of Crieff until you get to Dunira Street. Sincerely: Mary MacAlduie.* She folded the letter and put it in the envelope but didn't seal it as she wanted Henry to read it first. William was on her mind the entire day, sometime she felt angry at what he had done and other times she felt bad that he had not seen his dreams fulfilled; she wondered about the extent of his injuries. She made a special supper that night because more than anything she wanted to reassure Henry there was nothing that could tear them apart, not even William.

Kristine's letter to Mr. McGregor was simply an apology, not for what had happened but for hiding his identity after, and not contacting him to let him know what had happened. She enclosed a check from her own funds for what she calculated his loss may have been.

The third letter was to Harry, William's best friend. *Harry: You don't know me, I know this will come as a shock to you and I apologize but feel I must let you know what happened to your best friend William.* As in the other letters, she explained what had happened and why William had hidden himself from everyone. She continued, *I can't tell you how many times William has told me how much he missed you and how much fun you had as lads. I look at his two sons and can only hope they find such a good friend. I beg of you to find it in your heart to forgive him, he never meant to hurt anyone; he just didn't think it through. If you could meet with him sometime or better yet come to Crieff and visit us, I would be most appreciative. Sincerely: Kristine Stevenson.*

Harry cried like a bairn when he received the letter and he instructed Colleen to write back immediately and make plans to see him. There wasn't an ounce of anger in him, he was overjoyed. Harry and Colleen also had a young lad, two years old now. He knew exactly what Kristine meant when she spoke of the friendship between them. "I told you Colleen, he said, I was the only one who believed he was still alive, I told you I could still feel him." "Aye, you did," she confirmed. Colleen wrote back the next day and told Kristine that Harry was on top of the world at the news. *Please, she said, come as quickly as you can, Harry is so overjoyed that he can't stand it, he hasn't been the same person since we feared the worst had happened to William. Tell William that we have a son, Adam, two years old. Thank you for contacting us I will be looking forward to meeting you and your family. If you can't find us, just ask my parents next door, we are never far away. Sincerely: Colleen Rutherford.*

Agnes brought a letter back from town addressed to Kristine She sat on the porch and read it. The letter was from Mr. McGregor. *Kristine: Thank you for your kind letter letting me know what had happened to William. I blamed meself all these years thinking that I shouldn't have sent him to such a dangerous city; him just a country boy. Of course I am overjoyed that he is still alive but disappointed that he didn't let any of us know. I am enclosing your generous check. Mary Munro inherited a fortune and insisted that I accept funding from her to start the business that William and I had dreamed of. I am happy to report that it is doing well and thriving. Please tell William that I harbor no ill will against him, I would be happy to see him and show him the shop any time. Sincerely, George McGregor*

Kristine held the letter against her chest for some time after reading it then she folded it and placed it back in the envelope. She would show it to William, but not now, she was waiting to see if she received any other letters.

Margaret sat outside with the letter from Kristine in her hand, she was still dazed from the news and it had been a week now. She longed for him, her tall lanky, handsome son. Every day she insisted that Michael stop in town to check if a post had come and now it was finally here. *Dear Mr. & Mrs Stevenson: I can't tell you how overjoyed I am that you want to come and visit us. Please come as soon as you can, we have plenty of room so do stay a while so you can spend some time with William and the bairns; I am so anxious for you to meet the children. When you get to Crieff, take High Street to Perth Road until you come to Murray Drive, go approximately ¼ miles on Murray Drive and take a right. If you come to Callum Hill on Perth Road, you have gone too far. I will put up a sign on the drive by the road. You may notice his shop, Stevenson & Sons Men's Emporium on High Street when you go by. It might be better if you stop here first; I want this to be a surprise because he doesn't know that I've written to you. Love Kristine.*

Margaret couldn't wait to find Douglas and make plans to visit. She was busy in the kitchen baking everything she could think of that William liked; it was her release. The lads came in to dinner and she served their food then sat down and handed the letter to Douglas. She gave him a minute to read the letter and then asked, "When can we go?" "Sunday, he said, we can leave early on Sunday morning, the lads will have to see to things, and we will stay until Wednesday." "Aw Da, said Joseph, we want to see him too?" "I know, I know, he replied, let's see how things go on this trip, I'm sure we will see a lot of them in the future." He finished his dinner and then stood behind Margaret, threw his arms around her neck and kissed her on the head. "It won't be long, dear, it won't be long." She cleaned up the kitchen and thought how happy she was and yet sad for all the missing years that had gone by.

On Sunday, Margaret was up bright and early. She had everything packed and ready to go. Porridge was on the table and she had made enough food for the lads until Wednesday; of course Michael and Patrick's wives would see to everything, there was no need to worry. Douglas readied the carriage and they would take that, not knowing if it would rain sometime in the near future. He gave last minute instructions to the lads and then pulled up in front of the house for Margaret. He would never let on but he was nervous, not knowing what to expect; they didn't really know what condition their son would be in; obviously he was still able to Father bairns and it seemed he was able to run a shop. Douglas had been to Crieff several times before but not for several years so he knew where High Street was. It didn't take long to get to Crieff, it was only six miles away, to think he had been so close and yet so far and they didn't know it. "This is High Street, he said to Margaret, watch for his shop." "There it is, she said, let's stop, there won't be anyone around on a Sunday." He pulled up in front of the shop and they both got out and peeked in the windows. "It's nice, he said, it looks big." Margaret touched the door and held her hand on the handle for a moment. "I'm ready," she said. They got back into the cart and soon were on Perth Road, both of them were nervous and anxious. They saw Murray Drive and took a left, it wasn't long before Margaret spotted the sign; 'Stevenson' was all it said. Kristine had asked Martin to make a sign and put it out by the road and apparently William hadn't noticed it or just hadn't commented about it, because he never mentioned seeing it. Douglas turned into the drive and they both were surprised at what a nice place it was, "He must be doing well for himself, Douglas said, it looks impressive." "Aye, Margaret replied, lots of room for the bairns to play."

Kristine heard a carriage coming down the drive and looked out the window. William was sitting on the couch playing with the children and just relaxing for the day. She turned from the window and said, "They're here William." "Who's here?" he asked. "It's your parents I believe." William immediately rose from the couch and looked out the window, he saw his Da for the first time in many years walking around the carriage. "You did it then, he turned on her, I asked you not to Kristine." He went into the bedroom and shut the door. Kristine looked at the bedroom door and then at the front door not knowing where to turn first. As usual, Anna was one step behind her, clinging to her skirt. She put a smile on her face and then opened the door, "Come in, she said extending her hand, I'm so glad you've come, I'm Kristine." Douglas shook her hand and Margaret gave her a hug, "I'm glad to meet you, thank you for letting us know, we have spent years wondering." Douglas thought, "She's absolutely bonnie." The children stood like little soldiers wondering who these people were. "Children, said Kristine, I want you to meet your grandparents." "This is Daniel and here is Samuel." Margaret bent down and hugged them, "They look just like William." "Aye, Kristine said, they will be just as handsome as he someday, Daniel will be tall and lanky but I think Samuel will be smaller, like his mother." Kristine felt a pull on her skirt, she reached down and picked up Anna, "This is Anna, she laughed; she's always one step behind me." "Oh, she's adorable, she looks just like you." "Aye, William says she is a miniature of me." "Where is he, William?" Margaret asked. "Come, sit down, Kristine said, I will check on him." She walked to the bedroom door, looked at it and then opened it and slipped inside. Margaret looked at Douglas; they both wondered why he hadn't come out and were fearful that indeed his injuries were severe.

William was sitting on the bed hunched over looking like he was in pain. "What's the matter with you, she said, are you coming out, they are anxious to see you." He looked at her, she had never seen him look like that before, "Get out, he yelled, get out Kristine." With that, he emitted a groan and started sobbing, the likes of which she had never heard before. She walked over to him and touched him on the shoulder, "What can I do?" she asked him. He shook his head then snarled, "You've done enough, I said get out." She was crushed and tears flowed from her eyes so she exited the room and closed the door, then stood there. Douglas rose from the couch and went to her. "What's wrong with him dear, what can we do?" Daniel came up to her, "What's wrong with Da, why is he making those sounds Mum and why are you crying?" She touched him on the head and then turned to Douglas, "Please, she said, get Agnes in the kitchen, have her take the children to her house." She turned back to Daniel, "It's nothing dear, we're crying because we are so happy to see your grandparents, go with Agnes now, we will come and get you later." Agnes, clearly upset, mustered up and said, "Come on children, I've got some fresh baked oat cookies just for you, let's go and have some shall we." She hustled them out the back door. Douglas led Kristine to the couch she was barely able to stand. "He hates me, she cried, he told me to get out, I shouldn't have done it, I thought I was doing the right thing." Margaret wrapped her arms around her and stroked her hair. "I'm sure he doesn't hate you dear, he's just scared, that's all, you did the right thing, you did the right thing." She cradled her in her arms like a little child. Douglas couldn't stand it anymore he went to the bedroom door, opened it and stood inside. His son was on the bed, doubled over, tears flowing from his eyes and great sobs emitting from him. He sat down on the bed next to him, put his arm around his back and pulled him to his chest. "It's ok son; we're here now, your Mum and I, we love you, give it over, give it over." William clung to him like he was five years old again and the sobs got louder, they could hear him from the sitting room. Margaret continued to hold Kristine who was still distraught and she rubbed her back, "He's got a lot of years to get out of his system, she said, he needs to finally release it." Kristine looked up at her, "I love him so much, even when he was married to Abby I loved him. I won't stand it if he rejects me, I can't live without him." "Now, now, dear, don't get ahead of yourself, William isn't capable of hating anyone, he loves you, that's not going to change." "He's never raised his voice to me before, Kristine replied. "Give it some time dear, give it some time." Margaret wondered about their relationship but didn't ask, now wasn't the time; her heart was breaking for this bonnie lass.

They sat there wondering what was going on in the bedroom; they could no longer hear the sobbing. "I'm sorry Da, I was wrong, I know that now, I thought it would be easier for everyone that way." "It wasn't easier William, not knowing what happened, you must have known that." "I didn't want you to see me, like this." "It's over, you're home now, that's all that matters, the past is the past, we love you, we're not mad at you." He stroked his son's head; he did love this lad even though he rarely understood him. "Your mother is waiting to see you and your wife is upset do you think you're ready?" "Muster up son; we've waited a long time for this day." "Aye Da, I love you." "It's ok William, I love you too; no matter what you've done I'll always love you." "Da?" "Yes son?" "Can you send Kristine in first?" "I need to apologize to her." "Aye, she's scared, I'll send her in now, and the worst is over it will be ok." He hugged his son and then left the bedroom and told Kristine to go in.

Kristine stood inside the door not knowing what to do or say. William patted the bed next to him, indicating that she should sit down. She sat beside him and he pulled her to his chest holding her but not saying anything. He touched her hair and ran his fingers through it then took her face in his hands and ran his fingers over her nose, eyes and mouth. He kissed her, "I'm so sorry, Kristine, I didn't mean to hurt you, please forgive me." "Oh William, I couldn't stand it if you were angry at me, I love you, I thought I was doing the right thing." "You were, I wasn't angry, I was afraid, there is nothing that could make me stop loving you you're the best thing that has ever happened to me, I'm the luckiest man in the world to have you." He held her tight and stroked her back then kissed her, "I'm ready to see me Mum now, he said." "Thank you, she said, I've asked them to stay a few days, is that ok?" "Aye, Kristine, it's ok, it's good," he said.

Kristine came out and attempted a feeble smile. Margaret thought what a lovely lass she was, and she seemed to be sensitive like her son. Aye, she could picture them together quite well. She stood by Margaret and said, "He's ready to see you now, I'm sorry it's hard for him." "It's ok, dear it's not your fault, you've done all you can." "She rose and went to the bedroom door, took a deep breath and went inside. He was sitting there with his head hanging down, "I'm sorry Mum; I've let everybody down, it was wrong of me to do it." "Aye, it was, she said, we suffered William but it's over now, that's what matters." "You did what you thought was best at the time, right or wrong that's all any of us can do." "We still love you, you must know that." The tears flooded his face again and she took his face in her hands. "I'm so sorry you've suffered," she ran her hands over his face and touched the scar thinking it must have looked bad when it happened. "It's not that bad, she said, you're still just as handsome as ever." He tried to smile at her but the tears were still flowing from him. "Can you tell me what else happened to you?" He touched his arm, "Me arm was broke and me wrist, me fingers were crushed, I can't bend them." She took his hand in hers and rubbed the fingers, "Do they hurt?" "They ache Mum, they always ache." She had to stifle back a sob. "And your leg?" she asked. "It was bad, they almost took it but I can walk with a cane." "Good," she said. "We want to get to know our grandchildren, the boys look like you." He looked at her and smiled,

"Aye, they do, and Anna is the spitting image of her Mum, she going to be bonnie." "She already is, Margaret said, Kristine is very nice, I like her." "I wish you could have met her sooner, she was always at me about it but this time she took things into her own hands." "Well, she's a smart lass I'm very glad she did." "Me too, Mum." They sat and talked for a while longer and he told her about Abby and what had happened, how he came to own the store and how he met Kristine. She told him that he was an uncle now and he would have to come and reunite with his brothers and meet their wives and children.

Meanwhile, in the sitting room, Douglas was getting to know Kristine. She told him about her family, why they had moved to Crieff and what a wonderful Father William was to his children. "I can see that you adore him," Douglas said. "I do, does it show, she asked him. "Aye, it shows, he replied, he's a lucky man." "Thank you, she said, I feel like I'm the lucky one." "Would you like to see outside?" "I would," he replied. "Come with me then, we'll go out the back way." He looked at the livery and met Martin, then came out and asked about the cottages. "Agnes, our housekeeper and her daughter Gabby live here, they worked for us in Glasgow and we encouraged them to come to Crieff with us, I don't know what we would do without them." "Would you like to meet them, the children are there now." "Aye, I would," Douglas said, thoroughly enjoying himself.

Kristine knocked on the door and Gabby opened it. "Kristine, come in," she said. "Gabby, this is William's Father, Douglas." "Nice to meet you, Gabby said, come in and have a seat." They sat at the table and Agnes came out of the sitting room with the children behind her. "It's so nice to meet William's Da, Agnes said, I couldn't love him more if he were me own son." Douglas smiled, "It's nice to meet you Agnes it looks like the children are at home over here." "Aye, she said, there's not a day goes by that one or the other of them isn't here." Daniel stepped forward and Douglas had a flashback to when William was young, he looked so much like his son did back then, "You're me Grandda?" "That I am, Douglas replied, did you know you look like your Da?" "Aye, that's what everyone tells me; and Samuel looks like him too; but he's shy." "He is?" "Aye, but not Anna, Da says she's like me Mum, blurting out everything that comes into her head." "Is that so," Douglas said laughing. Anna peeked around Kristine's skirt, "No I don't," she replied. "Do too, do too," piped in Samuel. "Alright children, enough, your Grandda will think you don't have any manners." "It's ok Agnes," Douglas laughed, "Sometimes me wife says I don't have any either." They all chuckled at him.

"Let's all go back to the house, Kristine said, Agnes and I have to get dinner going and I'm sure Margaret would like to visit with the children." "I hope you're able to stay for a while?" She asked Douglas. "Aye, we can stay until Wednesday," Douglas replied. "Good, good, Kristine said, that makes me happy." They walked together back to the house, Agnes and the lads tagging behind and Anna one step behind Kristine. Margaret and William weren't in the sitting room so Kristine knocked softly on the bedroom door. "Aye, come in," Margaret said. Kristine stood in the doorway, "We're back; we took a tour outside." Kristine saw that William looked much better, Margaret was holding his hand. "I think we're ready, right son?" Margaret looked at William and he looked at Kristine and said, "Aye, me Mum and I had a long talk." "That's good, I'm going to check on dinner now would you like some tea." "I would, said Margaret, don't bring it out I'll come to the kitchen in a moment." Kristine left and heaved a sigh of relief, she felt like everything would be ok; the truth was finally out.

Douglas was seated on the couch and the children were playing around him, sometimes looking at him and offering a comment or two. He enjoyed watching them, so innocent, nothing to worry about at their young age. He looked up and had to choke back a tear as his son came into the sitting room walking awkwardly with his cane. He knew this must be hard for Margaret to see, she had always laughed about him being so tall and lanky, walking with those long strident steps. Still, he supposed he was lucky to be walking at all. William sat down on the chair and immediately all of the children ran to him, each trying to get his attention. "Da, are you ok," Daniel said. "I'm fine, son." "Why were you crying then?" "I was happy to see me Mum and Da again, that's all." "Ok," he said and sat down by his feet. Anna pulled at his pant leg until he reached down and picked her up. "Da, she said, touching his face." He leaned down and kissed her, "What my little angel." She pointed to Douglas, "Grandda," she said. "That's right, he laughed and Grandmum too." "Grandmum," she repeated. Samuel, the quiet one, stood behind William pulling on a lock of his hair.

"Tea's on," Kristine called from the kitchen. Margaret stood by the kitchen doorway and asked Anna if she would like to come and help. She looked at her Da and William nodded his head then lifted her onto the floor. "Give Grandmum your hand then," said Margaret. Anna put her hand in Margaret's and they went into the kitchen together.

It only took another day and the children were all over Douglas and Margaret. They caught up on news from Killin and toured William's shop; he insisted that his Da pick out something to take home with him for himself and for his brothers too. Kristine organized a picnic so that their friends could meet William's parents; no one mentioned the long absence since they had been together. It was a tearful goodbye, Douglas and Margaret promised to return soon, they had thoroughly enjoyed themselves. Kristine and William said they would come in the near future so that William could be reunited with his brothers. Margaret hugged both of them and told Kristine that William couldn't have found a better wife. William held Kristine tight and said he agreed wholeheartedly. Daniel and Samuel ran behind the carriage all the way to the road, Margaret looking out the back window and waving at them. That night Kristine lay next to her husband loving him even more than before although she wondered how that was possible.

The lads were waiting for them when they arrived home. "Is he alright," they asked. "Aye, he is, just a little banged up is all," Douglas replied. "He'll be home to see you soon." They lay in each other's arms that night, something they hadn't done for a long time. "What a nice family," Douglas said. "I agree, Margaret replied, a nice family indeed." The heartbroken years of the past were forgotten; all was well now.

That week the last two letters arrived and Kristine left them for William; no longer afraid that he would be angry. He read the one from Harry and then with a big grin handed it to Kristine. "They want us to come and visit, he said, I miss him so." "Yes, I know you do," she replied. "We can go whenever you want." "Let's go on Sunday, he said, we'll make a day of it and stop at home so I can see me brothers.' "Sunday it is," she replied.

The second letter remained on the counter unopened, Kristine wondered why he hadn't opened it but didn't say anything. Several days went by and the letter sat on the counter, then one night before bed Kristine saw him sitting there with the unopened letter in his hand. "You'll never know what it says until you open it," she told him. He looked at her, "No, I suppose not, he said. "Here, he said, handing her the letter, you read it first." "Me, she asked, I think you should." "No, you do it, please," he said. She sat next to him and opened the letter then read it, "Hmm," she said when she had finished. "Is it bad?" he asked. "No not really, she replied, I'm not sure what you were expecting her to say." "I don't know, he said, I'm surprised she answered at all." "Read it then, Kristine said, otherwise you will wonder what it says." "Should I do it?" he asked after he read it. "William, for heaven's sake, why are you asking me, if you want to meet her then do it, if not, then let her know so she doesn't sit there waiting for you again." "Are you mad at me now?" he asked. "No, of course I'm not mad at you but some things you have to decide for yourself, I can't tell you what to do." "I think I should do it, don't you think I owe her that much?" "I don't know, she replied, she seems happy now, I don't think she expects anything more from you." He folded the letter and put it back in the envelope making no further comment. Nothing was mentioned about it the following day.

On Sunday they got the children ready and headed to Killin. They had to pass through Comrie on their way and William couldn't help but think of Mary and wondered where she lived. This would be the first time William had set foot in the village since he left so many years ago. They reached The Falls of Dochart and William stopped the cart. "Give me a minute, he said, come with me lads, I want to show you something." He took one lad in each hand which was difficult with the cane and walked down to the falls with them, Kristine and Anna watched from the cart. "Why didn't Da take me," Anna asked. "It's a boy thing," Kristine replied, he wants to show them where he went when he was a lad." "I want to see too," she replied. They stood by the water's edge and William told them that they were going to visit his best friend Harry and this is where he used to go fishing with Harry all the time. "It's loud Da, said Samuel, the water is loud." William laughed, "Aye, it's the sound of the water hitting the rocks." "Come with me," he said. They walked back towards the cart and William called, "Anna, come by Da, I want to show you something." With a big smile, she turned toward her Mum and Kristine helped her off of the cart. She ran toward William as fast as she could on the uneven ground nearly falling before she reached him. He scooped her up in his arms and put her around his shoulders. "Look up there," he said pointing, do you see that big ben (mountain)." "Aye Da we see it," they all shouted. "It has a name, it's called Ben Lawers and right below it is Loch Tay." "Your Da used to look at it every day, I'll show you when we get to Grandda's house." They walked back to the cart together, Anna still on William's shoulders. William had all he could do to make it back, it was hard on his leg but he tried not to let it show.

They pulled into Harry's yard and, as usual, he was outside by his wood pile. He looked up and came towards them with a smile on his face and tears in his eyes. "William, my God, I knew I would see you again." "Just ask Colleen, I told her you were alive." He grabbed William's hand and shook it up and down then grabbed him around the shoulders and held him for a long time sobbing. They broke apart, Harry turned his head and wiped his eyes then William, grabbing his arm, said, "Harry, this is my wife Kristen and our children Daniel, Samuel and little Anna. "I'm not little Da," said Anna. "Oh sorry, William laughed, this is my daughter Anna, she is growing up just like her Mum" "Come in, Harry said, Colleen's in-side." He opened the door and announced that William and his family were here. "William," Colleen said and ran to hug him. "I can't believe it's you, Harry is like a new man since we received the post; he missed you terribly." "You must be Kristine, she said, it's nice to meet you." Colleen wasn't sure what to expect from Kristine, she was even more bonnie than Mary, if that was possible. "Colleen, I'm so happy to meet you, we were both excited when we got your post, you can't imagine how much, you must come to Crieff and visit us." "We will, Colleen said, Harry's already asked if there is somewhere to fish in Crieff." "Killin is beautiful, what I've seen of it so far," Kristine said. "I was here a long time ago but it's hard to remember." "We like it, Colleen said, of course I haven't been anywhere else." "I'm from Perth, so I'm not used to the country, but I like it so far, and I spend less money." laughed Kristine. "Gosh, where are my manners, Colleen said, have a seat, I'll go get the bairn, he's playing in his room." The children stood around William and Kristine not sure what to do in such a small space. "Harry fixed up the cottage before they got married, William said, I helped him." "It's very nice and cozy," Kristine replied. "We like it for now, replied Harry, but we'll have to expand or get something different if we have more bairns." "Speaking of which, this is Adam," Colleen said, coming hand in hand with their son. "Hi Adam, said Kristine, I'm so glad to meet you, this is Daniel, Samuel and Anna." "Hi," Adam said, peeking out from Colleen's skirt. "He's a little shy, Colleen said, we don't get out that much." "Samuel is shy too, Kristine replied, but only until you get to know him." Kristine knew that Mary and Colleen were best friends so she felt a little awkward wondering what Colleen's true feelings toward her might be; she couldn't detect any animosity from her, she seemed genuine and friendly. "Can you stay for dinner," Colleen asked. "I wish we could but William's parents are expecting us, he hasn't seen his brothers yet." "That's too bad, Colleen said, Harry would so like to spend the day with William." "Is Harry able to get off work for a few days, Kristine asked, William and I would love to have you come and stay, we have a cottage just sitting empty." Colleen was a little taken aback, she didn't know what William's financial status was but she was surprised to hear that they had a vacant cottage. "Harry would love it, I'll ask him," Colleen said. "Let's take the children outside, Harry said, nothing like a good run around the yard to get them acquainted." The men left with the children and Kristine remained in the cottage with Colleen. "He gets around well, said Colleen, we didn't know what to expect." "Aye, he's very lucky, Kristine said, it was pretty bad, he could have lost the leg." "Harry missed him so badly; he always felt like he was alive, he said that many times." Kristine smiled, "They have a strong bond, I never had a best friend like that; you did with Mary didn't you?" "Aye, I miss her, she lives in Comrie now." "Do you know him, her husband?" Kristine asked. "Not really, I know of him and his family, he's been in love with her for years but she didn't have time for him; he's very handsome, and educated." "I understand he teaches?" "Yes, he took a post in Comrie just to be near her." "You know she inherited a lot of money, a fortune really." "Yes, it's a small world, William ran a men's shop in Glasgow and it turns out that they ordered supplies from The Edinburgh Shipping Company." "One day the Imperial Administrator came to the shop and told him about the heiress, he was shocked." "You moved the shop to Crieff?" "Yes, Glasgow is a dangerous town and we wanted the children to grow up in the country, they had nowhere to play there." "When Abby died, William and I married some time later and neither of us really liked living there." "Don't get me wrong, he was grateful to have found a place when he got out of the hospital but he still longed for the country." "Who is Abby then?" "Oh, I'm sorry, you wouldn't know." "The lads, Daniel and Samuel are not my natural born children, William was married to Abby, she was a nurse at the hospital and she cared for him when he was injured." "She died in childbirth when Samuel was born; William was devastated about it, in a depression really." "Goodness, Colleen said, he has had a time of it, hasn't he?" "You could say that," Kristine replied. "How did you meet, the two of you?" Colleen asked. "We met on the couch to Perth when William first left for Glasgow; my Father gave him a ride to the Inn when we arrived." "I gave him my address and asked him to let me know how he was doing, he seemed so alone." "After that, we just kept in touch and became friends, Abby too." "I'm glad I met you Colleen, she said, truth is, I didn't know what to expect; you know, being best friends with Mary and all." "I understand, Kristine, I felt the same way." "Should we go out and see how the men are doing with the children?" Colleen asked. "Yes, Kristine replied, the men have probably had their fill of them by now." As expected, the children were playing together, Anna as the only lass, getting picked on as usual. William and Harry were sitting side by side on the cart drinking ale and rehashing old times. "How about having a bottle of ale, Colleen asked Kristine, it's much too warm for tea." "I'd like that," Kristine replied. They sat in the grass watching the children and talking for quite some time and then William said it was time to go. Harry grabbed him in another long hug and promised to come to Crieff when they could. "You'd better hang on to your woman, William, when I got the post from her it was the best news ever." "I will, you can count on it," he said. The children were loaded into the cart and they were on their way once again. "Bye, it was good to see him again," William said. Kristine smiled glad that the circle was almost complete it had been a long time coming.

They crossed the bridge and traveled on Pier Road, a road traveled many times by William. When they passed the turn to Mary's home William felt choked up but didn't mention anything. He pulled into the yard and sat there for some time. "Why are we sitting here," Daniel said. "Just looking, son, just looking," said William. Margaret came out of the house, "Grandmum," Anna squealed. "Welcome home, said Margaret reaching out for the lass, I missed you already." "We missed you too Grandmum," said Daniel, where's Grandda?" "Get out of the cart and run around, she laughed, your Grandda's down behind the shed somewhere." The lads ran down behind the shed and when Douglas looked up they yelled, "Grandda, we're here." "And so you are, he said, come here and let me give you a hug." William followed close behind trying to hide the tears in his eyes.

Kristine followed Margaret into the kitchen, "So this is where he lived, she said." "Aye, would you like to see his room?" "I would," she replied. She stood outside the bedroom door where William had grown up and tried to imagine him as a child like Daniel. She turned to Margaret with a tear in her eye. "What's wrong dear? "Nothing, nothing at all, she said, it's finally almost complete, now he can be a free man again with no secrets following him." Margaret took Kristine's hand and carried Anna in the other, "Come, she said, come with me." They went outside and sat on the bench. "This is where I used to sit and wait for him to come home, I could hear the cart coming before he got here." "He would always take the time to sit and talk with me." "I used to sit here with me eyes closed after he disappeared and I would imagine I could hear that cart coming." Kristine put her arm around Margaret, "You don't have to imagine it any more it's real now." Margaret nodded, too choked up to talk. They sat there for a while not talking until they looked up and saw the three of them coming toward the house. Anna let out a yell and ran to them on her little legs. "William and his children, finally home again, what a wonderful world," thought Margaret.

They decided to spend the night as the day had flown by much too quickly. William, Kristine, and the children had a lot of people to meet again; his brothers and their wives and children. The table was certainly much fuller than it had been when he left and it felt good, really good. The five of them squeezed into William's old bed that night, the children thinking it was the greatest thing in the world. After breakfast William told Kristine there was one more thing he wanted to do and he asked his Da if he could take the cart. He drove to the foothills of Ben Lawers and they all got out of the cart. "We'll have to walk the rest of the way," he said. It was hard for William but he was determined to reach the top of the hill that overlooked Loch Tay. "That's Loch Tay," he said to Kristine and he pulled the silver engraving out of his pocket. "It is, she cried, William it's breathtaking, no wonder you longed for it so." They stood there arms around each other, watching the children run in the grass and pick wildflowers. He couldn't help but remember that this was where Mary and he had spent part of their last days together. He turned to his wife and they walked hand in hand back down the hill. The children were running here and there through the fields just like he had done at their age. At that moment, he felt his life was almost complete but there was one more thing he had to do.

They reluctantly said their goodbyes and headed for home, William not concerned that the store would open a little late that day; the trip had been all he had hoped for. The children had bonded with their new cousins and were reluctant to leave. Everyone promised to come and see them, his brothers included. Agnes and Gabby were glad to see them back and life resumed as before.

On the Saturday before the last Sunday of the month William sat in the kitchen by Kristine. "I have to go tomorrow," he said. "Go where?" she asked. "To meet her, you know, Mary." "Yes, she replied, full circle." "Full circle?" he asked. She explained, "Full circle means when the beginning and the end meet." He smiled, "Oh, I understand." He took her hands, "You have nothing to worry about I love you." "I know, she said, I'm not worried."

She watched him drive away the next morning and for all of her confidence there was a small glimmer of doubt inside. "Stop that, she told herself, he'll come back, he loves me." She kept busy all day trying to put it out of her mind and touching the little gold heart between her breasts.

Likewise Henry was in a state of anxiety. Mary had insisted on taking the cart and going herself and he couldn't seem to concentrate on anything. He spent the day pacing from one end of the house to the other then would go outside and come back in. "Look, she told him before she left, I love you, I just have to see this to the end, that's all."

He sat there thinking about all they had done together in Comrie. Mary was committed to helping Henry with the school and he couldn't believe all the good ideas she had. Now that Mary had her oven, the lasses from school would come to the house for a cooking lesson each week and then take home what they made to their parents. Mary insisted that they build a library on the school ground and everyone from the village helped erect it and then came for the opening ceremony. They named it 'The McPhee Library of Comrie, Scotland.' It was open to children and adults alike and they started tutoring classes for any adults who wanted to learn to read and write as well as any children who needed special help. The substitute teacher was elated that he was getting to work more often and the school board funded the extra pay for him. They started a garden with a lot of work from the schoolchildren and parents; whatever was grown was shared with all of the families. They called it the community garden. Mary supplied the funds for a greenhouse and they grew seedlings for the garden as well as flowers. All of the kirks in the area benefitted from the beautiful flowers that were there and were donated for weddings, funerals and any other event in town that asked for them; free of charge. Mary spent hours writing scripts and coercing Henry to build sets for plays that the children could act out in an effort to make their history lessons more fun. The plays were held on the hillside in warm weather and the parents would be invited; the children would act out their plays and they would have refreshments afterwards. They organized trips to local businesses so the children could get an idea what opportunities were out there for them when they finished school. One day they all were loaded into carts and made the trip to Killin to see the blacksmith shop, hardware store, Ethan's tea shop and the bakery. They had lunch in the bakery after which they were served jam roly polys. They brought home tea, candy and pound cake for their parents. Attendance was greatly improved, the children not wanting to miss anything. Henry was working with the school board to bring a small college into the village. Mary had insisted that if the plan received approval and they could entice enough professors to come; she would fund the building and housing for everyone with her inheritance which was growing steadily. "Please, he thought as he waited there at the table, please don't let me lose her now, I won't be able to stand it."

If Kristine and Henry were anxious, it was nothing to what William and Mary were feeling. Mary arrived first and sat on the bench outside the kirk waiting to see if he would come. She could see the road and the bridge below. It wasn't long and she heard a cart approaching, when it crossed the bridge she could see that it was him, there was no mistaking it. Her heart leapt at the sight of him and her hands were shaking. He parked the cart and made his way up the hill, she could see that he had a cane and she tried to control the tears so he wouldn't see. She closed her eyes, afraid to watch until she heard a soft voice, "Hello Mary, it's me, William, I've come." To hear his voice again, she couldn't stand it another second and there was no stopping the tears flowing from her eyes. She bit down on her lip and turned her head, unable to speak. "Aw Mary, don't cry, I'm sorry, I'm so sorry, I didn't mean to hurt you, I loved you." He bent down and took her in his arms and she laid her head on his chest as he held her against him. A long time passed and then finally she said, "I was mad, happy and sad all at the same time when I read the post." "I know Mary, what I did was wrong, I was trying to spare you." "You didn't know me well enough or love me enough otherwise you wouldn't have done it." "I did love you, don't say that, please, Mary." "When you left I looked at the two stars night after night until I couldn't bear to do so anymore." "It's ok Mary I didn't expect you to wait." "Henry was there, he even went to Glasgow to find you, they told him there was a young man there, Shawn Ferguson, but he didn't make the connection." "How could he Mary, he wouldn't have known." "He felt bad when he came back, even though he knew finding you would mean losing me, that's when I realized that he had always been there when I needed him, I just didn't look at him hard enough." She sat up and wiped her eyes on her sleeve then she looked at him and let her fingers touch the scar on his face. "It's not that bad, you know, you are still handsome." He looked down and didn't say anything. "Your leg, it must have been badly broken?" "Aye, the bone was through the skin, I could have lost it, I'm lucky." "My arm and wrist were broken, they are ok now but my three fingers don't work anymore." She picked up his hand and caressed his fingers, then kissed them. "I would have come straightaway you must have known that." "Aye, of course I did but I didn't want that for you, what kind of life would it have been?" "It should have been my choice William, I wouldn't have minded, I loved you, I missed you." "You're happy now, with Henry?" "Oh aye, I love him, in every way." "Good, he said, I'm glad." "You don't hate me then?" "I could never hate you William, part of me still loves you and always will." "And you, Kristine, does she make you happy?" "Aye, she means everything to me she's a good mother to all of my children." "Go home to her then; it sounds like you found someone who cares a lot about you." They both stood in a tight embrace for several minutes and anyone watching would have thought they were two lovers. They kissed on the lips, she touched his face and let her fingers linger there and then they looked at each other for perhaps the last time. "Part of me will love you forever," he said. She nodded, "Me too William, me too." They turned and hand in hand walked down the hill to their carts, holding back the tears once again. They got into their carts and turned opposite directions to go home giving one last wave at each other. The closer to home William got the more he couldn't wait to grab Kristine and tell her how much he loved her. There was no doubt that he had loved Mary but his wild black haired lass had his heart now.

Mary pulled up to the house and could see that Henry was still sitting at the kitchen table. He looked up when she came in the house and the look on his face made her realize that he had been in agony since she left. "I'm home, she said, have you been sitting here the whole time?" "No, not the whole time," he said trying to read her face. "Come, she said, grabbing his hand, I want to tell you something." Feeling sick and scared he followed her into the sitting room and sat on the couch beside her. "Mary?" he asked. She took his hand and laid it on her stomach, then put her hand on top of it. She took her other hand and touched his cheek. "Say hello to your bairn; a little MacAlduie." He wrapped his arms around her, "A bairn you're pregnant then?" "Yes Henry, I'm pregnant and I hope the bairn looks just like you." "Oh Mary, I love you so much." "You better, because you're stuck with me for a very long time."

GLOSSARY

Bannock
A flat bread made from oats.

Ben
A mountain.

Ben Lawers
A mountain near Killin, Scotland that lies on the north side of Loch Tay and is the highest point of a ridge that includes seven munros. Estimated height is around 3900'.

Beverages
The main drink of the common people was ale and milk. I've incorporated tea drinking into my story. In actuality, it was called "highland tea" and was saved for rare occasions.

Black Pudding
Blood sausage cooked with filler until thick enough to congeal.

Comrie, Scotland
This is the town where my character Henry taught school and where he lived with Mary when they were wed. Located on the banks of the River Earn it is an affluent village in the Southern Highlands. It is situated on the Highland Boundary Fault and is nicknamed Shaky Town because of the many earth tremors it experiences. The railroad came to Comrie in 1893. In 1836 there were as many as seven schools in Comrie teaching various languages and mathematics.

Crieff

Crieff had a population of around 2,800 in 1801. Woolen manufacturing came around 1812. Sir Patrick Murray of Ochtertyre gave the town Lady Mary's Walk Around 1815. Crieff had a toll booth that was built around 1685 but it was destroyed in 1842. Queen Victoria visited Scotland on September 10, 1842 and passed through Crieff on her visit. Crieff finally had gas in 1842. The Caledonia Railroad opened the Crieff Junction in 1856 and the same year the Strathearn Herald Newspaper started. The next year, 1857 the Crieff Journal began publication. St. Fillan's Roman Catholic Church was erected in 1871 and St. Columba's Episcopal Church was built. Crieff also had a Free Church on Comrie Street and it was rebuilt in 1881. By 1872 Crieff had a main water supply and by 1881 the population had grown to over 4,000. Popular actor Ewan McGregor was born in Crieff.

Crofter

A person who occupies and works a small landholding known as a croft. The crofter pays rent to the tacksman or landlord of the croft.

Crutches/Wheelchairs

Crutches of the 19th century were not comfortable and could not be adjusted to the height of the user although they were made in different heights. These crude crutches were hard on the armpits and they did not have the rubber modern ones today have. Sometimes they would have to wrap rags around the top for comfort. The wheelchair was invented in the 18th century but I was unable to ascertain exactly when. The most common one was called a Bath Wheelchair but it was reported to be very uncomfortable. In the latter part of the 19th century, improvements were made to the wheelchair. Around 1869, a patent was obtained for a chair with rear push wheels and small front casters. I've incorporated this one into my story

Cullen Skink

Haddock chowder. Cullen is a town in N.E. Scotland.

Dolly Tub/Possing Stick

A wash tub for washing clothes is called a dolly tub, usually had legs. Possing sticks were used to agitate the clothes in a dolly tub; also called dollies or poshers.

Dunderhead

A derogatory comment that means someone is dumb or an idiot.

Falls of Dochart

Located on River Dochart in Killin at the western end of Loch Tay. If you cross the bridge as you enter Killin you can see the falls rushing over the black rocks and around the Island of Inchbuie which is the traditional burial place of the Clan MacNab.

Haggis

Contains sheep's heart, liver and lungs stuffed into a sheep or cow stomach with offal, oatmeal, spices and then boiled. Sometimes other meat is used.

Hen Night

Before the wedding the bride's friends take her to town and parade her around banging pots and pans. She is sometimes dressed up with streamers and on occasion sooted.

Killin, Scotland

There actually is a Killin, Scotland which is said to be one of the most picturesque places in Scotland and has a long history of legends and clans. I've tried to accurately depict the streets and their names during the 1800's.

One report states that around May of 1775 about 30 families, approximately 300 people met in Killin. To the sound of bagpipes and dressed in their best clothing they had booked passage to the United States and Canada. Some of them had as much as 200-300 pounds and no one had less than 30-40 pounds. It was said that they were joyous hoping to find a new place to live where they were free to practice their old ways.

Lister, Lord Joseph, Dr.

Joseph Lister was from England but he spent his adult life in Edinburgh and Glasgow studying medicine. He was instrumental in the development of antiseptics in surgery and the practice of washing hands before surgery. Prior to his work most broken bone patients developed either blood poisoning or gangrene. He found that carbolic acid would be absorbed by catgut from sheep and so it replaced silk for stitching. He was made a Lord by Queen Victoria after he performed a minor surgery on her. He was later a Professor of Surgery at The University of Glas-gow.

Loch Tay

Freshwater loch in the central highlands of Scotland. It is approximately 14 ½ miles long and 1 ½ miles wide. Killin is located at the head of the loch.

Lochay River
The river runs eastward toward Loch Tay joining the river Dochart at Killin.

MacAlduie
The name MacAlduie is associated with the Clan Lamont which was a target of Clan Campbell.

The Campbell Clan stole their lands and possessions and killed them. Sir James Lamont was Chief of the Clan and was well respected and a popular leader who was interested in the welfare of his people. He was held in a dungeon at Dunstaffnage in horrible conditions for over five years.

McCleary
Name is of Gaelic origin and can be either Irish or Scottish. Variations are O'Clery, O'Cleary, MacCleary, McCleery, McLeary.

Merchant City
Merchant city was developed around 1750 and became the residences and warehouses of the wealthy merchant "tobacco lords." It is located West of High Street, the street where O'Cleary's Emporium is located in my novel.

Munro
Clan Chief Donald Munroe was granted land in Rossire and a seat at Foulis Castle as a reward for helping King Malcolm II of Scotland to defeat Viking invaders from Scandinavia.

Naw
No

Nip
Shot of an alcoholic drink.

Nippin
Stinging. Or in sentence; quit yer nippin.

Oswald
Name is of Anglo-Saxon origin. Found chiefly in Northern England and Scotland. Derived from pre 7th Century name of Osweald.

Postage
Postage: Between 1812 and 1815 Penny Post Offices were opening everywhere

Powsoddie
A broth made from sheep's head.

Quaich
The loving cup, or Quaich tradition dates back to the 15th century and symbolizes the joining to-gether of two families.

St. Fillan's Episcopal Kirk
The 7th Marquis of Breadalbane was a hunter. In 1876 he built the church so that his shooting party had a place to worship. Some of the locals called it the grouse chapel.

St. Fillan's Mill
The mill where my character Ethan worked is located at the north end of the bridge on River Dochart. It is on the site of other older mills and was once a grain mill and also a tweed mill. St. Fillan preached near there on a stone (St. Fillan's Seat) under an ash tree. A flood in 1856 washed away the stone and a storm in 1893 blew down the tree.

Scunnered
To be sick of or to have had enough of something.

Sheilings
Huts build on summer pastures, some distance from town where woman and children would take the animals to pasture. It was a joyous event for them and sometimes the Piper would lead the group there. The women would spend their time churning butter and the children would scour the hillsides for medicinal plants and herbs.

Stag Night
Before the wedding, the groom is taken out by his friends and subjected to lots of harmless prac-tical jokes. Sometimes he would be stripped of his clothes, sooted and feathered and tied to a tree or post for a few hours or overnight.

Stevenson

Name means "son of Steven." First recorded in Scotland in 1388. Family farmed land in Neilston, Renfrewshire. Famous figure: Robert Louis Stevenson, novelist.

Stovies

Potaoes, onions, leftover beef, corned beef or other meat. Stove means stew.

Tacksman

Land holder of intermediate legal and social status who paid a yearly rent for the land let to them (tack). Their tenure might last several generations. They usually kept some land to work themselves and let out the land to sub-tenants or crofters.

Templeton Carpet Factory

A major extension was started on the building in 1888 and completed in 1892. The building was transformed into a work of art representing the late medieval Palazzo Ducale in Venice. It had red brick, terracotta, arches, turrets and circular windows. It was truly a beautiful work of art. While working on the building, on November 1, 1889 part of a wall collapsed due to windy weather. Over 100 women were trapped in the weaving sheds and 29 were killed.

Textile Industry

The textile industry started to change in the early 1800's. There was William Scott & Sons who were instrumental in the industry which started in Derry, Ireland. William became a master weaver. William Tille was a shirt and collar manufacturer in Glasgow; it was his vision to house all workers in one building. When steamboat service connected Derry and Glasgow in 1829 he started to sell his cloth to William Gourlie & Son and he dominated the shirt making industry. His success was the pivot that attracted other Scottish businessmen to Derry. In 1886 a railroad opened in Killin, increasing industry. Small mills were established and there were many home based weavers. The sewing machine was invented around 1856 or 1857.

The Glasgow Cathedral, Glasgow, Scotland

Located North of High Street and East of Cathedral Street beside the Glasgow Royal Infirmary. Allegedly located where St. Mungo built his church and the tomb of the saint is in the lower crypt.

The Night Asylum

The Night Asylum for the homeless was set up in 1838 as a charitable institution. They provided shelter for the homeless. The original location was on St. Enochs Wynd and could cater up to 100 people. The need for an additional site became urgent as the population increased so in 1847 the North Frederick Street Night Asylum opened and was instituted a year later

The Royal Infirmary Hospital, Glasgow, Scotland

This is where my character William was taken after his accident on Argyle Street. The hospital was opened in December 1794 beside the Glasgow Cathedral on land that once held the Bishop's Castle. A surgical block was opened in 1861. In 1856 Joseph Lister was an Assistant Surgeon there and in 1806 he became a Professor of Surgery.

Threshold

This was an old Scottish tradition. They believed that carrying the bride over the threshold would avoid any contact with evil spirits and if the bride should accidentally trip on the way in it would be unlucky.

Wee Clipe

Telling on someone. A tattletale.

Wheesht

Scottish slang usually accompanied by 'haud yer wheesht.' Means I'd be quiet or shut your mouth.